IN THEIR WISDOM

About the Author

Born in Leicester, England, in 1905, C. P. Snow was educated at Leicester University College and then at Christ's College, Cambridge, where he held a fellowship in physics and later became tutor. His first published works were scientific papers, particularly on infrared investigations of molecular structures. His serious career as a novelist began in 1934 with the publication of *The Search*; the next year he started to plan the *Strangers and Brothers* sequence of eleven novels.

At the outbreak of World War II, Snow entered public affairs; and for his services—as adviser on scientific personnel to the Ministry of Labour and afterward as a Civil Service Commissioner—he was knighted in 1957. In 1967 he became Lord Snow and served in the government as Parliamentary Secretary for the Ministry of Technology. He died in 1980.

C. P. Snow's works available from Macmillan Publishing Company include *The Realists, In Their Wisdom, A Coat of Varnish,* and the complete *Strangers and Brothers* sequence.

IN
THEIR
WISDOM

C. P. Snow

COLLIER BOOKS
Macmillan Publishing Company
New York

Macmillan Publishing Company
866 Third Avenue, New York, N.Y. 10022

Library of Congress Cataloging-in-Publication Data
Snow, C. P. (Charles Percy), 1905–1980.
In their wisdom.
Reprint. Originally published: New York: Scribner, 1974.
I. Title.
PR6037.N58I5   1987   823'.912   86-32710
ISBN 0-02-025400-8

First Collier Books Edition 1987

10   9   8   7   6   5   4   3   2   1

Printed in the United States of America

I wish to record several different kinds of indebtedness to Dr. Irving S. Cooper of St. Barnabas Hospital, New York City. He has taught me a great deal, directly and in other ways. Without him and his own writings, one theme in this book would not have been written.

PART
ONE

1

Mr. Skelding was doing what some men would have found more difficult. He was announcing, with an air of Adamic surprise, as though, he alone among men had been granted this revelation, news which at least two of his audience knew as well as he did. And which revelation, since Mrs. Underwood was to execute the will along with himself, he couldn't help knowing that they knew.

Still, there was well-being in some places round the room. Mrs. Underwood listened without expression, sepia gaze concentrated on Mr. Skelding, facial muscles firm, handsome, confident and commanding in her middle sixties, looking as though she should have been accompanied by a lady-in-waiting carrying her purse. Her son Julian was also well-preserved, seemed much less than forty, as he peered, light eyes wide open, enquiring, as though he too were startled by the Adamic surprise. But it was not from those two that well-being wafted back to Mr. Skelding, echoing his own. Apart from the Underwoods there were six others whom Mr. Skelding had asked to call on him that afternoon. Some were sitting on the window seats, others backed against the white painted panelling; the office was suitable for subdued legal interviews, not for a party this size. That, however, did not inhibit Mr. Skelding. He enjoyed telling people that they were due to receive money they did not expect. He also enjoyed issuing warnings about obstacles in the jungly path before money could be taken as

3

certain. For once, that afternoon the business was simple, his good nature was genuine and he could let it flow.

It was a warm day in October, one of the sash windows was open; through it, in the gaps between Mr. Skelding's modulated, rounded, deliberate lawyer's phrases, one could hear a muted background noise, which those who knew the geography would have identified as the sound of traffic in the Strand, getting on for half a mile away. In the court below the sun was shining. For an instant Julian Underwood, in the midst of his reckonings, caught a smell from the outside air, or thought he did. There wasn't a tree in the Old Court, but it might have been the smell of burning leaves. Whether he was imagining it or not, it brought back to Julian, who wasn't a nostalgic man, days, or perhaps a solitary day, when he was a student and had returned after travelling, back to England in time for term, with the autumn weather as benign and bright as this.

Mr. Skelding proceeded. His colouring was high, puce cheeks making small shrewd eyes sink deeper in. His lips were as fresh as a child's, and would have looked just as much at home sucking on a straw: which was the one respect in which Julian Underwood resembled him, for he too in his pale over-youthful face had childish lips, over-innocent they had sometimes been called, though others got the opposite impression.

Although Mr. Skelding was enjoying himself, he preserved a decent steadiness of tone and pace. After all, the old gentleman had been buried only a couple of days before. No doubt people in this room would be gratified by their legacies, but some, Mr. Skelding thought, might have had an affection for him. He hadn't been an easy man. Yet Mrs. Underwood for one had for years been devoting most of her life to him. Like a very good secretary. He had treated her like that, though Mrs. Underwood was what Mr. Skelding in his old-fashioned way would have called good county family, not outfaced anywhere. A secretary might have been forced to put up with it, but Mrs. Underwood had money of her own. Of course there had been sound reasons. Mr. Skelding wasn't given to passing judgments upon his fellow men, or at least if he did so he managed to conceal them from himself.

Gazing round the room he exuded a proper, subdued excitement as he broke morsels of news. He beamed, gleamed, and shone. The late Mr. Massie, he was saying, hadn't wished his will to be read at the funeral reception. That had never been a good custom. But he had given instructions for certain messages to institutions to be made known. These were included in his final will, which Mr. Skelding had drawn up. He had been present, when it was signed and witnessed a month before Mr. Massie's death.

"I don't think it's necessary to burden you with all the minor bequests. There are a number of objects mentioned which he had acquired over a long life time. Mrs. Underwood and I thought it would meet his wishes if I disclosed his statements about certain institutions to which I shall shortly be obliged to write."

Mr. Skelding pushed back his spectacles and drew the paper nearer.

"In effect," he said, "he required his school and college to be informed that he had at one period, a considerable number of years ago contemplated making testamentary dispositions for their benefit, and had entered into preliminary conversations with them on this subject. However, their lack of resistance to the stupidities of the present time"—he insisted on that form—"added to the irritation of living through his ninth decade. So he had decided to cease his connection with them, in particular to cease his connection with the Anglican church he was brought up in. He repudiated any thought of providing benefactions for them or any other institutions, and he expected those of similar opinions to himself to do the same."

Mr. Skelding gave this report without emphasis. He had trained himself to suppress any opinions of his own. That wasn't much of a sacrifice, if it meant his clients trusted him more. He glanced towards Mrs. Underwood, who was sitting near his desk.

"I think that is a reasonable summary?" She nodded, and said also without emphasis:

"Of course, you will send them the whole passage verbatim, won't you?"

"Of course," said Mr. Skelding. They spoke as though the recipients would resent being deprived of a single word.

5

"Well now," Mr. Skelding remarked comfortably, "we come into smooth water." He began to read from the second page:

"I wish to express my gratitude and give a token of recognition to those persons who have attempted to protect me from the stupidities and irritations of recent years." Attention in the room sharpened: this was getting warm. Some were thinking, the old man had sounded acerb, cross-grained to the last. No mention of his family. There were rumours that his daughter hadn't come near him. He had complained, someone had heard, at second-hand, of how she had treated him. She had been no use to him. None of them knew her, they had only become acquaintances of Mr. Massie in the last few years. A woman had been present at the funeral, pale, middle aged, solitary. That might have been her.

"Well then—" Mr. Skelding beamed at a large beak-nosed man. "To my doctor—" name in full, qualifications, address— "who has saved me from some unnecessary discomforts, I bequeath the sum of £5,000." The doctor did not beam in return but inclined his head.

"To my accountant—" a similar rubric—"who had dealt with incompetent officials, I bequeath the sum of £3,000." Four other legacies, one to his housekeeper, who had been with him only three years, also £3,000, one to his chiropodist, of £500. All six received their tips with decorum, like well trained hall porters at a grand hotel, with decorum and radiating satisfaction under the skin: except for the chiropodist, who couldn't hold back a large protuberant grin.

"To conclude," said Mr. Skelding, and returned to the text. "I wish above all to pay a debt of gratitude which I cannot properly express to my friend Mrs. Katharine Underwood for sympathy, support, and kindness beyond measure during my last years. At her request I do not bequeath her any sum of money. She has consented to act as an executrix of this my last will and testament. The residue of my estate, all preceding legacies having been discharged, I leave to her son Julian Stourton Underwood, Apartment D, 22 Philimore Gardens, London, W. 8."

Mr. Skelding had maintained to the last his aura of beatific astonishment, as though the final disposition was dazzlingly

6

fresh, not only to the Underwoods but to himself. Neither mother nor son stirred but Julian gave a blink, leaving his eyes, if that were possible, wider open still. There was a faint susurration somewhere in the room.

Mr. Skelding said: "I think that is almost all, then—unless anyone has any questions—? I do hope you don't feel that we have wasted your time." This was uttered earnestly, without any edge at all, the tone of one who had long ago ceased to obtrude himself upon apprehensive clients.

"Not in the least," murmured the doctor, like the chairman of a deputation moving a vote of thanks.

"Well—well—" Mr. Skelding said it restfully, a restful encouragement for them to leave.

The doctor took his cue and got up, and went over to shake hands. The others followed his lead as a social arbiter. Soon the Underwoods were left alone with Mr. Skelding.

"How much? How much will it be?" said Julian, while footsteps were still sounding down the stairs.

Mr. Skelding looked at Julian's mother, beaky of profile, eyes bird-like and brilliant. That was the one thing she didn't know; a solicitor whom Mr. Skelding had replaced still handled the old man's investments. She must have made her guess. She understood money as well as a professional. Caution intervened.

"It's early days to give any sort of figure," said Mr. Skelding. "And much of the estate is in equities, and of course the market is going down. I don't think we should be wise to give a figure."

"Don't let's be wise," said Julian with a sudden hooting laugh. "Just let's have an idea."

"We can do that, can't we?" said Mrs. Underwood.

"It's distinctly premature—"

"Not for working purposes," she said.

"If you press me—"

"Yes."

"Well then. Very roughly, though you mustn't hold me to this, the total estate may perhaps work out at a little over £ 400,000. The residual estate, when the other legacies are paid, might come to something slightly under."

7

"Much under?" Julian interjected.

"With good fortune, not so much under."

Julian made an acquiescent noise.

"But here's the body blow." Mr. Skelding, who relished speaking of large sums, also relished checking signs of undue grandeur.

"The realty isn't substantial, so the death duties are certain to be high. It would be safe to assume that they will swallow up half the final figure. We oughtn't to make calculations at having anything over £200,000, and it would be prudent to think more in terms of twenty or thirty thousand less than that."

Julian sat, lips parted, eyes wide. Mrs. Underwood went in for some brisk exchanges with the lawyer. Estimate of death duties? No, he couldn't get any nearer for the moment. Fall in value of the investments? Yes, it was important to get probate granted in quick time. Some of the portfolio ought to have been sold long before. They must be disposed of. The capital value had gone down by ten per cent over the past year. Mrs. Underwood nodded. She had realised that, or suspected it.

The only sensible step was to rush the probate through. Mr. Skelding would keep in touch. With that agreed, the Underwoods walked through the court in the amiable October air. Until they got into a taxi in Chancery Lane, Julian did not speak. Then he said:

"Sinful."

"What do you mean?" But she had been expecting this. She was on the defensive already.

"Those death duties."

"I told you."

"You didn't tell me they would be as high as this."

"That I didn't know. I'm sorry, darling."

"Shouldn't you have known?"

"It really was rather difficult, don't you see? I couldn't find out everything—"

His face was averted, staring ahead at traffic lights in the Strand.

"What's the use of a man making money? If they take it all away? Why do people sit down under it?"

"It's been going on for a long time, you know." She was try-ing to placate him, like a wife in a quarrel with her husband, hoping to bring out a smile.

He still wasn't looking at her, his profile stayed mutinous.

"Couldn't you have done something about it? There must be ways of shedding the stuff. This is pretty fair incompetence, it must have been."

"There are ways, darling, if you start soon enough. He'd have to have made gifts seven years ago. That was before I re-ally knew him. And anyway people always think there's plenty of time."

Julian showed a flicker of interest.

"Shall you think there's plenty of time? Shall I? Will it all go down the drain?"

At that, Mrs. Underwood, keyed to all his intonations, was encouraged. She began explaining some points in the law of in-heritance taxation. She did it more masterfully than Mr. Skeld-ing would have done, but she spoke in an intimate tone, or as though intimacy were returning. Then, a step more daring, she said:

"And after all you are not doing so badly out of the deal, are you now? When you add it all up?"

Suddenly he gave his hooting laugh, so loud that the taxi driver, going round Trafalgar Square, looked back over his shoulder.

"Ho! Ho! Like a man who has just been told," Julian was spluttering, exploding with hilarity, "that he has been pre-sented with a small fortune in New York and Paris. But is mis-erable because his account has been blocked in Addis Ababa."

He turned to his mother with an impudent, shameless, peni-tential smile. She smiled back, total complicity between them. It had been like this, his moods had changed as fast, since he was a child. Perhaps it was so, with the women he seemed to captivate. She didn't know he was capable of what sounded like ultimate confession and at the same time of keeping his secrets.

Anyway, with herself, she couldn't help but recognise, he had always been the dominant one. Since he was a very young man. It was she who was competent, to whom business came

9

easy, who could handle money and make it work: while he, though he was something of a miser, ingenious at not paying for a meal or a round of drinks, had never earned much of a living, and lived—again, how he lived she didn't know—on what she allowed him. It was also she who contrived for him, who made plans for what she imagined he wanted, all the time scheming for his love. Often she had been afraid that she would lose him. He hadn't given her much reason to be afraid. He sometimes was elevated on to what seemed like a cloud of his own, but mostly he was kind to her and, as now, sitting beside her in amity up Piccadilly, made her spirits light.

"What shall you do with it when you get it?" she asked.

He put a finger to the side of his nose.

"We shall feel our way."

"I think you might stand yourself a drink."

"Perhaps."

She had been teasing him. Again her tone was wife-like, but that of a wife now happy. He was abstemious, much more so than she was.

"Do you know?" All of a sudden he broke out in elation.

"What?"

"I shall buy a ham. A whole ham."

The curious thing, if she knew him at all, was that he might do just that.

"You could run to it."

"I've always wanted a ham."

The mouth of Knightsbridge. Friendly silence. Tentatively she said:

"You'll be able to marry Liz. If you want to."

"I'd thought of that."

This was a routine conversation. Conscientiously she had told him that she had longed to see him married long before.

She said: "I'd like to see my grandchildren before I die."

That also had been said before. He gave a soothing murmur.

Past Harrods. Friendly silence again. As they turned into the Kensington streets she asked if she was to expect him for dinner that night. No, he thought not, with a roseate secret smile.

They drew up in Victoria Road, outside her smart house,

shining with fresh cream paint, chrysanthemums in the window boxes. After he kissed her goodbye, out of old habit she paid the taxi to take him on to the other side of the High Street.

$$\text{\Large ❦ 2 ❦}$$

A fortnight after the meeting in Mr. Skelding's office, that is in the last week of October 1970, the House of Lords was debating the Queen's speech. That is what the Order Paper said; it was the second day of the debate, dedicated to economic and industrial affairs: but at five o'clock in the afternoon there was no excessive excitement. Benches gleamed empty and crimson under the lights, their occupants having gone to tea. On the Opposition side, a Labour economist was making a very long speech upon the history of trade union legislation.

On the Government front bench below the gangway, from which other ex-Ministers except himself had some time before departed, Lord Hillmorton stirred. He had been sitting with legs outstretched, and had to retract himself before he rose to his considerable height. Stopping on his way out, he spoke, audibly, socially, to Lord Ryle, on the last row of the cross benches.

"Bishops' Bar?"

Lord Ryle nodded. "In a minute."

Lord Ryle was remaining for politeness' sake, because in his academic days he had known the speaker. Having listened for thirty-five minutes, he decided that duty had been discharged, and followed Hillmorton out.

Anyone who had overheard the invitation might have imagined that the Bishops' Bar would be largely inhabited by prelates—possibly carousing prelates, rather like cardinals vermilion draped, sousing wine in lurid 19th Century paintings. That, however, was not the case. It was extremely rare to see a bishop in the bar, which was reserved for the private use of members of the Lords but without access to guests. Some time previously this had been the place where bishops robed: hence, with English inaccuracy, the name.

Lord Hillmorton was installed at the first table near the door. The room itself was small, half a dozen round tables down the narrow length, a settee at the end, darkish and confined in a comfortable clublike fashion. At the bar itself a saucer of sausages was simmering on the hot-plate. So early in the evening, only two other men were present.

"As usual?" said Lord Hillmorton. "A large Scotch and soda for Lord Ryle, please, that will be kind of you." He was smiling at the waitress. He was a prepossessing ageing man, hair still dark, with silver pigeon-wings over the ears, cheeks ruddy, eyes large and luminous. In a slightly quieter tone he said to his friend:

"This is pretty bloody dull, by any standard."

He was referring to the debate. Friend? Were those two friends? Perhaps, in the sense that men who have met late in life can be. It wasn't like the friendship of those who have been in touch since boyhood. There were facts about each other of which they were quite ignorant. They had become acquainted when they first entered the House at about the same period, a dozen years before, and some things about each other they had picked up. Some they had inferred or, neither of them inexperienced men, suspected. Maybe Ryle, chairman of Royal Commissions, one of the first Life Peers, historian by trade, inquisitive by vocation, had gathered the more: but Hillmorton was more observant than he looked.

There they sat, two substantial men in their sixties, Ryles' face flatter, more seamed, less bold-cut than the other's, but with its own authority. He had almost no bridge to his nose, rather like a picture of W. M. Thackeray or a retired boxer: which latter he wasn't. He said:

"Got anything pleasant to tell me about the world?"

Hillmorton replied: "No. When are you going to cheer me up?"

13

Ryle said: "That isn't going to be very likely, is it?"

It sounded like banter, but it wasn't so entirely. It was more like an attitude that had brought them together. In different fashions they had each seen a good deal. They had been interested in what went on around them, and still had a flow of interest, nearly as deep as when they were young: but interest was what they were left with most. Existing beside it, or lurking beneath it, covered up, there was something else similar in both of them—not quite sadness, not quite resignation, not quite pessimism, but as though their interest was edged with regret.

"As a matter of fact, James," Hillmorton was saying, "there is a bit of personal news. Not that it matters much, of course. But that's why I dragged you out—"

"What is it?"

"It's really very trivial, don't you know?"

"Come on."

A few instants previously the door had opened behind them and just at that moment a voice, gritty but tentative, sounded above their heads:

"May I join you?"

"Of course," said Hillmorton.

"You're sure I'm not interrupting anything?"

They both denied it, not in the least, not at all, denying the obvious with an air of maximum relaxation, composure and sincerity.

"What are you drinking, Peter?" said Hillmorton, and once more called to the waitress: "A large gin and tonic for Lord Lorimer, so good of you—"

Lorimer was a good deal younger, fifteen years, than they were. Although he was a constant attender they hadn't often talked to him, but sometimes, when there was a circle round a table, he lingered on the edge. As often with casual acquaintances there, Ryle knew some of the reference book data about him, and Hillmorton a few bits of gossip from hearsay. The first holder of the title had been an 18th Century admiral, who had won one of the West Indian victories. Since then the family, or at least the direct line of descent, must have become poorer—not a specially common performance, so far as early

14

19th Century studies had taught Ryle, who had written books about the Industrial Revolution. This man, dark faced, dark moustached, drawn, his movements as he lit a cigarette quick but jagged, hadn't had anything recordable in the way of a career: except in the war, when, as a soldier, though not a regular, he had held field rank and been decorated.

He spoke to Hillmorton rather than to Ryle: "What did you make of—?" He mentioned an Opposition leader who had spoken earlier in the afternoon.

"Good trade union doctrine, I should have thought."

"I don't like it," said Lord Lorimer.

"It's a fact of life."

"I don't see," said Lorimer, looking strained and also puzzled, "how the country can go on like that."

"There's not much choice, is there?" said Ryle in a consoling manner. "Which makes things easier."

"My dear Peter," said Hillmorton, "we really have to accept it, any Government that runs its head slap up against the unions is going to get us all into a mess."

Lorimer looked more puzzled. He was, as the others recognised, a loyal Tory backbencher, always ready to listen to the whip, now seeking a little comfort, a bit of fighting talk, from an elder statesman of his party. But Hillmorton, whatever he might say to Ryle in their own brand of intimacy, kept up a face of serene detachment with most others. And it wasn't only a face. To himself, he would have admitted that he was concerned about the future, not quite as simply as Lorimer: but also he didn't find it disagreeable to observe his successors in Government just as immobilized as he had been himself.

"We've got to do something," said Lorimer. "We can't let it all go to pieces."

"I suppose you mean, don't you?" Hillmorton surveyed him with an equable gaze, "that this kind of society is becoming ungovernable."

After a pause, Lorimer said, "Near enough."

"My dear boy, government's always been a bit of a confidence trick, you know. And when people begin to see through the confidence trick, then you tend to be rather in trouble."

Lorimer looked so lost that Ryle intervened and ordered him another drink. This man reminded him of his own brother-in-law, the brother of his wife recently dead. Simple, dutiful, utterly unironic, disliking most of what he saw going on around him. That brother-in-law had been a professional soldier all his life, brought up to a code of reticence, like Lorimer discomfited when others spoke without constraint. One night not long ago, in Ryle's flat after some drinks, he had confessed, as though it were the darkest and most shameful secret in existence, that he wouldn't like to go to war alongside the young men he met nowadays. They wouldn't pull you back if you were wounded, he had said, and then stopped and didn't say any more.

This evening Ryle tried to start some conversation with Lorimer, but couldn't make it flow. Soon Lorimer remarked that he ought to get back into the Chamber. When the door had closed behind him, Ryle glanced at Hillmorton, expecting what might have been the beginning of a confidence to be taken up, now they were again alone. Instead Hillmorton said, with an air of amiable reflectiveness:

"That chap puts in a fair amount of time here, doesn't he?"

"Yes."

"I have an idea that perhaps he needs his six pound ten, what do you think?"

"Quite likely."

"Still, I must say he sits round long enough to earn it. Very honourable of him, I should say."

The point was, members of the House were paid £6.10s* by way of expenses for a day's attendance. There were a number of penurious peers and some derelict ones. Of the latter, a few appeared in the Chamber for half an hour, maybe just for the length of question time, got ticked off on the attendance sheet, and duly claimed their pay. Which was noticed, and not approved of, by conscientious men.

Ryle was more direct, often more spontaneous, than his friend. He broke in:

* This conversation happened some months before the introduction of decimal coinage: later the Lords' allowance was raised to £8.50.

"What were you going to tell me?"

"Was I? Ah yes, I remember."

"It's not so very long ago." Ryle grinned at him and the other gave a curiously boyish smile, like one forced to admit that an onion skin of concealment had to be peeled away.

"You know my daughter Elizabeth, I think, don't you?"

"Of course I do."

"She's wondering whether to marry someone. No, that's putting it mildly. She'll have him if she can."

That sounded off-hand, but it was said affectionately. Perhaps there was an undertone which hinted that the speaker was fond not only of his daughter, but of women.

"Good luck to her," said Ryle. He had met Elizabeth once at the Hillmorton house in Suffolk, several times in the guest room in the House. She was a lively sharp-witted woman in her thirties, attractive, he would have thought, and he had wondered about her. Hillmorton had four daughters, of whom the youngest two were already married. Neither Elizabeth, who was the second, nor her eldest sister were.

"It's rather odd," said Hillmorton. "The fellow seems to have come into some money. He's older than she is. He doesn't seem to have done anything at all. He's not been married before, so I hear. I'd like someone to tell me, why he's waited all this time?"

They could both think of explanations, none of which happened to be the truth.

"You've met him?"

"She's brought him in once or twice. I didn't think it was serious."

"It looks as though you were wrong."

"I did think," said Hillmorton, "that he was rather engaging. Not too shy." He added, as though it was an explanation: "He's lost his hair."

He went on: "He's a man called Underwood. I don't know who he is."

This didn't mean what it appeared to mean. Lord Hillmorton was quite certain of Julian Underwood's identity. He was saying that none of Julian's family, relatives or acquaintances had had any connection in the past with any of the Hillmortons' family, relatives or acquaintances. In fact, Hillmorton being an Englishman, with the English antennae, had divined or discovered some material information about the Underwoods, such as that Julian's father, long since dead, had been in the old ICS and then later a member of Lloyds, and that the widow had been left—by the standards of those in Mr. Skelding's office two weeks before—more than comfortably off.

"Hal, you are not against it, are you?"

"It wouldn't make much difference if I were, would it?" Hillmorton leaned back, as though giving himself to rest. "A young woman her age ought to know what she's doing. Oh no, I'm not against it. I'd like her to have something for herself, she hasn't had much."

He said, with a frown at the same time ill-tempered and cordial: "We didn't educate them very sensibly, you know." (He was thinking of his daughters.) "It's nonsense that we didn't get them equipped for a career. I don't know what sort of world we imagined they were going to live in."

He went on: "They are bright enough. They'd have done quite well. Elizabeth is the brightest of them, as it happens."

"I can believe that," said Ryle, giving an astringent candour back. "The middle classes have been a shade more reasonable with their girls, you realise."

"I dare say. I dare say."

But that wasn't the real reason behind Hillmorton's neglect, Ryle knew well enough. Even if it were true that the middle classes had educated their daughters (what had happened to clever girls Ryle had known in Newcastle long ago, school teachers' daughters, bank clerks' daughters, the girls from the class from which he came?), and the aristocracy hadn't. That was too simple altogether. Hillmorton was an aristocrat. He was also a clever man and a far-sighted one. He would have taken trouble with his daughters—if he hadn't been obsessed by waiting for a son. Though he had affection for his daughters, he hadn't been able to resist bringing them up, or not bringing them up, as his grandfather might have done. A son had never come. Hillmorton's heir was what the reference books described as a 'kinsman,' not even a brother or a nephew.

18

Further research in those reference books would have revealed other things which, though more prosaic, were not so simple. Yes, Hillmorton was an aristocrat, more genuinely so than most people in the House, related to the old Whig grandees, with ancestors who had dined appropriately enough with Lady Holland. Before he succeeded to the title, he had, as Henry Fox-Milnes, sat in the Commons for what had once been something like a family preserve. As Henry Fox-Milnes he had had a place in the Macmillan cabinets, including a spell, which as he talked to Ryle that evening might have seemed inappropriate, as Minister of Education.

But the name of his paternal ancestors had not been Fox-Milnes. It had been Pemberton, and a Mr. Pemberton around 1820 had been the son of a Quaker banker. He had political ambitions, had married a Fox-Milnes girl and with celerity changed his name, as Englishmen on the make had never needed much persuasion to do. Usually in pursuit of estates or legacies, but not this time. Mr. Pemberton was considerably richer than Miss Fox-Milnes: on the other hand, she was considerably grander. If a connoisseur of social delicacies had been scrutinizing the high Whiggery, he might have concluded that even so she didn't quite belong, or perhaps belonged by courtesy. But anyway did Lady Glencora quite belong? For the purposes of a rising politician Miss Fox-Milnes was grand enough.

Hence office, hence the Hillmorton peerage. Hence after five generations the present Lord Hillmorton. In his own nature, even if he had been born in James Ryle's Newcastle street, he wouldn't have been easily put down by anyone. Still, it hadn't been a handicap to come from a family which had forgotten what it was to be socially put down.

There was one minor oddity, or indication to the contrary. For a while, now damped down, some of them had insisted on being more Whiggish that the Whigs. They had taken over the trick of calling each other by diminutives which were longer than the original Christian names: so that in his childhood Henry Fox-Milnes had to elderly relatives answered to the name of Hallio. In this House men who had been at school with him—hounds of smartness, preservers of a private world—sometimes called him that. Ryle never did. Antiquarianism was all right in its way, men with not much to hold on to held on to a private world, but this was a trifle more than Ryle could take.

"Mr.—what did you say—Underwood has been pretty lucky. How much is he getting, do you know?"

"Enough to live on, so I'm told."

"Do tell Elizabeth I'm very glad."

By now the room was filling up, men standing at the bar. Ryle said that it was a fine evening, he would walk home. They went out together, in the corridors red carpet underfoot, on the walls out-of-perspective pictures of the packed House at long-ago debates. With clubbish matiness, clubbish, impersonal, they called out the Christian names of men they passed and heard their own. At the tape machine they stopped and read, as they did by way of routine after a private talk, the news that was being tapped away. Nothing that mattered, on the tape that night.

❧ 3 ❧

I n her bed-sitting room in Barham Gardens, not far from Earls Court tube station, Mrs. Rastall was getting ready to go out. All was neat, as she was herself; so was her minuscule kitchen, and the bathroom, more precisely a shower room, her main luxury, from which she had just emerged. Once she had lived in opulence different from this, for she was old Massie's daughter, and was the woman whom the legatees had noticed, unobtrusive, unintroduced, at the funeral service. Not that she pitied herself overmuch because of the switchbacks of fortune. She didn't suppress her temper and her grievances, as she didn't consider herself a saint, but self-pity was to be pushed away. She could make do on very little, she had said for years: she had to and she did.

She was a small active woman, setting on for fifty, looking younger, keeping a charm about which she was diffident. This diffidence had been—though she didn't see it with the sharp eyes she used on others—a lifetime's handicap or wound. She wasn't sentimental about herself, and she didn't expend senti-mentality on those she visited. She visited a number of people, since she spent her days working for a society which looked after the old, some of them not poorer than herself, some sur-viving on old age pensions, a good many of them shabby-gen-teel, depressed by what had happened to them.

She wasn't paid for this job, the society was a voluntary one. Her visiting district was the area bounded by Gloucester Road on the east, Warwick Road on the west, Cromwell Road and Old Brompton Road, to the north and south. Layabouts, students, drug takers, all came her way, but they weren't part of her charge, which didn't start under the age of sixty. Above that limit she knew people in her district as well as any official or priest. It was harsh growing old in poverty and loneliness: that was about as much as one could safely feel, if one was to be any use at all, she sometimes thought, as she went off on her rounds. Loneliness was worse than poverty for most, anyway above the subsistence level, as some even in the 1970's barely were. One couldn't do much. Perhaps one could do a little.

This was early November, the week after Hillmorton and Ryle had been talking in the Bishops' Bar. Two mornings before, she had received a letter which had surprised, and, because she had a capacity for excitement, excited her. It came from the president of her society and read: Dear Mrs. Rastall, if you can make it convenient to call on me here on Thursday evening at 6:00 p.m. I should be pleased to see you. Yours sincerely, Reginald Swaffield. The 'here' of the address was Hill Street, and that must be his private house. She hadn't a vestigial notion what he could want her for. He couldn't be dismissing her (she was unconfident enough to have to reassure herself on that): voluntary helpers didn't get dismissed, and the association had to cling on to any bodies they possessed. She had met him only once, at a large reception, and he couldn't have remembered her. He was, she had gathered somewhere, one of the biggest of property developers, immensely rich, powerful, emerging from obscurity (though from nothing more mysterious than a small farm in Rutland).

It was nearly time to leave. She glanced again at the *Standard*, one of her evening comforts, on her income the only paper she let herself afford. She glanced at the sherry bottle: she liked a drink, but that was another expense, she had to ration herself, and presumably Swaffield would give her something in Hill Street. Hill Street—the logistics of travel needed planning when one used tubes and buses, and Mayfair was awkward. It would mean Green Park and then a walk.

When she arrived, through the drizzling night, she was let in by a male servant, the first she had seen for a very long time. He led her up the helix of stairs, wallpaper at the side Regency and striped, startlingly picked out in gold. On the piano nobile, the drawingroom, startling again: glazed chintz curtains, carpets from wall to wall like an optical demonstration in lines, squiggles and dots, more Regency stripes on chair and sofa backs, more stripes, a different species, on the walls: gilt framed mirrors, chandeliers, crystal lights over a mantelpiece. Mrs. Rastall's gaze boggled and dazzled as she saw amidst the illuminations a short figure moving towards her, arms widespread, saying: "Good to see you." He was short but square, thick legged, strong and quick on his feet. Over small features, large dark eyes assertively popped.

"What a lovely house," she said, social reflex returning.

"It's a nice home," said Reginald Swaffield.

She had to suppress a giggle, irreverence (of which she had plenty, subdued though she had come to appear) also returning. It was not a nice home. It was a horrible home. No one with her eye would endure it. She was searching round for an object to praise and saw a piece of porcelain.

"How very pretty!"

"Glad you think so. Sit down, sit down. Have a glass of champagne."

She liked the sound of that. Servant entered, her glass was filled, Swaffield's also.

"I always have a glass of this before dinner. Perhaps two. That's enough," he said, while the servant was still in the room. Swaffield was sitting beside her on one of the Regency sofas. If James Ryle, who had travelled up through layers of society, had been listening to them, he would have known that her voice was still undiluted upper-middle class, clear, unsloppy, not attacking but not a mumble, perceptibly louder than those of the contemporary young. While she, who had travelled down through similar layers, was puzzling about Swaffield's accent. She couldn't place it. Actually, the base was midland but overlaid by a veneer of Illinois American. Before the war, he had tried to make a living there, with no success. He had been a poor man in 1945, and the millions, a number of them, had all come since.

Once they were alone, he didn't waste time.

"I want to talk some business with you," he said.

"What sort of business, Mr. Swaffield?"

"Yours."

"I'm afraid I haven't any—"

"Oh yes, you have. You're old Massie's daughter, aren't you?"

"Did you know him?"

"No. I've heard about him." He turned full face towards her, with a hot imperious stare. "He left you out of his will."

She flushed with anger and embarrassment, but even more she was astonished. In her father's house she had met plenty of business men, but not anyone like this, who shot information at you as though it was his right to collect it, who produced it as though driven by an incomprehensible passion.

She tried to find some dignity to shelter behind.

"That's all over and done with. It's my concern, I think."

"Nonsense. What are you living on? I won't have it."

"This is my business. Nobody else's."

"You're not capable of looking after it. You're one of my people, that's why I sent for you. I'm taking over now."

She was affronted in two different ways. She was a proud woman, and had had failures which made her more so. Further, she had a feeling—and this might have been the thorn which went deepest into the flesh—that if she had been younger and prettier she wouldn't have been treated like this. Somehow failure and resentment and hope were all joining each other, so as to bring the tears humiliatingly near. Her marriage—that disaster had seeped her tiny store of confidence away. Marrying to cherish someone—and then to be left over-night.

And yet, though she wasn't sentimental about suffering, she couldn't stop herself being so about hope. Those who knew her thought she was realistic: in most respects she was, but not about her daydreams. Something wonderful might happen. Not this inflated power-drunk man wanting to look after her income. Patronising her, calling her one of 'his people,' acting out of charity. That wasn't part of the daydream. But someone wishing to look after her, just as herself (though her instincts

24

were strong, these dreams were pure)—that she would bow to, there would be no pride then.

She was shrewd, she often had good judgment. But she wasn't in a fit state that evening to judge Swaffield right. She had to admit to herself that he was a formidable man. The force that surged out of him, she couldn't miss. She did miss much of his ability, she wanted to despise him. And, though she wouldn't have liked him more if she had seen it, she missed altogether the passion to make a personal empire for himself, to run the lives of 'his people' and everyone round him, to be the patriarch of something like a family, a great extended family, among whom he was supreme.

There was another motive for his interference which she saw through almost at once. It was much more obvious, but less decisive than she thought.

"Why did he cut you out?" Swaffield's face came closer to hers.

"I don't want to talk about it."

"You may not want to, but you've got to."

"No."

"Don't be a fool. You're not a fool. What had he got against you?"

She didn't answer.

"You're a kind woman, aren't you?"

"I don't know about that."

"You wanted to be kind to him."

In a haze, she felt her will breaking down.

"I don't think," she said, "he ever liked me much."

"What about you?"

"I loved him. When he let me."

"What was the matter with him?"

She said: "Perhaps I disappointed him."

"You're smart enough."

"He'd have preferred someone who did him credit."

"What do you mean, did him credit?"

"When I was a little girl, he thought that I was plain."

"That didn't last," said Swaffield, with bullying kindness.

"He told me so."

"Blast him." He added: "This doesn't make much sense."

25

"He didn't approve of my marriage." By now she took it half for granted that Swaffield was informed about the marriage. Yes, he knew something. Marriage to a poor man: a clerk in what was then the L.C.C., and also unavailing, something of a waif. But also, and this presumably Swaffield didn't know, as egotistic as men came. At least, in retrospect (was she for once making an excuse for herself?) she believed so. Anyway he had left her. That, it went without saying, Swaffield did know.

"Jenny," (he even knew her pet name and she listened without resistance) "it doesn't add up."

He was exuding anger and energy combined.

"Of course, the old man was gaga his last few years."

She didn't reply, and he attacked her: "Wasn't he?"

"I have no idea. He wouldn't see me."

"Of course he was."

"It's not so likely. The family lives a long time."

"I tell you, he was. And that bitch of a woman stepped in. She's a double-dyed bitch if ever there was one. You'd better be honest. Try and tell me she isn't."

"I've never met her," said Jenny Rastall.

"Then you can believe me. She took her chance. She got him under her thumb."

"Mr. Swaffield, I've never met her, but he was my father, after all. He wasn't an easy touch for anyone."

"Any gaga old man is an easy touch for a woman like that. You can see what she did with him. Made him leave his cash to that son of hers. Who's a waster. He's a gigolo who talks women into bed and has curious tastes when he gets them there. I don't mind about him. It's the woman that I'm going to stop."

As Jenny sat within a foot of him, the seething of dislike—more spontaneous than dislike, nearer to hatred—was making him happier and more dominant. This was the motive that Jenny couldn't help but recognise and which, because she understood it, gave her a kind of familiarity or comfort. Though she couldn't know, she had no means of knowing, that, not so many years ago when Swaffield had first been asked to one of Lord Schiff's dinner parties, Mrs. Underwood had, so he imagined, snubbed him. Mrs. Underwood, in Swaffield's view, behaved as though she were conferring a favour on the Schiffs by eating their dinner. Much worse, he, Swaffield, was becoming eminent as a tycoon—and she asked him what he did.

Swaffield did not forget snubs even when, perhaps particularly when, he had invented them. He let them breed, and gained much pleasure from paying them out, the longer afterwards the more triumphant. Jenny didn't need to have any precise intimation of all that. The nerve showed through. But it was so sharp, it disguised from her a more interesting surgency beneath. She still had no conception what his kind of personal imperialism was like—nor how, if he had had no relation with Mrs. Underwood at all, he would nevertheless have been sitting with Jenny on his sofa that night, bullying her and taking charge of her affairs.

"There's no time to waste," he said.

She didn't meet the insistent positive stare.

"We're going to get that will overturned," he said.

She had been listening, mute and astray, resentful at being taken by storm, and yet defenceless, perhaps half grateful also.

"Undue influence the lawyers will call it," said Swaffield. "That's what they'll go for. It'll be a good old lawyer's holiday."

She had to make some sort of response, but she wasn't clear-minded.

"I'm not sure," she said, "that I want to drag my father's name through the courts."

"Nonsense, woman. You can't afford to be prissy." Though he was overwhelming her, he could read her expression and he changed his tone.

"If he hadn't been past it, he'd have told you to do exactly what I am telling you now. You just think of him before that woman took over. He'd have told you to look after yourself."

She was giving a lop-sided sarcastic smile, almost her first that night, and Swaffield wanted to make sure it stayed.

He said: "You won't be any good to anyone unless you do. That wouldn't be very clever."

He went on: "You haven't been very clever, always, have you?"

27

She said: "I can't say I have."

Then one of his barking, direct questions.

"How much are you living on?"

"Not much."

"How much?"

She made an effort to sound provided for. "I own the lease of my flat."

"How long for?"

"Ten years."

"Sensible." Swaffield, who could use good manners for a purpose, congratulated her as from one property owner to another.

"Apart from that, what have you got?"

"About £800 a year."

His only comment, and a quiet one, was: "I tell you, you can't afford to let those snakes get away with it."

There was a pause while he watched her. He went on in a manner brisk and impersonal:

"Getting down to business. I want you to realise, it won't be all plain sailing. There's a sizeable sum in the kitty, and they're not going to give it away just because we're making a fuss. Their lawyer is a man by name of Skelding, he's several kinds of old woman but he's not an idiot. So we shall have to follow suit. We'll have to go to a firm who knows their business. Robinson and Wigmore, they're goodish solicitors for this sort of game. They'll know what counsel to get their tabs on before the others have started."

In the same impersonal fashion he added:

"Of course, I'll take charge of the expenses. You can pay me back if and when we're home."

He gave her a hard encouraging grin.

"We shall get home all right. They've overplayed their hand. If only that bitch hadn't been so grasping, they'd be sitting prettier. If she'd just seen to it that there'd been a few thousand left to you, then they might have walked away. But she didn't know where to stop."

Previously Jenny had made one effort of pride about her living standard, and now she made one effort of self respect.

"I'm very grateful, Mr. Swaffield," she said, primly, and a

little thinly, "but I can't tell you tonight whether I shall want to proceed."

Swaffield looked at her with equanimity.

"That's natural enough."

"I really can't."

"You take a day or two and think about it. Then let me know."

He was a good negotiator, with women as well as men. It would do harm to force her. He understood something about her by now and was certain that the decision was already made.

He had filled her glass again during the conversation, but now, letting her go, he did not try to delay her with another drink. Her goodnight was constrained. His was cordial, not overdone and to himself relaxed and satisfied.

4

Once more in the Bishops' Bar, the following week, Hillmorton and Ryle were sitting together, this time with one of their closer friends. But they were, as they had often been in the past year, physically embarrassed. The table was shaking, each time Adam Sedgwick put his hand upon it. His glass had already slopped over, when he tried to raise it. There was no way in which they could help him, and he was offended, and hurt more than offended, if they tried.

It might have appeared that Lord Sedgwick was drunk. To some unobservant persons it did appear so, that night and other nights. Both Houses of Parliament were used to being charitable about drunkenness, and took it as an occupational hazard, rather like longwindedness in debate. However, to anyone who knew Sedgwick or even took a steady look at him, it wouldn't have occurred as a plausible explanation. The truth was, for some months past he had been, not immobilised but the reverse, with Parkinson's disease, and it was getting worse.

Beyond control his hands quavered and fluctuated as he attempted to light a cigarette. The only static area of his body seemed to be the muscles of his cheeks, deadened in a face which had once been both ascetic and humorous. While his right hand didn't obey, but jolted involuntarily about, with a clumsiness similar to that one sees in very young infants, he didn't look disquieted or lose his dignity. The other two were more uncomfortable than he was.

Sedgwick had had a career nearly as eminent as a professional scientist's could be. Alpha minus, he said, with sarcastic objectivity. He had been one of the founding fathers of molecular biology back in the thirties, before the decisive techniques were ready for him. Whether he would have had the wit to use them if they had been, he had also been heard to say, would fortunately never be known. He had in due course been given a Nobel prize, a little late. He had become President of the Royal Society. He hadn't made one of the ultimate discoveries, nothing in the class of Crick's couple, he used to remark, and was impatient if anyone contradicted.

Hillmorton and Ryle was familiar with all this, and with his personal style. And not only they, but many in the English official strata, were familiar with the Sedgwick group of families. This was something odd, insular, and academic. They had been prosperous and cultivated for a hundred and fifty years. (A great grand uncle of Sedgwick's, with the identical name, had been a Professor in Cambridge in the 1820's.) Wedgwoods, Darwins, Keyneses, Hills, Adrians, Hodgkins, Butlers, a few more. They had intermarried, obsessively and on the whole successfully, though the genes played tricks, negative as well as positive. The standards were austere. Sedgwick was fond of saying that it had its disadvantages to come from a family where, when one got a First, an uncle came up and observed that it was something to know you weren't altogether a fool. Similarly when one was elected into the Royal Society before the age of forty, if the uncle was feeling unusually complimentary—it seems you're not totally unrecognised, after all.

They had stayed in their own enclave, and in English terms had scarcely moved from the upper-middle class. They had never cared for any version of smart society, when that existed. Sedgwick was one of the very few who had, over a century, been appointed to this upper house, though one or two of them had turned an offer down. They had not had any but the remotest connections with Hillmorton's relatives: they didn't go to the same schools, they might have met at Trinity, but, so far as the records showed, there was not a single marriage between the Sedgwicks and their kind and the high Whigs. When the aristocratic country houses had entertained, the Sedgwicks did not go there. Adventurers did: even sometimes outsiders like predecessors of Ryle himself in earlier generations: but not these.

It wasn't that they were unsociable. They simply appeared to enjoy their own society. Before his illness, Sedgwick had been good company, someone people were eager to sit beside. Now he was putting up with his illness. But somehow—the more unexpected to those like Ryle who had known him longest—either his intelligence or his nerve had let him down. He had one of the most lucid minds extant, thought Ryle, and his courage wasn't in doubt, he had proved it on mountains and in war-time projects. Yet he wouldn't deal with his condition.

He had been given a new drug called L-Dopa. He had told the others how hopeful he was. They thought that a scientific education might have made him more sceptical, but he was like the simplest of persons with a miracle medicine. It worked on similar cases: he believed, or persuaded himself, that it was working with him. Neither Hillmorton nor Ryle could see any sign of that. Perhaps his speech, which had begun noticeably to slur, had somewhat cleared. On the other hand, his face was now being convulsed by twitches which might have looked like comic grimaces, and took away from its Red Indian distinction. Sedgwick admitted that this was a side-effect of the drug—"not specially becoming, I think." His hand movements, so far as Hillmorton and Ryle could see, hadn't become better. They judged that he was deteriorating, though not fast.

For those who didn't respond to the drug, there remained a brain operation which had been developed a decade or so before. It ought to give him years of remission and perhaps more than that. It carried some risks: but he had taken risks ten times acuter often in his life, and so had most men of his age. Most men wouldn't have hesitated for long. They might have had questions when they got into hospital, but they wouldn't have refused the operation. Sedgwick did refuse it. He persisted in believing that the drug would work.

The only thing not affected, the others thought, was his mind. It hadn't lost its edge, or scarcely at all. Sometimes the words were blurred on his lips, but they were still sharp. But, even there, was he becoming repetitive? That afternoon, he was talking about the educational policy of his own party, and they had heard him on this subject before.

Unlike the other two, he sat on the Opposition benches and took the Labour whip. That didn't inhibit him from saying that official Labour and T.U.C. statements on education were the most cretinous that had been issued in his time.

"It's extremely liberating for them to know nothing whatever about it. They've no more idea of serious education than you and I have of training ballet dancers."

"It'll take some time," said Ryle consolingly, "before they get what they want."

"I wish I could believe that. Elitism. That's the fashionable dirty word. It's a ninety-five per cent probability that anyone who thinks that elitism is the worst sin in the universe could never have belonged to any reasonable elite if he had tried for a hundred years. How does any sane man imagine this country is going to do any real science unless we train a scientific elite?"

"You're the authority," said Hillmorton. Neither he nor Ryle could totally suppress the consideration one showed when speaking to an invalid. "But I am pretty sure that we should go on doing it."

"I'm not so sure," Sedgwick persisted. "If these people manage to make education soft and easy and hygienic, and they may, then in thirty years real science in England will be on the way out. Less than half as good as it is today. It happens to be the one thing we still do well."

"Your colleagues will have to stop them," said Ryle.

"They've all lost their confidence. They're shouted down by stupid intellectuals. Stupid intellectuals are the biggest curse we've got. Clever intellectuals have their uses." (He employed the word clever in the old fashioned Cambridge manner, as a term of praise.) "Stupid ones are no good to man or beast. They're worse than that. They go about singing in unison, and everyone thinks that that is what the intellectual life is like."

"You know," he went on, "the intellectual life has got much sillier since I was a young man. The interesting thing is, how much sillier it can get."

His stoicism was hard, in health his contempt would have

33

been more relieved. The others wanted to divert him. Cambridge in the twenties—he was a couple of years younger than they were. Who were the real stars, looking back? Who was the cleverest man he had known? "Maynard Keynes," said Sedgwick, "without the shadow of a doubt. Not the greatest, by a long shot. Not the most agreeable. But superlatively bright. No one in that class now."

"By the by," said Hillmorton, trying another diversion, "when did you come here, Adam? I've forgotten."

That esoteric question was heard often in the House. It meant, when did you succeed to a seat or were appointed to one, but it sounded as though the man might have been actuated by a sudden whim, walking down Oxford Street, deciding that, instead of taking a holiday in Italy, he might as well join the Lords.

Sedgwick said 1966, just after he had finished being President of the Royal. Presumably all future Presidents would be asked, said Hillmorton. At that point Ryle, estimating that Sedgwick was getting ready to leave, got up quickly himself and said goodnight, while the others were sitting at the table.

The reason was, he was squeamish about seeing Sedgwick's run-and-shuffle to the door, bent over at an angle of forty-five degrees, centre of gravity in advance of his feet, like an old style music hall comedian coming on to the stage. Ryle wasn't made squeamish by blood, but sometimes he was by the grotesque. A man like Sedgwick oughtn't to be humiliated by the body in this fashion. It was grim to see him give a smile of shame as, at the end of his run, he butted into a wall.

Walking past Parliament Yard on his way home, Ryle had, not thoughts, shadows less clear edged than that, intrusions of mortality. Sedgwick wouldn't be seen in that place much longer. It was a place which kept reminding one that time, other people's, one's own, was drawing in. The average age was high, even though there were some young hereditary peers. The median age was much higher. When he looked round from his seat in the Chamber, he didn't see many people under sixty. As he watched those faces, he knew, with the certainty of a statistician, that some wouldn't be visible this time next year. Others would know the same, watching the faces on the benches where he sat himself.

It was a comfort to enter his drawingroom and switch on the lights. Through the stretch of window he gazed with approval at the collar of lamps across the river. He had lived here in Whitehall Court since his wife died the previous year, and he still didn't take the view for granted, he was still capable of thinking that it was one of the great townscapes. He left the curtains undrawn and sat on the sofa, looking out over the river and letting his reveries shimmer like the reflections on the water. When his elder son appeared punctually and by appointment he didn't want to be disturbed.

Ryle hadn't been close to this son since he was a child, although even now the father worried when he was ill or was flying in an aircraft. Ryle, used to being easy with people, was not so with his own son, and found himself, to his chagrin, becoming over hearty. Why this was so, he couldn't have said. Francis was an agreeable man of thirty, mildly eccentric, with a quirky sense of humour which his father found irritating. He was a principal at the Treasury, not likely, his father would have guessed, to reach a top job there, but capable enough. He spent a certain amount of time, which wasn't common in Whitehall, in devising proofs and disproofs of E.S.P., and this was another irritation to his father.

Ryle pressed a drink on him, feeling, as he so often did, like a noisy hairy Nordic barbarian outraging the sensibilities of a fine-nerved Hindu.

"I wanted to talk to you about the new arrival," said Ryle, referring to Francis's second child, born a week before, and using an arch self-conscious phrase as he would have done to no one else on earth.

"He's rather fun," said Francis. "I like very small infants."

"Do you?" said his father doubtfully. Yet he had done so himself.

"Original sin?" said Francis. "I think so."

At that his father became easier. "I think so too."

After a pause, he went on. "Well. I want to make some arrangement for him. Of course."

"You're not to stretch yourself. Really you're not."

"It doesn't make the slightest difference," said James Ryle. "You know that as well as I do."

This time it had been Francis who was over-considerate or

self-conscious. He gave a fresh shame-faced smile. He had been through all this before, when his first child was born. James Ryle had immediately set up a trust. He had been utterly unsecretive with his son, not only then but years earlier, about his finances—as he was unlikely to be with Hillmorton or Sedgwick, for there he had become acclimatised, on any question of private money, to a kind of automatic reserve. It hadn't been simply a flourish to say that Francis knew as much about his father's money as James Ryle knew himself. He did. He was surprised at how much there was.

It was all self-made. Comfortable professional jobs over a lifetime, but that didn't explain it all or nearly all. Histories which had sold well, especially in America, and used as text books. Consultancies with publishers. Investments which had started early, for a poor young man. It had accumulated and been well handled. If he died that night, Ryle's estate wouldn't be as large as old Massie's, but it might be something like half the size.

For years past he had been deliberately stripping it off. Often he looked less correct, more unbuttoned than his colleagues, but he could be just as precise an operator. The ideal, he had told his son Francis, was to die leaving nothing at all. Ryle equals nought, that was the formula for a decently calculated death. So there had been gifts with time to spare, trusts for both sons, trusts as the grandchildren were born, discretionary trusts to take care of other relatives and friends.

All that Francis had been informed of and understood. Frequently, though, he didn't understand his father. The theory was fine. Ryle talked of benefactions and made them. He didn't go back on his promises. And yet—there was no concealment, Francis had a clear idea of what was left, and he knew that his father had kept plenty at his own disposal. He wasn't getting anywhere near the formula for a decently calculated death. Francis would have expected him to be more ruthless with himself.

That evening, business was soon dealt with. Ryle proposed to do the same for this grandchild as for the first. Primogeniture, he remarked in an aside, was what had kept the upper class intact: but it wasn't for people like them, they weren't hard enough. So lawyers were already drawing up a new trust and it remained only for Ryle to live for the prescribed stretch of years.

"That's nothing for you. You'll only be, what, seventy-three," said Francis.

"We shall see, shan't we, one way or the other?"

"You're all right? When did you see your doctor?" For once Francis seemed not equable but anxious. In that interview it might have been a mercenary anxiety: but that it wasn't, or a long way after. "You are all right?"

"So far as I know." Ryle was dismissive and brusque. Then suddenly he broke into one of his outbursts, as cheerful, detached, spontaneous, as if he had been with a friend and contemporary, not with his son.

"Why should we go in for this nonsense? Will you tell me that?"

Francis gave a quizzical puzzled smile.

"I don't quite follow what you mean—"

"I mean, spending our energies, such as they are, thinking up financial settlements which are supposed to be useful in the 21st Century. It's nonsense. Whatever happens to this boy of yours, do you believe it's probable that any money we set aside for him now will be the slightest use to him in the year 2000? He won't be thirty then, I might remind you."

"Not very probable," said Francis. "But still, don't we have to—"

"It won't be any good to him," said Ryle with a loud laugh. "I suppose going through the motions is some good to us. It gives us the illusion that things are going on."

"Haven't people always needed that?"

"It's damned silly, but they've always acted as though they did."

Ryle, still expansive, reflected on the 18th Century Venetians. They were looking after their money and their descendants' money, just as the whole society was coming to an end. There were, said Ryle, some uncomfortable resemblances.

"I'm sure we're stabler. That is, if you put us in with America and Europe," said Francis, who had been trained as an economist.

"Well, you'll see. Anyway we go on making our nice little dispositions. Perhaps you're right, perhaps it keeps us from fretting. But it is damned silly, you know. Somehow we can't catch up with what's happening. Our emotions are always about a hundred years behind. A week or two ago, I was quite pleased because someone I know in the Lords told me about a daughter of his. She's going to get married, and the man's come into some money. I was quite pleased. Why the hell should I be? There's no sense in it. It's nonsense. Why should someone like this man who incidentally seems peculiarly worthless—why should he be appointed to live in the state of life that his relatives felt was designed for them a couple of generations ago?"

"I'll make you a small bet," said Francis, "that his father-in-law-to-be didn't feel it was quite so incongruous."

"The trouble is," said Ryle, "the young woman is very pleasant. I couldn't help being pleased."

When his son had gone, which was soon afterwards, Ryle was no longer thinking of Hillmorton's daughter, Julian Underwood, or natural injustice. That evening he had no intimation—and nor had the Underwoods or Hillmortons—that Reginald Swaffield had several days before summoned a partner of Robinson and Wigmore and set him to work. If Ryle had known of that, it would have seemed interesting but remote: for he, staring out over the streaming light paths on the river, was daydreaming, with some restlessness, about himself.

It might have seemed the opposite of his thoughts on mortality, walking home. The truth was, it was very close. It was the reverse of secretive talking of money to his son. But he would have been secretive about this, even if they had been intimate. One couldn't, he had long ago made it a rule, talk about marriage, much less an ageing man's sexuality, with those much younger than oneself: not even with contemporaries, if they were recent friends. He needed someone who had known him all his life, and there was none such within call.

He had had a happy marriage and he wanted something of the same kind again. Sex didn't cut off clean, as the young liked to think. Maybe it didn't cut off at all. Some day there would be a last time: but very likely one wouldn't know.

It wouldn't be easy to achieve what he was brooding over. Marriage was a language and a habit and he would have to learn them, and teach them, both again. To be an old man on the prowl, even if one weren't self-conscious and didn't feel it—did a healthy man ever feel old, except in moments?—was more ridiculous than one could bear. A woman too young would be no good for him. In the nature of things, it would before long become no good for her.

When he had wanted something before, he hadn't been held back, he had known how to act or at least how to put himself in the way of chance happening. Now he didn't. He wasn't used to being passive. It was like a regression into extreme youth, with its wild hopes and discontents. So he sat there, in a haze that might have been a youth's but without the limitless expectations. He had learned his way about, he had been active for so long. Now he didn't know his way, and sat there, daydreaming.

❧ 5 ❧

In Mrs. Underwood's bright, pot-pourri-smelling drawing-room in Victoria Road, she and three others were playing bridge. There was not much else to do. There was nothing more to say: which didn't prevent, as the game went on, a good deal more being said.

Round the table, the other three were Hillmorton's daughter Elizabeth, Julian Underwood and Mr. Skelding. The time was five thirty in the afternoon. That morning Mr. Skelding had heard that probate in the will had been held up: a caveat had been granted for six months. Six months was a long time, someone had said. Mr. Skelding had told them, with unctuous briskness, that they had to assume that there was going to be an appeal against the will.

All the information, which wasn't more than the legal exchange, had been given over tea. Since then they had proceeded with the rubber, some playing out of habit and discipline. Mrs. Underwood was an addict, and the table was appointed with pull-out slides on which the score-sheets rested and which also contained receptacles, as on an aircraft, for glasses. In Elizabeth Fox-Milnes's glass was gin and tonic. She was black haired, not showing much resemblance to her father's handsomeness, but with a kind of apprehensive mobile good looks, forehead carrying a premature line that night. But worry didn't affect her play. She was a long way the best of the four, although Mrs. Underwood was in good practice and, so it appeared, was Mr. Skelding, who was absorbing, also as in good practice, his second substantial whisky. The only non-drinker was Julian, who, partnering his mother, put down each card with dash and spontaneity, to be greeted by a frown because dash and spontaneity were not enough.

On the other hand it was Julian who was in higher spirits than any of them. Both women were depressed, and Elizabeth was having to hold down her qualms. Not so Julian, who wasn't holding down hilarious outbursts at the oddities of fate.

"There's nothing as scared as money," he said as a hand was being scored, with the air of one who was either financially in-different or alternatively could have made a fortune on the stock exchange. He had said it several times before, and his mother was irritated.

"That's not the point," she said.

"I keep telling you," he said, "just now there isn't any point at all. Is there, anyone?"

Mr. Skelding dealt sacramentally and spoke with caution and weight, discreetly satisfied because he was speaking with caution and weight.

"Of course there may be eventualities we can't provide against. But I hope you have all accepted it after the assurance I've given you, everything that can be provided against will be looked after in the next twenty-four hours. In fact," he said, as slyly as one coming to the climax of a card trick, "a certain amount was set going before I came here this afternoon."

"Lawyer's holiday," said Julian, not knowing that he was echoing a remark by another authority, Reginald Swaffield himself.

"It's bound to be done at a high level," said Mr. Skelding, who wasn't put off by Julian's euphoria. "We should be very. remiss if we didn't get the best opinion ourselves."

"I suppose that ought to be consoling." Elizabeth's tone was sharp. She tried to soften it, and addressed Mr. Skelding by his Christian name. Struggling with anxiety, her manners were good. She didn't like some of those in her own family. Her fa-ther's, since he had been a politician and was also affable by na-ture, were matey: but often enough she had heard relatives patting their own pet names across the room, patting the pet names of absent acquaintances with the same enthusiasm, who simultaneously would consider it fitting to say Mr. to someone like Skelding (sitting amongst them, doing them a service), even though they had known him for years.

"Eric," she said, "I wish to God that the old man had left his daughter something, just to look decent. Then we might have been spared all this."

She knew no more than Julian, moments before, that she also was echoing Swaffield. The fact was, that at this stage for normally shrewd people the position was not complex, and minds thought alike.

"It's going to come out right." Julian gave a cry as optimistic as Mark Tapley's in one of his less depressed moments.

"I think we had better call," Mrs. Underwood broke in.

They duly called, Julian again optimistic, and played. Julian and Mrs. Underwood went down once more.

Elizabeth was certain that Mrs. Underwood had deliberately stifled her question, and knew why. She was too much disturbed, she wasn't to be put off. She repeated:

"Eric, aren't I right? If only she had had a few thousand in the will—"

Elizabeth caught a glance between Mr. Skelding and Mrs. Underwood.

"That's as may be. I really don't think it's very profitable to hark back, Lady Elizabeth. We've plenty of better things to do, I'm sure you will agree."

Mr. Skelding had a regard for titles, enjoyed producing them, enjoyed hearing one of their bearers use his Christian name. Nevertheless he was being shifty. Elizabeth hadn't much doubt that he and Mrs. Underwood had been in disagreement, about the will. He was a sensible lawyer. He was likely to have suggested to her that it would avoid some comment if Massie 'remembered' his daughter. Mrs. Underwood was a sensible woman. It would have been easy for her—if she had been so close to the old man as Elizabeth imagined—to use her persuasions. Had he been obstinate? Or was there another reason? Had Mrs. Underwood been afraid of a quarrel with her son?

Elizabeth believed, though Julian had been secretive, that he

42

had known it all every step of the way. He would have been angry—Elizabeth didn't believe but knew—at sums of money being unnecessarily dispensed on persons other than himself. Elizabeth also knew for certain that, whatever sense and prudence told his mother, he would win in that kind of battle of wills.

Elizabeth sat at the bridge table, acute by nature, but also distracted and confused. She loved that man. She loved him to yearning point. She was in his power. The trouble was that she didn't trust him, or not with her mind. It had even occurred to her to suspect his extraordinary ebullience and bursts of hope that evening. Did they spring out because this news might give him an excuse to escape their marriage—or at any rate delay it? Procrastination, he loved. Any month or week or even day saved against not being committed—those he hugged to himself. Was that what he was doing now, blissfully outweighing the chance of money switched away? No, Elizabeth, though she was often lost in his mirages and quick change acts, couldn't think so. Her moves, intentions, desires, were straight lines, and his rarely were: and yet, she knew this much, in the end he looked after himself, few more devotedly, he had an instinct for self-preservation, and money was what one needed to preserve oneself.

Elizabeth had read somewhere that one couldn't love without trust. Whoever wrote that didn't know much, she thought: it must have been an ageing queer. When she let her acid thoughts about Julian crystallise, she said to herself that no one in her senses would trust him. Yet he had been much loved. Look at her own state.

But there was something else she didn't see so hard and clear. She had another feeling that later on James Ryle would recognise, but she scarcely could. On the surface she disparaged Julian. He looked like a wicked baby, she sometimes thought, and loved him so that she couldn't imagine loving any other man again.

Mrs. Underwood was saying to Skelding, "You're getting everything laid on, of course?"

"It'll take a little while, we can't rush things," he replied, fingertips tented together, expression bestowing security.

43

"It's all under control, though?"

"We hope so. We hope so."

"Everything?" said Mrs. Underwood.

"We shan't leave anything to chance."

Mrs. Underwood relaxed, satisfied, beak of nose less evident. She made some acquiescent remark about it all devolving on Mr. Skelding and the other lawyers. She gazed brightly round the table, and said:

"The rest of us will have to be shabbash wallahs. That's the best we can do."

This peculiar observation was incomprehensible to all the others, though it might have reminded some that she had lived in India. She explained that shabbash wallahs were spectators on the touch lines, cheering their side on. That was what they were going to be, she added in a commanding tone.

Meanwhile Elizabeth had had another suspicion, that Skelding and Mrs. Underwood had been talking in code. It sounded as though they were once more in alliance—but this time were they leaving Julian out? It could be that they (or rather Skelding) had learned a lesson, and weren't giving him advance information about tactics—so that he wouldn't be able to overpersuade his mother. Elizabeth could work out what one piece of tactics could be. It was obvious. And it was also obvious that Julian wouldn't like it, would make trouble, and that they were sensible to keep it to themselves.

Mrs. Underwood would feel guilty about it. Everyone thought her brassy, and maybe she was, except that Julian melted her. Elizabeth wasn't certain whether, facing the truth, she had any liking for the older woman. There was a farcical shadow of resemblance in the way they both clung to Julian, and that prevented any kind of ease. And yet Mrs. Underwood was her ultimate support about the marriage, Elizabeth believed, and so, though she might not feel any liking, she sometimes looked at her with the sort of dependence which isn't far from love.

"I don't know why we are all making such a fuss," said Julian, "I tell you, it's going to come out all right."

"Well," said Mr. Skelding imperturbably, "you wouldn't like your legal adviser to take that for granted, you wouldn't like it very much."

44

"I'm sure that things are going to come out all right, they always do." He turned, fresh, enlivened, to his mother: "Think of the times!"

From her expression, that touched memories.

Julian baited Mr. Skelding. "People make things too complicated. That's why they get them wrong. The only point is, we've got the will in our favour, and they haven't. At the end of all the flummery it will come down to that, you'll see."

"Oh, my friend," said Mr. Skelding, for once shocked, "that really is much too simple."

"Oh, my friend," mimicked Julian, "important things are simple. Otherwise they wouldn't be important."

As they started to play again, Elizabeth was wondering when if ever this rubber would end. And when it did—she was wondering what would happen. He might not choose to take her to his flat. For she never knew when he wanted to go to bed with her. Capricious, fanciful, there as everywhere, there more than anywhere. Among his charms, she had one of her acid thoughts, was a mildly luxurious hypochondria. He had told her recently that an orgasm spent as much energy as a three mile run. He might indulge himself into believing that.

At last the rubber did end. Mrs. Underwood said hopefully, more as addict than hostess, that there might be time for another. No one responded. The account was reckoned up. Mrs. Underwood and Julian had lost £7 between them. Mrs. Underwood paid for both. Elizabeth, despondent because she had received no signal from him, watched this happen. She had frequently done the same. He let her pay minor debts for him, though he refused to borrow money.

Then, casual, light, natural, came Julian's voice,

"Well, if you'll excuse us, mother, I think it's time Liz and I went home. She can make me a scrambled egg—can't you?"

He gave her his child-like smile. Suddenly she was totally happy, with the happiness outside of time or even of expectancy that might have lifted her when she was a girl, not a woman neither sweet natured nor gentle, getting on for middle age.

6

Six months is a long time, someone had said. In fact, no one knew for certain what the period of waiting would be, and it was easy to underestimate the resources of English law. So that a number of people had some more experience of waiting, expectancy, anxiety, and hope: and in the process one or two noticed some more of the curious properties of time.

Time was passing, that was dull, one realised it only when it was over and brought it back to memory, which was itself fallacious. One never realised what the actual flux of time had been like when one was living it: just as James Ryle might recall looking out over the river brooding on his celibacy, and cut off that recollection as though it were framed, like a period in a history text book: while on the actual evening, time had, not surprisingly, flowed on and in due course (and not so long after the brooding) Ryle had roused himself and gone off to have a meal at one of his clubs.

Time passing at a regulated pace was a nice, platitude-ridden, augustan thought, but it didn't really happen even to old men. Whether you were young or old, time in a period of waiting showed its relativistic possibilities, expanded or contracted or even stayed still, according to how you were feeling at that moment, how much you loved or dreaded the future, and what you were like yourself. For instance, of the principals connected with the will, Elizabeth distrusted the future most. She believed that the result of these legalities was going to deter-mine her life, one way or the other: and she didn't trust, and often didn't wish to know, the answer. So that on a good many nights, having spent hours making plans with Julian of how they would live when his money at last arrived, she would turn into the pillow and wish that this moment would never end. Did time duly stretch out? Sometimes she felt so peaceful just before she went to sleep that it seemed so.

Jenny Rastall was, on the whole, less transported. She had no one at that time in whom to invest her hopes. She wasn't frightened of the future, except of loneliness. When she had been through her second crisis of decision—which happened a couple of weeks after the bridge party at Mrs. Underwood's— there were mornings when she scampered off on her visiting round, half oblivious to any prospects from the will.

Occasionally, seeing a client or patient or charge (she never knew, even to herself, what to call them) whom she was fond of, she wished she had money to buy this old lady a present just to keep her interested, perhaps a television set. Then it occurred to Jenny that conceivably she might soon have money, and she felt excited with no misgivings at all. Frequently she woke in the morning, eager with the sense that something good might be coming her way. But that wasn't a novel feeling. It had come to her so often, cheated her, supported her, however drab her days were being. Maybe now it was stronger, with some realistic chance to think ahead. She enjoyed that, just as a gambler would: she would have been happier gambling than most of the others. She loved the excitement, like a gambler she loved to hope. On the other hand, she never made plans about how she was going to spend her money, if and when it ultimately arrived. Perhaps that wasn't a contradiction, perhaps that was another tic of hope.

Julian, who showed a good many tics, did not show that one. He made plans, in detail, of how the money would be spent. So much in detail that both his mother and Elizabeth tried to stop him, terrified that he would be disappointed, Elizabeth terrified for her own sake.

"Tempting fate, that's what you mean," Julian taunted them. "Never mind. Fate is what happens to me."

Those remarks, his listeners did not find tranquillizing. Nor

47

would they have found it tranquillizing if they had known that his plans as he had revealed them to his mother, though they sometimes included marriage to Elizabeth, were markedly different from those he revealed to his putative wife: and that both were different from a third, private or executive version possessed by Julian alone.

If she had known that, Elizabeth would have taken it as she did any fresh piece of dissimulation—at the same time surprised and not surprised, qualm-ridden, maddened, acceptant.

As for Mrs. Underwood, she like Elizabeth was afraid of the results, but not because she might see Julian extract himself from their relation. Though that thought had often worn her down, the old Japanese 'darkness of the heart,' it was something harder, more self-bound, that now made her angry as much as anxious, less depressed than Elizabeth, simply because she was angry and her self-esteem was fighting for her.

This matter of the will—it was something she had done herself, the most effective thing she had ever done for her son. Perhaps she had done it for a softer motive (at times she thought it might secure his love, never having learned or being capable of learning that that one could never do—in which she was not different from most of the human race), but this she had forgotten. It had been her doing, and it would be unbearable to have it taken from her in the end. She detested this unknown woman, whom she had never met, with lethal singlemindedness, and anyone who was helping her. Mrs. Underwood had forgotten her motive and also anything she had done to get that will achieved. It was now all innocent, all triumphant, all her own action. To have it upset—the adrenalin poured through her, she didn't turn into her pillow as Elizabeth did. Her will braced her, her will shouted that it would not happen.

Meanwhile the lawyers were working, more of them than laymen would have expected (Mr. Skelding's decorous and oldfashioned office concealed half a dozen partners and several qualified clerks) and—more so again than laymen would have expected—some of them getting their feelings involved on their respective sides.

48

It was not only that they were professionals and wanted to win, though that was true enough. Both Skelding's firm and their opponents had warned their clients that costs were mounting (they were already round £10,000) and put forward the arguments for settling out of court. That was a minimum responsibility. Otherwise the case had its legal interest and might also make some public noise, of which one or two counsel, already briefed, had a not displeasing premonition. Some young men, who wouldn't appear in court or even take part in conferences, nevertheless thought they might bite off some internal credit in their offices. But this wasn't the whole of it. It wasn't only Mr. Skelding who wasn't quite dispassionate. He himself had managed Mrs. Underwood's legal work for years. He had taken on Mr. Massie's a couple of years before the old man died on her introduction, and had drawn up the old man's will according to her instructions. She might have been more cautious, Mr. Skelding didn't let his criticism go further. He had wanted to keep her confidence, that was what he prided himself on and cherished. Perhaps he should have given stronger advice. Still, she could be headstrong, but she didn't overstep the guide-lines, and he wished her well.

Nearly everyone in his firm agreed. Some of the seniors, close to the family negotiations, regarded Julian with something near to physical distaste. This was a common masculine response. On the other hand, they tended to like Elizabeth, bitter tongue and all, and those who had been knocked about by passion wanted her to have her man, whatever he was like.

None of them knew Jenny Rastall, and a good many accepted the rumours that were clustering round her, just as rumours were always accepted (perhaps most willingly) by those who have lived in the world. She was an intriguer, she had been disinherited for financial fiddling or alternatively for unutterably callous behaviour, she was a tool of Swaffield's. Swaffield's intervention in the case had become known, and that tightened the solidarity of the Underwood party. To a good many people, whichever side Swaffield was on, the other must be right. He had a capacity for inspiring a kind of charismatic hate.

49

With some, though, he inspired passionate energy. Robinson and Wigmore were sophisticated lawyers, especially their chief working partner Symington, but they became as devoted to Jenny's cause as Swaffield himself. Whatever his other motives, he became convinced that Jenny was a nice and ill-treated woman, and he spread that conviction like a gospel. The lawyers met her, and thought her honourable and unassuming. Few of the rumours about her reached their side and when they did were kicked away. On the other hand rumours about Elizabeth began to circulate, encouraged by Swaffield, who had a voyeur's delight in sexual scandal. Stories of her and Julian—the enmity or contempt, with a simple change of object, became as strong as in the Underwood party, and the lip-licking more luxurious.

By the spring of 1971 there were perhaps about a hundred persons who were, some remotely, some as principals, affected by Massie's will, or at least who had some knowledge of it. Only a few were neutral. Even the outsiders weren't. Hillmorton might have said sarcastically that, in the parliamentary form, he had an interest in the case: but his friends Ryle and Sedgwick, who had no conceivable interest and were as capable of detachment as most men, seemed not to be capable of detachment about this. Sedgwick was weighed down by his illness, and yet, in ardent and paradoxically unselfish moments, he found himself indignant about Jenny Rastall, who he was unlikely ever to meet, and impatiently eager for Elizabeth to win.

That was so with Ryle also. In fact, those level-headed senatorial men (as others thought them) were being infected by clamour as thoroughly as everyone else.

Most of these participants, but not quite all, belonged to a privileged layer in an old and privileged country. Not quite all—for Jenny Rastall herself wasn't much luckier than the old people she cared for, though some believed that those who had been born well off, as she had, never completely forgot it and had a kind of protective veil whatever became of them. As for the rest, they were living more comfortably than most people, either then or ever, had been able to live. It was they who had become partisans—showing once more, as though that were

50

needed, that if men had a chance to become partisans, they couldn't resist taking it.

Some bits of partisanship had led to deaths in torment. This one was, to put it mildly, milder. And yet, a few reflective people were startled, and then embarrassed, to find that their emotions were getting bound up in a cause, not only minuscule, but which made them feel ashamed or in secret improper. For this was, there was no cover or genteel escape, a matter of money. Not even great sums of money, such as politicians like Hillmorton had once argued about, where sheer magnitude made it fairy arithmetic—but just naked personal money, the kind of money which affected a few day by day lives. They had all become curiously prudish about money. At the same time, they were singularly unprudish about sex. Within the human limits, few people were more unprudish about sex than Julian Underwood and Elizabeth and their younger relatives. There wasn't much that Hillmorton and the rest of his generation didn't tolerate—and not much, as someone like Swaffield might have discovered about their acquaintances, that hadn't been performed. Hillmorton and the others knew their own countrymen and wouldn't have been surprised.

Almost totally unprudish about sex: more prudish about death than their predecessors: and, as they didn't like to recognise, far more prudish about money. They didn't want to talk about it. They didn't want to face how much they cared and worried about it. They wished to pretend—to themselves as much as to others—that it affected them very little.

That was an hypocrisy. Like most hypocrisies it had something good in it. They wanted to disguise their motives, because they would have liked loftier ones. The actual facts, however, pointed otherwise. If anyone doubted that, he had only to read letters in the press or listen to the parliamentary debates. When first the news of Massie's will was broken, Hillmorton and Ryle had been listening to debates on economic policies. Later, as the will was challenged, their House, following the Commons, was occupied with the Industrial Relations Bill. A visitor from another civilisation wouldn't have been illusioned or disillusioned, but he would have picked out one simple theme. Most men thought about money more than they admitted, and badly wanted it. The only thing they wanted more, perhaps, was that other men shouldn't have more money than themselves: or ideally should have less.

There was some difference as to how to obtain these natural objectives. There were feelings in common, though. Hillmorton, not a self-indulgent man, would have taken a drop in what was called his standard of living more indifferently than most—provided there were others down on whom he could cast an appreciative eye. In not so different a fashion, trade union professionals devoted and ailing would wear themselves out in filibusters against the Common Market, in case the stratum of workers they used to represent might lose one step up the differential ladder.

It became a condition of daily life, as pervasive as fear in a cholera epidemic—but more enjoyable, for though there was fear in the climate, there was also a curious sort of excitement. For some, it wasn't at all unpleasant to feel ill-done-by about money or to be claiming it. A certain number were immune from this excitement, and they were often those who would have been immune from fear in an epidemic.

There were plenty of people who were breathing this air and didn't like it. Often if they were in touch with their own experience they felt shame and self-reproach. The time they spent with income tax accountants—this was a special addiction of the privileged. Income tax accountants as ingenious as theologians finding a way to salvation: which frequently meant saving, and being at the same time lawful about it, not very magnificent sums such as £400 per annum. Scrupulous persons kept from the Exchequer each penny they could, within the legal limit. They had suspicions, and more than suspicions, that others were not so scrupulous. Scrupulous persons, if they were middle-aged or more, felt that commonplace financial honesty had been on the slide in their own lifetime: just as Jenny Rastall, and an acquaintance she had not yet made, were to say to each other a few months later.

All this, the same persons sometimes thought in secret, was a symptom of a country in decline. Here they blamed themselves, the shame and self-reproach got harder, but they weren't being realistic. They were sensitive that the country's power had evanesced under their eyes. It wasn't contemptible that they took it to heart, and used it as an explanation for the discontent around them, and their own failures. But as an explanation it wasn't always or often true.

When their country had been at the peak of its power, just over a hundred years before (the decline had set in long before it was visible on the surface), there had been just as much rapacity for money—maybe slightly less manoeuvring, less hypocrisy or façade words. And in their own time, the late 20th Century, there were countries with structures like their own but not yet manifestly on the way down, which in the chase for money, or anything it symbolised, could give them ten yards in a hundred and a beating. This was endemic all over the rich world, and over some of the poor world too. They blamed themselves a bit too much, perhaps so as not to see something more difficult or foreboding.

The trouble was people, any people, people like themselves, couldn't forget themselves for very long. In the first years of a great religion, or of a revolution, or of a total war, people could forget themselves almost completely, except for their own souls or the vast hope of the future. But not for long. All societies had discovered this, after a revolution. Hence the disappointments of tender-minded men. There wasn't much stamina of the soul: there was almost infinite stamina of the ego.

Yet most men, even the disappointed and the most self-bound, still at moments had hankerings after a different life. How to find it? A religion couldn't be invented. Once a religion wasn't credible, it didn't exist. Maybe some of those, now foraging among the money claims, might have found a kind of grace in attempting to wipe out some of the revocable suffering and poverty in the world. Jenny Rastall was trying, in her local fashion. The children of people on the other side, Sedgwick's, one of the Hillmorton's, were devoting themselves outside the country, and had elysian hopes.

If that were ever achieved, by any means on earth, and if in a couple of hundred years, long after these people were all forgotten, most human beings were living half as comfortably as they had lived—then what? Would they get into the same state? You mustn't ask, disciples of action would have to say.

What are the human limits? They could see only their own time. The answer oughtn't to stand in the way of good will, but it might. It might prevent the chances—and no one could reckon them, they hadn't so far been great—of good action.

7

Jenny Rastall's second decision was forced on her as gustily as the first. To an extent she was getting used to Swaffield's telephone calls—the one word 'Swaffield,' then an instruction, then, instead of 'Goodbye,' a final 'Bless you' which didn't sound like a benediction. So, on an afternoon in December, when she picked up the receiver and heard the surname, voice vibrant, she thought she was prepared.

"I have to see you."

She asked, when, finding it as always difficult to put him off.

"Six o'clock." She sighed. It was a cold day, she had just returned from a couple of visits, she was looking forward to an evening with a book.

"You are to come to the House of Lords," the Swaffield voice went on. "Ask for Lord Clare. He's a friend of mine. I put him on one of my boards." Swaffield, not expecting her to reply, told her which door to go to, with the complacency of one who knew his way about.

"Six o'clock," he repeated and dismissed her, not even with a blessing.

Jenny gazed at the silenced telephone with irritation, amusement and, she couldn't resist it, a flash of excitement. He might be doing things for her, he was the only one, she couldn't be too delicate—but she still had the touchiness of the unlucky. On the other hand, she found herself grinning, the

House of Lords was one up to him, one up as a meeting place even on the Hill Street mansion. How had he managed it? and why? She had never been inside the place herself, and that was why she was excited. It wouldn't have been in her style to pretend to be superior. She wasn't an intellectual, she wasn't given to progressive opinions, she came from her own race and class, she had a soft spot for royalty and for lords.

More than a soft spot, in fact a vestige of thrill. As she got inside the door and told the attendant she had an appointment with Lord Clare she felt the nerves at her elbow tingle: just as men from families like hers, were seen to tremble as they went to receive decorations from the Queen. Jenny was a reasonable woman, and she would have been puzzled if she had reflected on these phenomena.

When the attendant, large, soldier-like, be-badged, led her into the guest room, which was the bar where strangers were admitted, the man slipped away, for Swaffield advanced on her, mouth wide-smiling, like a magniloquent frog.

"Jenny, I want you to meet Lord Clare," said Swaffield, not fussy about the finer points of etiquette.

The room was large and very bright, tapestries on the end walls, an array of small tables as in a London café, most of them occupied that evening, as many women (Jenny thought, visitors like herself) as men. Swaffield and Lord Clare had established themselves at a table by the window, from which, looking over the river, they had a view suitable for Monet and in a tone, with half a mile of geographical displacement, identical with that from James Ryle's drawingroom.

Lord Clare, blond hair swept back, shook her hand with his own left one (the other was covered by a black glove) in a manner assured and at the same time slightly uncoordinated. He was earnestly polite to Jenny, apologising for the room being so full, explaining that 'the other side' had put on a three line whip. The other side, Jenny took for granted, as Tory as he was, would be the Opposition: but she didn't take for granted much else about him. She glanced at his hand, and thought she remembered that he had done something gallant—not in the German war, she fancied. The name, yes, the name might have some sort of misty aura.

56

Jenny preserved her generalised regard for the House she was sitting in, but didn't know much history. She didn't realise—though she would have liked it if she had been told—that this was one of the old names, probably the only pre-1660 title in the noisy room. This man was a remote relative of Byron's Clare, one of the boys whom Byron hankered after, not that that demarcated him clearly from other boys, nor, as far as that went, from other girls.

Lord Clare had another distinction, curious though minor. He was one of the few peers with a territorial title who actually possessed land in (or to be exact in his case, within three miles of) the place from which the title came. Unlike the Hillmortons, who hadn't owned a house or an acre within fifty miles of the little Warwickshire village for generations.

Ignorant of these embellishments, Jenny was watching, her eyes alert and concentrated, the man himself and his exchanges with Swaffield. Swaffield hadn't yet given a hint of why he had brought her there. As a rule, he broke news without preliminaries or warning, and she knew him well enough by now to be suspicious. If he wasn't being imperious, there was a reason for it. Meanwhile, he wasn't being imperious with Lord Clare, far from it; and neither was Lord Clare being imperious with him. Jenny, personal irreverence becoming more powerful than institutional reverence, was soon finding a certain beauty in this mutual civility.

At times, it became even more soothing than that, something like a mutual sycophancy. Lord Clare called Swaffield 'Reg,' teased him about his tycoon activities, flattered him about the objets d'art in Hill Street, and, politely not leaving Jenny out, invoked her in aid as another of the applauding cherubim. In return, Swaffield slid in admiring references to Clare's interventions on the board ("It's only three years since I put you on, Edward, you picked it up faster than any of them"), his success on a postwar mission ("He'd have made money anywhere, any time, I tell you." Swaffield turned to Jenny. "He knows more than I do about things it's my business to know, and there aren't many I'd say that of, which is lucky for some of us").

Impatience to hear whatever her own news could be was

damping down. Excitement at the occasion was damping down still more. Irreverence was winning. Two or three men came up, Clare invited them to 'enlarge the circle,' Swaffield looked disappointed when they said they had to leave. Jenny was coming to two conclusions. The first was that Lord Clare, old-style he might be, elegant in his classical fashion, possibly heroic, was also remarkably enthusiastic about keeping his director's fees. He must be well off, quite likely rich, but he would sing a good many praises of Swaffield if that meant holding on to what he was paid. The second thought seemed less plausible to Jenny, who wasn't certain how these institutions worked, and she didn't find it agreeable—but it didn't need super-human divination to guess that Swaffield was aiming at a place in that House himself and was using his considerable resources to get one. She hadn't seen him at the suppliant end before. It wasn't overdignified, but he didn't lose any of his force, his capacity to exude energy—and, though she didn't wish to recognise it, underneath the brashness his smooth and lubricating subtlety.

Another man stood behind their table. It was James Ryle, but, before Clare could introduce him, there were shouts of 'Division,' scraping of chairs as people rose, shrilling of bells. Ryle, whom Jenny might have talked to without this interruption, said that he had better go and vote. There was an amendment to a government bill in the committee stage, and Clare, a conservative devotee, went off automatically to do his duty.

Left alone with Swaffield in the window corner, Jenny looked at him expectantly. Now was the time. Instead, Swaffield returned her look with tantalising, impudent or leering cheerfulness, and said that he wished he could buy her another drink—but he had discovered that as a guest he couldn't.

"I tell you what," he observed. Once more she thought, this might be the time.

"Yes, Mr. Swaffield?" No one had ever made it so difficult for her to keep still.

"I don't think much of the hereditary peerage. It's a load of nonsense."

After his purring over Lord Clare, he was, with his usual energy, having it both ways. This outburst was sincere enough: the curious thing was, the purring might be sincere too. That was hard for Jenny to accept, thinking him constantly cool-headed, the cynical operator. And yet, side by side with that, there could co-exist another quality, which was that he believed in what he was doing while he was doing it, though sometimes not for long.

He stared round the room, places left vacant at the tables, women chattering, here and there a solitary male.

"Why in God's name should they be here?" said Swaffield with a disapproving grin, as though addressing the vacant seats or proposing a cantankerous health to absent friends. He went on:

"What good do they think they're doing here? You tell me that."

Just then—they had been away only three or four minutes—Clare and an acquaintance re-entered the room, followed by others. The acquaintance was Lord Lorimer, as lonely and out of place as when he had seated himself beside Hillmorton weeks before. Ryle had not returned, but Clare began collecting chairs and assembling them round their corner. Swaffield was known by sight to people who looked at photographs in the financial columns: a Jewish peer, Azik Schiff, maybe even richer than Swaffield, joined the party, together with his wife and step-daughter. As well as Lorimer, several men, including a newly elevated bishop, began to listen on the fringes of the group. Jenny couldn't help but realise, as had happened to her before, on visits to Hill Street, the magnetic attraction of great wealth: the rich might not be different from us, except that the most unlikely men gathered round them. People seemed to like being courtiers, even at the oddest of courts.

In a moment, she realised something else. When Swaffield suddenly accosted her, in a tone jeering and protective—

"Well, Jenny, my girl, I have a message for you—" she knew that he had been waiting for an audience. He had done this to her once before, out of the blue questioning her about her father and the will, at a large dinner party in his own house.

"Can't it wait?" she muttered, blood flooding up, defenceless. She had been prepared for much, not for this. Even he couldn't discuss her private business before a group of strangers, in a place where he didn't belong. She still had something to learn.

"Not on. You'll have to make up your mind. Anyway Edward will be interested, he ought to hear." Swaffield was speaking to the group at large. "Edward's going to be one of my vice-presidents, you see, and this is one of my girls." Expansively Swaffield explained that he was talking of his society for old people: it wasn't his only charity, he said, but it was his favourite one: "We shall all come to it soon, you'd better face it, we shall all know what it's like to be old." His eyes flashed round among the men, with his matey taunting defiance, as though inquisitive as to whether they were still virile or had ever been. Then he gazed at the women with similar interrogations about their husbands. As it happened, Lady Schiff and her daughter were about as likely to be out-faced or discomfited on such a matter as he was himself.

He reverted to being cordial. After the challenges and the salacious eye, there were emollient listener-magnifying words returning, warming the moment. Yes, how good it was that Edward Clare was going to help him.

"Very good, very good," said Bishop Boltwood, not overfond of rich men, liking them better if they showed a tinge of human feeling.

"Of course," said Swaffield, "Edward has been helping me with some of my business games. He's been a great help, I don't mind telling you."

Murmurs of assent. Clare sat, pale eyed and not self-concerned, unselfconscious with the placidity of one who was used to being praised from childhood, not minding if Swaffield went on claiming what friends they were. Then Swaffield broke off. He said, startling and also embarrassing Jenny once again:

"This girl has been a great help too. We couldn't run the charity without people like her. And she's about the best I've got."

"Very good," said the Bishop, a small bright-eyed figure, giving Jenny something like a wink of encouragement. She was distracted, chips on shoulders leaping up at being patronised: and yet, it wasn't all patronage, some of it was kindness, he had cut off sucking up to peers, stopped his manoeuvres on his own account—as though he were momentarily contemptuous of these people round him—and concentrated on her.

"It's something to do," she said in a muted tone to the Bishop, who was sitting closest to her.

"It's more than that, I know, I know," the Bishop replied, hearty and north-country but also quiet, getting his hands free from the clutter of official garments. A connoisseur of English nomenclature might have observed that, while red tape turned out not to be red, lawn sleeves were certainly lawn. No one else had been listening to them, but Swaffield seemed to have directional hearing, however many people his eyes were flickering round or were being kept under his dominion. In his loudest attention-compelling voice he said:

"There's something else for you to do, dear. You'll have to make up your mind." Yes, he had compelled attention. Glances were fixed on her, sympathetic, curious, or amused.

"What about, Mr. Swaffield?" Her own voice had become harder. She wasn't going to be beaten down.

"I heard from old Symington" (Symington was a partner in the firm of Robinson and Wigmore, the lawyers he had found for her) "this afternoon. That's why I brought you here." He paused, staring at her with hot ungentle fixity which might have been—though she knew with her it wasn't —a stare of lust. Then he said, suddenly casual and off-hand:

"The other people are trying to buy you off. You'll have to make up your mind."

He addressed the group sitting round the table with utter equanimity, as though it were entirely natural for them to hear about a stranger's affairs:

"She's being done down over her father's will. I thought it was time someone got things right."

He went on: "Well, Jenny, they've offered £10,000. That's net, they'll pay all the costs."

She had been told to expect some move like this, but still wasn't prepared.

"Old Symington," said Swaffield, "thinks we might jack them up a thousand or two. Not a lot. This is about what they think it's worth to keep you quiet. You'll have to make up your mind."

Sometimes she trusted him. Was he being ambivalent now? She asked, as if she depended on him:

"What do you think?"

"It's not a win for us. It'd mean they're getting away with it very cheap. They're getting away with murder. I'd like to see some of that crowd begging in the street."

That was too violent for his audience. He sensed it, he was letting too much of his aboriginal fury break through. With a quick change act, he became once more a benevolent, protective and indulgent benefactor.

"Still, you know, we can't have everything, sometimes you have to sit by and see a set of crooks making a meal of it."

Someone asked a question about the legislation. Swaffield didn't answer, but spoke without emphasis to Jenny:

"You'll have to make up your mind about the offer. I advise you to take it."

She had a strong feeling that he didn't want her to. He might be trying to influence her by contraries, he was fluid enough for that, she had seen him bring it off. Yet somehow— she trusted him more than she let herself think—she believed that he was being responsible. At least he was making an effort to be responsible. After all, he knew the difference this money would make to her. She had been reckoning that it would increase her income by fifty per cent.

"I advise you to take it," Swaffield repeated. In a moment he spoke to Azik Schiff: "Isn't that what she had better do?" Lord Schiff shook his large Judaic head, as melon-mouthed as Swaffield's own:

"No, I don't know anything about the circumstances." He smiled amiably at Jenny. "I'm sure she will be perfectly sensible, whatever she decides." Azik Schiff liked the look of Jenny and wished her good luck: but in fact his faith in other people's sense about money was minimal, and he had a mild unemotional desire to get her out of Swaffield's control. He had to admit that Swaffield had made a large fortune, but Azik Schiff thought he was a philistine and that his operations, though presumably legal, ought not to be so. Sometimes there was a freemasonry among successes, even financial successes:

but not with Azik Schiff, who in secret admired only intellectual men, preferably scholars, such as he might have been.

Shouts of 'Division' again and insistent bells. "Must be Clause Stand Part," someone said knowledgeably, but not in the language in which Shakespeare wrote. Clare and Lorimer departed to vote for the government: the Bishop departed to vote against. Azik Schiff, detached about all governments and used to giving sceptical advice to any, did not vote at all. Instead, now that the room was partially cleared, he caught a waitress's attention and ordered more drinks, but, once more standing outside, did not drink himself. On the other hand, when he managed to acquire a plate of sandwiches he ate his share.

Apparently, Jenny speculated, that was all any of them would eat till late that night. How long was the debate going to last? "Arrangement to stop at 1:00 a.m.," said the knowledgeable person. No dinner laid on, why not? The knowledgeable person, who like Azik was not voting, had an explanation. To Jenny it all seemed singularly ascetic.

For a while Swaffield was leaving Jenny alone. The Schiffs beamed at her with good nature but didn't refer again to her decision. Partly out of delicacy. Azik Schiff was a better mannered man than Swaffield, which wouldn't in itself have made him a Lord Chesterfield: but, by loftier standards, his nerves were fine and he had refined his wife's. They wanted this peculiar exhibitionistic scene not to start again. But they had another reason for wanting that.

They both knew what it was like to be poor. Azik had arrived in London in the thirties with a hundred and fifty pounds: Rosalind Schiff came from the back streets of a provincial town. She had married one wealthy man and later Schiff, after he had become very rich: she was the best dressed woman in the guest room: that didn't prevent her studying Jenny's clothes with the costing eye of forty years before. As for Azik, it came as easy to him as walking—that is, to reckon what this money meant to her. Reaching the same conclusion, they both made the same response, wishing to hear no more and have no responsibility. It was a withdrawal, coming out of

63

prudence and memory of self-preservation. It was an unexpansive withdrawal which happened naturally to a good many who had once had to think about petty sums.

Rosalind's daughter—not by Schiff—was braver. Pretty but not outgoing, divorced at twenty-two, still under thirty, living by herself on an independent income, she had been inspecting Jenny with cool curiosity. Taking advantage of a conversational flux among the others, she asked, in a quiet clear tone, intended only for Jenny and herself:

"I take it this offer they're making you—it's not much of a share?"

"Not very much."

"That makes sense." The young woman nodded.

She said: "Say you turn them down and go ahead. Couldn't you get someone to invest in you, and take a cut if you scoop the pool?"

"I shouldn't like that." Jenny didn't like the young woman either, too ornamental, self-possessed, remote.

"It might be worth thinking of."

Jenny didn't like her, bridled at any more intervention, but was becoming excited, something between happy and exuberant now that the company seemed to be simmering round her. The room was suddenly full again after the division. The loudspeaker announced the result, which wasn't a source of surprise.

Soon afterwards, as though without realising that she was making an announcement or a choice, Jenny said:

"Mr. Swaffield, I'm not playing."

"What do you mean?"

"I mean, I shall say no. I'm going to refuse."

Jenny noticed a glint in Muriel Calvert's (the young woman's) eyes and was for an instance chagrined. Was she conceited enough to think her comment had anything to do with this? But Jenny was buoyed up by the surge of hope and personal superbity which infused one who had taken a decision.

"I advise you against it," said Swaffield. He gave her a smile, his expression difficult to read.

"I'm sorry. I'm going to refuse."

"I advise you against it. So will old Symington. You'll have to talk to him tomorrow."

"I'm quite certain," said Jenny, voice loud, authoritative, heart-and-soul at home. "It doesn't matter what he says."

"Mrs. Rastall," said the Bishop warmly, "you can't decide anything on the spot, you really can't."

"No," said Lorimer. It was almost the only word he had uttered, since he joined the party.

"I can, you know."

"Well, you can't say she doesn't have spirit," said Swaffield, with what sounded like proprietorial pride.

"You'll have to listen to your lawyer," said Azik Schiff, trying to put the discussion to one side.

"Oh, I'll listen. But that doesn't make much difference as a rule, does it, Lord Schiff?"

That reply was bright, half-cheeky, but he respected her. It wasn't to be his concern, but he was vestigially uneasy. Others had been uncomfortable at Swaffield's behaviour, but Azik Schiff alone had, along with Jenny, wondered whether there was a purpose behind it.

"I've known it do so now and then." It was not to be his concern, and that was all he permitted himself to say.

In his polite style, Clare raised his glass to her, and remarked:

"Good luck to you, whatever you do."

Lorimer muttered a shy Hear, Hear.

The interest in Jenny's news was fading, contentedly, not dramatically. For some of them, it had been an interlude, mildly diverting, soon submerged in the long night's stretch, anything welcome which helped pass the time. The Bishop, who had spoken on several clauses, felt for conscience' sake obliged to stay until the end. So did those who were obeying the whip. A new speaker was announced by the address system. The Bishop, peering at the list of amendments, said that he wanted to listen to the next but one.

Lord Clare, for once unceremonious, said that he could endure staying outside the Chamber until B——— 'had a go.' Jenny had a half-thought that that sounded a peculiar expression, as of people leaving all their utterances to blind chance. Clare was continuing, in an aside to Swaffield, that it was going to be a long haul: he'd be glad of a little support, if Swaffield could bear it. Swaffield could bear it.

He was cheerful at the prospect, basking there. So Jenny saw him, not knowing whether to resent or admire him for not being tired, for not caring whether he ate or slept. He was getting old, but he was no different now, pursuing a desire, from what he must have been as a young man. He was going to make some more acquaintances that night, meet more associates of Clare's.

Men came in, more congratulations on speeches. Noise, wafts of laughter, more drinks, people bringing up chairs and then away again. Jenny began to find the talk vaguer and the lights brighter: she couldn't think when it was time for her to leave. At last she said—it came out as unprepared as her declaration to Swaffield—that she must go. No one paid much attention. Swaffield gave a proprietorial nod, kissed her cheek, recollected himself and reminded her to speak to the lawyers in the morning.

Lorimer said that he would show her the way downstairs. He was obstinate when she tried to put him off: no, it was a confusing building, anyway he wanted a few minutes' breather.

They went through the corridors, over the carpets, crimson, thick, shut off from the outside world as in a womb, or Jonah's whale, or this particular piece of Westminster: past, though Jenny didn't notice, a door with a small notice Peers' Bar, which was the official name for the Bishops' Bar. There Ryle was at that moment sitting, though not with Hillmorton, who was in his place in the Chamber and shortly to make a speech.

Jenny, spirits still high, excitement bearing her up, was conscious that Lorimer was a nice, gauche man, diffident in spite of his grimmish soldier's face, but she felt in herself a blankness in his company, a kind of disappointment that he didn't attract her.

❧ 8 ❧

Old Symington was not old. Only Swaffield thought of using that particular appellation about him. This year he was still not forty. He did not look old. He did not even look vaguely paternal or as though administering pastoral care, as Eric Skelding did. At first sight, or more sights after that, not many would have guessed that Symington was the most active partner in a firm of solicitors, one respected in London whose reputation, thanks to him, was growing: or that he had climbed to that job by merit, leaving school at sixteen, the son of a clerk in a local government office.

Not that he was unimpressive to look at. On the contrary, he was spectacularly handsome, but not in the fashion of an efficient professional man. Glossy haired, lustrous eyed, pillar-necked, he might in Edwardian days have been taken for a successful actor manager. If all the people involved in the Massie case, close to or remotely, had been collected in one room, he would have been the one to whom eyes kept turning. Hillmorton had remained good looking, and, in an austere way, so had Sedgwick before his illness struck him. Liz was a sharply pretty woman and Mrs. Underwood in her youth had been more than that. Some of the others had the presence which authority and recognition could bring with it, or which helped to produce those effects in the first place. All those physical manifestations were in the normal run of things, you would find something like them in any privileged group anywhere at any

67

time. But you were unlikely to see anyone as picturesque as Leslie Symington. It was a rare gift, probably rarer than Sedgwick's intellect, certainly rarer than Ryle's sense.

Women noticed him, as a matter of course. Some connoisseurs in such matters might have suspected that, with those looks, he would turn out narcissistic and either wouldn't be given to sex at all or alternatively would marry a plain woman who wouldn't interfere with his own glory. Those connoisseurs would this time have been wrong. Symington's wife was as beautiful as he was, or something near it, and together they gave out an aura or a field of force, that could come from no other origin than married joy.

On a February evening (there were still three months to go before the Massie case came up) they were sitting in their drawingroom in The Vale, and they were discussing, as they had been on and off for the past year, whether to have another child. It was, as it had been all along, a luxurious discussion, sensual, sexual, child-loving. They already had two children, with their usual good luck (which they knew as well as acquaintances who envied them) a boy and a girl both abnormally handsome, which they didn't pretend to be surprised at, the boy aged fourteen at Westminster, the girl aged nine at Frances Holland.

Ought liberal minded parents to buy private education? They lived in a prosperous liberal circle, and most of their friends thought not. Even the Symingtons, who were a robust couple, were sometimes uneasy, sitting in that comfortable Chelsea room, appreciably less violent on the eye than Swaffield's drawingroom, white rugs on the parquet floor, tweedish curtains, tobacco-toned chairs in the Hille style, the only primary colours from some diagrammatic paintings on the walls. They might have been comforted if they had heard Lord Sedgwick on modern educational theory, but they would still have had pricks of conscience. Alison had been calming these, since her daughter went to school, by working with mentally handicapped children. That would have sounded priggish, outside their circle: but good works always sounded priggish, and anyway there was nothing priggish about another preoccupation of theirs, which they alone knew. Although he masked it under his sumptuous exterior, Symington was a hungrily ambitious man, and ambitious with a sharp focussed aim. He wanted (and this was a liberal cause too) his own junior branch of the law to take its share of judgeships and the rest: he wanted to be one of the first solicitors to become a judge. He and Alison were happy enough, and that would make them happier.

What about another child? They knew the arguments by heart, had gone over them pleasurably, repetitively. As with most arguments close to the nerve, as with Jenny Rastall's internal ones, the answer was formed before they admitted it. They were familiar with the risks. She was only a year younger than he was. With a mother that age, the statistics were stark, and they had studied them. The chances of bearing a mongol were becoming too high to be relaxed about—higher than any physical chance one took in the ordinary run of life. Which is a fatality I shouldn't cope with decently, Symington had said before this. Of course, I should put a face on it, on the surface. So would you. But when we looked at each other— On the other hand, there appeared to be a statistical chance, nothing like so sharp edged, nothing like so high, of a child unusually bright. Hubris, he had said again that evening. Well, we've always gone in for hubris, haven't we? Others had had the same thought about them, with a different kind of wish.

As they talked, enjoying themselves though there wasn't anything new to say, an observer would have noticed the difference from their seniors, such as Adam Sedgwick or Ryle, or from their juniors too. They showed none of the forebodings of the older men. Of course their society was changing round them, but they felt it was, by and large, changing for the better. Anyway their children would get used to it, they would breathe a happy-go-lucky air. In this, they might have missed intimations from certain of the harder-minded young, who would have liked a climate altogether bleaker: but that was something that no-one had yet calculated or foreseen.

Alison loved her husband. She was so happy that evening that she seemed to hear her mother telling her to count her blessings, but she had, as on other evenings, one complaint about him. He was working obsessively, as he had always done. Once it had made his career, but now it could have been tapered off, enough for some free hours. Ambition or no ambition. But it had become an addiction, and it would distress him, and not alter the habit, if she put in a plea. He allowed himself the single drink before dinner, as now, the hour's conversation. Then dinner, or rather food, for he might as well have eaten charcoal: then back to work until eleven. She had to accept it. It was like being married to a high class surgeon.

They had no secrets, and she knew in detail what he would be working on that night. It was policy to keep on terms with Swaffield, and that was why he had from the beginning taken a personal oversight of the Massie business. Later on he had become interested, not just for policy's sake. Now, and for an evening or so past, he was involved with records of an interview with Massie's last housekeeper but one. Mrs. Underwood had removed her and most of the others who had looked after him, but she had been the housekeeper until three years before he died. What use, if any, could they make of her as a witness? How far was it safe?

"You said," Alison remarked, used to sharing his addiction, "that she didn't seem to like Mrs. U. all that much."

"That's the understatement of all time."

"She got edged out of course."

"But, I've told you, she didn't seem to like him much either."

"Nice little family party."

In fact, for both of them the Massie household had taken on a kind of anti-glamour, at the same time gothic and prosaic, embossed with the improbability of everyday events. They had had the curiosity, one weekend that winter, to go and inspect the house from the outside. It stood back from a side road, half a dozen miles outside Haywards Heath: from the road, though, they could see nothing except the darkening barrier of pines. Up the drive, quite a long stretch (Symington was making an estimate of how much this land would appreciate in the next decade), until they might have expected a neat reposeful Georgian front.

They might have expected it, but they didn't get it. What they got was an assembly of red brick castellation, turning into itself because of trees confining the lawn, looming sombre in spite of the glaring brick. Early city style mansion in Sussex, they thought, period about 1890. It was in one of those downstairs rooms, which had a flourish of windows, none of them matching, French, ogival and in one room casement, that old Massie had lain in the terminal years. According to the housekeeper, Mrs. Underwood kept him immobilised in that room though "it wouldn't have hurt him to go out." According to the housekeeper again, it was from that room that he shouted at night "loud enough to bring the house down," for someone to go and talk to him.

It sounded as though he had the night insomnia of great age, though he dozed most of the day. "She got on to that. She got on to that before I left. She was ready to talk her head off any night. Mind you, she made up for it in the day time." So then, quite soon after Mrs. Underwood took to sleeping in that house most nights of the week, he began crying "Birdie! Birdie!", which appeared to be his name for Mrs. Underwood. To the Symingtons it had an affectionate ring. Not perhaps to the housekeeper, who repeated it without comment.

That night-time shouting, the Symingtons accepted as without doubt authentic. But were some of the housekeeper's other stories authentic too?

"Would Mrs. U. have been badgering the old chap to marry her—even while that woman was still hanging about?" said Symington. "I still think that's a bit too hard to take."

"It's so hard to take that I don't see her inventing it."

"She wasn't indiscreet, by all accounts, in anything else she did. She may be a harpy but she wasn't indiscreet."

"She hadn't settled the will then, of course."

"She seems to have been pretty confident that she'd get everything she wanted—"

"She might," said Alison, "have had a few doubts about that son of hers. She could have preferred to have the money for herself."

Alison did good works, she was optimistic about other human beings. She might even think they were perfectible—but not now. When it came to a case like this one, she was as realistic as a lawyer. On that specific point she happened to be over-realistic or at least dead wrong. But her husband listened to her. The housekeeper's stories were hard to make sense of. Some of them had the strange unpredictable echo of true stories. The old man lying—as he had apparently done long before he needed to—on a camp bed in the downstairs room, lights on all day. Bellowing,

"Change! Birdie! We must get ready for change!" He was always talking about change, said the housekeeper, change for them, change for everybody. Once he cried (she reported):

"It'll all come right in the end." And again, after Mrs. Underwood had mentioned that she might speak to the local vicar he cursed the church, which was one of his rituals, and said: "There's time enough for that. It'll all come right in the end."

The housekeeper might be over-colouring everything she heard, and yet there could be underneath some basis of truth. She wasn't clever enough to see that those sayings of Massie's might be interpreted as proof of something else. On the face of it, they indicated that, within three years of death, he was neither senile nor incapable of resistance. In fact, the housekeeper's stories were full of the noise of his voice, perhaps slightly crazed, but still booming insistently away. His voice, not the other's.

Symington became more dubious of how safely he could use the housekeeper in evidence.

The plinths of the case had settled themselves long before this. Mrs. Underwood had been altogether too decisive, for a sensible woman. That was going to be used. Bringing in her own lawyer, Skelding, not long after the housekeeper was dismissed: getting hold of previous wills with their formulaic beginnings, the old man's message of disapproval against schools, universities, and the Anglican church: getting rid not only of domestics but of people who did him any service. She might have been a shade less precipitate. It had been a mistake not to summon Jenny when the old man was at last getting near his death. All that was enough to build the case on. Symington's chief doubt at this stage came when he picked up suggestions of the old man's assertiveness, dislikeable self-willed assertiveness, right into his last year.

Symington had had the curiosity to identify older servants

who had known Jenny, when, as a young woman, she was still living at home. He found what his experience had made him used to, but to others might have seemed curiously contradictory impressions. One or two loved her, without knowing anything about Mrs. Underwood. Jenny was always kind, she kept your spirits up, she took care of you, she was a very human person. Others were reserved, not speaking their criticisms but not at ease. She liked everything just so, one woman had said, and gave the impression that Jenny had been touchy, and fretting to her own and others' nerves. That was before she got married, not that that seemed to settle her, from all they heard.

Before the war, Massie had employed a butler. That old man had developed a vein of preciosity. He reflected on Jenny, and with an air of pride produced the word perfectionist. "That's what I should call her—a perfectionist." It was not clear what this conveyed, except perhaps that she had been turned down in a love affair when she was a girl, and had kept hope alive, fending other men off, for years.

That evening the Symingtons went on to talk about Swaffield, and how he had reacted to the rumour of marriage, old Massie being chased to marry Mrs. Underwood.

"Well—" Leslie gave a large-eyed grin— "he couldn't help getting excited by the idea of Mrs. U. jumping into bed with the old man the night before he died."

"He couldn't think that!" Alison was grinning as widely.

"Couldn't he hell. He'd heard of the Bourbons, which was it, Philip V, God knows how!"

Swaffield was not educated, so far as they had discovered he had read almost nothing: and yet there weren't many tales of sexual oddity, and even fewer of sexual enthusiasms, that he hadn't mysteriously acquired.

Of course, Symington was reflecting, Swaffield would like the story of the marriage-design to be used. It would be a knife in the ribs for Mrs. U.: but not if the lawyers judged it dangerous.

In the long run Swaffield could always cut away from his flights of salacious imagination, or even from his vendettas, and do what he was constantly advising Symington, keep his eye on the ball. He knew when to be single-minded. That had been one of his strengths. The ball he was keeping his eye on was simply and solely to win the case. Nothing more, nothing less, though he had no objection to accumulating a little credit on the side.

The Symingtons were among the few who had a liking for Swaffield—an indulgent liking, but still genuine. Others, many others, hung round him, flattered him, became members of his court, some like Lord Clare for the benefits, some not receiving or having much chance of benefits, but somehow happy to bask in the odour of power. They got satisfaction out of basking there, remained in the ambience as long as he let them, and nevertheless, often not admitting to themselves, detested him.

It was singular for these two to like him. True, Symington had profited by a good deal of patronage. Work had flowed to the firm through Swaffield since Symington came to London. For a solicitor on the rise any patron was better than none, even if he did exhibit vagaries of temperament. But that wasn't the whole of it, not even most of it.

No, they were ready and willing to go on liking him—although, or because, he had tried to interfere in their marriage. He had, it was a matter of course with his young friends, citizens of his empire, stood them holidays. He had visited them on those holidays, private aircraft touching down, private catechism in hotels, off with demoniac restlessness in forty-eight hours.

He had wanted to make them confess how they 'got on' in bed, how often they made love, how they were going to space out the children, the full late 20th Century examination, Kinsey plus Doctor Spock plus Reginald Swaffield. Sometimes he looked disturbed, like a doctor not actually detecting but suspecting a premonitory sign, and appeared to feel that they would be better off with other partners.

They weren't so much as harassed. They happened to be on their home ground, and they were invulnerable. They could stand all the prying. In fact, they would have given it back, but that they reserved to themselves. With Swaffield it was

74

more fun, and possibly kinder, to lay trails to set that indomitable detective off in wrong directions.

When they were alone, they speculated about him. The obvious answers were not only too simple, they were wrong. He was neither innocent nor impotent. He had been married twice and had children, and that was only the official part of his story. He had more libido than most men, pressed down and running over. Somehow his libido hadn't found its proper home. Maybe for him there was no proper home.

This didn't make them sorry for Swaffield. Over-compassion was a mistake they were trying to avoid. He was a natural force, and they respected him for that. In secret, in their own bedroom, he became an aphrodisiac joke.

Nearly half past seven. Dinner time. Then three hours work on the papers before they met again.

❦ 9 ❦

Lord Hillmorton was considered by most people to be urbane and civilised, rather better natured than the general run of men in public life. But there was one person who didn't think so and had some reason for not thinking so. That was his heir, Doctor Thomas Pemberton.

Doctor Pemberton was too active and combative a man to indulge himself with fantasies. Day after day his big form hurtled itself through an existence without leisure, more chased by the minutes than most middle-aged men. A round of patients early, examinations for an insurance company in the middle of the morning, private patients between noon and two p.m. (no lunch), instructions to stockbroker two thirty to two forty-five, casts of two shows to inspect for medical condition before tea time, calls to pay on the theatres, back in the Fulham Road surgery between six and seven (passive panel of patients waiting there, frightened of him), a meal with his wife and the son still living at home, more visits five or six nights out of seven, a glance at his favourite reading, that is the Stock Exchange quotations, bed, sometimes not to be left undisturbed.

He was a powerful man, built like a heavy-weight boxer, and he had stamina as well as muscles. Even so, he wasn't left with much free energy, certainly not for useless psychological speculation, which he despised. And yet—he had a capacity for rancour, there were times when disciplined thoughts were broken up and he couldn't exclude visions of himself in a triumphant denunciation of Lord Hillmorton.

Lord Hillmorton had seen him twice. The first time was when Pemberton was fourteen years old, and at school—at a school which took in sons of doctors at reduced fees. Pemberton's father, who had been a G.P. in Birmingham, had died young ten years before: it had been a coronary, he was as massive as Pemberton himself became, a combination of facts which Pemberton did not, in later years, find heartening. Suddenly Lord Hillmorton wrote to the Headmaster announcing that he would like to visit the boy.

This was during the war. Lord Hillmorton (at that time Henry Fox-Milnes, M.P., without a courtesy title except the Hon., for the Hillmorton peerage was a Viscountcy until he himself won it a step up) was already a Minister of State. For the school, not used to eminences, official or social, not used to lords or heirs, it was a good deal of an occasion. Lord Hillmorton walked round the playing fields, inspected the laboratories, talked to the staff and the Sixth Form, behaved with his usual grace and amiability. Except when he was alone with the young Pemberton, to whom he forced out questions as to how his work was going, but so mechanically that acquaintances would have scarcely recognised his tone of voice.

If the boy had heard the expression, he would have thought that Lord Hillmorton couldn't bear the sight of him. Pemberton was not physically self-conscious. He knew already that he had his share of rough masculine good looks. Of an odd colouration, not uncommon in England, dead pale skin under jet black hair. But he couldn't blink away the coldness of this distant relative, the something other than coldness. It rankled, he couldn't understand it. He was still at a loss, the second and last time he spoke to Lord Hillmorton, nearly ten years later.

His family had been left with very little money, but he had managed to get scholarships, not to a university but to a teaching hospital. He had done well. He had unusual self-confidence and had decided that most people were feebler and an order of magnitude more timid than he was himself. He didn't doubt that he could be a success at any branch of medicine. He had—though this was concealed by his abilities both for generalised contempt and for financial bargaining—something of a vocation. At that stage he wanted some money to support him.

He needed another couple of years in hospital. He had never made use of being the heir to Lord Hillmorton, except in young man's boasting (some of his acquaintances didn't believe him, and he had to buy a second-hand copy of Debrett). Now surely this was the time.

It was the early fifties, and Hillmorton had become a full minister, though not yet in the Cabinet. Pemberton was shown into his ante-room, private secretary, girl secretaries, Hillmorton entering from the inner door, a smiling public man, liked by them all, easy with them all.

But, as soon as they were alone in his office, he wasn't easy with Pemberton. Without any of his habitual fluidity, without even his courteous evasive wariness, he said: "I don't quite understand—"

Pushing, wooing, brash, importunate, the young man loomed on the other side of the desk. Not to put too fine a point on it, he said, he required money: another qualification and he was well away. But he couldn't afford even one more year, unless he got some help.

"What a pity."

"It would be a pity."

"I don't quite understand, though," Hillmorton spoke with a mixture of impatience and strain, "why you wrote to me."

Pemberton gave a smile, forceful, cheeky, such as women found engaging. He said: "There is a connection, isn't there?"

"I suppose you've considered, Doctor Pemberton, that we've all got a set of common ancestors. That sort of connection we all possess with everyone. I'm bound to have it with each person on my staff next door—" He gazed at Pemberton as from a distance, speaking with academic thinness.

"In my case, though, it's all on paper. You know that," Pemberton said.

"You attach importance to this, I gather."

"It's on the record. And we can't get away from it, there are plenty of people who would think you have some responsibility—"

"I'm sorry, Doctor Pemberton. I can't regard that as decisive. I hope you find some method of continuing with your training. And now, perhaps, if you'll excuse me—" Hillmorton was already feeling for a button underneath his desk. The private secretary entered, as polite as Hillmorton in his normal form, and within seconds Pemberton, bitter, furious, mind stormy with plans for revenge and also for another approach, this time victorious, found himself in the Treasury corridor and within minutes in Great George Street.

Hopes didn't die quickly in a man as prepotent, as used to bullocking his own way through, as Pemberton. He tried to interview Hillmorton again: letters of refusal from the secretary. It took some time, years rather than months, before Pemberton accepted that he was not going to extract one penny. Rage smouldered. He regarded his relation, his very distant relation, with angry loathing. In occasional reflective moments, he did think that this behaviour was eccentric by any standards. But Pemberton was not much interested in people who got across him when he couldn't bully, coax or win them over. He didn't speculate much about why Hillmorton was behaving so, and didn't worry himself to find an answer.

The answer was simple. He was Hillmorton's heir but not his son. Hillmorton hated him, or at least was affronted by his existence—because of that. It wasn't subtle: it was instinctive: it was primitive, irrational, atavistic. It was utterly unlike, different in kind from, any response of his since he was growing up. No human being had seen anything like it in Hillmorton, except perhaps some women who had known him when he was young. It was the opposite of everything he approved of in the way of human virtues. He admired endurance, good sense, realism, a kind of courage, a kind of irony. In his meetings with his heir, and much more in his thoughts about him, he had exhibited none of these.

There was no one who could have observed both him and Pemberton. Anyone who had been able to and was fully aware of Hillmorton's feeling would nevertheless have thought him still the more urbane and civilised. That wasn't high praise, because Pemberton didn't begin to be either. But if you forgot or overlooked this rift in Hillmorton's temperament, he could be said to be civilised, more so than most men. It might have been more an effort of control and conscious style than of natural goodness, but somehow he had brought it off, which wasn't a major feat of moral gymnastics, but at least a modest one.

Pemberton didn't see any necessity for moral gymnastics. If he had been curious enough to perceive why Hillmorton had shown such meanness, he would have despised him: but not because it seemed savage but because to him it seemed almost the reverse. To Pemberton, caring about who was one's heir was would have appeared as a drawingroom emotion. And Pemberton, who not only despised vigorously but was good at contempt, had considerable contempt for those who indulged themselves in drawingroom emotions. What did it matter who one's heir was? What did they matter, most of the emotions people wrote books about? If you had been a doctor and lived your life in the presence of the primary emotions, then the rest of people's worries and hopes were trivial—bits of playing, luxuries you could afford because you had nothing serious on your mind. You needed to be close to people in the fear of death. If his own sons were near death, he would be as passionate as any man: but it didn't worry him that one presumably some day would get the Hillmorton title, and his favourite wouldn't. Death is the one thing that is a hundred per cent certain, reflected Doctor Pemberton, and gave a thought, not a notably compassionate one, to Hillmorton.

What in God's name, he had frequently asked himself and his wife, was the use of a title without a penny coming with it? In earlier days the estates would have been entailed: not now. Pemberton had a knack of picking up financial information, and believed that the property would pass to the eldest daughter, a curious example of purposeless primogeniture. For himself, the bare title, a seat in the Lords, what use was that to a doctor?

Well, he wasn't a delicate fibred man, and he could get something out of it. He thought Parliament was a farcical institution and the Upper House the most farcical part of it. But other people didn't, he would get more respect, which would be ludicrous but could be valuable, he should be able to extract grants. There might still be time to do some research, he was going to make contact with some of the best Americans. No doubt also, directorships would be offered to him. He had far more knowledge of the Stock Exchange than a man like Ryle, spent far more gusto and energy in playing it, and yet puzzlingly hadn't shown anything like the profits. Still, after all that effort, directorships would seem only just.

Death was a hundred per cent certain, Pemberton consoled himself. Unless something odd happened (he was unqualmish about his own mortality), Hillmorton, twenty years older, would die before him, and in the foreseeable future.

As well as having a knack for collecting financial information (he wouldn't take advice about investments but gave instructions), Pemberton also had the same talent with medical information. For this he was better placed, and the judgments he made of it were appreciably less adventurous.

About Lord Hillmorton, the information wasn't exciting and didn't need conflating with articles in the medical journals. It came from a doctor acquaintance of Pemberton's who had met Hillmorton at meetings of the governors of one of the London hospitals. He reported, not inquisitive as to why Pemberton should be making these enquiries, that the old boy seemed in the best of form, mental and physical.

A pity. Pemberton wouldn't have suppressed the thought if he could. He had seen people waiting at death beds for patients of his to die. He was as conscientious as a doctor could be, prolonged lives as far as his skills let him, and wasn't unaccustomed to looking at disappointment ill-concealed. It was ridiculous to pretend. Pemberton wouldn't pretend about anyone else or himself. This robust health of Hillmorton's was an irritation, a minor irritation, but still enough to make his temper worse. He might have to wait another twenty years. Whatever bit of profit this wretched title might bring him now, it would have vanished by then. He would be in his sixties and too old.

The big man was a familiar figure at the end of the Fulham Road. Here and there in those streets houses were being smartened up, but not the doctor's. He lived a life austere, comfortless, hardworking, and enjoyed it. In introspective moments, which were few, he wondered why he had not been more successful. He knew that he was a first rate professional, more experienced and more in touch with modern medicine than most doctors of his age. Except to those who didn't like to be over-powered, he was a comfort to his patients—the more so the more they were suffering and the nearer to the extreme conditions.

Any persons who had been allowed to share his thoughts on peerages, Parliament, the follies of the national scene, might have judged that he was a committed radical. They would have been wrong by a hundred and eighty degrees. By his side, not only detached conservatives like Hillmorton, but also right wingers, devoted lobby pedestrians such as Clare or Lorimer were compassionate liberal thinkers full of warm sympathy for all their fellow men and anxious that their lives should be transformed. Pemberton's view of his fellow men couldn't have been lower without being pathological. Perhaps a doctor saw them at their worst. One tried to cure them. Sometimes one felt animal kinship. It was a satisfaction to be some help. But most days Pemberton was in contact, as close as flesh to flesh, with fright, often with cowardice, selfishness, deceit, venality, petty fraud, attempts to cheat him out of drugs, all the shifts of the craving, the stupid and the terrified. For a man as disposed to contempt as he was, the spectacle was not likely to remove it. Life was a poor affair at best, he had thought since he was a boy, human beings were a poor lot. After twenty years of medical practice he believed that he had been right, but a shade optimistic. He fell back on his favourite curse-word of abuse and hadn't a doubt that anyone who thought more loftily must have lived their entire time in drawingrooms.

Ah well, decent kinder people like the Symingtons would have said he didn't know anything about the working class. On the contrary. He knew far more about them in the sense of physical contact, touch, hearing, sight, smell, than they did or anyone connected with old Massie's will. Hillmorton in his political career had met working class constituents and confronted others as a negotiator across tables in Whitehall. Similarly with Ryle and some of the rest. Whereas nearly all of Pemberton's patients—not the private ones, from whom he made some money—came from the proletariat of southwest London. When they were ill they were like everyone else, no more admirable, no less, Pemberton thought. When they weren't ill, as a group he detested them.

His appetite for contempt was formidable. He used it with enthusiasm on any social group that existed. But it was more undiluted for the working class than for any other, if that were possible. They were shamelessly lazy, almost clinically lazy (that affronted his hardworking soul). They wouldn't stir themselves to earn an extra pound for their children, except by passively joining a hundred thousand other layabouts in coming out on strike. They couldn't act as individuals, they were dead wood, they had no concept of the individual life (that affronted his individualistic soul). As usual, he didn't make his own thoughts softer or less brutal. He merely detested such people.

When they came to him in illness, they found him understanding and a support. Which was a dispensation of fate that would have gratified Lord Hillmorton, whose sense of irony missed something through not knowing his kinsman. If he had, however, and even if there hadn't been a barrier of instinct between them, Hillmorton would have reacted as others did to Pemberton, and would have dismissed him as a savage.

Sitting in his bleak surgery, Pemberton, studying the medical journals, totting up his investments, had not the slightest intimation that anything was being decided about one of Hillmorton's daughters. There his intelligence service didn't operate. He wouldn't have been interested if it had told him about the Massie will. That was trivial. What did one more marriage count, among people for whom he cared nothing except to bear a not uncherished grudge? It was to be a year or more before he heard anything relevant about the family and longer than that before he introduced himself to Liz.

❦ 10 ❧

Until that summer neither Jenny nor Liz had been inside a court of law. Julian had, since as a young man he had read for the bar, with the secret intention of never practising. To both Jenny and Liz, it all struck strange, with the kind of discomfort an apprehensive person feels on entering a sick room or happening on a service in a foreign church.

In the court room, on a midsummer morning, there didn't seem much to inspire any superstitious dread, yet Liz was feeling something close to that. True, the room, one of the courts nearest to the Strand, was the wrong shape, much too high for its floor space, like a basilica gone mad: but, waiting for the judge, the officials, the barristers, the solicitors, most of the spectators, including Hillmorton, looked comfortable enough. The benches were hard, it was going to be a long trial, trust this judge, someone was chattering, it was going to be hard on the backside. On opposite halves of the room, though separated by only three or four yards, Jenny and Liz were glancing at their solicitors for reassurance.

There sat Symington, reposeful after a word with the silk in front of him. When she noticed him, even Liz, who wasn't struck by handsome men, for an instant thought that he was worth looking at. But she and Jenny, in this alike, as in other responses that morning, more than they could know, were feeling as other litigants had often felt. They didn't enjoy the sight of the lawyers being so jolly among one another. Hadn't they any nerves? Didn't they imagine that others might have nerves?

The silk on the Underwoods' side was porcine, Jenny's silk was aquiline: they were having a cheerful insulting match, like undergraduates. As though the result of the case didn't matter to them or anyone else—they weren't even funny. Liz's temper was sullen, why did they fancy themselves as humorists? Someone was still complaining about hard benches, as though that were the issue to be decided. At ten thirty precisely, a chime from a church outside could just be heard, an inside door opened, feet shuffled as people stood up, the judge came in, walked along the dais, gave an affable plump man's bow. Then he settled in his seat, with the air of one not at all impatient, contented to be settled there for a good long stay.

Mr. Justice Bosanquet had, in his own modest realistic view, a good deal to be contented about. He had become a High Court Judge distinctly late, so late that he had resigned himself to being passed over: no earnings to fret about now, and a more serious fret removed by a satisfactory pension at the end. The Family Division was a nice terminal job for anyone like himself, not much of an abstract lawyer, but still inquisitive about people. In fact, he was a shrewd and able man, with more than his share of human interest.

He had a round face, with small, very bright eyes, who vaguely suggested either a Dickensian philanthropist or a Chinese statesman Chairman Bosanquet. Or, since the Chinese teachers sat on mats, not chairs, the title should really have been translated, matmaster—Matmaster Mao, Matmaster Bosanquet. It would have fitted him. He would have sat on a mat, or on anything else possible to sit on, for any length of time he thought necessary to reach a judgment.

To those not domesticated to the courts, quick thinking women like Jenny and Liz, and even to acquaintances such as Lorimer, who dropped in to give Jenny inarticulate support, the entire process seemed oblivious of time—and they felt like that before the end of the first day, not to speak of the days that followed. It was the impression which also damped down strangers, when they first listened to the parliamentary

85

process. Were these people operating in periods of months or years? Or eons? Or were they merely timeless?

The trouble was, of course, that for business purposes spoken speech was by now an anachronism. One was conditioned to reading: and one read three or four times as fast as anyone could speak. Jenny had read all of Symington's briefs to counsel. He had come to respect her sharpness and precision. She wouldn't tolerate any nonsense or blearing over or anything she couldn't make sense of in the witness box. The final brief was the basis of her counsel's opening speech that day. To read, it had taken her about half an hour, which included time for her own questions. In court, it lasted almost all of the first morning: that included time for gentle, pertinacious, twinkling questions from Mr. Justice Bosanquet, and a few objections, part of the game, private badinage, incomprehensible to all but the lawyers, from the Underwoods' counsel.

Listening to the opening speech Jenny at moments felt sensations of déjà vu, and at others of being a chilling distance away. This man, whose name was Lander, under his wig young-looking for a middle-aged man and in private entertaining, was talking of her father and herself. It was as though she had been dead some time, and someone had unaccountably written her biography and then adapted it for the stage: someone who didn't know her, and had got a few things right and some grotesquely wrong. In this respect unlike Liz, no one was less superstitious than Jenny, but she was near to seeing ghosts, but not the authentic ghosts. She found herself painfully nervous. Whether it would have been better if there wasn't a decision hanging on all this, she couldn't have told.

Actually Lander was being entirely competent, though in the newspapers next day the extracts made him appear either foolish or preternaturally bright. "Cordelia cut out by King Lear," said a headline: it was true that he hadn't been able to resist a bumbling allusion. When she heard it (it was a product of counsel's own genius, not Symington's) Jenny blushed as she hadn't for twenty years, and was thinking with snapping rage that she was as much like Cordelia as she was like Brigitte Bardot. She thought this more bitterly when she read the paper next day.

Lander began by saying that Massie when he made his last will was a very old man.

"Old age is relative, but perhaps we can all agree that the late eighties is genuinely old age." It was the plaintiff's submission that this was a case of undue influence. "In general old people are often susceptible to the pressure, influence and persuasion of those round them.

"It is common knowledge that, if we live long enough, we find our memories likely to deteriorate, and also our resistance to influence likely to be weaker. And so this is a familiar story, one that many of us have heard of, a very very old man being grossly over-influenced, being psychologically coerced, I don't wish to go further than that at this stage, by a very determined lady."

That lady, Lander explained, was not his daughter. To Jenny, this was the passage, lasting perhaps only five minutes on the clock, where her skin grew thinnest and she couldn't have given a précis of what she heard.

He was carefully not covering up the breach between father and daughter, and other lawyers thought that this was good pleading. There had been a breach: Mrs. Rastall would be the last person to deny it, she would make it clear when she gave evidence. She couldn't explain it: there hadn't been a definite quarrel: her father didn't approve of her marriage but that was long since ended, fifteen years before, and she had not married again.

His wife, her mother, had died when Mrs. Rastall was in her teens, and had left her a small settlement. One couldn't explore human motives, but conceivably that had begun to jaundice him (this was an interpretation of Lander's own which Jenny did not for an instant believe). She had seen little of her father for years, simply because he demonstrated that he didn't wish it. She had done her best to restore their relations but without success. It was here that Lander interpolated his patch of eloquence, smiling with vicarious regret, about Cordelia.

"Mrs. Rastall wishes to conceal nothing about this personal sorrow. On the other hand—and I now come to the real hard and in my submission completely unshakeable substance of her case. Many years after this break between father and daughter had come into existence—until quite recently, until the last will of all, made so shortly before his death—years after the last time he had seen his daughter, Mr. Massie was still making will after will leaving considerable portions of his estate, never less than half, and more often the greater part of it, to Mrs. Rastall. There is nothing surprising about that. It is what most fathers, however eccentric their behaviour, would consider it fitting to do for an only child."

Lander broke off into an exposition of Massie's will-making proclivities. The judge was smiling placidly, and there were similar smiles in the court. Jenny had ceased to wince: here was business, here was neutral territory. "Yes, the old man had enjoyed making wills," said Lander. It was not uncommon to meet this habit among the old, particularly among what he might call the rather cantankerous old. They had a sense of power and they relished tantalising people round them who had expectations (this was another of the quotations in the next morning's papers). There was a burst of laughter in court, audibly from Julian Underwood, and tight grins elsewhere.

There would be evidence about this series of wills from Mr. Massie's former solicitor, Lander laid a stress on the adjective. They had some features in common. They all began with a formula saying that the testator had no intention of leaving money to any institution, any place where he had been educated and specifically not to any establishment remotely connected with the Church of England. (Mr. Justice Bosanquet asked impassively,

"Am I right, Mr. Lander, in getting the impression that the late Mr. Massie had been a member of the Anglican church, but had rather lost enthusiasm for it?"

"Quite right, my lord." Deadpan reply, another burst of hilarity from Julian.)

Then various charities, appearing in one will, disappearing in the next as he became displeased with them. Bequests to personal attendants, doctors and the rest.

"But we shall learn that the particular persons, the physician who attended him, his housekeeper and other servants, were all in due course changed as Mrs. Underwood took charge of his household arrangements. Then at the end a bequest, and always a very substantial bequest, except in the last will when it was removed altogether, to his daughter."

When Mrs. Underwood took charge there were changes. They began, it was difficult to fix the exact month, but sometime in 1966, four years before he died. The medical practitioner was changed.

"I should say at once that we have nothing whatever against the competence, responsibility or good faith of any of the persons appointed. In particular there was a change in Mr. Massie's legal adviser. His former solicitor, Mr. Balderstone, who had served him for a lifetime, was replaced to all intents and purposes by Mr. Skelding. Mr. Skelding happened to be Mrs. Underwood's solicitor, as of long standing. I have to re-iterate that Mr. Skelding is a well known lawyer of high professional reputation. No one has the slightest intention of detracting from this. It was Mr. Skelding who drew up the final will, learning from Mrs. Underwood that these instructions were those of the testator. Mr. Skelding was given copies of three of the previous wills, and was instructed that the initial formulae should be preserved including the remarks about the Church of England (laughter). There was however to be a major alteration. The residual estate, that is the largest part of it, was no longer to go to Mrs. Rastall, whose name as I have mentioned before disappears entirely, but instead to Mrs. Underwood's son. Mr. Skelding in person took this will to Mr. Massie and it was signed and witnessed a month before Mr. Massie's death."

Then Lander went off on a disquisition which connoisseurs of such speeches judged unnecessary, or badly timed. He was talking of Mr. Massie being immobilised in the downstairs sittingroom. For the last two or three years, that is, during the tenure of the new housekeeper, he had remained in that one room, and only Mrs. Underwood and the new doctor had free access to him.

Though connoisseurs thought that this passage was at best tedious and added nothing, they might have been wrong. The case was being decided by the single judge, and this particular judge was the most tireless of men. It was conceivable that, in his career as a counsel, this was how he would have argued the case himself, not only leaving no stone unturned, but turning each stone several times. Certainly he showed no sign of boredom, and went on making notes as devotedly as a student in the last week before his examination. He looked up once, and asked:

"Do we have any information about visitors to Mr. Massie during this last period?"

"I believe that visitors of any kind had to obtain permission from the doctor or Mrs. Underwood, but that can be confirmed."

"That would be quite natural in his state of health."

Jenny, with the suspiciousness of stretched nerves, heard that as a defence of Mrs. Underwood.

The morning was pounding on, the audience was getting restless for lunch. But Lander's last words were suddenly succinct, and attention stiffened.

"I have to say one thing which may seem suggestive. At no time during Mr. Massie's last illness did Mrs. Underwood communicate with Mr. Massie's daughter. Even when he was without any shadow of doubt approaching his end. There was no communication of any kind. Mrs. Rastall had no warning that he was approaching his death. She had no opportunity of coming to his death bed. The first she knew that he had died was through the death notices in *The Times*."

Liz had known all this, but rather as one knows a historical fact. She had been certain that it was a mistake. Ever since the will was challenged she had looked back over these mistakes. And yet to hear this out loud—it sounded different in kind, not a mistake, not even any of the things it might have been, a calculation or a sign of coldness, callousness or pure indifference, but more like a crime or worse still a shame. As though one had been turned down by a man and he was bragging about your offer to his friends. Liz had a prickle of gooseflesh, cold with fury and shame.

She glanced along the seat towards Jenny. Neither of them had seen each other before that morning, any more than had Mrs. Underwood and Jenny. They would go on seeing each other in court and then perhaps not again. Liz felt nothing but dislike. Jenny felt dislike, with the faintest edge of curiosity. They were both passionate women, capable of hatred, and when they hated they had no room for efforts of refinement. And yet, since no one in court or anywhere else knew them both, or was ever to do so, there was no one to notice, much less to tell them, in what ways they were alike.

Ryle, who might have been perceptive enough, if he had met Jenny, was sitting behind Liz and trying to tell her that no points had been scored for either side that morning. Hillmorton, who might have been detached enough, had his interest otherwise engaged. What he actually said was, as at last the judge had given his bobbing bow and made his exit,

"Well, I suppose everything has to have a beginning."

Julian let out one of his hooting laughs. Hillmorton went on, gazing at the ultra-gothic ceiling as though architectural taste was the only conflict dividing the assembled company:

"I must say, when our grandfathers were vulgar, they were remarkably vulgar, or perhaps you don't agree?"

11

As the days in court became a habit—though a good many onlookers, of whom Hillmorton was one, took to attending only for odd sessions or even single pieces of testimony—one detached person said that whoever arranged the trial had no sense of drama, it was very poorly staged. It was too much like the Church of England marriage service, the exciting bit came far too early.

The commentator was Muriel Calvert, who added that so far as her own marriage went she would have done better without any exciting bit at all. This kind of brightness didn't amuse Jenny, who disliked the young woman for herself and disliked anyone who came to the court as she did, not alone in this, out of sheer cool curiosity. Yet she had a point. She was meaning that Jenny's evidence, which might be critical to her own case, and maybe seem even more critical than it was to onlookers moved by that same sheer curiosity, came early on the second afternoon. After that, a flow of evidence on the plaintiff's side, days of it with no climaxes, the verbiage of evidence that in the verbatim record stretched out over page after page of typescript.

Muriel Calvert, not disposed to spoil her sarcasm, didn't recollect that Mrs. Underwood's evidence was bound to be critical too: and then at the end however execrable the staging they would all be waiting for a resolution, they would have to hear the judge decide. Still, it was fair comment that, from ten thirty to one and two till four thirty, on many days there were the long passages of anti-climax or more truly of sustained lack of climax.

That applied to evidence about old Massie's state of mind, though to the lawyers and a few attentive laymen, it caused some interest. It came from the doctor who had been in charge of Massie's health before Mrs. Underwood's regime. He was a diffident witness, but his answers were straightforward. The old man had some unusual physical quirks. He had the strongest neurotic objection to having his blood pressure taken. He was an unusually firm-minded old man.

To the lawyers, that wasn't an answer to be neglected: but its effect was rubbed away when in cross-examination the doctor averred just as firmly that when he last saw Massie, three years before his death, he judged him to be getting somewhere near a state of senile depression, with possible, not absolutely definite, clinical indications.

Evidence about Mr. Massie's series of wills, from his former solicitor, Balderstone, who was trying to prove that he hadn't lost the old man's confidence and had continued to handle parts of his business. That the court scarcely listened to, but when he described the wills a kind of subterranean hilarity spread through the room. The Christmas wills, the New Year wills, all dated like vintages of claret. Apparently the old man had been in the habit, by way of celebrating Christmas or New Year, of making a new will, and then informing both the gainers and the losers of his intentions "in time for them to start the New Year straight."

Gainers nearly always had only a temporary status. Next Christmas, as the wills demonstrated, they were likely to be written out. On one occasion, bequests made in the Christmas will of 1962 were cancelled in a New Year will of 1963. All this was on the files of Balderstone's firm. The judge had already received copies. He asked if the defendants wished to have them confirmed. Their leader blandly said that he would challenge none of them, and in cross-examination asked the solicitor only a few perfunctory questions. This disappointed some of the more inexperienced on the Underwood side: but actually nearly all the facts mentioned in Lander's speech or anywhere in the case were 'common ground' and it rested on how Bosanquet would interpret them.

Jenny went into the box at two forty-five on the second afternoon, after the finish of some testimony by a gardener, curiously like parliament, Ryle thought, in which the announcement of a national calamity was likely to be delayed by the answer to a question about travel facilities in the Kyle of Lochalsh. This was the first time Mrs. Underwood and Liz had had a clear view of their enemy. She stood there, face sensitive, finely drawn, incongruously so over good strong shoulders. A man might have found that incongruity pleasing, but Mrs. Underwood wanted to dismiss the sight of her and Liz viewed her with as much distaste as though she had been one of Julian's women.

Deliberately Jenny had refused any coaching as to how she should give her evidence. Swaffield had bullied her, forcing advice upon her, but she had resisted, in the end brusquely. Symington had been more subtle, but to him she said—she liked him, though, with another resemblance between enemies, she no more than Liz was beglamoured by his looks—that she must do it her own way. She must say what she had to say. She told him that politely, almost regretfully. In fact, she had resolved to tell the truth so far as she was capable. In that, although she didn't know it, she had made the same decision as competent people made before a security interrogation. In her realistic mind she didn't expect it to be easy.

Lander, whom she had met only once and then in a conference with Symington, began with a quiet question:

"Mrs. Rastall, if your father had asked for your presence at any time you would have gone to him?"

"Of course."

The court record went on:

LANDER: "You would have stayed with him?"
MRS. RASTALL: "Of course."
LANDER: "I want his lordship to be clear on this. If your father had asked you to be at his disposal at any time during his last illness or before, you would have gone?"
MRS. RASTALL: "Yes. Naturally."
LANDER: "For any length of time?"

94

Mrs. Rastall: "Yes."

[Those answers came easy, nothing but the truth.] *

Lander: "I have to ask you this. What were your relations with your father?"

Mrs. Rastall: [She felt more nervous, but her voice was strong.]

"Not good."

Lander: "Recently, that is?"

Mrs. Rastall: "No, for most of my life."

Lander: "Did you love him?"

[She hesitated.]

Mrs. Rastall: "I think I loved him so far as you can love anyone who doesn't love you back." [She hesitated again. She wasn't going to be extravagant.] "I think I had a daughter's feeling for a father."

[Lander had been ready for responses similar to this. Symington had told him that she was an unusually honest woman.]

Lander: "I want to take you back to your childhood. When you were young did your father love you?"

Mrs. Rastall: "He didn't show much sign of it. No, I doubt whether he ever did."

Lander: "Did that upset you?"

Mrs. Rastall: "Very much, when I was a girl. Later on, I had to live with it."

Lander: "Has it been a sadness to you, though?"

Mrs. Rastall: "Yes, I can say that. It has."

Lander: "Do you remember him showing you signs of affection? When you were a child perhaps."

[She gave a sudden smile, as though boasting and ashamed of it.]

Mrs. Rastall: "I did rather well at school. He seemed to like reading my reports, and when my results came through. He seemed to be proud of me, a little, then."

Some in the court who were well disposed to her and one or two who weren't had a glimpse of a clever girl, amusing, demurely cheeky, expecting happiness, before life sobered her.

Mr. Justice Bosanquet, entirely amiably, destroyed that mo-

---

* Interpolations in square brackets were not part of the record.

ment through his addiction to detail. Leaving nothing to chance he asked what those 'results' had been, 'O' levels, 'A' levels?

Jenny, smile retracted again, said "Both."

After that Lander took her through her biography. She hadn't gone to a university; it had been discussed, but the war started and she got a job in a Government office. Her father had made her an allowance until her mother died. After she came into a settlement, the allowance was stopped. If she had asked him for money—? He might have helped her. She had never tried Marriage. No financial support. After the separation ("My husband left me," said Jenny, defiantly flaunting the truth) she was left on her own. Yes, on the occasions she saw her father—they were very few, once a year or less—he referred to his estate and what he was leaving her. "You may as well have it, there's no one else," was her recollection of one of his remarks: she couldn't be sure of the exact words. "You'll be able to spread yourself when I am gone." He had said something like that to her certainly three times, possibly more, the last on their final meeting. That had been not quite five years—as usual her memory was precise—before he died.

Finishing, Lander asked her whether she had heard that he was dying.

"No, not a word." That was said sternly. She saw the announcement of his death: nothing to do except attend the funeral.

When David March, the leading counsel for the defendants, got up to cross-examine her, he seemed to her less porcine. He had a face oddly and unreadably mobile, in the American sense homely, in circumstances other than the court, a comfortable face. His eyes, though, were as sharp as her own. He had a thick deep voice, and some of his questions were innocuous and bumbling. She had to tighten her control, so as not to vacillate between agreeing with him too easily (yes, there were times when she was tempted to do that) or claiming too much for herself.

On the record, her answers, especially the more relevant of them, stood out clear enough. Thus, after a long desultory exchange of no significance, March's question was abrupt and not prepared for:

MARCH: "Did your father talk to you about his will? About any intentions for you?"

MRS. RASTALL: "Yes. I said so."

MARCH: "You told my learned friend so. But it is easy to get a wrong idea of a conversation, wouldn't you agree?"

MRS. RASTALL: "Sometimes."

MARCH: "We are all liable to wish-fulfillment, aren't we? You could have formed a definite impression out of something extremely indefinite, couldn't you?"

MRS. RASTALL: "I suppose I could have, but I didn't."

MARCH: "You said, if I remember rightly, that your father made this kind of—what should I call it?—indication two or three times—"

MRS. RASTALL: "Certainly three. Perhaps more."

MARCH: "But your memory could be exaggerating, possibly, and making it all more definite. That is, there need never have been anything really like a statement of intention, if you genuinely search your memory—"

LANDER: "My lord, I must object. My learned friend appears to be imputing mis-interpretations or inventions to my client. At the time she reported these interpretations, and years afterwards, we have the clearest possible documentary evidence that Mr. Massie in his wills was making Mrs. Rastall a principal legatee."

MR. J. BOSANQUET: "I don't think that Mr. March was making implications. I certainly hope not. In any case, the wills are in front of me."

(To MARCH): "I suggest that it isn't profitable to pursue this topic any further."

A later extract from the record. As a matter of tactics, March wasn't following a chronological order, and again broke out with one of his abrupt not-led-up-to questions.

MARCH: "I put it to you, from the time of your marriage, you were completely estranged from your father?"

MRS. RASTALL: "Not so far as I was concerned."

MARCH: "I put it to you, it takes two to make a complete estrangement?"

MRS. RASTALL: "That's not what I've found."

MARCH: "And also it takes a cause? Something happening between you—"

MRS. RASTALL: "I haven't found it so."

[Two pages of the typescript record further on.]

MARCH: "You didn't really try to look after him at any time, did you? When you once left home—"

MRS. RASTALL: "I offered to, several times."

MARCH: "How did you offer to?"

MRS. RASTALL: "Usually I wrote."

MARCH: "When was the last time you wrote?"

MRS. RASTALL: "1960."

MARCH: "Ten years before he died. Not afterwards?"

MRS. RASTALL: "No."

MARCH: "Why not?"

MRS. RASTALL: "After one has made so many offers there comes a point when you can't do any more. When you can't inflict yourself any more."

MARCH: "Inflict yourself? Is that the voice of total filial affection, should you say?"

To that there was no reply on the record. March knew as well as she did that when she said "inflict yourself," she meant something harder, she meant humble yourself. Last pages of Jenny's testimony:

MARCH: "You told my learned friend that you knew nothing of your father's final illness. There was nothing to prevent you telephoning his house, was there?"

MRS. RASTALL: "I didn't even know that he was ill."

MARCH: "Come, he was a very old man. It would have been natural—wouldn't it?—to make enquiries from time to time?"

MRS. RASTALL: "I knew no one there."

MARCH: "You did nothing at all?"

MRS. RASTALL: "I wrote."

MARCH: "When?"

MRS. RASTALL: "April 1970. Some months before he died. I got no reply."

The last questions concerned the final will:

MARCH: "Did you expect to benefit?"

MRS. RASTALL: "Yes."

MARCH: "Were you certain?"

MRS. RASTALL: "His death came as a shock to me."

MARCH: "That sounds a little dubious, if I may say so."

MRS. RASTALL: "I hadn't thought about any prospects of money for a long time."

This answer was to many people in court the most surprising she had given. Some, perhaps most, didn't believe it.

MARCH: "Well. So what steps did you take?"

[She had rung up Balderstone, whom she remembered from the past, and who put her onto Skelding's firm.]

MARCH: "And you were told you were getting nothing?"

MRS. RASTALL: "Yes."

MARCH: "Wasn't that a blow?"

MRS. RASTALL: "Of course."

MARCH: "What did you do then?"

MRS. RASTALL: "I've had other blows. I thought I had to take it."

MARCH: "I should like your lordship to pay particular attention to that answer."

(To MRS. RASTALL:) "Your first impulse was not to contest the will. Why not?"

MRS. RASTALL: "I know very little about these things."

MARCH: "You mean, you thought the whole situation perfectly reasonable."

MRS. RASTALL: "I mean nothing of the sort. I didn't know what had been happening to my father, I didn't know any of the people round him."

MARCH: "In fact, you knew nothing at all about him, and didn't expect to be remembered?"

MRS. RASTALL: "I didn't know the people round him, but I happened to know a certain amount about very old people."

It looked neutral on the record, but it wasn't said like that: it was said with her kind of lively defiance, sarcastic, provocative. She was glad that she had, just by straining herself, kept to the truth, especially in the answer which March invited the judge to notice and which wouldn't do her good. Now she was entirely prepared to talk about the old, and how she had seen some of her pensioners prevailed on to will their bits of money away. March had an instinct for danger, and stopped short.

MARCH: "You didn't contest the will for some while?"

MRS. RASTALL: "I think you have the date."

MARCH: "There was quite a long interval before you did. Perhaps you had advice in the meantime?"

MRS. RASTALL: "Of course I had advice. I've never contested a will before."

Her spirit was emerging now, demureness had retired. March judged it safer to let her go. She went back, with the elation of one who has just finished a speech and is delighted with it, to her place, among the people supporting her.

"Not bad, not bad," said Swaffield, but looked at her only briefly and then glanced away. From a couple of rows in front, Symington turned round, smiled a social smile, nodded, and turned back. That was all. It wasn't so much the breath of blame, it was absence of praise. She felt extreme let-down. Only Lorimer, as the session at last ended and he walked beside her in the grandiose central hall, chilly as a cathedral in the summer afternoon, managed to mutter:

"You did fine."

She was so grateful that the tears pricked. She went on being grateful when, just as lamely, he asked if he could give her dinner that night (in front, Swaffield, arms gesticulating, was making a vehement noise to Symington, but none of them minded leaving her alone). Then Lorimer asked if he could call for her: that sounded to Jenny like old-fashioned manners, very old-fashioned, though she wasn't so much the younger.

As she gave him her address, she said: "It isn't very grand, you know."

He showed a grain of humour. "Nor's mine." He told her he had a small flat in Pimlico.

When Jenny got home, still only half past five, Lorimer not due for a couple of hours, she did what she hadn't done for years. She lay on her bed and cried. Tired, disappointed, criticised, by this time conscious that she might have played it wrong. But she hadn't been trying to play it, she began to encourage herself. She had enough spirit to become angry, and that warmed her. If they couldn't understand that she was being honest, so much the worse for them. What was it all in aid of? Her realistic soul reminded her, a considerable sum of money. What was that worth? What a world. These people were playing a game according to their rules, but it wasn't her game. They weren't her kind of people. It was good to be going out to dinner. She might have wished it was with someone more exciting. She would put on her best dress for him.

It wasn't very grand, she thought sarcastically as she took it out of the cupboard, any more than this bed-sitter was. It was as good as she could do. She would try to be some sort of company.

❧ 12 ❧

Lorimer took her in a taxi from Earls Court to Soho. It was a longish fare, and when she watched him ordering dinner she wished that she had insisted on travelling by tube. For she knew as much as anyone in London about the devices of the genteel poor. She saw him pressing nice things on her, and choosing the cheaper ones for himself. No, he didn't eat much at night, he didn't want that to put her off: perhaps he'd just have soup and an omelette. But she must have a decent meal. Wine? She pretended not to have any palate, and suggested a carafe of vin ordinaire. When she noticed that he liked his drink, she hesitated about how much another pound would hurt him and then let him order a second. Herself, she was in need of alcohol that night.

She wasn't finding it, however, too much of an effort to show gaiety or at any rate interest. Particularly when he had said something which pleased her. He was a most inarticulate man. He did force himself to say something about her performance in the witness box, but he did so in the identical words he had used four hours before. He said:

"I thought you did fine this afternoon."

"I'm glad."

He paused for a long time, framing some words.

"I don't know much about it. But you didn't try to make things better for yourself, did you?"

She shook her head.

"I liked that."

"How nice of you."

She was surprised, by this time astonished that anyone should have any glimmer of what she thought was decent: astonished that it should come from a man as dumb as this. He wasn't alluring, and yet she was moved.

It made her eager to cheer him up, and learn about him. Nevertheless, there was no doubt whatever that he was, if not dumb, then unquestionably mute. He was also, she would bet, very little used to women. He was certainly poor. Here her judgment would be more accurate than that of his House of Lords acquaintances. He was probably a shade better off than she was, not much. He had been married once. A failure. He hadn't succeeded anywhere. He wished he had stayed in the army. He might have "done all right" there. Of course, he said, he would have been "on the shelf by now." Yes, he'd just about have made colonel, thought Jenny.

She asked him, did he often go to the House of Lords?

"Nearly every day when they are sitting," said Lorimer.

"Do you often speak?"

"No." He looked constrained, or embarrassed. "I haven't started yet." He burst out: "You know, I'd like to have a go."

She said (and in a moment wished she hadn't, finding it was her turn to be embarrassed), "How long have you been there, in the Lords, I mean?"

"Eleven years."

When they left the restaurant it was still daylight outside, though her watch said nearly half past ten. She wouldn't let him take another taxi, and so they walked to the Leicester Square under-ground. She felt quite peaceful, after the day's strain and hurt. She had had a good dinner and enough wine to give her a lift. This man didn't make her footsteps light, but he had understood something and that still heartened her.

They gazed at the striptease posters, the pornographic book-shops. Sleazy, as sleazy as any capital on earth. He remembered coming to restaurants round here when he was a young man: it was better then. She had been here too, once or twice, in her teens. Yes, it had been better before the war.

Of course, they were romanticising a little, putting the

sweetness of life, the douceur de la vie, back into their own youth along with all the decorum. In historical fact, this street had been moderately sleazy in the thirties, though not as shameless. They were romanticising with the homesickness, the indulgence, with him the subdued bite of rancour, of those who had themselves in their own lives seen better days, and whose kind (one might say class, except that they came from two sub-classes, delicately different) had also seen better days, never to return. However, some of their regret was unselfish. They each had what Lorimer as a boy had been taught to call a code, and their codes were very much the same. One hadn't to go far in central London that night to feel that such a code— like the class who formed it, whether they kept to it or not— had gone for ever.

Jenny was used to viewing the scene round her with distaste and not repining. She wasn't repining now: the day, the nervous day, was over, that was a blessing. She was asking a casual question, looking up towards him, when she saw him gazing at the bright sky.

As usual the words didn't come.

At last he said: "When I was in the desert, that was the one thing I missed."

"What was?"

"Nights like this. The short summer nights. Northern summer nights."

For an instant, she thought he was attempting to distract her, and then decided against. No, he wasn't thinking of her, it was the only independent vestige of poetry she had heard him mutter.

A few minutes later, as they were walking down Cranbourn Street he had the same reflection again. Once he had found words he didn't let them go, and so he said, pointing to the sky: "When I was in the desert that was the one thing I missed."

"You told me that before."

"Sorry. But I did miss them. Short summer nights."

"They'd be even shorter in Iceland, wouldn't they?" she said, bright-eyed, deadpan.

He said, without humour: "I suppose they would."

At about the same time another couple were walking in the lucid midsummer evening. These were the two leading counsel in the hearing, Lander and March, and they were walking from their club, which was the Reform, along Pall Mall. They were intimate friends, intimate to a degree that, say, Hillmorton and Ryle could not have been. People often wondered about them. They seemed an ill-matched pair. Apart from their professional skills, they were very different men. March came from an old established Jewish family, something like Jewish Forsytes: he was wily, tactful, guarded, intuitive, overmature and often gave the impression of dilapidated phlegm. While his friend, by a fluke looking much more like a Jewish stereotype than March, who didn't in the least, was vivacious, a bit of a dandy, bright-tongued, in private likely to give offence by the same bright tongue, though he was by a long way the kinder and more dutiful of the two: entirely English, though foreigners expecting the English to be stiff and silent didn't believe it.

Why should these two be so intimate? The explanation was commonplace. They knew, and had known since they were at school, the secrets of each other's sexual lives: and, as young men, had had features of a sexual temperament in common. These weren't sensational features, and nowadays the two of them had half forgotten or submerged even the memory, though Lander, not excelling in tact, sometimes reminded his friend. Simply, they both had been unusually insecure and unconfident, too long so for their own composure, doubtful of their virility, uncertain whether they would satisfy women or be loved by them. All that was odd to recollect, now that they were middle-aged men, long since married, sons grown up, the tentativeness belonging to other people and a dead past, both used since they had become star barristers to admiration from women, whom once they might have been frightened of. It was that kind of similarity, and the knowledge that each had of it, which had made them close, for life.

They had been talking of a dinner in the City which they had to attend on the coming Friday night. March discussed their transport with gravity, as though planning a difficult military campaign:

"The streets may be clear as it's the weekend. But using ordinary prudence we can't rely on that."

"Oh, for God's sake don't let's use ordinary prudence." Irrepressibly Lander added: "Just for once."

March gave a deflated, lop-sided smile. Soon they went through the palace gates and crossed into St. James's Park. There they sat down. It was a warm and tranquillising night. They both lived in Belgravia close by. March was a shade more talkative and unrestrained than usual, the only external effect of his having drunk enough at the club. Enough, in his case, was a fair amount. Of the two, Lander, bright and loving entertainment, was the abstemious one. He thought that March drank more like a Scandinavian than a Jew: and not given to holding his tongue was accustomed to say so. That evening March had drunk a bottle of Burgundy and half a dozen stiff whiskies. Lander, after a lifetime still not entirely used to those habits, viewed with envy how his friend was entirely unaffected, except perhaps rather more fun.

Up to that time of night they had not exchanged a comment about the Massie case. The truth was, it did not matter to them overmuch, except in the line of duty. They were not involved with their own principals, they invested no emotion in their side—unlike the solicitors, who in both camps had become more partisan as the months passed.

Lander and March were quite outside all this. Certainly, as the case stretched on their own fees stretched out (the costs had now accumulated to something like £25,000); but again that, though mildly gratifying, didn't matter to them much. Each of them was among the leading chancery barristers of the period, earning a minimum of £40,000 a year, sometimes much more. March was tipped to become, and soon, a High Court Judge. Lander might have to wait a while because of his excessive sparkle, but he too, the pundits said, would finish on the Bench. Money didn't matter: this case didn't matter: and it was casually, as they sat beside the ornamental lake, that March asked:

"What's the betting on this present job?"

"Which job?"

"What we're supposed to be performing on this week."

Lander, who never betted, had learnt his friend's language. He said: "I'd have thought something like evens, isn't that it?"

"That's about right."

"Perhaps a bit in your favour."

"Perhaps six to four on."

"Of course," said Lander, "no one knows what passes through what the old Tortoise [Bosanquet] is pleased to call his mind. I wonder if he does. He might decide almost anything. But if I had to judge it I should want some proof that the old man Massie was capable of being influenced by anyone."

Lander was arguing his friend's case, but the point was obvious. They knew each other's quality, even when competing there was no value in keeping secrets.

"He was obviously an old horror," Lander went on. "I wonder if he was compos at the end."

"I wonder," said March, "if he was compos at the beginning. Or any other time."

"Come to that," said Lander, "your woman [he meant Mrs. Underwood] must have behaved like an unspeakable fool. If you were going to bamboozle an old man out of his money, would you make it quite so public? Politely eliminating everyone who ever came near him. It does give a slightly unfortunate impression. Don't you think that might have occurred to her?"

"We'll see what you do to her." March wasn't implying physical assault, but cross-examination. In fact, in their different techniques either of them, cross-examining for the plaintiff, "would have done to her" very much the same. There wouldn't be much room or need for finesse.

"Good God alive, most people don't deserve to come into money!" Lander cried. That was a poor man's (or a relatively poor man's, his father being a Cambridge don) cri du coeur. "I take it you've seen her, what's she like?"

"Not my cup of tea," said March. "Hard. Simple. Haute bourgeoise. You might meet her at a Tory party conference with feathers in her hat. Devoutly believing in hanging and flogging as a kind of moral exercise. To be restored, not for prosaic practical reasons, but for their own delightful sake."

"That son of hers," Lander was still musing on his cri du

coeur, "stands to gain a quarter of a million." Then, as though there was some obscure connection, "I take it he's a pansy." In which Lander, like a good many others, was possibly in theory correct, in practice remarkably wrong.

In a similar equable disconnected fashion, March said, "What did you make of your woman?" (This time it was Jenny Rastall who was meant.)

"She wasn't a bad witness, except when she presented you with something on a plate. God save us from our friends."

"Did you care for her?"

"Would she care for me?" Lander grinned. "She's a bit tight lipped, isn't she? She'd decide that I was frivolous and light weight. The old old story."

March was meditating, but not on misjudgments about his friend. He said: "I have a very faint idea that she might be rather fun in bed."

"You have odd tastes, you always have had. Still, you may be right, you sometimes are."

"Well," said March, "we shall never know. And we shall never know why her father wished that she were dead. That must have been true, mustn't it?"

"I'm not so sure." Sometimes Lander was the more cautious of the two.

That was all they said about the case that night.

They sat, comfortably tired, relaxed, gazing at the water.

"It's a beautiful night," said March.

"That's not exactly a contribution to thought," said Lander.

Once more March gave a lop-sided grin, and obstinately repeated the remark. Not long afterwards, they got up and, with an outward appearance of middle-aged lawyers of some eminence, walked home.

✤ 13 ✤

March did not open the case for the defendants until the end of the week. When at last he did so, he simultaneously looked more deliberate and actually was more succinct than his friend. He disclaimed any special interest in Jenny: she was someone, and there were others, to whom money might have or not have been left according to what the old man finally desired. The essential things, March broke out, with the sudden thrust and bite which was one of his techniques, were what his state of mind was, whether he knew what he wanted or was being told: and whether Mrs. Underwood's intervention in his last years wasn't just a simple act of kindness. March said that that was the most natural explanation, and the most natural explanation was usually the best. Here was an efficient woman who couldn't bear the sight of the old man's solitariness, and set about clearing it up. A well-run home wasn't everything in one's eighties, but it was preferable to squalor. All she could give him was her energy and her time and this she had done.

That was unsensational, deliberately so, and so was the evidence he called that Friday. The doctor who had been present in Skelding's chamber the previous October, head on one side in court like an exceptionally judicious bird or a politician being interviewed on television, pressed by Lander in cross-examination about Massie's state of mind—at the end of which some observers in court weren't going to be moved from the opinion that the old man was senile. A good many others thought that he was using old age to get his own way, and that he had a kind of self-willed, dislikeable cunning. None of the evidence, either that day or on the following Monday, cleared up the discrepancy.

There were other witnesses who had attended to him physically, humbly or not so humbly. A surgeon who had operated for a prostate, the chiropodist, a barber who saw more of him than the doctors, shaving him three times a week and cutting his hair once a month. "He was one of the old school," said the barber with irrepressible cheerfulness. "He couldn't stand his hair being long: not that there was much danger of that, to tell you the honest truth." Which remark, the humour of the court as of all assemblies being elementary, gave much simple pleasure.

During the weekend which interrupted this stream of prosaic evidence (marshalled by David March to give a sense, even a dulling sense, of comparative normality), Liz and Julian Underwood spent their time in Julian's flat. It was a flat which at first sight, and certainly at second sight, a perceptive woman would have found discouraging if she was set on marrying the man. Liz had felt so, before she got herself entangled.

Not that the flat was degraded, or suggested corruption, or was even untidy. On the contrary, it was only too immaculately kept. Julian was very good at looking after himself, far too good, Liz had judged in her less hallucinated days. Books all dusted, pictures well lighted, a view over the gardens at the back, sunlit that weekend. In the pantry his own food, hygienically chosen so as to prolong life, including a remarkable quantity of yoghurt and garlic. No drink for himself, a bottle of sherry for his guests, with which Liz, a non-ascetic drinker, had to be content whenever she stayed with him.

Between them, on the Saturday, was a question of judgment and a question of superstition. Liz believed that his mother's evidence, which must be heard early the next week, might be decisive. Julian, who was being unusually thoughtful and protective, doubted it. Not in this kind of case, he argued with her gently. Nothing is as decisive as all that. And if it comes to an appeal even less so. Then it is all read on paper and it looks very different.

"Appeal," she said, "are we going to have any more of this?"

"Anyone's guess," said Julian. "We shall win, but we ought to be prepared for anything."

Liz was not convinced. She could resist him when he was being sensible. Perversely, she couldn't, or she had to struggle, when he was elevated into one of his fugues—fugues of talk, un-reason, pseudo-science, clouds of shimmering psychic explanation. Then he dominated her. He had made her as superstitious as he was. That Saturday she was being more so.

Julian was a superstitious man, and one of his superstitions was attached to sex. At the beginning she had thought this was part of his sadistic play. Later she believed it, or wasn't certain when to disbelieve; what was in his mind was hers. Openeyed, solemnly, fluently, absurdly (was he jeering at her, provoking her, making fun of her?), he had lectured her. Copulation on a Tuesday meant bad luck the following day. Or even milder sexual pleasures. It had happened to him more than once. It had become an absolute tabu.

Now it was her turn. It might have been revenge, but it didn't feel like that. Before an ordeal or a crisis (and his mother's appearance in the box had for Liz become unshakeably just that)—if they had enjoyed themselves, then all would go wrong. No, she wouldn't risk it. They would feel guilty afterwards. This would all soon be over, and then they would be released.

Julian tried to talk her round. Himself, he felt distinctly like it. Magnificent weather, pleasant to look at the sky from bed level, after they had had enough. No one to disturb them for forty-eight hours. Shame to waste the time. Crisis, anxiety, brought him on, and so (he knew all her nerves) they did her too.

Her expression was dark, loving, determined. He could possibly have coaxed her. He could have forced her. She was in his power. But he held back. He was as selfish as a man could reasonably be, or perhaps not more than other men but more shamelessly so. At the same time, he had his own kind of good nature. He enjoyed understanding her moods. She would enjoy herself frenetically and then the instant they finished feel bad. And feel worse when they got into court again. Perhaps he enjoyed making up for times when he had ill-treated her. So he was gentle to her all the weekend, did the cooking and, as an unprecedented concession, went out and bought her half a bottle of gin. He was more gentle, she thought, than he had been when he was first seducing her: when, despite or because of all his practice, he had been deliberately slow—soon, so slow as to test her patience—in making the first move.

After this curious piece of delicacy (drawingroom emotions, Doctor Pemberton would have said with more than his usual scorn) Mrs. Underwood, giving her evidence on the Tuesday morning, did not appear delicate at all. She was handsome, authoritative, smartly dressed, warm-voiced. She gave no sign of doubt or what she might have described as butterflies. And yet, though only Julian knew it, she had been sick twice after breakfast. She was one of those on whom strain acts directly on the body, not on consciousness: like Polish officers in the war, among whom the rate of anxiety neurosis was vanishingly small by comparison with the Anglo-Americans, that of heart conditions much higher.

David March wasn't above learning from his opponent and friend, who had carefully not covered up the breach between Jenny and her father. March, after planning his examination over the weekend, adopted a similar tactic, but was bolder, asking the thin-ice questions himself.

Mrs. Underwood's first statements were simple and undecorated. With her husband, she had met Mr. Massie once or twice in the past. When she met him again, years after, it was through being taken by neighbours of his to his home in Sussex. At that time he was merely an old acquaintance. It was later that she came to regard him as an old friend.

She didn't like the state he was living in. She had time on her hands. First she visited him frequently: then she took to staying in the house. It needed a little while for her to understand the whole position. She decided that the doctor was a good competent man, but not the right doctor for Mr. Massie's temperament. The housekeeper was not satisfactory: he

wanted food at strange hours, not much food but snacks, often
in the middle of the night, and the food wasn't provided. He
needed alcohol and that was permitted to run out. He didn't
drink excessively, but on and off throughout the twenty-four
hours. It was one of the few comforts he had left.

Court Record:
> MARCH: "It would be fair to say, would it, that for the last
> three years or so you devoted most of your life to him?"
>
> MRS. UNDERWOOD: "That's not for me to say."
>
> MARCH: "But you came to be on call day and night?"
>
> MRS. UNDERWOOD: "Yes, that is true."
>
> MARCH: "You sacrificed all your ordinary life?"
>
> MRS. UNDERWOOD: "It had to be done."
>
> MARCH: "So you did devote yourself to him?"
>
> MRS. UNDERWOOD: "I was obliged to, I felt—"
>
> MARCH: "You did it out of duty?"
>
> MRS. UNDERWOOD: "Oh well, he was sad and lonely and I
> wanted to help."
>
> MARCH: "Tell us this. When you began to devote yourself in
> this fashion, did you have any idea of his testamentary
> intentions?"
>
> MRS. UNDERWOOD: "Absolutely none at all."

Yes, she had realised that he had some money. She didn't enquire where it was going. She knew vaguely that there was a
daughter. She had never met her. The daughter was not mentioned. Mrs. Underwood assumed that she had gone right out of
his life.

> MARCH: "You didn't talk about her?"
>
> MRS. UNDERWOOD: "Of course not."
>
> MARCH: "You didn't remind him about her?"
>
> MRS. UNDERWOOD: "He didn't want to be reminded."
>
> MARCH: "You didn't communicate with her when he was
> dying? Or when he actually died?"
>
> MRS. UNDERWOOD: "She was a complete stranger to me.
> And by that time I took it for granted that she was to
> him also."

113

Yes, in that last year or thereabouts he had discussed making a new will. By that date he had accepted Mr. Skelding to do some of his legal work. His other solicitor was very busy, and sometimes Mr. Massie wanted information (she obtained it herself on the telephone) at short notice, or an interview late at night. Mr. Skelding was someone in whom she had complete confidence and Mr. Massie soon felt the same. In the end Mr. Massie described to her what he wanted the new and final will to contain. He wished to repeat the rubrics from some of his previous wills, of which there were copies in his files. She relayed his instructions to Mr. Skelding. He came down in person with the document, Mr. Massie had it read to him and signed it in the presence of witnesses. It was as simple as that.

MARCH: "Tell us one last thing. Anyone can understand that Mr. Massie should wish to show appreciation for all your sacrifice and devotion. But it might seem a little strange that he expressed this by leaving most of his estate to your son?"

MRS. UNDERWOOD: "That is very simple too."

MARCH: "It would be helpful to get this entirely clear. How often did Mr. Massie meet your son?"

MRS. UNDERWOOD: "He came and stayed in Mr. Massie's house several times when I was there."

MARCH: "They talked?"

MRS. UNDERWOOD: "Yes, but the reason for Mr. Massie's bequest was very simple. I was sixty-five and it wasn't sensible to risk two sets of death duties. Also I am moderately well provided for so long as I live, but most of my income comes from pensions and annuities which won't go to my son. I made the whole position clear."

[After March's sustained piece of pre-emptive tactics, which all the lawyers appreciated, his rival wasn't left with many points of entry. For once, though this wasn't apparent, he was somewhat at a loss. He had long ago decided that he daren't touch the old housekeeper's story of Mrs. Underwood's plans for marriage; neither he nor Symington could bring themselves to believe it, and it hadn't been mentioned in evidence. Instead he had to retreat into a repetition of Mrs. Underwood's changes in the household. She answered as confidently as to her own counsel; she wouldn't accept any implication, they were what any responsible person would have done.

Lander had to force a sharper tone.]

LANDER: "You wouldn't deny, Mrs. Underwood, that you had great influence on the old gentleman?"

MRS. UNDERWOOD: "I really am not quite certain what that means."

LANDER: "Look at the facts. You got him to do precisely what you wanted, isn't that so?"

MRS. UNDERWOOD: "Not at all. He was a very strong willed man."

LANDER: "But Mrs. Underwood, may I remind you, he let you—or maybe he wasn't in a state to resist—he let you introduce a new doctor, a new solicitor, a new housekeeper, all before you had been in his house a year?"

MRS. UNDERWOOD: "I have explained already that that was absolutely necessary."

LANDER: "Whether it was necessary or not, it happened. We agree on that, don't we?"

MRS. UNDERWOOD: "I am very glad that it happened."

LANDER: "No doubt. But he couldn't resist you doing it, could he?"

MRS. UNDERWOOD: "He took some persuading, of course."

LANDER: "Persuading? Persuading, Mrs. Underwood?"

MRS. UNDERWOOD: "Certainly persuading, what else could I do?"

[Lander tried other versions of the question but got no further. He had to switch his thrust.]

LANDER: "Mrs. Underwood, you have lived in this world. You can't have been in Mr. Massie's house for long without realising that he was distinctly well to do."

MRS. UNDERWOOD: "I didn't give it much thought."

LANDER: "But you did realise it?"

MRS. UNDERWOOD: "He was living like a man of some means."

LANDER: "And in the not too distant future those means would inevitably have to descend on other people."

MRS. UNDERWOOD: "I did not give that any thought at all."

LANDER: "Does that sound entirely probable?"

MRS. UNDERWOOD: "Certainly. I saw a job of work that I could do for him. Making his last years more bearable, that was what I thought about."

LANDER: "Nothing else?"

MRS. UNDERWOOD: "Nothing else at all."

[More pressure, satire from Lander, confidence from Mrs. Underwood and no give whatever.]

LANDER: "Yet, even you have to recognise there is a faint difference in his final will? From anything before you took charge?"

MRS. UNDERWOOD: "Naturally, I was glad that he wanted to show some recognition."

LANDER: "Equally naturally, you discussed his will with him?"

MRS. UNDERWOOD: "He told me what he wanted to do."

LANDER: "After you had persuaded him? Or influenced him, shall we say?"

MRS. UNDERWOOD: "He had made up his own mind."

LANDER: "You didn't think of dissuading him? You could have influenced him in other directions. You might have reminded him that he had responsibilities. His daughter, for instance."

MRS. UNDERWOOD: "He didn't feel any responsibility for her."

LANDER: "No discussion, no influence. You might have influenced him against such a curious will, mightn't you?"

MRS. UNDERWOOD: "I was very grateful. That would have been a ridiculous thing to do."

LANDER: "After all your efforts."

MRS. UNDERWOOD: "I think it would have hurt his feelings."

Lander pressed on, asking how many times the old man had actually seen Julian in the flesh. Perhaps three or four. Towards the end he wished to see only her and the doctor. She was still invulnerable. Dissatisfied with himself and his technique, quite uncertain about what impression she had left, Lander had to let her go.

In fact, on most people in court she had made a strong and favourable impression. A great many on her own side were certain that she had clinched the case. Even Liz, hypersensitised, had phases when she dared to think so.

There were a few sceptical thoughts. It was all so tidy, so rationalised, so free from hesitation: did anyone behave or think like this? But then, in such an audience, there were bound to be a few who didn't give anyone's self-explanation the benefit of the doubt. A few more were speculating on what the conditions had really been, inside that gloomy-sounding house. She had made it seem too like a nice orderly business meeting, someone observed. It couldn't have been quite like that. Whether the old man was senile and defenceless or not. After all, she had said herself that he had been an obsessive drinker, his glass ready at hand night and day. To which the answer was that she had no conceivable need to bring that out. It was another proof of how straightforward she was.

In the final tailing-off of evidence, there was one glimpse of a scene in that terminal downstairs room. Mr. Skelding answered questions, composed, quite unperturbed, about his connection with Mr. Massie. Yes, he had been introduced by Mrs. Underwood. Yes, he had advised her for a good many years, and her husband before that. Yes, he had had conversations with Mr. Massie. Yes, Mr. Massie was entirely capable of attending to business. Yes, Mrs. Underwood had instructed him of Mr. Massie's wishes about his last will. Yes, he had been shown copies of previous wills and asked to preserve the identical form. The signing and witnessing of the will was, of course, all in order.

Lander made no attempt to challenge any of Mr. Skelding's previous evidence and his cross-examination was short.

Court Record:
> LANDER: "Did you ask Mr. Massie whether he understood his will?"
>
> MR. SKELDING: "No. I should have thought that was impertinent."

LANDER: "Did you have any conversation with him?"

MR. SKELDING: "It wouldn't have been suitable. When I arrived the witnesses were already present in the room."
   [The witnesses were father and son from a house close by.]

LANDER: "Was anyone else present?"

MR. SKELDING: "Mrs. Underwood was there."

LANDER: "What happened then?"

MR. SKELDING: "I presented the will to Mr. Massie. He looked over it."

LANDER: "Could he take it in?"

MR. SKELDING: "To the best of my knowledge and belief, of course. He signed. His writing was good and firm right up to the end. The witnesses signed."

LANDER: "Did anyone speak?"

MR. SKELDING: "So far as I can recollect, no."

LANDER: "You mean, all this took place in complete silence?"

MR. SKELDING: "I think I remember Mr. Massie at the end saying something like thank you."

✤ 14 ✤

On the Thursday morning, after counsels' speeches, Mr. Justice Bosanquet announced that he would take the rest of the day to reflect and give his decision the following morning. Another night of waiting for the anxious: and they went on waiting during the first careful, noncommittal hour or so of Mr. Justice Bosanquet. Sitting contentedly in his place, teacher-like, he began with a homily. He didn't fancy himself as an orator, and actually there was a marked lack of resemblance between his effect on an audience and that of Trotsky at his most inspired. Nevertheless, Bosanquet was not deterred from utterance and in secret enjoyed it. His homily was, like all his other homilies, sensible, indefatigably so. It dealt with the unwisdom of going to law whenever the legal process could be avoided. Cases like the one before him could and should be settled between the parties: compromise was to be preferred to legislation.

That wasn't said so simply, and the clock ticked on. Then he approached somewhat nearer the point. Undue influence. That was the bone of the plaintiff's pleading. Of all the cases that came before this Division of the High Court, those of undue influence were the most difficult, and sometimes it seemed the most unrealistic, to decide. Undue influence, what did it or could it mean? There was no satisfactory definition. Imagine that he (Mr. Justice Bosanquet) is a very old man to whom in the nature of things death cannot be far away. There is no relative close at hand to minister to him, but there is, shall we say, a nurse. A nurse who is always available, makes him feel less lonely, understands his worries. She will talk to him about whatever is on his mind and will help him make his decisions. Is that influence, can it become undue influence?

He may easily become grateful to his nurse and ask her how he can express his gratitude. He may easily ask her if she would care to be included in his will. She may tell him that there is something that would make her happy. Is that undue influence? She may of course take advantage of a decline in faculties, and put suggestions into his mind which wouldn't have been admitted when he was fully capable. That one would regard as undue influence, but where and how is the line to be drawn? Most people appeared to respond strongly to those nursing them in their final illness—sometimes with great dislike, usually with trust.

Usually there was bound to be influence, undue or not. It was unsatisfactory to have to make a decision in law about anything in this misty landscape. Still, that was his duty this morning.

At which Mr. Justice Bosanquet at last got down to the case. He said firmly, impassively:

"I listened with great respect to the evidence of the plaintiff, Mrs. Rastall. I have no hesitation at all in saying I believed every word she said. She was, in my judgment, telling us the entire truth of a very painful situation, as it affected her." This sounded ominous in some ears, not in March's, who had known him before he was a judge. It was still anyone's bet, March was thinking, how he would come down. March knew that Bosanquet, who though prosy was less vain than most men, had one spot of vanity. He was vain about his human sense.

He might have said, and had sometimes done so, that his snap-judgments about witnesses were likely to be only a little better than an even chance, he was perhaps a shade more likely to be right than wrong: but to himself he trusted his insight more than that. That morning he was using it with confidence. March listened with some interest. He thought that the judge wasn't clever and not his favourite dinner companion. But was worth listening to about people.

Bosanquet was describing the father-daughter relationship and its effect on Jenny.

"I completely accept that she couldn't persist in forcing herself upon him. Some women would have done so, but, so far as one can interpret Mr. Massie's personality, one of the more obscure features of this case, I believe that he would have rejected her. I further believe that he had inhibited his daughter's display of affection, not the affection itself which she naturally possessed."

More about Jenny, temperate and kind. Then:

"However, none of this is central to the core of the case. It is common ground that Mrs. Rastall and her father were on distant terms. It is also common ground that nevertheless in all the series of wills, the rather peculiar series of wills which Mr. Massie executed, Mrs. Rastall was always the principal legatee—in all that series of wills until the last one. So the relation between father and daughter is not of the first relevance. What is of the first relevance is how Mr. Massie came to change his mind in that last will."

That brought Bosanquet, carefully unemphatic, to the actions of Mrs. Underwood. No one had tried to deny, or could possibly deny, that she had "dedicated almost all her time and energy" (that was the phrase he continually picked out, as though with a pair of tweezers) for nearly four years to this old gentleman. Four years was a considerable stretch in anyone's life, the more so when one was not in one's first youth. It was not entirely easy to reconcile the medical testimony, but at the very least Mr. Massie was by this time physically frail, and mentally his moods appeared often to have been clouded.

The judge went on: "He was much alone, and Mrs. Underwood had gone out of her way to relieve that loneliness. But [at that moment the 'but' was left in the air, and there were some whose attention tightened]—it is possible to consider that some of the steps she took may have increased his loneliness. She has explained her reasons for dispensing with doctors and others who had served him for so long. However satisfactory these actions were to Mrs. Underwood, the effect must have been to isolate this old man from all those he had normally been connected with. Getting rid of one professional adviser or attendant could be a coincidence, getting rid of all of them might appear to bend coincidence rather far. Mrs. Underwood may very well have persuaded herself that she was doing it for the best. The conclusion, however, was that she was left as the only confidante or, even more, the only source of influence surrounding the old man."

An eye flash passed between March and his opponent. By this time, they—and other persons with a share of perception—had realised that the judge mistrusted Mrs. Underwood. He hadn't been overpowered by her confidence or conscious rectitude. In retrospect, some thought that though he was straining himself to be fair in his own mind, he wasn't—or rather that this was someone who, in private as well as public, he couldn't have had sympathy with. He said, and repeated it, and refined what he had repeated, that she could have believed that she was acting with the best of intentions: but in his heart he wasn't moved by that excuse. He had decided that she had carried out a planned and calculated campaign. He probably thought that she was more of a piece than she actually was: he had never seen her craving for her son's affection. But, as March and Lander argued later with a detachment not granted to others in the case, it was a nice problem in psychological disparity.

The judge was a man in touch with his own experience. What he felt, he recognised without cover. Mrs. Underwood was a woman of action. Between the introspective and the person of action there was one of the oldest mis-comprehensions. Persons of action were good at not letting the right hand know what the left hand did: and often, with ardent and genuine sincerity, denying it. "In this case," said Lander to March, "the right hand was getting the old man his bedpan night and day: and the left hand was making sure of the dibs. Is that hypocrisy? Quite possibly not. Horizontal fission, if you like." In that amicable conversation, Lander added cheerfully, "Still, for my money, the old Tortoise was in the right of it. Come on, David, you're not a specially good man, but you've never deceived yourself about a motive in your life."

In court, the judge had made it clear that Mrs. Underwood had deceived herself about her motive: or at least that that was the most charitable assumption. "The lady has told us that, when she took up residence in Mr. Massie's house, and for a considerable period afterwards, she had no knowledge of, or even interest in, how he was proposing to dispose of his estate. In its full significance, that I do not find entirely easy to accept, though I am sure Mrs. Underwood was making a conscientious attempt to recollect. . . ." (A few minutes later.) "We have to bear in mind that Mrs. Underwood is quite patently a most able and efficient woman. She is used to handling money. She is used to meeting people like herself, who have to give thought to their financial affairs and their final disposition. It is not easy to accept that this experience didn't lead her to acquaint herself with Mr. Massie's mind about his own final disposition. . . ." (Later.) "All this evidence appears to me cumulative and leads me, despite the reservations I made earlier about the uncertainties of this kind of case, to one finding. I have decided that one cannot study the final will without seeing in it the influence of Mrs. Underwood. In the light of all the weight of the cumulative evidence I have decided further that one cannot avoid seeing undue influence. I have therefore to declare that the will of September 6th, 1970 is invalid."

He added, in a reflective tone: "For the present I shall suspend the award of costs."

Muriel Calvert was not present in court that morning. Though she had a glacial interest in some of the personalities, she had none in the result. If she had been there she might have observed that Mr. Justice Bosanquet had no sense of dramatic shape: for, instead of stopping short at his decision, he spent a further five minutes repeating his strictures on unnecessary legislation and the desirability of rational compromise.

Listening to the judge's verdict, which in fact she along with the lawyers had anticipated many minutes before, Liz felt a flood of dark flushing anger, together with a curious naked shame, as though she as well as Mrs. Underwood were being exposed to jeering censorious prurient gazes. But the shock, the bitterness of disappointment, made her more active. Before the judge had finished, she was already stirring with a sunburst of plans. It was no use being quiet any longer.

Meanwhile Jenny had heard the verdict and had, for an instant, felt an extraordinary and to her unknown sensation, as though she had been transformed into a vacuum inhabited only by herself. Then the blankness passed and she listened to the judge prosing away with a warmed and almost patronising satisfaction, wishing to congratulate someone in the vicinity, someone not herself.

As they got out into the hall that well-being was soon nibbled away. Swaffield and Symington were talking together, Swaffield caught her watching them and said he was taking them out for lunch, Symington pressed her arm and said, "So far, so good." It did not need a woman as fine-nerved as Jenny to detect that that wasn't the voice of unmitigated triumph, of struggles packed away and won.

Swaffield had them all driven to Prunier's in one of his grand cars. On the way he was in the best of tempers, which meant there were glints of happy malice.

"That woman [Mrs. Underwood]—not quite enough people to hear, not quite enough. Still, she heard, unless the Lord suddenly made her deaf. That's something." It wasn't until they were sitting at their table that he congratulated Jenny.

"Well, my girl, you did your stuff with the judge. I didn't think you could have done. That shows how wrong I can be."

For Swaffield, this was apologetic and handsome. He went on: "But you mustn't throw your hat in the air just yet."

"That's about the last thing I feel like doing," she said with acidity.

"What's the matter?" said Symington.

"That's the question I ought to ask, what is the matter?"

"Oh, we were more or less prepared for it, there's some talk of an appeal."

While they were still standing in the Law Courts' hall, he had left them for some minutes, she now realised it was to confer with the lawyers, their side and the other's.

"Is it sensible?" said Swaffield. But as rapidly as anyone in court, he had realised the significance of the judge's last decision, or rather non-decision. He wouldn't have held up an award of costs if an appeal was only the slimmest of chances.

Symington regarded Jenny. Both men knew her well enough by now to know that she could stand the truth. "The old judge said today that these cases are anyone's guess. Another judge might just have tilted the other way. As for being sensible, it depends on how much money everyone is prepared to spend. The costs are going to be quite impressive."

Swaffield said: "I can stand them." He reflected, powerful, relaxed, great mouth up-curved. "We've done very well. Perhaps you and I had better see what's the best arrangement now." He had spoken across the table to Symington, and Jenny missed the point of the remark, though Symington didn't. She was thinking about time and certainty.

"How long is this business going to take?" she cried.

"If it comes to an appeal," said Symington, partially responding to Swaffield also, "we'll have to reckon on waiting for another twelve months. At least."

"Good God Almighty," she said. "Will this thing go on for ever?"

"Almost for ever," said Symington with affection. He not only knew that she could stand the truth but in her own fashion had great endurance. Swaffield knew the same but was feeling benevolent that day and so more than usually interfering.

"I'll stake you, of course, Jenny. But you're not to run me in for more than an extra thousand. For your pocket money!"

"I can't do anything like that." With him she couldn't manage to be haughty enough.

"Yes, you can. And you can buy yourself a new dress, you need one."

Symington was thinking, as they sat over a delectable meal which no one but Swaffield was enjoying, did this man arouse Angst in everyone? Even when he was at his kindest. He was promising to send Jenny a case of champagne and a case of whisky that afternoon, just to keep her going.

That same afternoon, in the late edition of the evening papers there was an announcement that Mrs. Underwood's lawyers had already given notice of appeal.

✥ 15 ✥

The case, or some of those most affected by it, moved into a kind of limbo. Not the judge, of course, who sat placidly in the Law Courts trying other cases, and then went home to Highgate without giving a retrospective thought to this one: nor March and Lander, who were earning their big livings and had their customary dinner together at their club once a week with the Massie case compartmented out of mind. But Skelding and his partners on one side, Symington on the other, still had occasional hours in occasional weeks when they were drafting briefs for the appeal—in the stretches of limbo-like time before it could happen, if there is time in limbo and if there was ever going to be an appeal. For that Symington was, while going through the exercise of preparing for it, simultaneously and much more enthusiastically planning to avoid.

The more Symington studied the record of the case in Bosanquet's court, the less positive he was about their chances in a higher one. The time might soon be coming to put out the first feelers towards the other side. "Leave them guessing," said Swaffield, who had performed more negotiations than most men, "the more they want to settle the better, they must be more anxious than we are, let them worry. Above all they mustn't get the slightest idea of what we'd settle for."

Swaffield had respect for Symington, but he wanted another opinion. With a rich man's superbity, just as he had told Jenny that Symington's was "the best firm in London" for their case

126

and just as he might have shouted for "the best man in London" if he had had a twinge in his chest, so he asked for names, the loftiest names possible, and the papers were being read that August by a former Law Officer of the Crown.

They involved Jenny in none of this, or more exactly didn't communicate it. "She's a sensible woman," said Swaffield with proprietorial approval, and then went on, "she'd damned well better be content with what we can get her, she ought to get down on her knees every day of her life." He had involved her, however, in another fashion. Either because he couldn't resist getting some return on the money he was spending on her, or because he equally couldn't resist having a protégée under his eye, he had asked her to put in half her time at the charity office. Asked her in his ambivalent manner, and she couldn't refuse.

To her own surprise—she had not done any executive work, even on operations as modest as these—she liked it and was good at it. Not so much to the surprise of Swaffield. Just as he had the knack of judging the Symingtons, so he had with women like this: functional judgment if you like, not Dostoevskian, but useful to him nevertheless. The job was good for her morale, he thought with self-satisfaction. His motives as so often were a welter, undisentangleable, incoherent: possibly bringing about a lift in Jenny's morale might have been mixed among them.

Waiting for the law to finish with her, waiting for a future which seemed never to arrive, well, she could get used to that, it wasn't so different from so much of the sostenuto of her life, often she forgot it altogether. The day after Mr. Justice Bosanquet had given his verdict, Lorimer had written her a short awkward note, saying that the House would be sitting late three or four nights a week all through July, they were on the Industrial Relations Bill, and it would pass the time and give him some support if she could "drop in" occasionally, that is if she wouldn't be too bored. He was copying the form which he had heard Clare use to Swaffield. This she did, and sometimes sat through a couple of hours of the debate, her English soul enjoying the flummery, her debunking mind telling her that the first necessity of the Parliamentary life must be an inordinate capacity to put up with boredom, with sheer jaw-aching boredom. Lorimer had spoken truer than he knew, but it would have upset him if she told him so.

Anyway, though he was the most dutiful of men and voted in each division, he didn't carry duty so far as to listen much in the Chamber. They spent most of those long night sessions in the bar, and there Jenny wasn't bored at all. Sometimes a well-known face: usually faces not so well known which she came to be familiar with, such as Schiff's: the curious relaxed climate which seemed to pervade the place, though she couldn't define it: a fair amount to drink (she reassured herself that Lorimer was getting a day's extra expenses each week).

On the other hand, it was Liz, who, from that first blaze of rage or resolution in the court, wouldn't adjust herself to limbo or let herself enter it. On the instant, she had promised herself that she wouldn't sit back, she wouldn't let time run on, she wouldn't take delay without end. She would force Julian to marry her. It wasn't to be borne, hanging on for the case to come to a climax, months ahead, longer than that, maybe a year or two. It wasn't to be borne, a woman's life was short, his would go on without change, already she looked her age, more than her age (in that her introspection was morbid). She had to make this man marry her.

That meant some practical steps. It meant, first of all and most important of all, getting hold of some money. Without that, she was sure that she stood no chance. Liz prided herself on her own kind of realism, cutting away the frills, no non-sense or illusion. She would have been grateful if people told her that she thought like a Norman peasant. And yet, some might wonder whether she was as realistic as all that, with her looks and charm, never winning what she most wanted, while she was pursuing an infatuation for a man others despised. And this was a recurrent situation: she had had a long-drawn-out affair, as desperate on her side, with a man who wouldn't divorce his wife.

She believed that Julian would have married her if he had come into the Massie money. He had said so, as definitely as he ever said anything, and though he had hypnotised her before now with clouds of tantalising words, she believed that this time he intended it. Further, she believed—and here was her kind of realism, she thought she was seeing him straight— that Julian would marry her if she could bring him money. So it was for her to produce it. She had little of her own, yet. It had been enough for a bachelor woman, since she earned a fair salary in the employment agency where she worked. Although she wasn't close to her eldest sister they shared a St. John's Wood flat, and that didn't cost much. All her life she had lived in a condition where, though she might not have money, there was money around. It was time that she did what she hadn't done before, and talked to her father.

He had always been an amiable father. When she was a girl she had thought him charming, he was as easy mannered with his family as with friends, and yet she could scarcely re- member talking to him seriously, at least about her own con- cerns. She had very little idea of how he planned to dispose of the Hillmorton estate. She did know, what Dr. Pemberton had discovered a good deal earlier, that he had made over the Suf- folk house and land to her eldest sister. That wasn't a special surprise. Death duties existed to be out-manoeuvred by fami- lies like hers. These transfers were played like one of her hands at bridge or perhaps more like solo-whist, for she had heard of people with five times the property of the Hillmortons boasting that they had divested themselves of all of it, and had reached a state of successful misère, sleeping by sufferance under roofs now owned by their sons or grandsons. It didn't make any dif- ference to them. The Suffolk home might be in her sister's name, but their mother still lived there, and didn't appear to be aware of the change.

Liz knew, or had noticed, one other thing about her father. He had become, the more so as he grew older, curiously stingy to himself. He might stand you an expensive dinner and many drinks, but after he said goodbye he wouldn't consider indulg- ing himself with a taxi, but stood patiently waiting for a bus to take him home. As for home, he had none in London. He wouldn't stay at one of his clubs, having presumably decided that their price had gone too high. When he had to remain in London for the mid-week nights, after sitting at the Lords, to the best of Liz's information he borrowed a bedroom from her youngest sister, married to a young architect, not yet established, living in a small terraced house in the hinterland behind Talgarth Road.

However, when Liz went to meet him as they had arranged, he received her like one who enjoyed being hospitable, not only to his daughter but to anyone in the neighbourhood.

"My dear girl! How very nice! It's far too long since I saw you. Have a drink at once. A large gin and tonic," he called out. "Isn't that what you like?"

This took place in the long drawingroom at Brook's, about five in the afternoon, a humid July afternoon, jar and grind of traffic, smell of petrol, ascending from St. James's Street below. Liz, who had an interest in her heritage, which she disguised by her sharp sarcastic tongue, might have recalled that some of her ancestors must have sat in that room, probably, if they shared the habits of other eminent Whigs, more than a little drunk: but she was too intent on her mission. She had been uneasy on her way there, not entirely easy now. His kind of imperturbability didn't make others as imperturbable. But yes, he was as usual enjoying providing drinks. She hadn't been alone with him for months. Maybe he looked a little older, cheeks not so pink and full, but no change in manner, none at all.

"Look," she said, "I want to get married. I want a bit of help."

She said it without any lead in, handsome face set, dark greenish eyes unblinking, fixed on his. There was the faintest shift in his expression. His old colleagues could have told her that his antennae were wary, he didn't relish being taken by storm.

"Ah well," he said. "I hope it's all right. I do hope it's all right. Still, you've always been able to look after yourself, haven't you?"

There seemed no answer to that. Then she was staggered. As from a kindly distance, he enquired:

"Tell me, is the man anyone I know?"

Eyes snapping, she burst out: "You know perfectly well he is!"

"Do remind me of his name."

"You know it perfectly well. Julian Underwood!"

"Of course, of course." After an appearance of meditation he remarked, under a hooded glance:

"So I gather the result of that curious case—you know, that business about a will—must have been something of a disappointment to you."

He had heard, the previous autumn, of Julian's putative legacy. He had been in court, this June, for several of the sessions. He had chatted with Julian. He was one of the most competent of men. He preserved an excellent memory, which he went on to demonstrate. In the presence of this performance Liz was not so much maddened as lost. She felt that she had never known her father. Façade after façade seemed, with the utmost candour, to be stripped away: just to reveal another underneath. With lucidity, with the kind of detachment with which he baffled political acquaintances, he was giving her his opinion of the case. Naturally, he was a complete ignoramus, but on the whole, though he had heard lawyers, good lawyers, hold, rather strongly, to the opposite view, and with a slight margin of doubt himself, he was inclined to agree with the judge.

Once more his glance flickered towards her.

"Though I dare say you wouldn't feel the same?"

His disquisition had taken some time.

She said: "What I feel about that, it's neither here nor there."

"My dear girl, do have another drink." His voice, a public speaker's voice, surprisingly resonant after his modulated intonation, rang through the room. "Another large gin and tonic." Then:

"I'm not sure that I took to—Julian's mother, not all that much."

Liz didn't comment. She was screwing herself up for another attempt at a breakthrough.

"You've known him some time, have you?" her father said.

"You remember. A couple of years."

Sharply, flannelling discarded, he asked: "What does he do for a living?"

"He doesn't do anything for a living."

Flannelling, amused smile all back again. "My dear girl, surely that's rather—uncontemporary, I should have thought?"

He supposed that Julian had means of his own. No, said Liz, telling him again what he already knew, but his mother wasn't poor.

"He seems to be bright enough."

"He hasn't done anything with it so far, has he?" she replied.

"No doubt he's nice."

She gave him a fierce grin. "I shouldn't say that."

At that he didn't smile back, but his interest sounded genuine:

"How well do you know him, then?"

"I've lived with him since soon after I met him."

Hillmorton nodded.

"On and off," she went on, "I've had to chase away other women."

"It'd be worse," he said, "if you'd had to chase away boys." She smiled, her first real smile since they began to talk.

"Women fall for him, as a matter of fact. I don't imagine you'd understand why."

"No one ever does. About anyone else. But if you want to marry the man, it might have been a mistake to live with him, you know."

"I've wanted to marry him all along," she replied. "More so now." She added: "I love him. I love him very much."

Her father said: "I see."

Between them those last few minutes there had been a thread of understanding. She assumed—why she couldn't have told, but in this she was right—that he was invincibly acquiescent about anyone's sexual life. For an instant, the only one in that conversation, she had a flash of disinterested curiosity about his own. About his past, or even his present. There were stories of a long-standing affair, which her mother had put up with for the sake of politics. There were other stories which might not have reached Liz, not so romantic, of casual pickups. He hid so much; whatever had happened, he would certainly hide all that. Soon the thread of understanding became frayed. Liz wouldn't or couldn't leave him to musing reflections about her love affair. Instead, she started forcing him again.

"It's about him that I want you to help me," she said.

He seemed to foresee what was coming. Delicately he began to execute the first of his sidesteps.

"If ever I could, my dear girl—but I can't imagine what use I can be, I really can't imagine—" His voice trailed away.

She said: "There's the matter of money."

"Money," he said, as though that were a word he had scarcely heard before.

"Anything you were going to do for me later. It might make all the difference if you did it now."

"There are a certain number of difficulties I won't bore you with." He launched on one of those explanations designed not to explain, and then suddenly became direct again.

"Even if money were forthcoming—I doubt if you could buy him."

"It's worth trying."

"I must say, I doubt if it is."

"I know him and you don't."

"I can't help thinking, if you could buy him he might not be worth having."

"I'm the only one who can answer for that."

He said: "There's such a thing as masculine pride, you know."

She laughed, freshly, not sarcastically.

"He doesn't need that to get along, I can tell you."

"Well. He sounds a remarkably lucky man."

"He's a very happy one," she said. But she wasn't letting her father get further away. "You can see, I wouldn't ask you for this money unless I wanted it—badly."

"To tell you the truth, I'm in a curious position financially, I'm a great deal more powerless than one would think. I've been making, or at least I've started to make, some rather complicated adjustments." He was off on another elaborate façade-stripping expedition in which nothing, or only another façade, was revealed. He moved from exaggerated detachment to exaggerated candour and back again. He used a trick, natural to anyone who had lived in politics, of telling her, under a demand for secrecy, something which she was already well aware of. Which was that the family house and land had some time ago been transferred to Georgiana (her eldest sister). He had, also some time ago, explained to them all, he said, that it was necessary to act on the principle of unequal shares. (When had he explained that, she thought. And if he had, it explained nothing at all.) So he felt for the time being unusually powerless.

"But you must know," she interrupted at last, "what you are thinking of for me."

"These things aren't as straightforward as they might be."

"You can make it straightforward if you want."

"Of course, I wish I could."

She had never conceived that a man, any man, let alone her father, could be as elusive as this. Julian was as devious as most people, but when he was being devious it was with some satisfaction of his own in view. But all her father's tactics seemed quite motiveless; it was like being beaten over the head by a very soft pillow. Yet he was imperturbable. It was she who ought to be taking the moral initiative, but mysteriously it had escaped her and slipped away to him.

The most she could extract was a promise. A promise given with much outgoingness, and accompanied by a reservation given with the same outgoingness. He promised to consult his lawyers and his accountants. They would examine the entire situation of the family money. This should be done at once, and it was all he could guarantee that night.

He might have been eluding her in the mind, but he didn't make any excuse to elude her in the flesh. His manners were still impeccable, she thought with frustration. He was prepared to sit in that elegant gambling room as long as she cared to stay, listening politely, amusedly, yes, affectionately. But she could get no further. Not until she said that she had better go did he mention that there was a whip on in the House.

Having kissed his daughter goodbye, Hillmorton made his way down the street towards the Park and Westminster. It had been one of his favourite walks for half a life time. The cloud ceiling was very low, it was a heavy London summer night. He wasn't thinking of Liz, he had the knack of boxing commit-

134

ments away. It had been a necessity, or at least a help, in his kind of life. Instead, he was thinking, as he walked across the corner of the Park, that people talked of the town becoming more dangerous, but in this part of it you were much more likely to be manhandled a hundred years before. That is, if one could believe the literary evidence.

Detached reflection as usual soothed him. It was pleasant to arrive at the Lords, but also soothing, being given the comfort of a club, an island of peace. Actually, when he found his friends having a drink before dinner, the place wasn't up to its highest standards of peace. Committee stage on the Industrial Relations Bill, divisions expected until one or two in the morning: tempers nearer the surface than urbane men liked. Among the thoughtful, there were expressions of disquiet. Someone said, did anyone begin to know how to run their kind of industrial society? Certainly not, said Hillmorton, with his elder statesman's equanimity. As a rule persons engaged in politics, even in senates such as this, didn't indulge in long views. Yet, someone else was speculating whether other countries, as they got rid of sheer animal need, would run into the trouble this one had.

There was something stirring at the nerve ends that night, rather too much like pre-war nights or the time of Suez for Hillmorton's taste. Still, it was pleasant to find Sedgwick and Ryle at dinner-time, pleasanter still to find the long table full, so that they could sit by themselves, close to one of the incongruous tapestries. That night, with a late sitting predictable, the standard cold supper was laid on. Ryle fetched beef and tongue for Sedgwick, and, watching the uncontrollable hands, would have liked to cut it up. As it was, Ryle carefully stopped pouring the wine when Sedgwick's glass was only half full.

Their talk would have been disconcerting to enthusiasts on either side, as disconcerting as if Jenny and Mrs. Underwood had overheard their counsel conversing in the Park. Sedgwick, despite his disease, was attending today as often that summer, to walk through the lobbies till midnight: this was as late as his body could bear it. He would vote for the labour amendments. Old habits, old loyalties, he couldn't break at his age. "That doesn't mean," he said, "that this bill is the greatest outrage since the crucifixion. Which is what people on my side appear to be persuading themselves."

Hillmorton, more habituated to political emotion than his friend, having spent his life among it, couldn't resist the oracular occasion. He didn't recall any Parliament, he said, in which either side—it didn't matter which—had been a hundred per cent set on a course of action without being utterly and absolutely wrong, and inside a remarkably short time demonstrated to be wrong. This bill was a nice example.

"Our chaps really do think that it's going to produce a new heaven and a new earth. While anyone with the political intelligence of a newt ought to realise it can't possibly do any good and may do a finite amount of harm. There's too much innocence knocking about, and that's more dangerous than wickedness or anything else."

This statement of his own seemed to induce in him a subdued elation. The burgundy was rather good, he said, and ordered another bottle. Further, whatever anyone else suggested, he would do a certain amount for his party, he would stay till the end and vote for their ridiculous bill, but listen to a meaningless debate he would not.

Liz might have found her father in this mood unfamiliar: and maybe just as unfamiliar when a little later he mentioned her own name. The three of them had moved into the bar, in time enough to secure a corner table, and it was there that Sedgwick, who hadn't met Hillmorton since the finish of the Massie hearing a fortnight before, asked him a question.

"Was it a surprise?" he said. In fact, he and other acquaintances of Hillmorton's were displeased, partly because the gossip writers had begun to throw out hints, having acquired suspicions both of the Swaffield connection and the 'friendship' of Julian and Liz.

"I suppose it must have been a surprise to some of them," said Hillmorton with statuesque calm. "It's always a bit of a surprise to have a few hundred thousand whisked away from you, shouldn't you say?"

Then he added: "I'm afraid it's rather upsetting for my daughter Liz. I had a word with her before I came along, as a matter of fact. She's tied up with the man who was left the money, don't you know. I must say, I'm beginning not to be specially keen on the sound of him. I'm rather sorry for her."

He had spoken as though with off-hand irritation, but there was more feeling than he had shown to Liz herself.

"I'm very sorry for her," said Ryle. Suddenly Hillmorton gave him a glance inquisitive, acute, no longer lazy. But soon he reverted to disinterested observation. "It's very curious, you know, how some of the cleverest women are astonishingly bad pickers of men. Far worse than we are, I think, the other way round."

The bar filled up, and a group gathered round them. Hillmorton usually collected an audience there and so, among the cultivated, did Sedgwick. Hillmorton was not indisposed to entertain and talked at large, but Sedgwick, long before it was time for him to leave, fell silent, hearing his speech go slurred, not able to trust his tongue and lips. For Ryle, it was sad to watch that classical mind muffled like this. And afterwards Ryle recalled feeling angry out of proportion when, round eleven o'clock, Hillmorton complained of being tired, saying these sittings were harder to get through than they used to be. Healthy men, thought Ryle, oughtn't to complain like that in the presence of the ill: it wasn't like Hillmorton, usually sensitive in these matters.

Yet Ryle, when he recalled that incident, recalled also thinking, not for the first time, how relaxed this minuscule society of theirs still seemed to him. Much more so than any place he had known. Jenny on visits there had had the same impression, though she couldn't explain it. Ryle could get nearer. Elderly men, of course, were good at making existence tolerable for themselves, but it was not only, or chiefly, that. It was much more that in the whole House ambition, that is vocational ambition or competitiveness, was as good as spent. A few men there had their private games to play, or private aspirations, but there were only two or three dozen out of hundreds who were still professional politicians, working out the chances of jobs and office.

A good many more had been professional politicians, but that was safely in the past. None of them had reached the top places, but the disappointments, like the ambitions, were over.

A few felt that they had achieved less than they started out expecting: perhaps Hillmorton had instants naked to himself when he felt that kind of pang. Some hadn't got what they expected. But many more, humbler and more easily satisfied, believed that they had got more than they expected. The luck had been kind to them, and that helped make them more relaxed and the climate which surrounded them.

Now the expectations, like the ambitions, disappointments, bits of luck, were over and done with. The expectations, that is, of striving struggling men. Other expectations, though, remained with them—far more actively than they would have guessed when they were young—and wouldn't, so it seemed, flicker out until they died. Often they would have been hard put to it to recognise what these expectations were, or embarrassed to confess them. With Sedgwick the hopes were limited and clear, just surcease from being crippled. With Ryle, they were clear too, though he would keep them to himself. Hillmorton was not such a candid soul, and sometimes he had visions of the future, his own future, which he wouldn't admit to his own mind. Yet, though those visions might be inexplicit or even absurd, he wouldn't live without them.

The last pair left the House that night as Big Ben was striking two. They smelt the sprinkle of rain, the settled dust: and, as at any other time in their lives, the smell touched them with wistfulness, a kind of remembering, and hope.

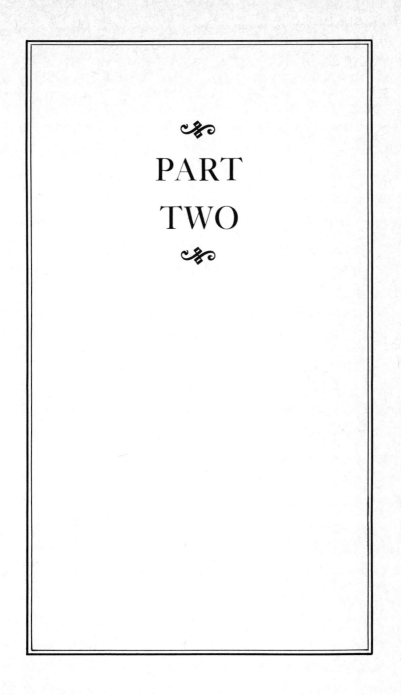

PART
TWO

❧ 16 ❧

That summer, Liz was discovering for herself what had been written about, a generation or two before—that all resolutions are taken in a mood which will not last. People thought she had a strong will, but to herself it seemed to operate only in intermittences and often left her limp and unavailing. After her father's magisterial deployment of the intricate defence, she heard no more from him through the weeks of August, and wasn't confident enough to ask again. As for telling Julian that he had to marry her, that she couldn't do now, whatever resolution she had made, any more than in the past.

She needed support from somewhere, and it was in that state, more or less carelessly, she telephoned James Ryle. She might have said that he seemed warmer and more forthcoming than most of her father's friends. She didn't give it any more consideration than that, and asked, could she come and see him, she wanted some advice.

Ryle, taken by surprise, pleasurable surprise, fixed an appointment for that same night, and sitting in his drawingroom in Whitehall Court became irked, or perhaps apprehensive, when half past five arrived, the minutes ticked by, and the woman hadn't come.

A quarter of an hour late she rang the bell, began apologising in her firm and unapologetic fashion:

"I'm so sorry, Lord Ryle, there wasn't a cab for miles—"

But then the meeting disintegrated. Though her assurance wasn't dented, she had entered fast, as though to make amends, and within fractions of a second glissaded on a mat which slipped on the parquet floor. She cannoned off Ryle, who had been greeting her a foot or so away, and then, elegance all gone, singularly clumsy like a child finishing one of its first walks, she stopped herself with both palms pushing against a looking-glass hanging on the wall. From there she gazed back over her shoulder at Ryle with a smile meaningless, abashed, even fatuous, as of someone who had run to catch an underground train and seen the doors closing in her face.

Ryle gave his loud unrepressed laugh. She said "Oh dear," and for once he saw her face not intent, not so good looking either. Shortly afterwards Ryle's son Francis called in to take a book, and saw the two of them, Ryle in one arm chair, Liz in another, Ryle smiling, Liz concentrating, remarkably like teacher and pupil. Francis, who had never met her, thought she was a decorative woman, and wondered what was happening, particularly when his father appeared both elated and impatient for them to be left alone.

Actually what was happening was, on the face of it, simple, just an elderly man listening to a young woman's confidence. She had imagined that she was going to ask him business-like questions about her father's money. She started with one or two, dropped them as though that wasn't anywhere near the point, and fluidly, spontaneously burst into talking of her conflict over Julian. Often she set out to say the same things as she had told her father—and yet it sounded different in kind. She might have been crying or laughing: her eyes snapped, there was a crackle of devilment about her. Ryle got the impression that she didn't have close women friends. She talked as though this was the first time she had let her splintered temper, her pining, all break loose.

"How do I get out of it?" and then, almost as her next words: "Can you give me one sane reason why he shouldn't marry me?" As to the first question, Ryle said he could tell her all the old recipes, don't see him, don't hear about him, don't write, but he had never known anyone act on them. But that was the only piece of sarcasm he felt like making.

He didn't want to intrude, he was listening to her story, picking up fragments, hints which tantalised, explicable only if one had installed a microphone for their bedroom talk. Ryle had made his own observations of Julian during the court hearing. Unwillingly he had smiled at his gibes, unable to recall in all his existence having met a man so cool, so uninfluenceable. He had gathered more about him than Hillmorton had, and liked him less. When Hillmorton in the Lords' Bar had expressed mild concern and Ryle had echoed it—which the other had noticed—his was more than mild. This man was self absorbed, not affected by others, but constantly aware of his effect on them and good at using it. He was solipsistic, if you like, no feeling except for himself, but nerves responding to the women round him, sensitive to sensations. That was a powerful combination. It was obvious enough that he basked cool and sultan-like, in domination.

But Liz was telling Ryle, or not so much telling him as conveying, something different. Her actual words about Julian were very much those she had used to her father. She was honest and direct, not the person to alter what she thought to be true because she was talking to another man. Nevertheless, without realising she changed her tone. With her father, detached, amused by other people's sexual tastes, she had spoken as though she scarcely liked her man but was simply in the clutch of an obsessive passion. She didn't know much about Ryle, but somehow she talked to him as though he were a man of feeling who cared what a man and woman felt for each other, as she felt for this one.

It was part of her honesty and directness that she often misled herself. She was proud of seeing with clear eyes. Not only with her father, but in her own mind, she found words for a cold view of Julian, not only cold but disparaging. Of course he wasn't to be trusted. Of course he was mercenary beyond any limit. (And yet, saying exactly the same to Ryle, she added that he was also strictly honest with money, never borrowed from anyone and hadn't taken a penny from her, except perhaps by letting her pay for a taxi or a meal—and though she had produced the clinical statement, by now she was speaking with urgency, begging Ryle to believe.) Of course Julian never did anything he didn't want to. Of course he wasn't any good.

Those were the clinical statements. That was what she thought she felt. It didn't take a man as alert as James Ryle to learn that she felt something nearer the complete opposite. What she most deeply felt for Julian—against most of her own utterances, and, it is true, against most of the objective evidence—was close to passionate respect.

As they talked, excitement in the air, talking about emotion inducing its own emotion, Ryle was learning something else about her. She wasn't much as she appeared. No, that was being too soft-minded. For nearly all her workaday life, she was as she appeared, positive, decisive as her hard clear profile, not diffident about her own authority. She would have made—possibly was, for all Ryle knew—a good business executive. She was a shade sharper and more domineering with him than most women of her age would be with a man of his. Nevertheless there was a fissure. Underneath, in her longings, there was something not so much tender as abject. She was born to be a pushover for a man like Julian, and no doubt that was why he had selected her at sight.

There had been another love affair on the same pattern, she more loving than loved, surrendering from the beginning, the self-chosen victim. Repetitive patterns tell their own story, Ryle had accepted long ago. What you want is what happens to you. Would he have seen this defenceless quality in Liz if he hadn't also seen that custard pie scene when she slipped on the mat, and then the smile of absurd humiliation, disproportionate to any such occasion, as humiliated as Adam Sedgwick when in disability he butted against a door? Any indication helped, any indication however silly, Ryle thought later, but in time he couldn't have missed the rift within her. Only a fool trusted his guesses too far, but of that he was moderately sure.

Talking about emotion induced emotion. There was a charm for Liz in speaking of the man she loved, analysing her love to another man. Her love in its present state might not be bringing her happiness, but talking of it that evening was very near a happiness, as though telling someone what she wanted made it seem that it was about to happen—or in some timeless universe had already happened.

It was Ryle, not she, who broke the charm. Abruptly, almost brusquely, he said:

"You came to find out something definite, didn't you? Didn't you mention something about your father's money?"

She was surprised, disappointed, thwarted at being cut off short. With a frown, she stared across at the seamed expressionless face.

"Yes," she said.

"Well, go on."

She collected herself. "I should like some idea how rich my father is. Do you know?"

Roughness put aside, Ryle had once more taken on his easy, comfortable, avuncular manner.

"He's never told me. He's not the most confiding of men."

"Haven't you any idea?"

"I can only guess."

"Then please guess."

That was her peremptory tone. Ryle said that he expected a good deal of the estate was in land. Land had appreciated wildly, but this was Barmecide money. Presumably Hillmorton wouldn't sell it. Still, if one assumed that his grandfather was well-to-do at the turn of the century, which was almost certain, it was difficult to imagine him being worth less than a couple of hundred thousand in 1900, probably twice as much—then it would have taken consummate mis-management not to be many times richer by now.

"You can work it out for yourself," said Ryle.

That was near enough to Liz's own estimate.

"Mind you," said Ryle, "he might possess in theory several million pounds, but he wouldn't have much of that as disposable cash."

"But he could afford to detach a slice of it in my direction. He needn't wait till it's too late."

Liz put in another sharp question. Had Ryle any notion of how her father was leaving his money? None at all.

"You really haven't heard anything?"

"I said before," Ryle replied, "he's not the most confiding of men, now is he?"

Liz, picking up her gloves, said:

"I've been taking too much of your time, Lord Ryle. Thank you for putting up with me."

She hadn't recovered from being cut off short. She had the ratty air of one who felt she had outstayed her welcome. She gave him a firm, commanding smile. It might have belonged to a different face from the abject one which had moved him an hour and a half before.

After the hall door had closed behind her Ryle walked across the room, gazed with blank eyes to the lights across the river, and then slumped down on the sofa. It was a let-down, now that she had gone. It had been an impulse—unpremeditated, leaping out of caution—to break it up. They were running into danger. Not for her, she was in enough danger of her own. But for him. It was an idiot's trick, letting your imagination crystallise over a woman totally involved with another man.

Yes, attending the court hadn't been just an elderly acquaintance giving her support. He had thought of her, not trying to interdict himself, in her absence, and that was an idiot's trick too. Yet for a while, before the thoughts seeped up too often, it had been a pleasure, getting on towards a joy, to recognise the springs of feeling. They could still transform the day. Hillmorton, who was not uninterested, had noticed that something was happening: that was the meaning of his glance during the late night sitting.

In the let-down Ryle was taking a kind of comfort. This was a classical trap, a touch of comedy for anyone watching from outside. Let the feeling go on crystallising, and there came a point of no return. One didn't learn much from one's experience, but one learned a little. He was warned in time, he was managing to stop it. Otherwise he would be in a state of hopeless love, so ridiculous that he couldn't even admit it, more ridiculous than being hopelessly in love when young.

He might be congratulating himself too early. When a man has told himself that he has escaped the danger, the danger might already have gripped him too tight to escape at all. That thought didn't cross Ryle's mind, or was kept out. He had some faith in his own resources. He was practical, he had an active temperament. He would search round among women who used to be fond of him. That might not satisfy his soul, but it could take away one part of the tension. He ought to have done it before, then he wouldn't have been so vulnerable.

It would have been no different if Liz hadn't been totally wrapped up elsewhere. She would have been much too young, no future for her, not much for him. Had he, without accepting it, been already thinking of her, when he was brooding on women too young for him in this room the autumn before? She wasn't even really in his taste. Too sharp, too narrow, not free enough. He hadn't been meeting many women, it was a chance and a pity that she had come along. She wouldn't have suited him, nor would he have been much good to her.

In all that he was probably right. There was another reflection which wouldn't have consoled him. The chances of possible partners whom one met produced a sense of fatality: so ought the chances of possible partners whom one didn't meet. The division bell had rung just as Ryle was about to be introduced to Jenny Rastall. As it happened, and it was pure chance, they didn't speak to each other that night, and were not to meet again until it was too late, though they would see each other across a room.

It was possible that they were, as Ryle's old mother would have said, made for each other. No one could predict that for certain, there was no one alive who knew them both well, and there was only one test, which they alone could have proved. From their habits, affections, tastes and natures, though, it seems more likely than not that they could have fitted one another: certainly more completely than with anyone they actually found. Which, in his mood that evening Ryle, not a specially sardonic man, would have considered not a specially good joke.

❧ 17 ❧

It was not early October, and Reginald Swaffield was giving one of his dinner parties. He was in his most expansive—his enemies would have said inflated—form. Wearing a purple smoking jacket, he stood in his morning room, which opened off the hall in Hill Street, and gave his own kind of welcome to his guests, barking at them with a mixture of interferingness and blarney, the proportion blended according to his intentions on the guest.

Since Parliament wasn't yet sitting, a cabinet minister called Haydon-Smith was able to attend: nothing surprising in that, cabinet ministers were used to accepting invitations from tycoons. He and his wife were received with a fairly high proportion of blarney, though Swaffield had been known to express judgments on politicians in general which were robust but not over-enthusiastic. One of the top Treasury civil servants, Sir Ernest Packe, got perceptibly more blarney, young and unobtrusive as he was. The Symingtons, being old acquaintances and protégés, got almost none, but Swaffield was immediately giving advice and instructions about Alison's pregnancy. That debate had at last been settled, and, both of them looking more sumptuous than anyone else in the room, she was three months' gone. Jenny, bringing Lord Lorimer with her according to orders, got nothing but a pat and a conspiratorial leer in the direction of her partner. Jenny hadn't been astonished that Swaffield's intelligence service had come up with

the name of Lorimer. It was like being on the edge of an enor-
mous spider's web, she grumbled to herself, but the grumble
was nominal by now. Sooner than one realised, one ceased to
resist.

They stood round in the morning room, furnished like the
great drawingroom above, according to Swaffield's conception
of what a beautiful room should be. They were drinking the
first of his statutory two glasses of champagne before dinner.
Other guests arrived, the Clares, who were received with
slightly more ceremony than the Symingtons, but not much
more, being by now part of Swaffield's empire. Clare remained
statuesque, rather like an image of Nordic man or a real-life
Baltic baron, but his wife was small, exophthalmic, excitable,
and looked as though all this was more stately than she was
used to, which was the opposite of the truth.

Finally, the Schiffs appeared, a quarter of an hour late, so
that Swaffield was fretting with impatience and temper. Schiff,
however, was the one person in the whole company whom
Swaffield admired, and so he was allowed one glass of champagne and given the chance to refuse another. Rosalind Schiff,
more expensively jewelled, scented, accoutred than any of the
other women, and more alluringly, looked round the room in
search of the most interesting man, and moved off towards the
cabinet minister.

Swaffield, in spite of his admiration for Lord Schiff, was
restless, one foot tapping the floor, dinner being held up, perfect arrangements discommoded. The instant, or a milli-second
after, Schiff waved away his second glass, Swaffield was
reaching a finger behind him, pushing a button concealed as in-
visibly as those which Hillmorton had once had in a ministerial
office, designed to bring in, and hasten out, visitors on the con-
veyor belt.

This time the butler was brought in.

"Mr. Swaffield, dinner is served."

All ceremony, Swaffield himself was as ceremonious as a
performing animal. The party was led across the hall to the dining room, also on the ground floor, according to the old London practice. Swaffield, still performing, stood at the end of
the table while the others studied the placement diagram and

sat down. Then Swaffield, continuing to stand, announced with an elfish grin:

"Thirteen at table. I hope no one's superstitious. I don't consider superstitions ought to be encouraged."

That was the kind of antic he liked devising, Jenny thought. Possibly there was someone there who didn't appreciate it. The party settled down to the food, Swaffield's vibrant voice predominating.

Almost any commentator in that period, surveying the table, would have acted on a conditioned reflex and mechanically typed it as an establishment dinner. It was nothing of the sort. Commentators had the knack of taking the meaning out of words: perhaps, Lord Hillmorton might have observed, that was why they were commentators. So far as the establishment meant anything, which wasn't much, no one there belonged to it, not even the minister, not the Treasury boss, who had a curious oblique function right outside the decision-making groups. Schiff had occasionally offered economic advice to succeeding governments. None of them had taken it. You could say, if you wished, that it was a prosperous dinner. Everyone there, except Jenny and Lorimer, had a five figure income, most far more, but that didn't give them influence over opinions, much less decisions. As for Swaffield, no inner circle in England would have employed him—unless in war time, when his daimon might have been too strong for them, and he could have carved his way.

This didn't imply that he was becoming subdued. He was actually saying:

"I think I shall always give large dinners in future. Not little ones like this. I don't call this a dinner. Large dinners, that's what I shall give. I hope you all agree."

Some of his guests in private did not agree. What could you do with a man like this? If they had his millions, they wouldn't live in a house as hideous as his (this dining room was decorated in his own eye-dazzling style). They would know how to entertain.

The curious thing was, though they had to admit that the food and drink were passable, they didn't give him credit for his taste. A gourmet would have realised that both food and

wine were as good as in any private house in the town—
especially the wine, for Swaffield had the palate of a professional. He had served champagne, as it were contemptuously,
for those who didn't know, and most of them were drinking it.
For himself, it wasn't a drink to go with a dinner, and he kept
to a good Pomerol, in which his only company was Sir Ernest
Packe. Others scoffed away, under the illusion that vulgarians
never learnt.

It wouldn't have improved Swaffield's reputation much, but
it might have been subtilised if he hadn't been one sense
short. That is, he had no—or else an extremely abnormal—
visual sense. Hence his house. That fitted all that people expected of him. His other senses were both acute and delicate,
but they didn't notice that. It is true, booming away like an
emperor that night, he gave them plenty of excuses not to notice.

As usual with any of his fiestas, there lurked a purpose or
purposes beneath. One of the purposes, in the midst of a non-
stop allocution, was to arrange his holiday. He had decided
that he needed a change, and with dromophilic energy was
planning it. That meant planning an entire caravanserai, for
Swaffield couldn't bear being alone. Some of the present company knew what it was like to be summoned late at night: if
the house was not otherwise occupied (they all suspected that
there were visitors unknown to them), then some of his court
had to be collected.

On his holidays the court was once more required. Transport was laid on, he was hectoring the table. His private jet
would fly anyone anywhere. He proposed to start in the Dordogne: he had hired a house that afternoon (some there guessed
that he wouldn't rest still three days). There wasn't a modern
airport near, but cars would be available night and day, whenever the jet flew into Toulouse. It remained only to dragoon
the Clares, the Symingtons, Jenny, Lorimer, any of the appropriate cherubim within sight. For Swaffield not only needed
people round him, he needed people for—what? applause?
recognition of debt? reminders of his power?

Strange, Jenny had thought, now she had seen enough of
this process, that a man who would take on the toughest cus-

tomers alive should need this reassurance. Yet she couldn't see any other explanation. He didn't feel fundamentally safe outside his own environment; and his own environment consisted of people whom he was looking after and who had a suitable sense of favours to come. That was the proper environment for a restless man. When he went on holiday, he carried his environment with him.

At the dinner table, Lady Clare on his right, he shouted down to Clare at the other end.

"You two'll come, of course, Edward." Clare wanted to go: it was a free holiday, and no doubt a luxurious one. On the other hand, he wasn't practised at coping with such an invitation, which had been given rather like a benevolent employer offering a bonus to a faithful but ungifted employee. Since he had become inextricably entwined in Swaffield's net, there had been a distinct change of manner towards him.

He looked along at his wife, and began a kind of impassive havering.

"That would be very nice, of course, but, you know, we have some commitments—"

"Commitments," said Swaffield, "look after themselves."

He suddenly switched to the Symingtons. "You two as well," he said matily.

Unlike Clare, Leslie Symington didn't want to go: unlike Clare again, he had had practice in receiving such invitations.

"We'd love it," he said lustrously, and Alison said the same. "But," Leslie went on, and she nodded her head. They were conveying enthusiasm, affection for Swaffield, not cupboard love. There was an element of truth in this, for they were easier with him than the others there.

Swaffield was a move ahead. Yes, he had thought of the difficulty: they were thinking something might go wrong with the child.

"Three months is a dodgy time," he said, giving a knowledgeable impersonation of a midwife, and identifying himself lavishly with the flesh. He had everything provided. There was a competent doctor in the village, already bespoken, guaranteed to be on call. In case of need, two specialists in

Toulouse were also bespoken. They could reach her inside three hours.

"You'll be a hell of a lot safer than you'd ever be in Chelsea. I can't bear Chelsea," he added, as though he would propose to plough it with salt.

"You shouldn't do all this," said Alison, awkward, laughing, touched.

"Do you think I should let anything go wrong?" he snapped.

Then to Jenny: "You come. You come. Bring him." (He grinned at Lorimer, and contrived to invest the thought with remarkable suggestiveness, which continued in the next unremarkable words.) "Quite comfortable. All modern conveniences in all rooms. Nice views from the bedrooms."

"No, Mr. Swaffield," said Jenny, in a voice as resonant as his own. "I can't get away now."

"In Christ's name, why not?"

"It's too early. I've only been working in the office a couple of months, and I haven't got things quite straight."

Swaffield gave her a fixed eye—protruding stare. But he didn't say what he might have done, that the job wasn't all that significant. He was, in his own fashion, too considerate for that. Instead he gazed at Lorimer and said:

"Tell her she must go. Order her about. Good for her."

"No, I can't get away yet," Jenny repeated. "It would upset the others."

"She's right, you know," said Lorimer, voice creaking in the effort to articulate. "She's thinking of morale. She's right, you know."

The two of them showed a united front, Jenny sensible, Lorimer disjointed in support. Pressure, bullying, quasi-genial demands from Swaffield, but they didn't budge, and with an expression more stupefied than angry he seemed to leave it there.

They all climbed upstairs to the kaleidoscopic drawing room. Parties of Swaffield's, as the well trained knew, were not expected to split up. The chairs were duly set within eye-range, conversation-range, of a focal point, so that Swaffield could preside over one of his favourite entertainments. There was just time, while drinks were carried round, for a short exchange between Haydon-Smith and Lord Schiff. The minister had decided that Schiff appeared agreeable, but hadn't caught his name—it couldn't be Sheep, it might be Sheean. Shipp? The minister was a liberal-minded man, in charge of overseas development, and liked dilating on pleasant topics to other liberal-minded men. He proceeded to tell Schiff how much the country owed to the latest wave of Jewish talent. Financiers, enterpreneurs, industrialists, all coming over in the thirties or even later.

"They've done more for this country than the old Jewish families, and they did a lot," said Haydon-Smith. "I really don't know how we should have got on at all without these clever Jewish gentlemen."

Lord Schiff gave a large courteous smile.

"Minister, we think we have something to pay back, don't you think that's reasonable?"

Tactlessness of a tactful operator—Haydon-Smith was filled with ultimate chagrin. He needn't have flushed, though. Azik Schiff didn't keep on watch for affronts, he had less touchy spots than anyone there.

Swaffield was dispensing vintage port after dinner—vintage, because he liked being luxurious and also because he had a taste for it. Then he got down to amusing himself. Jenny had seen this happen several times before. His particular diversion was to discuss the affairs of one of his courtiers or dependants in public, just as he had done with hers that evening at the House of Lords. From this he derived a considerable and complicated pleasure. The best game of all was to make someone analyse his or her present love life, especially when it was tinged with sexual misadventure and when the company contained persons who were eminent, shockable and stuffy. It was that which Jenny was anticipating, but it didn't happen. Perhaps because the dependants present weren't suitable subjects, or the others weren't shockable enough, and some of them he had another use for.

Further, Jenny had resisted him over the holiday and it was desirable to demonstrate what was her proper place.

Without a preliminary he stared at her, spoke straight at her, as though they were the only people in the room.

"Your bit of business," he said, "I may as well tell you what to do."

Jenny, though she hadn't been tactless, flushed as the minister had done a few minutes before. She wasn't prepared for this. He was doing it all over again. In that drawingroom, in front of a party half of which were strangers whom she hadn't previously met, including the cabinet minister and Sir Ernest Packe, Swaffield recapitulated the history of the will, his own insistence that it had to be reversed, the court case, now the appeal. This didn't take over long, despite snatches of Swaffield-esque mischief. Although Jenny was not in a mood to appreciate it, it was a masterly piece of exposition, as compact and well ordered as Sir Ernest would have been capable of.

There was just one oddity, which Symington alone could appreciate. They had now received an opinion from distinguished legal authority, and Swaffield had talked to him that week. In fact that opinion was suitably ambiguous. It could be read as inclining to the view that the appeal wouldn't be allowed. Swaffield, like a Prime Minister studying a paper which wasn't exactly what he required, chose to interpret it in his own way, that is in favour of an immediate settlement. Swaffield was ordering Jenny to call it a day.

"They offered us a price to buy her off," said Swaffield to the party, who appeared interested, not only for politeness' sake, Haydon-Smith nodding a sapient head.

"But it wasn't big enough," said Swaffield. "Well, we'll up that offer, enough to keep them quiet. Three quarters of a loaf is better than no bread. It's time we were shut of the whole business."

"My girl," he shot a command at Jenny, "that's what you do."

He gazed at her with triumph, wanting her to be obstinate, ready to ride her down.

Strange faces were looking at her with curiosity.

"Of course," said Jenny. "I'm sure you're being very wise."

She didn't say it with especial grace. She had more than her

155

share of counter-suggestibility. Often she hated the man. Yet she also respected him. Whatever his whirlpool of motives was, she had learned that his judgment—even when he made it sound brash and grotesque—was curiously cool.

"I'm sure that's right," said Symington. "You do agree, don't you?"

"Of course I do." She was sharper with him than with Swaffield, regarding him as a friend, thinking she ought to be protected more. "You're preaching to the converted."

Lord Clare intervened: "We all hope this can be pushed under the carpet now. We really don't want any more in the papers."

Lord Clare said the obvious with loftiness, and others acquiesced. Journalists had been following up the Julian Underwood-Liz-Hillmorton connection, and among that party journalists were not popular.

Swaffield was still gazing at Jenny, and fired off another interrogation. Flushed again, she replied, not over-gently but with something like submissiveness and deference. He couldn't draw her. She agreed, she would do what she was told. Swaffield gave a shrug, as though deflated and at a loss, like someone who had pushed strenuously against a door and found it on the latch.

Soon afterwards, though it wasn't eleven o'clock, early for a dinner which started at half past eight, Swaffield was showing signs of impatience again. Just as he had been tapping a foot because his guests hadn't arrived, now his foot was tapping, his eyes growing hot, because they wouldn't go away. Those who had most to do with him suspected that he was expecting another visitor that night, or maybe there was another visitor already in the house. That aspect of Swaffield none of them knew. He enjoyed living everyone's lives in public, but there was one exception, his own.

Some of the party recognised the signs and began to say goodnight. The Haydon-Smiths, the Packes, somewhat surprised, stood up themselves.

"You have to go, have you?" said Swaffield, not making a more resolute attempt to detain them. "I know, I know, I'm not a pradge owl myself."

That singular phrase, a relic of Swaffield's past, was unintelligible to them all. It seemed to mean that he didn't go late to bed: which, to the Symingtons, was also unintelligible, since it wasn't long since they had been requisitioned for a supper at one in the morning.

As the party was standing about the room, door open, leave-taking complete, Swaffield made a last gnomic remark.

"Glad you came. It's been nice listening to you."

Was that great smile malicious or naive? Did he really not remember that he had been talking himself eighty per cent of the time?

The Packes moved to their official car outside. The Haydon-Smiths, with benevolent goodnights, moved to theirs. Mrs. Haydon-Smith, who considered the evening had been bizarre, asked her husband what he thought of Swaffield. In private Haydon-Smith wasn't devoid of humour, but he had a politician's gift of not condemning a man until he was safely finished, even to his wife or in his own mind, particularly if he was a man of power like Swaffield. Haydon-Smith considered, and then replied:

"I think I should say, he's a distinctly unusual fellow."

✤ 18 ✤

The Chamber was abnormally populated that evening, so were the library, the guest room, the bar, and surreptitious lurking places. Peers' wives sat on one side of what was also called the bar, and other guests opposite to them. At the further end of the Chamber, elderly dignitaries from the Commons sat on the steps of the throne, bottom by bottom with the sons of peers, one or two in their teens. Spectators looked down from the galleries.

As in a theatre with a certain hit, sheer numbers produced their own excitement. There was more laughter than the House was used to, even the vestigial trace of hysteria, which an actor would have recognised, underneath the phlegm. A skilful speaker could have played on it. No one did so. The courtesies flowed out. Speeches were being read from sheaves of what might have been notes, but were delivered intact to the Hansard reporters. Reading speeches was forbidden by a rule of order which was always being broken. There was another rule of order against acerbity of speech, and that was usually obeyed. It was being obeyed that evening. It was October 28th, the second day of the debate on the intention to enter the European Community. The vote would be taken later in the night.

About the result, there was no suspense. It required invincible ignorance to feel any. Anyway, it didn't matter, since the Commons had been debating for five and a half days, and were

about to vote handsomely in favour. The only perceptible suspense was about the size of the majority. In the bar, some
cheerful betting had been going on, on the lines of an old style
transatlantic crossing, high field, middle field, low field. High
field was 400 and above. That's about right, said someone, as
confidently as he would have done a generation before in the
Queen Mary. "This is a classical case of over-kill," said a more
judicious voice.

The whips weren't on, and so most of the Opposition were
voting with the Government. Although the whips weren't on,
discreet notices had gone out and, not entirely as a coincidence, faces which weren't familiar had appeared for those two
days, also to vote with the Government. The argument over
Europe was shadow-boxing. The political nation was for entry;
and, very strongly, the educated young. All cool-minded observers knew that a referendum would have decided against it.
So also, said liberal persons in the bar, would a referendum
have decided against the abolition of hanging. So also, said
conservative persons, would a referendum have decided
against fighting in 1939.

There were dissidents scattered round the House that night.
As wasn't uncommon, the extreme right and the extreme left
were speaking the same language. As was less common, a few
professional economists, though not speaking the same language, joined them. And there were one or two, like the un-
quenchable Lanjuinais throughout the French Revolution, who
said no to everything.

In the guest room a dispute broke out, half gibing, half intense. As the evening went on, most people present felt that
the air, though not undisturbed, was on the whole benign.

From the opening on the previous afternoon the speeches
were running nine or ten to one in favour of entry. Not many
of them were exultant. The tone stayed sober, practical, sometimes qualified (il faut parier, the old Pascalian phrase), once or
twice idealistic, from men taking colour from the young.

It was the only time Hillmorton, Ryle, Sedgwick, could
remember all three of them speaking in the same debate: and
all three on the same side.

As a luminary in the House, ex-senior minister, Tory elder

statesman, Hillmorton was number four on the list for the first afternoon. His speech had been singularly unlike his private conversation, not in the least ironic or detached, and only intermittently reflective. It might have been designed to give comfort to the Clares and Lorimers of his own party, but the curious thing was, he hadn't any such intention, he had always been more orthodox or commonplace on his feet than anyone who heard his ruminations would believe.

This was right, he said, as enthusiastically as at a Conservative garden party, the Government was right, there was no other way. He didn't wish to live to see the people of this country getting poorer than their fellow Europeans. This was the only way to prevent that. He thought it his duty (said gravely) not to minimise the difficulties. In his judgement there would be some years of hardship, and perhaps sacrifice for many, immediately after entry. But any spirited people could take some sacrifice in the present, when that was the condition of a better future. A sturdy rumble of hear-hears as he sat down: also notes passed from the front bench, to whom in private Hillmorton's scepticism from above the battle was frequently not a source of encouragement.

In this House, unlike the Commons, the order of speakers was fixed in advance, by an apparatus solemnly referred to as 'the usual channels,' which actually meant the party whips, with ancillary help from the leaders. 'The usual channels,' trying to take care of Sedgwick's physical state, put him in early on the second afternoon. He had insisted on speaking, which was something of an embarrassment, and those who had once heard his crisp patrician English were embarrassed most, listening to the fumbles of his tongue. But the speech itself was as crisp as the utterance used to be. Most of the elder statesmen, and many who hadn't been statesmen, let alone elder ones, devoutly believed that the importance of a topic bore an exact relation to the suitable length of one's speech. Hence in this debate it wouldn't have been proper to speak for less than half an hour. Sedgwick thought that ten minutes was as long as anyone ought to speak on anything, including the end of the world. Ten brisk minutes. He believed in entry into Europe as incisively as anyone there. Almost all scientists did. They were by vocation internationalists. The nation-state seemed to them, at best, obsolescent. Europe was only a starting point. It would be significant if it were the sign of a movement towards a more rational world.

Relaxed applause when the effort of speaking was finished, interspersed with mutters that this was too academic, scientists wouldn't get down to bread-and-butter.

Ryle, who had no claims to special consideration, got up at an uninvigorating time—just before eight o'clock on the second evening, most members out for dinner, fatigue descending on the dutiful—and proceeded to make a bad and confused speech. Partly it was that, though in terms of action he had decided on this matter years before, he was, somewhere behind the will, more divided than his friends. Was it his historian's training, was it temperament, was it, curiously enough, not being an aristocrat or an intellectual patrician that tied him to the past more than they were tied?

Anyway, he made a bad speech which attracted no interest and wasn't mentioned in the parliamentary reports the following morning. It was a muddled historical disquisition. In the 18th and 19th centuries, this country had been lucky beyond the limits of luck (so earlier on had the Venetians been, that old echo wouldn't stop recurring, though he kept it to himself). During the last hundred years, the luck had run out. At the peak of the country's power our predecessors, including predecessors in this House and the other place, had shown preposterously little foresight—not for want of being told. Now we were back in something like our natural power position—but with historical legacies lingering over and imperial debts to pay. So we had to make the luck for ourselves, carve out a realistic position. Of the possible choices, none of the others was now realistic—except Europe, it was left as the only choice.

Ryle sat down, dissatisfied, not over-concerned about the effect of a speech, but feeling that this was worse than most. Acquaintances in the House went in for lavish congratulations to anyone on almost any speech, rather as though oral expression were a new and astonishing accomplishment, and, as he walked down the corridors and sat in the bar, he received a few that night. With Hillmorton in a corner, however, Ryle, like

Jenny after her evidence in court, was conscious of an absence of praise. Hillmorton coped with the occasion by generalised comments on the whole debate. "I doubt if anything specially novel has been said, wouldn't you think?"

"Possibly," Hillmorton mused, "after all this time there isn't anything novel left to say. Possibly," Hillmorton mused more lengthily, "it would be a mistake to try."

Which was as near as Hillmorton would come to evaluating the performance of James Ryle. The bar was so noisy that they moved to the guest room, but that was as noisy and more crowded. People were waiting about now until the closing speeches from the front benches.

The House became as packed as it had ever been: men were sitting in the gangways and on the cushions in front of the Lord Chancellor, standing all over the Chamber, the galleries full: all to hear the winding-up utterances, which, though satisfactorily long, quite long enough for the gravity of the proceedings, did not, as Hillmorton might have been prophesying, strain after anything novel to say.

At last, at the drawn-out last, the motion put. Large roars of content. Scattered defiant rumbles of not content. "I think the contents have it." Defiant rumbles again. "The contents will go to the right by the Throne, the not contents will go to the left by the Bar." It took over a quarter of an hour for the contents to traipse through the lobby (it was the biggest vote in the House's records, partly for the undramatic reason that the number of members had not previously been so high).

"The contents have voted four hundred and fifty one. The not contents have voted fifty-eight." Rollicking reverberating hear-hears. The euphoria, the relief of a consummation. Someone observed there was as much excitement as though (a) the result signified, whereas the Commons had settled the matter (b) this particular vote was in doubt, instead of being inevitable all along. But the person who observed that wasn't capable of group emotion.

Excitement continued. Men celebrating in the bars as others like them had done at the end of wars. The guest room became so hot with the fumes of alcohol, tobacco and victory that the windows were thrown open. Hillmorton and Ryle were standing near by, and they looked out for a breath of air. Over the river was a temperate, misty, wistful autumn night and Ryle looked back to the celebrations.

"Not exactly a case of the pathetic fallacy," he said.

"Not exactly," said Hillmorton. He knew that the other man wasn't at his most tranquil. Casually, easily, Hillmorton went on: "I think we've done enough for honour. Let's go along."

So they went along in the mist, past the railings of Parliament Yard. They could have called at Ryle's flat, which was near, or at one of his clubs, which wasn't far away, but it was to Brooks's that they walked. To Ryle, after that evening, it might have seemed a suitably elegiac choice. On the other hand Hillmorton didn't reveal any elegiac thoughts.

He said, again casually, "Well, that's settled."

"I suppose so."

They were standing at the crossing, waiting for the lights to change.

"Give it ten years. It will be interesting to see what comes of it."

"I must say," Ryle broke out, "that's a very profound remark." Hillmorton gave an affable smile, not showing his reflections as directly as his friend. In case of doubt or feeling, detachment was a good cover, so were lofty platitudes, either would do.

They went on with their walk to St. James's Street, taking nearly but not quite the course which Hillmorton used in daylight. Instead of turning alongside the park, they went down Whitehall, deserted at that time of night, only one light shining high up the Treasury.

When they were young men, this street had had some charm for them, the charm of authority, perhaps for Hillmorton the charm of something like power. Memories didn't come back to order. There they were, two substantial elderly men walking slowly, thoughts drifting through their minds, Hillmorton saying something, not significant, about the future. Past Downing Street, but he didn't recollect the first time he had been summoned there. Nor did Ryle recollect an acquaintance, back in the thirties, saying with enthusiasm, "Do you realise, this is the most important street in the world?" That hadn't in cold fact been true then. At one time, at one privileged time, it might have been. It wouldn't be true again.

All that, those two had accepted long ago. You came to terms. They had been coming to terms those last two days. You didn't overstay your welcome, or pretend for ever that you were stronger than you were. And yet, though Hillmorton hid it, there was regret somewhere in their mood. At the same time they had the confidence of those who had had the luck and had known what it was like to be listened to. That didn't forsake you so easily.

They walked along, not noticing places they knew so well, comfortable enough in this familiar part of the town.

❧ 19 ❧

O n evenings that autumn Liz lay in Julian's bed, darkness pressing against the window, conserving them from all others, giving her the comforting moments, stress cleaned from her forehead. When he had become satisfied, he was kind to her, being a man who was pleasant in the epilogue of sex. His favourite time for sex, to which she had fitted herself, was between tea and his evening meal. Having shown himself unascetic in one domain, he was glad to lie beside her and then wait placidly to show himself ascetic over his supper.

In due course he liked to watch her get it ready, going naked round the flat, another liking of his, setting out the yoghurt, cheese, garlic and wholemeal bread, and, if he was going to indulge himself, cooking him an omelette. Well, that was all right. She hadn't expected to produce such a meal for any man, but she took it for granted now.

That was all right. And yet, her own campaign wasn't making much progress. There was a little news, some which seemed good, some fretting. She hadn't dared to try and force Julian, as she had her father. Usually she could trust her courage, but not there. Sometimes she made approaches, so tentative and timid that she despised herself. On these occasions Julian put up a cloud of mystification, but there was nothing about her that he didn't understand. Often he replied, with a blaze of innocent-looking blissful optimism:

"Let's have a little patience. Let's wait till the business is settled. Then all will come out right."

On the spot, in his presence, Liz—and in this she was like other suspicious, jealous persons—was easy to pacify, even easy completely to reassure, much more so than a simpler woman would have been. Away from him, however, the doubts and disbeliefs swam back and there were times when she found herself muttering sombrely:

"You can lead a horse to the water but—" Then she would make herself remember what he had said, and become once more loving and happy. Further, she had achieved something, so it appeared, with her father.

That was her piece of positive news. He had summoned her again, this time to the guest room in the Lords, a couple of days before the community debate. He told her, with considerable weaving and sly probing darts, that he "saw his way to making a modest contribution." Not immediately, but as a gift which would be realisable when he had lived seven more years: if need be, it could be drawn upon two years before that. It might be "some slight assistance" to her to know that this contribution was coming.

How much, she asked him, straightforward as she couldn't be with Julian. There Lord Hillmorton weaved and elaborated. There wasn't a simple answer, it depended on the value of certain securities, it would be a modest addition to her portfolio, it wouldn't make her rich, but it mightn't be altogether negligible.

He seemed to enjoy obfuscation for its own sake and simultaneously to enjoy doing something for her. While he was repeating those themes, James Ryle entered the room and joined them. Suspiciously Liz wondered if this were prearranged, a clinching piece of obfuscation. She wondered also if Ryle had been told of her father's new arrangement. As it was, confidences languished. Ryle looked at her with more concern than her father did, she thought, but didn't so much as mention Julian's name.

During those autumn weeks Julian was cheerful, which was nothing strange, but secretively cheerful, like a minister who is holding back a piece of information which will demolish the opposition, or an income tax inspector who has after years of searching found a method of catching a rich man out. Julian was greeting the unseen, that is the future, not exactly with a cheer but with benign approval.

Straight from the meeting with her father, when she and Julian were lying in bed, she told him—having saved up the news for the peaceful moments—of the financial promise. Julian greeted that with benign approval too. He kissed her (not as he had been kissing her a quarter of an hour before), and said "Clever girl." Then he hooted way, and gave her a lecture on the falling value of money—"We have got to get hedges all the way round, your father mustn't lose most of this stuff for us, I don't know how sensible he is."

Despite that lack of faith in Lord Hillmorton's acumen, Julian was gratified. But there was one feature, just one feature, of that autumn with which Julian wasn't gratified. Nor was Lord Hillmorton. It might have surprised both of them to find a subject on which their minds were at one.

The trouble, as Lord Clare had indicated at the Swaffield dinner party, was journalists. Families like the Hillmortons had lost their power and functions, but they hadn't lost their allure for the gossip columns. The name of Lady Elizabeth Fox-Milnes was good for a line or two in several papers. It didn't take much detective work (a reporter had started it by seeing her beside Julian in court) to connect her with the losing party in the Massie case. Though owing to Julian's parsimony they so rarely went out together, their names kept being dragged into the press. Julian began to develop the paranoia of one under surveillance. He believed that the Phillimore Gardens block of flats was being watched: or alternatively that the caretaker was in journalists' pay: or both.

Lord Hillmorton, to himself blaming Julian for it, also disapproved of this publicity. To Ryle and others close to him, he disapproved with something like rancour. That could have puzzled those who remembered that he was a worldly man and had been a professional politician all his life. But professional politicians, though they lived on publicity, didn't get inured to it. Most of them became more thin-skinned, not less, as they grew older, and underneath the cordiality distrusted journalists more. And sometimes this was true of some of whom one would have least expected it, some who could give a fair impersonation of Lord Melbourne's devil-may-care, such as Hillmorton himself.

Julian disapproved of the publicity with approximately equal rancour. That could have puzzled anyone who knew him, any of his women. It did puzzle Liz, who had the best of reasons for knowing that he was totally shameless. Anything which gave him pleasure, provided it didn't get in his own way, was a good idea. Yet he was affronted, morally affronted, at sly little paragraphs inferring that he and Liz were living together.

He had once, ten or so years before, been cited as the co-respondent in a divorce case. It didn't strike him that, with natural justice, he could have been cited in others. This intervention he responded to at the time, and still did, with a deep, shocked sense of moral outrage. It shouldn't happen to him. Hypocrisy? But Liz had to recognise that there was no one less hypocritical. She thought she understood each change in his expression, and yet she couldn't understand him at all. She found herself driven back on banal explanations, such as that he didn't like any public exposure which might give pain to his mother. Even though nothing in Mr. Justice Bosanquet's statement about his mother had (Liz was certain she could read him there) moved him in the slightest.

That old divorce case had been revived by a journalist. It was moderately scabrous. It had been with the wife of a still-prominent Tory politician. Julian was angry, not only angry, but hang-dog and penitential. Liz had seen him mock-penitential when he had hurt her, but this seemed genuine. She was lost.

Lord Hillmorton was also angry about that resurrected story, but not in the least penitential. There had been plenty of divorces among those round him, and plenty of marriages (political gossip said his own among them) which had been preserved as a front for the sake of the public game. On the other hand people didn't get into this kind of scabrous mess, at least not in the open. Lord Hillmorton could bear with anything as long as it wasn't in the open. Then he was as conventional as the rest, though there was realism in it. It was desirable to keep some kind of decorum. It you didn't, the whole structure might begin to fall round your ears. He therefore had further reasons, not for disliking Julian—in ultimate privacy he had a soft spot for another devious and unbudgeable soul—but for wishing him to get out of Liz's life.

Lord Hillmorton had no means of knowing that, at this same period and as a consequence of the publicity, Julian had suggested to Liz that, at least in form, he should do precisely that. Perhaps they ought to have a diplomatic break. Perhaps she ought not to come to his flat any more. They could of course meet elsewhere, or they could stop seeing each other until the stories had died down.

If Hillmorton had overheard that proposition, would he have been soothed? The answer was, of course, no. Hillmorton had seen too many men and women playing this sort of love gambit. Julian genuinely believed that the flat was being shadowed, he even brought himself to identify a man in a mackintosh, walking about outside, hours a day (this was a delusion). So he would have preferred another place to meet.

Otherwise, in making the proposal, he wasn't doing much more than enjoy his power over her. Listening to them, Lord Hillmorton would have heard his daughter passionately crying. Hillmorton was not a warm-hearted man, but he wouldn't have liked the scene: and he would have realised, which was the most relevant point, that neither of them had the slightest intention of parting.

Mostly, they weren't quarrelling; Julian was getting his way, she wasn't crossing him. She picked up something about the legal negotiations, though she heard only at second-hand about any meeting with the lawyers. She gathered that not only Skelding, but also counsel, were against pressing the appeal up to the court itself. What was needed was a decent private settlement, they were all urging—just as Swaffield had been urging Jenny at his dinner party. A decent bargain out of court—compound for that. Each side might be left with twenty or thirty thousand to pay in costs, the kitty was being whittled down. Even so, all sensible persons were talking of a settlement.

Hillmorton wanted it, no more gossip, no more trouble. Though he didn't often write letters to his daughter, he wrote one now. Mrs. Underwood, so Liz was told by Julian, wanted it. What did he want himself? Money, he said, and she was reassured, and certain that he wanted a settlement too.

She received one vague intimation from Julian's mother that the lawyers had collected a piece of new evidence. Apparently the local vicar had called on old Massie shortly before his death. This sounded incongruous, and the lawyers didn't expect that the Court of Appeal would allow any extra testimony. Still, it might strengthen their bargaining hand, and their morale rose, though Julian's had been high all along.

There was another pair who discussed—though the discussion was one-sided—a settlement that autumn. Several nights during the long debates Jenny sat with Lorimer in the Lords guest room, and when the House wasn't sitting she went and cooked supper for him in his Pimlico flat. She had heard over the telephone from Symington, back from the Dordogne holiday though Swaffield was still on his restless travels, that they were "feeling their way" towards the settlement.

She was now taking this for granted and told Lorimer so, reminding him of Swaffield's advice at the dinner and saying that the final share she received didn't matter much, she would be glad to hear the last of it. As usual, Lorimer was reticent if not mute, and yet she felt, being able to distinguish between his silences by now, that there was reserve inside him, but one which her sharp questions didn't disinter.

His flat was, as he had said the first time he took her out, "not very grand either." It was on the ground floor of a narrow fronted 1840ish house in Lupus Street, built during the Cubitt attempt, which didn't succeed, to make Pimlico smart. Now the house was in decay, and so was Lorimer's flat. He had one room more than Jenny had herself, a bedroom with a curtained off bath as well as the sitting room, outside which the traffic swirled along the street. When she first saw that room, the mantelpiece, the glass fronted bookcase (an edition of Kipling's stories, some books of Winston Churchill's, a collection of Thomas Hardy, a few paper backs, not much else) was gritty with the London dust. She soon made a difference there: just as she made a difference to his food, setting about with eggs and cheese and meat she bought nearby, producing edible dishes not only for his sake, but, since she had a healthy appetite, for her own.

He had no instinct for comfort. There were no pictures on the walls, just one or two photographs of officers in the desert, a group photograph of a public school she hadn't previously heard of. He had no money, and, with his straight simplicity, told her he had never had any. In the mornings he taught at a day preparatory school, taught French which, when she heard him utter a few words, made him seem sadder. On Mondays and Fridays, as a rule non-sitting days in the Lords, he took a form by bus to a playing field in the suburbs. This job brought him a little income. The Lords expenses brought him a little too. He had been left a few government securities which he hadn't known how to reinvest. The two of them were much of a muchness, Jenny told him, and that made him laugh, which wasn't a common sound. When he did laugh, however, it was whole-hearted, and the bitterness passed away. There was bitterness whenever they talked about the world they were living in. They agreed about it, it gave them consolation to agree, but Jenny viewed it with regret and he with something closer to hate.

She understood a good deal about him by now. Her first impression, that evening in Soho had, she was certain, been right. In some fashion he was fond of her—that she didn't expect from anyone, but she couldn't help but recognise it was true. Still, he was abnormally diffident with women, certainly with her, presumably with any woman. He had been married, he wasn't a virgin, and yet he was as timid as one, more timid than some male virgins she had met. Jenny knew more about men than most observers would have guessed. David March, speculating about her to his friend Lander in the Park, hadn't been a long way from the mark. Shrewd, active, not giving people the benefit of the doubt, Jane Austen like—that was how people who liked her were liable to judge her. In fact, Jenny hadn't lived a life of maximum chastity. She hadn't had so many opportunities, she had been discreet, but she had made the most of them and often enjoyed them.

In many ways she was remarkably like her enemy Liz, which was one of the perversities of their situation which they couldn't know. She might have borne the resemblance of a sister fifteen years older—except that Liz's eldest sister wasn't at all like her, and Jenny was. But she was less obsessive and more sensual, and that made her both warmer and wiser. It would have been difficult for Jenny to get into the kind of relation that Liz had with Julian. It wasn't that Jenny was prouder. In that respect there wasn't much between them: but Jenny's body, emotions, nerves, senses, were much more at one. It was only by mis-chance that she wasn't a high-spirited and happy wife. No one but a fool, and a conceited fool, James Ryle had been known to observe, doubted the part luck played in one's life. Ryle was not so cynical as Hillmorton, but like Jenny was in tune with his own nature. It was possible that sheer chance had once more intervened, in preventing the meeting of those two.

Jenny came to admit to herself, Lorimer might even love her. If he had made an advance, however diffident, she would have agreed. Out of curiosity, of which she had her share, as well as kinder feelings. Yet she hadn't encouraged him in that sense, or brought him on—which she would have done, she told herself, tolerating no nonsense, if her feelings for him had been different. Yes, she was beginning to have an affection for him. Yes, she was sorry for him. But (and here her thoughts turned bewilderingly stilted) she told herself that she didn't begin to love him as a woman ought to love a man. It might have been a Russian heroine thinking or talking. Liz would have received that reflection with jeering scorn, and re-phrased it for her in terms more suitable for a stable lad. Liz didn't wrap things up.

Yet Jenny wasn't any more sentimental, knew as much about the sexual life, and had more intuition about it. But then, like a good many realistic people, Jenny had a sense of when not to let her words and thoughts become too sharp, even to herself. It might make her sound less earthy than Liz, which she wasn't. It was a protection.

Jenny didn't mind sounding miffish to herself. No, she didn't love this man as she wanted to love someone. But she began to admit another thought. She was coming to believe that he wanted to marry her.

Jenny didn't think she could be wrong. At that point her own species of diffidence got between them, prevented her being spontaneous. Men had occasionally wanted to go to bed with her, that was in the nature of things. But men hadn't liked her all that much, men had certainly not wanted to marry her. Why should they, what had she to offer?

It occurred to her, and now her diffidence was as morbid as it used to be, that soon she might have money to offer. Looking round this poor flat, she thought that money might solve some of his problems. It was conceivable that he had thought so. It was conceivable—her suspicion was alive, destroying the peace of the moment—that that was why he wouldn't talk about the settlement.

So, on more than one evening, she stopped him when he seemed to be starting to confide, or begin any sort of declaration. It was better for them to stay just where they were. Let them remain static, not break it up. They were lonely people, there was comfort in looking after him, they were company for each other, it was better than loneliness.

❧ *20* ❧

By the middle of November, all Swaffield's guests had returned. Jenny saw Swaffield himself in the charity's office looking like a high powered and sunburnt frog. He had a few words with her, cordial and casual, saying something which implied that he, like everyone else, was taking a settlement for granted. He had ceased to be specially interested. That was last year's hobby. He didn't invite her to his house so often. At the moment he was organising an appeal for his charity. This was the newest, grandest crusade, and he expected all his entourage, Jenny included, to be as absorbed in it as he was himself.

Eleven o'clock one night in November, almost exactly a year after she had received the first letter from him. Jenny was sitting in her room, having not long returned from Pimlico. The cold had been raw and searching on her walk back from the underground, and she thought that it would be pleasant to tuck up in bed.

Telephone. The one word, Swaffield.

"Yes, Mr. Swaffield?"

"I'm sending a car round for you."

"Oh—"

"I shan't keep you long. I'm in a hurry."

"It's rather late, Mr. Swaffield. Can't it wait till tomorrow?"

"No. I'm sending another car for old Symington."

"What's happening?"

"I'll tell you in half an hour. Bless you."

As the big Daimler swept her along the Cromwell Road, feeling as though she were being driven to a police station, Jenny tried to nerve herself by grumbling. This is a bit much, she wanted to say out loud, this is more than one can stand.

He needn't have left her in suspense. With Symington dragged in too it was something to do with the case. She couldn't imagine what, gazing out at the brilliant shops. No answer, imagination beating in a vacuum, when the car turned fast along the dark and empty Mayfair streets.

Swaffield let her in himself. He was wearing both a dinner jacket and a wide assertive smile. Leading her into the morning room, where he had greeted his guests at the party only ten weeks before, he announced that he was going out in a few minutes. Symington had already arrived, no one else but the two of them. Though neither knew it until the following morning, when Symington received a telephone call, Swaffield had also attempted to recruit Lander. But successful counsel were more independent than most men when dealing with financial magnates, and this successful counsel had bourgeois habits and liked his bedtime.

It was soon clear that Symington had been told no more than Jenny. But, though Swaffield had kept them waiting up till now, he did so no longer. They were all standing. He didn't ask them to sit down.

He said: "You can forget all the talk about a settlement. We're going through with it."

Symington and Jenny looked at each other, expressions washed blank with surprise. It was Jenny who spoke first.

"But you said the opposite, you remember, you said it as strongly as anyone could, in this very house—"

"I've changed my mind."

Symington, much more quietly than Jenny, asked Swaffield if he was taking account of the former Law Officer's opinion.

"That chap," said Swaffield without inflection. He then went on with a remark—having previously behaved like a Prime Minister interpreting intelligence in one way, he now behaved like a Prime Minister finding it convenient to read the appreciation in the diametrically opposite sense—that "that chap" had given them enough to go on.

"You can't deny it," he said with potency.

Symington hesitated. There was truth in it, the opinion was finely poised.

Then Symington, smiling, said with a nice mixture of professional authority and deference to a patron:

"As your lawyer, I think I'm obliged to give you my advice, aren't I?"

"That's your privilege."

"I don't think I've ever known you make a bad judgment. But I must say, to the best of my knowledge this one is."

Swaffield said: "If that's what you think, you're right to say so."

"So you will re-consider it, won't you?"

Swaffield gave a fighting grin. "Not on your life."

"I'm sorry, but I feel obliged to press you."

Swaffield said: "I may as well remind you, whose show this is. I'm picking up the tab."

Inflamed, Jenny was just about to flare out, but she caught a warning glance from Symington and managed to bite the words down.

Swaffield said: "Well, that's all for now. I'm going out."

In silence he took them to the Hill Street door and in a tone of obscure triumph said again: "Bless you."

Symington, apparently self-possessed, talked to the chauffeurs outside, and said that one car was enough to take them both home. When they were sitting inside he muttered:

"Jenny, this is serious," and put an arm round her shoulders, for his consolation as well as hers.

It was a consolation that this man, whom she had not seen put out until now, seemed as sore within as she was. It had been an indecent display of power. She was rankling more, the further they got away. They had both seen Swaffield exulting in indecency before: they had seen him indulging one of his preposterous whims at another's expense. What they hadn't seen before was a whim, when it came to serious business, getting in the way of calculation. He had calculated their strategy over the settlement, and now—without any reason to offer—he was turning it on its head. They couldn't understand.

They each sat silent on the drive to Chelsea, although getting out of the car Symington forced himself to add to his good night:

"Don't worry too much."

Without realising it, they were under the first stress of a similar feeling. It wasn't entirely humiliation, or puzzlement, or even misgiving. Symington had already defined it for himself, though not in terms of action. That night, Jenny was lost, not only about Swaffield's motives but her own.

Swaffield hadn't offered them a reason, but he had one. He never told them, and they never knew. If it had been one of his ferocious reasons, such as taking maximum revenge on Mrs. Underwood, he would have told them, blatantly enough. But this was one of which he was, in some secretive fashion, ashamed. He confided it to no one, at any stage in the future. Not even the two men who had taken part with him in a quiet little scene the day before had any conception of the truth. All they knew, and then not immediately, was that they hadn't achieved what they came for.

Giving Symington and Jenny his ultimatum, Swaffield was not being so spontaneous as he appeared. He had let his impulses rip, but only after he had decided to. It had been a day and a half since the quiet little meeting. It had happened like this. Swaffield received a letter from a high functionary of the Tory party, with the good old City name of Meinertzhagen. Could he make it convenient for a couple of friends to wait upon him? Swaffield was somewhat less stately, and by telephone invited the couple of friends around that afternoon to his office in Victoria Street.

Swaffield did not believe in conspicuous consumption when it came to offices. He worked in a small mustard-coloured room which might have been rented by a very minor consulting engineer, and there came the two friends. In fact, Swaffield had met Meinertzhagen precisely once: the other was Haydon-Smith, presumably chosen, Swaffield thought later, because they wanted a Cabinet Minister, and this was one whom he was known to entertain.

The meeting lasted less than an hour. There wasn't a voice raised, nor what Meinertzhagen might have called a word out of place. When he judged it desirable, Swaffield could be as polite as the next man, and on this occasion he was as scrupulously polite as the other two. For the deputation, Meinertzhagen did most of the talking. He was a large man with a cylindrical head, bald except for the ear fringes. His tone was subdued, husky and high pitched, like that of some great athletes such as W. G. Grace, but considerably more cultivated. He began by thanking Swaffield for all the services he had done for the party.

"We really do appreciate that," he said. "We wanted to tell you how grateful we are."

"Yes, we wanted to," said Haydon-Smith.

"We do need people like you. We do hope you realise how much we need you. We haven't so many friends who can do what you can, you know."

"I've been very glad to make a little contribution," said Swaffield, catching the tune.

"You've done a great deal for us," said Meinertzhagen with earnest persistence, as though Swaffield required much convincing. "Everyone realises that. I know that all my colleagues wish me to tell you so."

"Certainly," said Haydon-Smith.

It wasn't difficult for their colleagues to realise Swaffield's services. He had given a hundred and fifty thousand to their party funds during the past three years. There was nothing mysterious about this. Swaffield might not be in the least impressed by politics or politicians, but he was a capitalist, he didn't indulge in over-refinement, capitalists supported the Tory party. For his support, he expected recognition in return. Not that anything had been spoken or written on his side or theirs. There hadn't been a word said, much less, to repeat a beautiful phrase, a word out of place. The most that had been delicately suggested, as by one speaking at a distance or in code, wasn't any more brutally forthright than a remark by Meinertzhagen now.

"You are always in our minds," he said, with more weeping earnestness. "We do want you to understand that. You are always in our minds."

"It's good of you to say so," said Swaffield, also with earnestness.

Further insistence about the retention of Swaffield in the leaders' collective mind. Then a shy, tentative smile, and a sincere, firm, intimate address.

"Now, Reginald—if I may call you so—we have a little favour to ask you."

It was uncommon of Swaffield not to see the point of a meeting or negotiation. But at this stage he still didn't.

"Go ahead," he said.

"This is all extremely ticklish and strictly confidential. Within these four walls—"

"The room isn't bugged, as far as I know," said Swaffield. The other two broke into excessive amusement at this delectable piece of humour.

"Within these four walls," Meinertzhagen persevered, "some of our people are getting embarrassed. Which is the least we can say. And you know, as well as anyone alive, how the news gets around. We don't ask you to confirm it or deny it, but there is a general feeling that you have been helping, I'm sure with your usual generosity that we have been trying to express thanks for this afternoon, and I'm sure with nothing to gain yourself, the people who upset that Massie will."

As a negotiator, Swaffield was practised at saying nothing.

"We want to impress on you, Reginald, that this is all turning out very embarrassing. You know that the press are getting hold of the story. It's beginning to involve some very senior members of the Party." (That meant, Swaffield decided later, not only Hillmorton but the minister whose wife Julian had slept with.) "It might do harm politically. We don't want any more talk about sex and money anywhere near the party."

"It can't be all that significant," Swaffield said in an impartial tone. "Aren't you over-stating your case?"

Meinertzhagen said: "Perhaps I'll withdraw a little, but I want to impress on you that some of our most senior people are very seriously distressed. That is absolutely certain, and I hope you will accept it from us."

"Who are these people?"

179

"No, I think you would be surprised if we told you that."

"I've seen one woman's name mentioned. I don't know anything about her or anyone connected with her." Swaffield showed no feeling, and was speaking without assertion or rasp. He was referring to Liz, but by now he had caught on to the other, older affair. He knew as well as they that the press would have plenty to play with if stories broke out about Julian's women, particularly that damped-down scandal of ten years before.

"Reginald, this is where we want your co-operation. The worst thing for everyone is for this business to drag on. We are asking you to see that it's all tied up as soon as may be. Don't let it get to court again. If it's handled quietly now, then it will only be a nine days' wonder."

All the vibrance was suppressed from Swaffield's voice, it was kept as gentle as the others.

"I really think there is a little misunderstanding, isn't there? I'm a complete outsider in this case. I'm not a litigant, I'm not a principal. So it's not possible for me to pack it up, you see?"

Meinertzhagen gave a large slow managerial smile.

"A few minutes ago," he said, "you told us we were doing a little over-statement. Aren't you doing a little under-statement now? I fancy we might suggest that if you used, what shall we call it, your influence, that that could have a distinctly positive effect."

"If you used your influence," said Haydon-Smith, who seemed determined to act as an agreeable chorus.

"I'm sure you wouldn't suggest, though, that if I had any influence I ought to do anything unethical with it."

"Of course not," said Meinertzhagen, with a shocked expression.

"Some people might possibly consider," Swaffield spoke deeply shocked as though meditating, "that it was unethical— To ask a woman to share out her money after the courts had decided it was hers. All to avoid a bit of commotion."

"Forgive me, but we don't see it quite like that."

"How do you see it?"

"We see it," Meinertzhagen replied, supremely reasonable,

"as a matter of mutual sacrifice, all for the sake of good relations."

"Who's making the sacrifice?"

"She would be giving up a little money. You'd be exerting yourself and using valuable time and energy. We should call it sacrifice all round."

"All to keep names of eminent people out of the papers."

"No, Reginald, no, Reginald. All to keep relations as good as they ought to be. As good as we want them to stay."

Swaffield didn't reply. Meinertzhagen said, at his most gentle,

"That's why we are asking you this little favour. We feel that it's not asking you too much, to use your influence. It would be a great pleasure to some of us who, I said before and I repeat, are always thinking of you."

Again Swaffield didn't reply. Meinertzhagen smiled at him and went on:

"As friend to friend, you know, we consider it might be in your own best interests too. That is, we're inclined to think that if you didn't see your way to give us a little help it might slightly affect your relations with some of our people, not seriously of course. Everyone knows what you've done, everyone is grateful. But it might make for a little constraint, you know better than I do how people get upset when they feel neglected—"

The interview went on some minutes longer. Meinertzhagen returned to the topic of Swaffield's good nature, generosity, and the sweetness and light which he would confer by this small service, Swaffield produced general reflections on the difficulty so often of deciding where one's duty lay. At last Swaffield promised to think the whole problem over "with maximum care." He would let them know shortly, within days, whether there was anything he felt able to do. They parted with handshakes, cordial greetings to other acquaintances, and expressions of regard.

Would the other two have guessed Swaffield's mood as soon as the door was closed? It was a mood of rage, of smouldering, erupting, smouldering, erupting rage: and since Swaffield despite his whims and wilful antics was a man whose real emotions stayed constant, more so than most men's, that mood lasted all through the next day, was still dominating him when he gave his orders to Symington and Jenny. Much of this would have seemed farcical to anyone who wanted to minimise him. For Swaffield, when in one of his passions, had a habit of talking to himself and speaking of himself in the third person. "Christ almighty! So they think they can buy off Reg Swaffield. Reginald—no one's called him that since he got married in church. They are telling Reg Swaffield to play ball, and then they might consider giving him something. God damn them to hell."

That same evening, "That chap Hillmorton had better look out, so had Edward Clare. Snakes in the grass. They've got the nerve to tell Reg Swaffield that if he doesn't play ball they'll cut his throat and he'll get nothing. That was a threat if ever there was one. People don't threaten Reg Swaffield and get away with it. God damn it, he hasn't been threatened for thirty years. Reg, my boy, now's the time to see them in hell first. You tell them you're not playing, and then rub it in. What a blasted crowd. You've got on without them. You can get on without them now. You might pull down the whole rotten show."

The listening enemy would have found it singularly ridiculous. After all, this kind of implicit deal wasn't exactly a novelty. Swaffield must have gone it himself times enough. Great magnates shouldn't take offence like this. Great magnates shouldn't indulge in gestures at their own expense. They shouldn't do any of those things, but Swaffield did them all. After a day's brooding (his calculating mind cool, co-existing with the rage) he wrote a note to Meinertzhagen, that he still couldn't see his way entirely clear about the suggestion made the afternoon before. That was a prim little note, but he was anticipating a scene later on, and it was a rousing thought.

He had made his decision, sent off the note, before he gave any intimation to another person, either to the lawyer or Jenny, who later that night were hearing what he had already, to his own satisfaction, settled flat.

❧ 21 ❧

There were times when Ryle couldn't repress asking Hill-morton a question about Liz just for the pleasure, or the mirage satisfaction, of mentioning her name. He knew that he could only get evasive exercises in reply, and he knew too by now that Hillmorton had his own private entertainment be-cause his old and sensible friend was not behaving like an old and sensible man.

Ryle didn't excuse himself: though in fact, apart from those questions to Liz's father, he didn't commit other follies in ac-tion, even if some filtered through his mind. He had once given Liz advice on this same topic: he must have been one of the few men, it occurred to him, to follow his own advice him-self. Yet, sitting in his drawingroom at Whitehall Court, he sometimes felt the spring of the nerves when the telephone rang: only to find that it was his stockbroker or accountant.

Still, he was learning, late in life, what less stable men dis-cover earlier, that any expectation, even a frustrated one, is—at any rate in its first stages—better than none. His spirits were higher than the year before, when he was at peace, anticipating nothing. A couple of days before the Christmas recess he was settled in his place in the Chamber, listening with some ap-proach to content as fellow members expressed themselves.

Ryle sometimes grumbled—rather as Jenny had thought to herself—that to endure the legislative process, either in that House or in the other, you had to be brought up a parliamentarian man and boy. Committee stages, amendments, reports, parliamentarians were unborable or appeared so, and Ryle wasn't. Still, that was how the work got done. On Wednesdays they could talk at large, someone introduced a general topic and moved for papers (having to withdraw his motion at the end, otherwise there might be embarrassment, since no one knew where, if anywhere, the papers were).

That particular Wednesday they were talking about conservation. As usual in these debates, one or two speakers had expert knowledge. Ryle was learning something. As usual also, one or two speakers were not specially relevant. One peer delivered a very strong allocution about Eskimo languages.

To Ryle's surprise, he had found that Hillmorton was down to speak. As a rule, elder statesmen, like the working politicians they had once been, didn't take part in such a discussion. Nevertheless, uncharacteristically, Hillmorton chose to make a speech. He also made—even compared with his October utterance on Europe—an uncharacteristic speech. It wasn't long, but it was curiously sentimental. Hillmorton was speaking in praise of the English countryside, demanding that it should be left, so far as they could contrive it, exactly as it was.

Now Ryle had heard Hillmorton, when conversing with his normal detachment, remark that that same countryside was every square foot man-made, and that no revenant from as recently as the seventeenth century would be likely to recognise his native spot. Further, Ryle knew for sure that Hillmorton detested the countryside as a place to live in, and had, all the time they had been friends, used any excuse to escape from his home in Suffolk.

Ryle was thinking, involuted and deeply forested men like Hillmorton seemed to be able to let themselves flood into sentimentality—at any rate in public—as more open characters seldom could.

After his speech, Hillmorton stayed, according to etiquette, to hear the next one, and then walked out. As he passed Ryle's place, he said, fingers stroking one of the unicorns on the wooden bar:

"Have you had enough of this?"

When they reached the lobby outside, Hillmorton asked if

Ryle felt like coming to Brooks's. On the way—this time, as it was early evening, they took Hillmorton's favourite and nostalgic promenade, walking across the corner of the park—Ryle, still diverted, was gibing at some of the afternoon speeches. Then he referred to Hillmorton's own.

"New line for you, Hal."

"You thought so, did you?"

"How much do you believe of all that?"

Hillmorton's face was bland in the winter dark.

"How should I know?"

They walked on, up the Duke of York's steps, into Pall Mall. Ryle could hear, without looking, that the other man was limping, scuffing one of his feet. He had noticed the same effect during the past week or two, without paying much attention, and without mentioning it. Elderly men, especially elderly men proud of their condition, didn't welcome being told of minor disabilities. They were on the south, the club-filled, side of Pall Mall: the other was bright, Dickensianly welcoming with the Christmas illuminations, false and also cosy, artificial Christmas trees bedecked with coloured bulbs shining out among guns and fishing tackle.

Hillmorton made an effort at disinterested observation.

"Should you say that was jolly?" he remarked.

"Perhaps it is."

"In my house, when I was a boy," Hillmorton kept up the same tone, "we always had roast beef for Christmas dinner. Just roast beef."

"One-upmanship," Ryle commented. "Showing that you went back earlier than those vulgar Victorian inventions. Like turkeys."

"I dare say, I dare say."

In the club, in the same long room in which Liz had asked her father for money, Hillmorton ordered drinks and drank his own off fast. Then he limped across to fetch another, dragging his right foot, the toe of his shoe trailing along the carpet. This had become so obvious that Ryle decided it was uncivil not to say a word. He asked, when Hillmorton had regained his chair:

"Is this sciatica you've got?"

"I dare say." It sounded another mechanical response.

The room was about half full, somewhere near the right density, not too full to be oppressive, men drinking as comfortably as themselves.

"Is it painful?" Ryle was referring to Hillmorton's leg.

"Not so as one would notice."

"These things disappear as suddenly as they come."

"I dare say." Hillmorton added with an air of casualness: "As a matter of fact, I think I've been feeling slightly under the weather."·

"What's the matter?"

"Oh, nothing to speak of. Just slight malaise."

"What does that mean?" Ryle asked.

Either there appeared to be no definable symptoms, or else Hillmorton was dismissing them. Ryle, inquisitive about most things, was not specially so about clinical troubles. But he said, out of duty:

"Perhaps you ought to see a doctor."

"Oh, I'm not much good at seeing doctors, don't you know."

"Perhaps you'd better."

"We'll see. If it doesn't clear up."

They had another round of drinks. Ryle was invited to stay for dinner. In the dining room, Ryle, after appreciating that Hillmorton was eating a fair meal, didn't give any further thought to his health, or to anyone else's. In fact, he was wondering, and speculating across the table, about something considerably less vital.

They had each sat often enough at club dinner tables like this, eating a meal like this (that night they had ordered lamb chops and devils on horseback). It had sometimes been a soothing way to spend an evening. But how long could these clubs last, Ryle was letting fall a commonplace question among men similar to themselves. The cost of manpower would sink them, no machines in the world were substitutes for human hands, the present-day young would never know what a well-run club could be. Anyway the present-day young weren't fond of joining them and certainly didn't use them to dine in. Hillmorton replied with an indifferent offhand remark—perhaps these clubs would follow the American pattern and become luncheon houses pure and simple. Better to close them, said Ryle.

His old historical curiosity was stirring, as he looked round the agreeable decorous masculine room, decanters on tables, lights beaming off cutlery and peach-fed cheeks. Why did such clubs originate in England? Bourgeois prosperity, of course. No, that was the answer for the 19th Century clubs, which meant nearly all of them: but, as it happened, not for this one. The gaming clubs had become domesticated by bourgeois prosperity, though. If resurrected fifty years after death, Charles James Fox and his friends would have found the architecture of this club familiar, but not the company: too staid, too respectable, in some respects too grown-up.

In English prosperous life—this was another thought of Ryle's—the clubs a man belonged to told one something. Hillmorton—Brooks's, Turf, Pratt's. But he had recently resigned from the Turf, one of his economies. Adam Sedgwick—Athenaeum alone. Swaffield—none. Lorimer—at one time the United Services, now resigned. Clare—White's, St. James's, Carlton, Pratt's. Ryle himself—Athenaeum, Garrick, Beefsteak. If one could read the fine print, those details had a certain eloquence, just as accents had.

Hillmorton and Ryle didn't stay late in the club. After a glass of port upstairs, Hillmorton said that he ought to be making his way to his "little place." This reference Ryle didn't understand, but it meant the bedroom at his youngest daughter's house. Standing outside the cool façade in St. James's Street (the pair of them looking quite unlike Gillray's Sheridan and the Duke of Devonshire, outside the same façade) they said goodnight.

They wouldn't see each other until the new year, after the recess, said Hillmorton: he wouldn't be in the House the next two days. They didn't shake hands, but Ryle replied:

"Thank you for dinner, then, and see you in January."

Hillmorton walked up the rise and into Piccadilly, going towards the tube station. Ryle turned the other way, down across the Park.

✥ 22 ✥

For nearly all of his acquaintances, there was no news of Hillmorton over the Christmas holiday and the start of the new year. Ryle heard nothing. Nor did his daughter Liz, safely cocooned most of those short dark winter days in Julian's flat. There was one person who did have news, though he was scarcely even an acquaintance. This was Doctor Pemberton.

Hillmorton, not only evasive out of habit, had been disingenuous when he seemed to answer Ryle's questions about his health. He was stoical, unusually so, but not as stoical as he pretended. He had not gone to a doctor to be examined, but he had, before that evening in the club, spoken to one of his fellow members on the hospital board of governors. He had spoken as it were nonchalantly. He was having "a bit of discomfort." It was nothing to bother people about, but just possibly it mightn't be a bad idea to be "looked over" when that didn't interfere with anything else. He spoke so indifferently that the other man, who knew him only as a public figure, was taken in.

Ryle would have realised that Hillmorton was shirking being examined, wanting to be reassured, but also wanting to put it off, avoiding the evil eye, frightened. Just as frightened as anyone less trained to hide his feelings. He didn't confess, any more than he had done to Ryle, that for some weeks past his right hand seemed to be half-numb, and that the numbness wasn't passing. In private, he exercised the hand a good many times a day, trying to persuade himself that it had more sensation than half an hour before.

The result of that conversation, as casual as Hillmorton's own tone, was an arrangement that he should go to the hospital for a check up (if Hillmorton had been free from qualms he might have felt even more distaste for that mechanical little phrase). The arrangement wasn't hurried. Thus it was Christmas Eve when Hillmorton went to the hospital. That evening, after seven o'clock, the last patient having been dealt with, Dr. Pemberton was sitting in his surgery when the telephone rang.

"You're interested in old Hillmorton, aren't you?" This was the voice of his medical contact at the hospital.

"You know I am."

"He's been here today."

"Business or pleasure?"

"No. He's been gone over by the neurologists."

"Has he, by God?"

"It doesn't look too good. I hope this doesn't upset your Christmas—"

"To hell with Christmas." Doctor Pemberton in no circumstances bore much resemblance to Tiny Tim. "What have they found?"

"Oh, there's a mass of tumour on one side of the brain."

"Which side?" Clinical question without point.

"Left."

"What do they think?"

"Well, what do you think?"

Doctor Pemberton didn't reply. Anyone's spot diagnosis would be about the same.

The other doctor said:

"He must have noticed something before this. He ought to have come in months ago."

"If it's what it's most likely to be, that wouldn't have made one per cent difference."

"True enough."

Doctor Pemberton said: "They must be doing the obvious tests?"

"Chest X-ray tomorrow."

"Why wait that long?"

"Holiday season. Bit of dislocation."

"Christ Almighty." Doctor Pemberton uttered a few crisp words about the general efficiency and industriousness of the country.

"Yes. But what you said before—if your man has had it, it won't make one per cent difference. Or point one of one per cent, come to that."

"Someone ought to be sacked. It would encourage the others. Anyway, let me know what happens. I am interested, I told you that."

"I'll keep in touch."

The other doctor duly kept in touch. The following night, when Pemberton was sitting at dinner with his wife and younger son, he was called to the telephone. He was drinking the single glass of port he allowed himself on festive occasions. That rationing of his alcohol still didn't come easy to him. He was wearing a paper hat, which didn't come easy to him either.

The conversation was short.

"Your man Hillmorton."

"What about him?"

"Two spots on the lung."

"That ties it up, then."

"You were afraid of it, weren't you?" said the other man. Pemberton thanked him for ringing and said that he must get back to dinner.

For some minutes, though, he didn't do quite that. In the hall, antiseptic smelling like all that house, he sat beside the telephone, absently draping his paper hat over it. This meant that Hillmorton would die before long. How long, was anyone's guess. Pemberton was a careful doctor, not an intuitive one. He had no use for intuitions, anyone else's or his own. The only guides to be trusted were one's knowledge and one's mind. These carcinomas which the hospital had traced must be secondaries: there was a primary somewhere, and they would find that soon enough. That night Pemberton's speculation—it wasn't any more than that, but he thought dismissively that it was as good as anyone else's—was that in about six months Hillmorton would have to go into a nursing home for the last time. After that, he would die in—maybe another six months, maybe a year, only a fool predicted the course of terminal cancer.

Doctor Pemberton felt little emotion of any kind, certainly not pity. He would have despised anyone who, in his situation, pretended to feel pity. He scarcely knew the man. All the man had done, in their couple of confrontations, was to humiliate him. Doctor Pemberton, not vulnerable to a good many of the human wounds, was vulnerable to humiliation. He hadn't forgotten and wouldn't forget.

This man's death would bring him some advantages, already imagined and reckoned out. That brought a certain, not excessive, gratification. More gratifying, so far as he was feeling anything, was the warmth, something like a moral warmth, of an injury being disposed of. Doctor Pemberton would have considered it hypocritical to pretend.

Doctor Pemberton considered it hypocritical to pretend pity or concern about most deaths. In his experience, people didn't often feel either. They pretended to, but instead they felt slightly more alive because someone else had died. Most displays of mourning were so many shams. The only human beings whose deaths would move him were his wife and sons—and perhaps someone he had slept with. He had decided that in essence the same was true of all men.

If people really cared as they pretended about others' deaths, human life would be unendurable. It wasn't. Just look at their faces at a funeral. Few men were less religious in spirit than Doctor Pemberton, but no one believed more completely that in the midst of life we are in death: and that we bear it more complacently than the most minor upset of our own.

Doctor Pemberton also believed that we are all common flesh. He assumed that no one had told Hillmorton the truth about his condition. He had himself had to tell such news to others. They might put on an act, some made jokes and tried to make it easy for the doctor: but everyone was afraid. Hillmorton would be. Doctor Pemberton had heard many people say that they wished to know the truth, so they might, provided it was pleasant. No one wished to know the truth, when it was news of his own death. Any doctor had learned that.

Sometimes one had to tell it. But anyone was cowardly if he had to listen, Doctor Pemberton was certain. We are all brute flesh, he would be cowardly himself. So, even though he was thinking of Hillmorton whom he hated, perhaps there was a mutter—impatient, pushed aside—of visceral sympathy.

If he had been attending him as his doctor, he couldn't have suppressed that. This was likely to be an unpleasant way of dying. Dying was a messy business anyway, far more often than not. One couldn't tell with terminal cancer. Not even when they had investigated the primary source of Hillmorton's, one still couldn't tell. Sometimes his kind of cancer was merciful. As a rule it was a more messy way of dying than most.

That might be the case with Hillmorton. If it were so, Pemberton had a hope. It wasn't gentle, it was fierce with Pemberton's usual opinion of his kind. He hoped that Hillmorton had a doctor without any scruple about putting him out. The only pity worth having was practical. The rest was maundering and false. Doctor Pemberton had killed a number of sufferers in his time. He wouldn't have thought much of a man who had done otherwise. To anyone he could trust—which considerably reduced the number of possible confidants—he wouldn't have softened either the word or the fact. People maundering on the sanctity of life—Doctor Pemberton regarded them with more than his normal degree of contempt. They didn't know what life was like: or what dying was like. Let them watch some ways of approaching certain death. Then, if they could still think of their individual salvation and didn't do what he had done—well, human beings were miserable creatures and these were more miserable than most.

As usual, Doctor Pemberton became invigorated when he had found extra reasons for being scornful of the species. He picked up his paper hat and returned to the dining room. His wife asked:

"Oh dear. Do you have to go out?"

"No, no. Nothing like that. Nothing much."

The family knew, of course, about his heritage, but for years it had lingered like a vague and distant prospect, not coming nearer, not likely to come nearer. Pemberton would tell his wife the news later that night, but not in the presence of his younger son. Pemberton wasn't so tough minded within his family, and he was even worried at the thought of resentment between his sons. After all, this one would get nothing out of it except a courtesy title, which in Pemberton's view was more of a nonsense and distinctly more useless than the rest.

So Pemberton sat down, and, though he kept to his own rule, he pressed them each to have another glass of port. They were hearty people who liked their drink as he would have done, and they took these with pleasure and without wondering what the telephone call had meant. Mrs. Pemberton was wearing a purple crown and the son a tricorne hat. They were both big and handsome, the son, twenty years old, a couple of inches taller and not many pounds lighter than his father. Pemberton viewed them with benevolence. The son had received a cheque for £20 as a present that day, and Pemberton, who had a passion for instructing, proceeded to give a clear, Christmassy, after-dinner lesson on the principles of short term investment.

❧ 23 ❧

In that Christmas season there was no one, except those at the hospital and Dr. Pemberton, who knew of Hillmorton's state. There were, however, others who were having what some—though not Dr. Pemberton—would have called crises of conscience. Dr. Pemberton believed that persons' decisions were formed before they admitted them. They did what they wished to, and all the arguments with their consciences were so many minutes which never influenced actions by a millimetre.

That was not the view of the Symingtons, who had, since Swaffield's volte face, been talking to each other about what was the right thing to do. On the night of Boxing Day, they were having another of those conversations, not arguments, for they were trying to reinforce each other. It had been a cheerful Christmas, the children had gone to bed, they were in their own bedroom, Alison lying back against the pillows before she undressed, her husband having drawn up a chair by the bedside. He looked with love at her blooming face: it was being a good pregnancy. But, though he looked at her with love, he spoke with exasperation.

"I must say, I think we might have been spared this."

He had said that a good many times before.

"If you can't see the way clear, I don't think anyone could."

They were talking in married shorthand, and repeating what they had said often in the past days. "This" was the consequence of Swaffield's ultimatum. Since then, unknown to him, negotiations with the other side's solicitors hadn't been cut off short. Symington was too experienced for that, and legal probings had their own dynamic. By this time, he was convinced that Skelding would do a deal. Exact figures shimmered—like a proposal of marriage between a tentative middle-aged couple—among the cautious talk. But Symington would have guaranteed that the other man would settle for forty per cent—adding, just to touch wood, plus or minus a few per cent. This meant, with all costs paid, Jenny would receive something not too far from eighty thousand.

"She'll be happy with that," he said.

"So she damned well should," said Alison. Though the Symingtons lived prosperously they had little capital.

"If anything went wrong on appeal, she'd be sunk. And I'd be responsible."

"Not only you."

"She's my client, and no one else's."

There was no doubt what any respectable lawyer would advise. Or in fact insist on. But there was also the existence of Swaffield. He had given his orders.

"He's as obstinate as a pig," said Leslie Symington.

"He's a megalomaniac," said Alison.

"He's a very able man."

Neither of them had found any conceivable motive for Swaffield's conversion. They had no idea, and were not to have, of how simple it might be. All they could think of was that if they won the appeal he would be triumphant, Swaffield pantocrator. If they lost, he would, they kept persuading each other, take care of Jenny. After all, he had his generosity—that was an act of faith, insisted on a shade too strongly to each other. Were men generous, when they had made a mistake—worse than a crime, a silly error—at someone else's expense? That was almost the one doubt which Symington concealed from his wife, but she knew he had it.

None of that was relevant. There was no doubt what a respectable lawyer should do. At least, up to a certain limit.

"One has to go on telling him that he's dead wrong. About as wrong as Wilde v. Queensberry, though for a slightly different reason."

"You've told him that."

"Well, the old image certainly ought to know. He is an old priapic image, isn't he?"

"There's nothing to do but keep on."

"Which will leave us in exactly the same place."

Some lawyers—he had said so several times, but not that night—would have threatened to throw up the case. Swaffield's reply wouldn't have been unduly elaborate: "Then I'll hire someone else." Some lawyers, perhaps not so many, would have let him. Would that have shown an excess of scruple? Professional duty said that you gave your advice. If it wasn't followed, you did your best with what your client wanted. Swaffield wasn't Symington's client. Did you do your best for what someone else wanted, a potentate who was paying your client's bills? Particularly if that potentate was your own most powerful patron.

It was a nice problem in what academic acquaintances were calling situation ethics: or what Bishop Boltwood would have called the ethics of cases, saying blandly that the old catholic name was casuistry, before protestants took that over as a term of abuse. Those reflections the Symingtons would not have found specially encouraging.

"Say I clear out altogether. It will do no good to Jenny. Swaffield can dig up a decent stooge of a lawyer at the drop of a hat."

"We might feel a bit of relief."

"We might feel it was a luxury, keeping our noses clean if it did no good to anyone else."

Symington added: "And I'm not even sure it's right. A lot of lawyers wouldn't think so."

"And a lot of lawyers, let's face it, wouldn't pay the price."

That wasn't cynical, though it was said smilingly, edged with awareness of the two of them. She knew that he had as much scruple as she, and as much as most moderate men. It was easy to make passionate exhortations about scruple, if you lived a life which couldn't offer choices, as it did in theirs. They would, or at least they might, pay a considerable price if Swaffield got tired of them. A sizeable part of the firm's work, and of Symington's influence there, and possibly of Symington's long-term ambition, depended not so much on Swaffield's personal concerns as on the litigation which, as with Jenny's, he steered towards them. The curious thing was, they couldn't decide whether, if Symington defied Swaffield to the limit and resigned from this case, he would get tired of them. The likelihood was yes. Emperors existed to have obedient admirers round them, and there were plenty more where they came from. And yet, this particular emperor was a capricious man. He might make more fuss of them than ever.

No reasonable person would have bet on it. That didn't make the choice any easier. But they were a buoyant couple, and before they got to sleep that night, they still had a hope that the point might not arise, and that, if Symington used all his skills on Swaffield, sense had a further chance to prevail.

A few days later, in the first week of the new year, a conversation on a similar subject took place. It happened in Lorimer's sitting room in Lupus Street, and it happened about an hour after an outburst of sheer virtuous rage from Jenny, which began as soon as she got across the threshold. She had come straight from Swaffield's office. Half turning, she was shaking her umbrella in the dingy little communal hall outside. She was flushed, rainswept, looking young and bright-eyed.

"This is about the end," she said.

Lorimer was not good at dealing with angry women. Lamely he said: "What is?"

"What do you think has happened?"

Lorimer had no reply.

"You know that man Lord Clare?"

She had heard Lorimer greet acquaintances, and speak of them, either by the full title or the Christian name, nothing in between, and she had picked up the habit.

Lorimer could reply to that. Yes, he did know Lord Clare.

Jenny said: "He's a shit."

Lorimer did not often hear her speak in those terms.

"Is he?"

"You know, nearly all the money for Swaffield's charity is collected in small sums." (This wasn't strictly accurate. Swaffield had made large donations himself, and squeezed others out of fellow magnates.) "From people who can't afford it. Elderly people who haven't much themselves. They're the ones who are sorry for other old people. The ones who haven't anything at all." (This was nearer the fact. The charity collected a large number of small covenants, £10 a year and so on.) She went on:

"Every penny ought to go to the purpose they are giving it for."

"Point taken," said Lorimer.

"Well, Lord Clare doesn't take it. Damn him to hell. He's just going off to California with his wife, first class all the way, plushy hotels when they get there—and every blasted bit of his expenses charged down to the charity. He's had the neck to write a letter saying that he'll be doing some propaganda and so he assumes that it is all in order."

"Oh, I say, that's not good enough."

"It's rotten. And he'll get away with it."

"Will Swaffield let him?"

"What else can he do? After all, the bloody man will swear black and blue that he's doing a mission for the charity."

Lorimer suddenly had a patch of eloquence.

"In the Lords, you know, we speak on our honour. No oaths or anything like that. We don't have to declare an interest unless we want to. We just speak on our honour."

Jenny smiled at him with something like tenderness. He was so much in earnest—and he hadn't made his maiden speech after eleven years. Then she became outraged again.

"Lord Clare doesn't know what honour is."

"That's going a bit far—"

"If people like that don't keep up standards, how do we expect anyone else to? Come on, we've sat here and said there's no common honesty any more, haven't we? Is there anything wonderful about that, when there's no common honesty at the top?"

She gazed straight at him. They were sitting on the sofa. Her spirits had become higher, the more she let her anger fly. He looked so gaunt and sad that she put her hand on his sleeve.

"You wouldn't defend him, would you?"

"No, I don't see how I could."

198

"It makes me feel absolutely bolshie."

"I feel bolshie too."

They understood each other, regressing to the idiom of their youth. Lorimer muttered:

"I don't know how we keep up standards. We've got to."

After that, for a long time afterwards, Lorimer was silent, even for him. That is, though he made noises of acknowledgement as she talked, laying the table for their meal, he didn't volunteer a remark. When she again sat down beside him, he still stayed dumb. This wasn't just ordinary inarticulateness. Jenny was irritated, and at the same time strained, by the trouble inside him. She stared at the clock on the mantelpiece, its back reflected in the mirror (where had his bits of furniture come from?), ticking away. At last she broke out:

"Whatever is the matter, tell me?"

"We've got to keep up standards."

It was like him, having got hold of some words, not to let them go, Jenny thought with irritation. There he was, opening his mouth without speaking, like a fish, Jenny thought again, more irritated still. When he opened his mouth and did speak, she wasn't prepared.

"Are we? Keeping up standards, I mean. I mean to say—you know—are you?"

He was looking grey and embarrassed. At first she didn't catch any sense of it, and then half understood.

"You'd better go on," she said.

"I mean, are you sure about your father?" He was getting a trace more fluent. "Are you sure he wanted you to have all his money?"

"How can I be?" She was suddenly as embarrassed as he was.

"Are you sure he didn't want that woman to have it her own way?"

"How can I be?" she repeated. Then she reached inside for an honest answer.

"No I'm not."

"I've never been happy about it. I couldn't tell you, you know."

At last she understood why he had shied away, when she

199

talked about settlements and the appeal. She had misjudged him. Her diffidence had misled her. Whatever he wanted from her, it wasn't the chance of money.

"I rather wish you had."

"I couldn't manage it." A long awkward silence. Then:

"Jenny," (he scarcely ever called her by her Christian name, or, as far as that went, by any other appellation) "I don't think I like this Swaffield business."

"Nor do I."

"I mean, he may win the whole thing for you. But I don't know whether you ought to take it, you see what I mean."

"I see."

"I don't know about Swaffield. I shouldn't like to be in business with him, I do know that."

Dear God, Jenny was thinking to herself, that was pathetic. Swaffield would eat several brighter men than this any day before breakfast. And yet she was respecting him.

"What do you think I ought to do?"

He couldn't make himself clear. He seemed to be stuck with her father's intentions.

"That's impossible," she said. "We can't find out, we never shall."

Another silence.

"Can you stand up to Swaffield?" he said.

"I can stand up to anyone. If I'm certain that I have to."

"Well then, I'm trying to say that you shouldn't take more than your share."

"Who's to decide what is my share?"

"You'll have to do that for yourself, won't you?"

Jenny was practical. She wasn't going to make a martyr of herself, she said that martyrdom wasn't on. She didn't propose to give up the whole show, and let the other side win by default. But—he had touched a nerve. On the way back from that midnight soliloquy with Swaffield, Symington wasn't the only one who was struggling with disquiet. So was she.

For Symington, there was no question why he shall be. It was a matter of professional responsibility or, if you preferred a more grandiloquent name, of conscience, such as Symington had since been thrashing over so often with his wife. For Jenny there was nothing so sharp. She was being disturbed by motives she couldn't place. Maybe she wanted to behave according to her idea of decency, or even according to Lorimer's idea, stiffer than her own. Maybe this was some kind of conscience too: though Dr. Pemberton, if in possession of the facts, would have brusquely pointed out that Jenny, being a realistic woman, didn't like running perceptible risks when she might have a reasonable settlement for the asking. That was when people called conscience to the rescue, Dr. Pemberton would have remarked.

Jenny wouldn't have been got down by Pembertonian exercises in reduction. As she saw it, she and this man she trusted were trying to find a tolerable way to go. She didn't want to behave like a card sharper. On the other hand, there was no call for wildness. Those earlier wills were enough justification for keeping one's head. So she came back to the compromise which Swaffield was ordering her to throw away. She, and Lorimer too, were badly off. They were beginning to understand about inflation and soon they would be worse off. Compromise money would keep her from poverty for the rest of her time. It was honest enough, it was common sense.

So she and Lorimer were talking like the Symingtons. They had their own problem in situation ethics, though they hadn't heard the term. She could give instructions to Symington, whatever Swaffield said. What would be the price of that? Not so heavy as to Symington if he withdrew. Swaffield might turn vindictive, sack her from the one job she had enjoyed, demand his money back. Still she would be left with a considerable sum. The quarrel would be unpleasant. Shamefacedly, she would miss being on the fringe of Swaffield's court. It wouldn't be a disaster. As she explained this to Lorimer, telling him stories of Swaffield's entertainments, Lorimer said:

"I don't think I would like to shake hands with a man like that."

She believed that Lorimer was jealous and felt pleased. Perhaps by this time she had submerged a thought which earlier hadn't troubled her at all—that, though he was upright and wouldn't have performed any shady trick he denounced in others, there was bitter envy mixed up with the uprightness.

Now she wanted to think well of him, she liked to believe that his decency was pure.

She mustn't hurt Swaffield unnecessarily, she insisted. Oh yes, he was capable of being hurt. Much more important, she mustn't force Symington's hand. She owed something to him. Whatever happened, she mustn't involve him in difficulties with Swaffield.

Since they were in a similar situation to the Symingtons, they not surprisingly arrived at a similar conclusion, or absence of one. They did so no more repetitively than the Symingtons, though Symington was a trained professional. Trained professionals when arguing their way through ethical mantraps were as repetitive as anyone else. In fact, Lorimer, much the stupidest of the four, was the one who havered least: but he was also the one with least to lose.

In the end, they agreed, like the Symingtons, that it was wise to play for time. Jenny thought, rather less hopefully than the others, that Swaffield's present storm might subside. If that time didn't come, then, one way or the other, she would have to make the decision.

24

During January and February, Dr. Pemberton received more reports on Hillmorton's condition. The primary carcinoma had been discovered. It was in the prostate gland. That was no surprise, said Pemberton. But he might have noticed something wrong when he urinated, before the other signs developed? Not necessarily. Anyway, old men took that as a matter of course and didn't go to a doctor. More fools they.

He was being treated with deep X-ray therapy, Pemberton heard and gave a sceptical grunt. That meant more discomfort, and in his experience did no good. He saw no reason to alter his prognosis. He still guessed that Hillmorton had another year's grace, if one could call it grace. It was all going according to form.

Had he been told yet? The hospital doctor wasn't certain, but thought not. Or at least (he used a civil servant's phrase) not in terms. Pemberton had seen it all. He expected that Hillmorton saw the truth, and then had phases, quite long phases, of deluded hope. These terminal conditions, this one as much as others, more often than not carried fits of euphoria.

That wasn't so far from the truth. In his mind, suspicious, acute, not self-deceiving, Hillmorton hadn't any doubt. Yet sometimes doubts encouraged him, rosy doubts, the encouragement of mornings when he felt pretty well, mortality far away, still incredible.

What Dr. Pemberton didn't know, and wouldn't have been over-interested in if he had known, was that Hillmorton was behaving with a special kind of ruthlessness. In his mind he was preparing to die. That led him to display his stoicism, but a stoicism which spared no one round him. At last, he could dispense, after a lifetime of control, with the conventions of affection. He kept hold on his manners, but they were the manners of style, not the manners of the heart.

When he was not being treated in the hospital, he returned to the little bedroom in his youngest daughter's house. He made it clear, with detached politeness, whom he wanted to see, and even clearer whom he didn't want to see. So far as that daughter knew, her mother, his wife, came to visit him precisely once. She went away without tears, her expression unyielding, but her daughter believed—was she being sentimental, herself starting a happy marriage?—that she felt it the final disaster, that of being useless at the end. Another woman, whom the daughter had never seen before, came often, stayed long, and, though she called sometimes in the sitting room on her way downstairs and asked questions about nursing him, didn't give, or else concealed, her name. She seemed to be quite broken.

Hillmorton was as ruthless about which of his friends he chose to see. James Ryle, hearing by casual gossip in the House that he was ill, discovered from Liz (it was his only source of information, he could excuse himself) where her father was staying. Ryle wrote a note, full of hope for a quick recovery (at that time neither he nor Liz nor any of her sisters knew the truth) and offered to talk to him, read to him, do anything to pass the time. In reply, he received a letter in child-like calligraphy which he did not recognise.

"My dear James. How very kind of you! How typically kind! I must apologise for this scrawl, but I'm having to write with my left hand. But no, I cannot think of taking advantage of your good nature. This affliction of mine promises badly, or at least so I infer. I am really rather like a sick animal, and I don't wish to impose myself on anyone. I am better left alone with my thoughts, such as they are. However, thank you again for your kindness. Yours ever, Henry Hillmorton."

Ryle was snubbed and chilled. Even the signature was remote. He was used to Hillmorton signing himself Hal. He was more snubbed (such a wound still rankled, even though he now realised that Hillmorton was very ill) when Adam Sedgwick mentioned that he himself had written a letter, and had been immediately invited to call round. Ryle had to take it as a dismissal after being a friend for nearly twenty years. He believed that he had been a loyal friend. The only explanation he could find agreeable was that he was a man in robust mid-sixties health (anyone would have said the same of Hillmorton the year before). Maybe Hillmorton would be affronted by the sight of a healthy man but could bear that of a sick one. Or maybe Hillmorton had always thought that friendship was a pleasant civility, no more, and Ryle had only imagined that he possessed it.

Sedgwick had to hire a car to get himself driven to Beryl Road. It was a sunny February afternoon around three o'clock, the red brick houses behind Barons Court glaring in the level light, terraced houses built early in the century for the lower middle class now being smartened, property values rising. The house in Beryl Road was just one such. Sedgwick wasn't a rich man, he lived in a donnish house in Cambridge, but he had not been inside one like this since his undergraduate lodgings.

The driver had to help him along the crazy pavement. There was a decoration in coloured glass above the front door. Hillmorton's daughter let them in. From what Sedgwick recalled of Liz, whom he had met once or twice, this sister wasn't as pretty, or as strong featured, but gentler in manner.

"Lord Sedgwick? It's very good of you. My father is expecting you." She looked at him, timid because of his disability. "I'm afraid the stairs are rather steep."

"He'll get me up somehow." This wasn't a time to be proud: and the driver as good as carried Sedgwick up the flight of stairs. The house had two rooms and a kitchen on the ground floor and a symmetrical set above. Mrs. Dennis (Sedgwick had only just learned her married name) led them to the back bedroom, and there Sedgwick was lifted to a chair by the bedside.

"My dear Adam! This is very nice!" Hillmorton's voice had lost none of its resonance, but there was a trace of indistinctness in his speech, though not so marked as in Sedgwick's own.

The other two left them alone, Hillmorton waving a hand, saying that he would ring when Lord Sedgwick felt inclined to go.

As Sedgwick watched him—one mustn't watch too long, the glance was drawn and then turned away—Hillmorton did not appear gravely ill. His cheeks were thinner, perhaps there was a trace of yellow colouration near the bones, difficult to identify in the afternoon light. The flesh under his chin was sagging and the corners of his mouth pulled down: but Sedgwick had often seen them pulled down in detachment or sarcasm. He was lying on his back, impassively still.

On the bedside table there was a stack of books, the topmost of which was a volume of Greville's diary. This seemed a curious choice. To break the silence Sedgwick asked:

"Are you enjoying that?"

"It passes the time." Hillmorton added: "I shouldn't have expected it, but the time doesn't go very fast. Would you have expected that?"

"I don't know. Not yet."

"How are you?" It was a polite question, not interested in the answer.

Sedgwick said: "Much the same."

"Oh yes."

In fact Sedgwick felt better, sinfully better, warm with relief, sitting by this bedside: like someone who had been dragged from a car crash, knowing that his companions were still inside.

So as not to watch too much, he was glancing round the room. It was a neat spare room, something like fourteen feet by ten, a chest of drawers along the far wall, a dressing table parallel with the single bed: above the chest of drawers, a Utrillo reproduction. Through the window, at the far end, was a placid skyscape, cloudless, beginning to be gilded as the afternoon drew in: one turret was, not reaching into the sky, but standing firm against it.

"What's that?" said Sedgwick, making conversation again.

"Hospital. Fulham Hospital. My last stopping point, I think."

It was nearer, more convenient than the one where he was being treated, Hillmorton explained. Anyway, what did it matter? He spoke indifferently, not going out of his way to make the other comfortable.

"I suppose," he said, indicating the bedroom, "this is the last stopping point but one."

"Are you sure?"

"I should think so, shouldn't you?"

Even then, there was the faintest vestigial searching for reassurance, but Sedgwick couldn't give it. All he could say was:

"I hope not."

"It does seem rather strange, don't you know."

What? Coming towards death in this tidy suburban bedroom? Just dying? It had been said with an edge of incredulity, without fuss.

Hillmorton said: "I can still get about a bit. On good days I can walk to the pillar box. Not far. I might be able to come to the House again."

"Is that worth the effort?"

"I might manage a speech. Not long. I'd like to do better than last time."

Extraordinary, it seemed to Sedgwick, that that thought rankled now.

In precisely the same tone, level, matter of fact, slightly speculative, Hillmorton said:

"I don't want to die."

After a pause he went on: "Do you?"

"No."

"Are you afraid of death?"

It was some time before Sedgwick answered. He said:

"I'm certainly afraid of dying."

Another interval. Sedgwick went on: "And I think, I think, I'm afraid of annihilation. At least I don't like the prospect."

The thoughts were clear. The speech wasn't clear. A listener would have found it difficult to pick out what they were saying, either the impassive figure on the bed, or the twitching face above. But each could understand.

"You don't believe there's anything to come?" It was said dispassionately, but again there might be vestigial appeal. If so, Sedgwick was not the man to answer it. Did Hillmorton have any kind of faith?

Sedgwick said: "What can that possibly mean?"

"Most people have believed in an after life, haven't they?"

"I can't give it any meaning."

Hillmorton broke into a smile, a genuine malicious smile.

"You're not the most cheery companion for this particular occasion, are you?"

He went on: "That's why it's rather bracing to have you here, don't you know. After all, you must have thought about these things."

"Quite a lot, this last year or two." Sedgwick produced an equivalent smile.

"Adam," said Hillmorton and stopped. Then he said: "Why do we cling on to life so hard?"

"You've enjoyed yours, haven't you?"

"I'm not so sure."

"I've always thought you had."

"I suppose it's been an interesting life. That's as far as I should go." He added: "I've not done much, you know, I'm not leaving anything behind. That's where I envy you. You have your kind of immortality."

"No." Sedgwick was as positive as before. "I can't give that any meaning either."

He had known, he said, men who had sacrificed much to leave a memorial behind them, scientists, writers, the rest. It was as romantic as the hope of personal immortality. No scientist this century, not even Einstein or Dirac, would be more than a page or so in a text book in a hundred years. Science was an edifice, people like himself had added a small brick. With luck he might be a foot note in another text book.

"Call that immortality?" he said.

"You are pretty bleak with yourself, aren't you? I wish I'd known you better."

Hillmorton went on: "And yet a minor politician hasn't even that. That's all I was."

Each of them would have shrugged off kind words. Sedgwick said that it was unthinkable that anyone they had known would be remembered, genuinely remembered. The world had gone too fast for them. And yet, he confessed—and it was a confession—that he wanted to finish a piece of work before he had a brain operation.

"After what you've been saying—why? why?" Hillmorton was amused.

"Pride, perhaps. Or a silly bit of hope. It would be nice to bring something off to finish with."

"How long will it take?"

"I'll give myself till this time next year. I can't leave the operation any longer. It's my last chance."

"I suppose it is."

"I'm frightened of that too. I've been frightened all along."

Hillmorton said, looking up at the ceiling:

"Everything they've written about dying is no good. It's too pretty, it's nothing like the thing itself."

"I agree."

"Didn't someone write, Life to be sure is nothing much to lose. If he had known about dying he couldn't have written that. And doesn't it go on, But young men think it is, and they were young. Nonsense. Young men don't care about dying, they can't imagine it. I wasn't very brave when I was young, but I was much braver than I am now. And I expect you were too."

"Yes, I was."

"Books have nothing to tell us about dying. That's why I read Greville. Trivial stuff, but that's better than being pretty about—" he didn't finish.

"Do you have much pain?" said Sedgwick.

"Not much so far. Plenty of discomfort. General fading out. But if I have more pain, I shall want to live."

"I'm frightened of the operation. First of being put out for good. Secondly, being left worse than I am now. That could happen."

Hillmorton did not respond. At that point they were speaking without reference to each other, as though each were alone.

Suddenly Hillmorton had a return, perhaps to politeness, perhaps to companionship.

"Don't you find you become simpler, the closer it comes? I think one does as one gets older anyway. One hardens, one hasn't any use for the frills. But certainly I find it now. One doesn't care about anyone else."

Sedgwick was thinking of other persons mortally sick, behaving differently from this.

"Perhaps," said Hillmorton with a surge of cheerfulness, "that's what we are all really like all the time." He relaxed into what could have been either contemplation or hebetude.

After some moments Sedgwick said:

"I'm tiring you."

"No more than I'm tiring you."

"I'd better go."

Hillmorton said, "The moral of this is, there's nothing to look forward to. Have you thought of that?"

"Not yet."

"I'd like a pleasure to look forward to. I can't find one."

Again Sedgwick said: "I'd better go."

Hillmorton, expansive style resurrecting, pressed him to have a drink before he went. Sedgwick said that it was a peculiar time to drink (it was nearly half past four).

"Oh, time doesn't mean all that much to us now, should you say?"

He felt for the invalid's bell push his daughter had rigged up, using the thumb of his left hand.

"I rather fancy opening a bottle is beyond us, is that right?"

He was smiling with complicity, open about his incapacity and the other man's, rubbing it in that they had one working hand between them.

"Alcohol used to be a pleasure," he remarked as they were waiting. "It isn't now. I can't touch spirits. Not at all."

His daughter opened the door. His voice rang out, as it used to in the Bishops' Bar.

"Oh, my dear girl. Will you be very kind and open a bottle of champagne? It would be extremely kind of you. You're allowed a glass yourself."

The cork popped, glasses were filled, Sedgwick asked the young woman to bring up his driver in a quarter of an hour. She went away.

"Good health," said Hillmorton, using a greeting entirely out of character, as though deliberately chosen for the occasion.

Sedgwick managed, with two hands, to get his glass to his lips, spilling some on the way. He took a gulp. He had never drunk as heartily as Hillmorton, but he enjoyed champagne and did so now. Hillmorton sipped as though at a wine tasting, and shook his head.

"No," he said. He couldn't keep querulousness out of his tone. "I don't like the stuff. I never have. I can't find anything I like."

As they remained there, not speaking, once more his concept of hospitality took over. He rang for his daughter and asked her to fill Lord Sedgwick's glass. He said,

"Come again, Adam. If you can stand it, that is." Then he gave a final goodbye smile, half amiable, half sadistic. "After all, I'd do the same for you."

The night air was cold as Sedgwick, fending off the driver's arm, made his scurrying run along the strip of pavement to the front garden gate. Back in the car, he felt a kind of relief, but not quite the relief he had known after visits to other sick beds. He was thinking, how was he going to endure it? When he knew—which that night he didn't for certain, as Hillmorton must—that his term was fixed. Anyone could put on a show in public or with someone to watch. It wouldn't be difficult for most people to die with spirit on the scaffold, spectators down below. But when one was alone?

❧ 25 ❧

By a sheer and meaningless coincidence, on the afternoon when Sedgwick was paying that visit to Hillmorton's bedside, there was a conversation proceeding in which when healthy Hillmorton might have taken some interest. Symington telephoned Jenny to say that the "showdown" couldn't be delayed much longer. He was proposing to have one final frank (not really frank, for he would have to conceal the not irrelevant factor that Swaffield might still veto any settlement whatsoever) exchange with Skelding, to see—when all the palaver was dispensed with and the ceremonies properly performed—what figure, yes, crude figure, the other side would settle for. Of course, Symington and Skelding knew almost exactly, and had known for months, what was in the other's mind. Symington had told his wife so, in their arguments at Christmas. But there had been no hurry, and a few per cent either way meant thousands of pounds.

Now Symington was in more of a hurry. He wanted a definite lawyers' bargain to confront Swaffield with. He and Jenny would struggle to make him give way. If he wouldn't—but that Symington left in suspense, still not resolved about how he should act himself and believing that Jenny wasn't either.

It was a disadvantage, in this kind of bargaining as in most, to be more pressed for time than your opposite number. Symington knew that as clearly as any lawyer practising. He gave a good impersonation of a man without impatience, the exchange with Skelding was unwoolly, succinct and amiable, and they reached an agreement to present to their clients. Maybe—Symington was self critical about any of his professional jobs—he had given away a shade too much, a shade more than if he had been at leisure. Still, Swaffield apart or forgotten, it was an agreement that he would be happy enough to recommend to Jenny.

Skelding was happy too. A nice picture, two happy lawyers, one old established, one on the rise. Skelding wanted to make his own recommendation quickly. That meant a meeting with the Underwoods, and Skelding decided to ask Liz along. To give weight to the proceedings he invited their counsel David March to summon a conference. Skelding was proud of the amount he had secured. It satisfied his kindness, his concept of pastoral care, and also his modest self-importance, all at once. He not only wished to have the whole business signed and covenanted, he was not disinclined for a little subdued pomp and fuss. Accordingly they all met in the counsel's chambers in the Inner Temple a couple of days after Skelding had agreed on the bargain. March had asked them for five thirty in the evening, and one of his pupils was pouring out drinks, a large one for March himself, substantial ones, not quite so large, for Mrs. Underwood, Liz and Skelding, nothing for Julian.

That room in chambers was as shabby and dilapidated as March's own dress (now that he had taken off the gown he had been wearing in court, his collar was seen to be rumpled, his shirt not fresh), a room which only a successful counsel would afford. It had no more an air to impress than a station waiting room. Even the bookcases were half empty, and if inspected revealed only a few law books, more novels. Just for once, that might have been an affectation of an unaffected man. There was a library of law books in the ante-room close by. But March had an abnormally precise memory, something like a trick memory, and in his younger days had shown it off to clients and their solicitors. It had been part of his stock-in-trade at the Bar. As for the novels, that wasn't an affectation but a habit. They were the classical 19th Century novels in old editions, Tolstoy, Dostoevsky, Dickens, Trollope, Balzac, Galdós. Again in younger days, he had found them a comfort, allied with a good deal of whisky, when he was struggling against one of his depressive phases. No writer this century, he had been heard to announce in his Johnsonian fashion, had taught him anything about people that he didn't know better than they did: but he had learned quite a lot from their predecessors.

"Well," he said, bulking above the rest, at the same time slack and massive, "shall we get round the table?"

The table was large, covered with green baize as though in a bureaucrat's room in Eastern Europe. Apart from March's desk chair and a wide settee on which he liked to lie and read, it was normally the only piece of furniture in the room, though that evening other chairs had been brought in from outside. They sat round it, March at one end, Mrs. Underwood on his right, Julian on his left, Skelding opposite to him, Liz and a couple of his pupils seated in between. There was dim lighting from a chandelier above the table and a green shaded reading lamp on the desk. One of the pupils switched on the standard light beside the settee and that shone upon the faces of those on March's right.

"You had something to tell us, Eric, I think," said March down the table. Skelding had, and proceeded to tell it. He was not deterred, any more than he had been at the disclosure of the will eighteen months before, by the fact that he had already reported the terms of the offer to Mrs. Underwood. That is, she, Julian and Liz already knew all that he was saying, and March—with whom he had had a telephone conversation—most of it. This did not deter Eric Skelding, nor detract at all from his simple pleasure. He was speaking with the enthusiasm, as though astonished himself at what he had just discovered, of one who is at liberty to confide a state secret.

He was not going to be fretted into cutting his pleasure short. March, who accepted that Skelding was a most good-natured man, far more so than himself, thought it was a pity that good-natured men could be so preternaturally boring. This could have been said in five minutes. It wasn't. Preliminary talks with 'young Symington,' putting out feelers, premature talk of figures, hints of Symington suggesting twenty-five per cent, all explained with merciless love, like water dripping in a bedroom. Story of the local vicar, everyone agreed that the court of appeal wouldn't admit the evidence; further, if it had been given before Mr. Justice Bosanquet it wouldn't have convinced him.

"Which seems rather to reduce its relevance," March couldn't resist inserting.

Skelding gave a broad beaming smile. He disarmed criticism when he was being tedious by saying that he was. That didn't make him hurry. He went into intricacies about the second round of bargaining.

"I could feel I was upping them. Upping them," he said, proud of his command of the modern language. "I could feel in my bones that they were ready to go up to thirty-five per cent. One feels one's way. That wasn't the time to seem to argue. We went into a state of suspended animation."

That concept appeared to Skelding very funny, more so than to his audience.

"Then young Symington happened to come across me in the club, accidentally on purpose if you follow my interpretation, and this was a different cup of tea. He meant business, and I would have bet my boots that if we didn't settle now we never should. Cards on the table. This time he didn't mind mentioning figures. Forty per cent he said, that's a fair offer. I'd always had at the back of my mind that we should ask for half and then expect that at the end of the day we should have to come down. Not quite good enough, I said. Fifty per cent would be more suitable. I knew, and he knew, that that wasn't really on. In their position they couldn't do it. No responsible people could. Young Symington is quick off the mark when he wants to be. He said, 'I'll meet you half way. Forty-five per cent.' I didn't want to be precipitate, I thought I might stand out for another one or two per cent. I explored a bit more, but then I thought, was it wise to open our mouths too wide? To cut a long story short, I told young Symington that I would be prepared to lay that offer in front of my clients."

Skelding subsided, like an exceptionally modest conjurer, trick triumphant, backing into the limelight.

"To cut a long story short," said March, elephant-eyed. "I must say, Eric, it sounds as good as we shall get. Better than I reckoned on."

He meant that. The method of slow talk, they would call it: but it often worked. The unborable made good bargainers.

"Yes, it is," said Liz with urgency.

"Well done," said Mrs. Underwood, also with urgency.

One of the pupils asked if this type of negotiation often required so many steps.

"One feels one's way," said Eric Skelding, again with modesty.

"Give Mr. Skelding another drink and a pat on the back," said March to the other pupil. "Well, this is about the end. We seem to be home and dry. With a certain amount of honour."

Julian threw back his head and gave a long, hilarious, hooting laugh.

"I've been doing some sums," he announced, with his most infantile expression.

"Have you?" said March, off hand and uninterested.

"I'm not very good at arithmetic, of course," Julian went on. "So I hope I've got it right."

Actually, his mother and Liz both knew that he had gone over his calculations like old Gobseck counting pieces of gold, or an addict checking his football pools on Saturday night: but neither knew what he was going to say next.

"I make it that, all the pennies paid out, all of you getting your whack, including the Senior Partner—"

"Who the hell is the Senior Partner?" March was getting restive.

"The Chancellor of the Exchequer, of course. Well, when you've all dipped your fingers in, I stand to collect about £60,000 clear. And our dear friend Mrs. Rastall about £70,000. Do correct me if I've done it wrong."

"It's early days to make an estimate," said Skelding, prudent and paternal. "But perhaps one can say that's somewhere near the mark."

"All agree?" said Julian, brightly smiling.

No one disagreed.

"Yes." Julian gave another laugh. "Then I'm very sorry to

disturb the beautiful harmony of this beautiful afternoon. I am so very sorry. But I'm not playing."

"You can't do this," cried Liz. She had been anxious all along. He had said nothing to her, but she had learned the air of satisfied salacious delight with which he kept a secret.

"You don't know what you're talking about," said March.

"I really think I do. After all I'm the principal beneficiary. That gives me some sort of standing, shouldn't you say?"

"I'm afraid," Skelding remained reasonable, "you haven't considered all the consequences."

"I rather think I have. All we have to do is to go on with this appeal. We shall win it. And Bob's your uncle."

"You're not a lawyer," March was now exerting himself. "You'd be foolish if you didn't listen to lawyers."

"Oh, I am very foolish, very often, ask anyone."

"For God's sake stop it," said Liz.

"Just for the record, I did read law, a little, once." Julian gazed open-eyed at March.

"That's worse than useless, as you ought to know."

"No, I learned one thing. Everyone always gets everything wrong."

That was said with consummate cheek. March, for once misjudging an opponent, brushed him off.

"Any lawyer in England will tell you that the appeal is more likely than not to fail. Appreciably more likely than not. Your opinion isn't worth wasting time over."

"Please listen," said Mrs. Underwood to her son across the table.

"Darling. Be said," begged Liz, in agitation regressing to an old lower-class idiom that she must have picked up from a nanny.

"This isn't your affair," he said with sexual contempt. It was said quietly, but for an instant the table was silent and constrained.

"You had all better leave this to me." March took command. In the doughy face the small acute eyes were fixed on Julian.

"I tell you, this cock won't fight. The odds are against. The appeal hasn't a good enough chance. We have an excellent settlement."

"Not excellent enough."

"It's time you used a little common sense, which I hope you possess."

The struggle had become confined to the two men. Because that was so, to the others it appeared to last longer than the clock time showed. On one side, March, massive, weighty, bringing out all his personal resources, as a matter of technique letting his sarcasms fly. On the other Julian, talking like a playboy, facetious, not respectful, not appearing to care what March thought of him. Between them there weren't even the amenities. March didn't conceal, not only disregard, but scorn or something like revulsion.

Julian wasn't moved. He mightn't know much law, he said, but he could read. Any appeal judge reading the court proceedings would get a neutral impression. Personalities wouldn't enter, the facts would tell. The facts were strong.

"For God's sake," replied March, "do you think you're capable of judging?"

Julian replied, "Do you? Does anyone?"

"I'm trying to decide," said March, "whether the course of action you'd like to persuade us into is more irresponsible than just plain stupid."

March sounded reflective. He was in control of his tongue as he was in court, but there was temper smouldering underneath.

He said: "I do find it difficult to decide. I'm trying to."

"Go on trying," said Julian encouragingly. "But I don't think this is getting very profitable, do you? Anyway, I really fancy I've had enough of it. I may as well give you a reason you might possibly be able to understand. You see, £60,000 odd is no good to me. I can't live on that as I should rather like to live. I can just as well potter on as I am. If I collect the whole pool, that makes a difference. So it's worth going all or nothing. Anyone understand?" He gazed round the table and then back to March.

"Oh, and by the way, you said something about me persuading you into this. That's not quite the position, as it happens. I hate to be crude, but I'm not persuading you, I'm telling you. Sorry."

Liz plucked his sleeve, her face white, lines deep in her forehead. She whispered, and others caught the word "realistic."

"No." Julian spoke to her audibly, quite gently this time. "I'm much more realistic than you when it comes to the point."

His mother, who had scarcely uttered throughout the altercation, looked in what seemed hopelessness or surrender towards Skelding. He stirred from his seat like a man making a formal statement:

"I have to say to you that this would be a dreadful mistake."

"That's the least of it," March said.

"Well, you can always get out, you know." Julian's innocent eyes were bright and shining. "I'm sure I could find another counsel who won't mind dipping in for his whack of the costs. I'm sure I can find another solicitor too, Mr. Skelding, if you really find it too intolerable. And we shall all perfectly understand."

March gave a rough outburst of a laugh.

"No. Speaking for myself, if you insist on throwing good money after bad, I'll take it. I'll do the appeal as well as anyone else you'd get. Any competent man would be about as good. But it wouldn't be sensible to switch horses now."

That was the end. No further argument. Skelding said that the other side would have to be informed. Negotiations had failed. No settlement was acceptable. Skelding said that in the rounded tones of a life time's practice, and no one gave a thought to what he was feeling, or imagined that he might be feeling anything.

March nodded without expression or even interest, dismissing the case from his mind. After all, this fool was his client, he had none of Symington's professional complications.

As the others broke up and left the room, March was sitting at the table and pouring himself a drink.

At their ritual dinner that Friday he told his friend Lander about the conference, the result of which Lander had, through Symington as Jenny's lawyer, already heard.

"It was a triumph of will. Just sheer will," said March, with a puzzled candid smile. "I didn't think I was easy to get down.

But that wretched layabout had more will than I had. Much more than anyone there. It shows how wrong you can be."

March, though he had an honest mind, didn't relish confessing defeat. It might have been a consolation, if someone disinterested had told them that, in a certain restricted sense, Julian had a stronger will than anyone connected, even peripherally, with the Massie business. Stronger than those of eminent worthies such as Hillmorton or Ryle: stronger perhaps than Swaffield's, who might be the nearest competitor. It took an abnormally strong will to live as Julian had lived, doing nothing which he didn't want to do. It wasn't admirable, it could be at the same time silly and destructive, but it was there. His mother knew this. She had lost in every conflict of wills since he was a child. His women knew it, Liz most clearly of all. Maybe it gave him his power over them.

Neither March nor Lander had any idea of that particular power of Julian's. They wouldn't have liked him better if they had. Over the dinner table Lander was expressing the simple desire to kick his arse. They speculated a little on the motive behind his final piece of obstinacy. It might be simply the money, as he had declared. Mixed with motiveless mischief? Or was it conceivable that he wanted revenge—revenge for his mother being humiliated by old Bosanquet. "Too subtle," said Lander. "That's giving him too much credit."

Then March was ruminating on the part will played in human affairs. Far more than personal relations, he had long ago decided. People didn't do anything for you because they were fond of you. That was what the unworldly thought. Or because you had done something for them. There was an old folk saying—was it Russian?—'Why does he hate me so much? I've never done him any good.' No, affection didn't count much, except with exceptionally fine characters. Will counted much more; so did fear. If they knew your will was stronger or were afraid of you, you sometimes won. It was even better if they knew or felt that you were cold inside. That was the sort of man who, for many, captured loyalty. Probably it was true of "that beastly creature" (Julian).

"Not much hope for us," said Lander, as usual rubbing it in.

As a result of Julian's victory, the two of them would be opponents again in the Court of Appeal. They knew each other's talents to the syllable, and there Lander would have a slight edge.

"Want a small bet on it?" he said, not being a betting man.

"Perhaps not this time," said David March, who was.

Swaffield had to be informed by Symington that their own conference, which would have been convened within a fortnight, was pointless now. Swaffield was furious. Furious with Symington for bringing such news, responding like other potentates to anyone who brought bad news. Swaffield also had a shrewd idea that Symington hadn't obeyed his instructions, or had been trying to slip through them.

Swaffield, whose impulses didn't die down but reinforced themselves, had been looking forward to a final act of assertion. He had also been looking forward to a scene with Meinertzhagen, Haydon-Smith and anyone whom they chose to bring along, not a nice quiet gentlemanly scene this time. That would have given Swaffield considerable satisfaction. As it was, he had made a gesture, a poor half-hearted gesture, for nothing. Doing himself some harm.

Swaffield frequently wanted to make gestures, but except among his dependents restrained himself. They were an indulgence, and in action, though not in his rebellious outsider's soul, he didn't go in for indulgences. So now, fuming internally, taking it out on any member of his court within hearing, he set to work to repair channels of communication. Meinertzhagen, Haydon-Smith, half a dozen other bleeders and their bitches of women (Swaffield was talking to himself) had better be invited to some function they would be too mean to give themselves.

Meanwhile, Symington and Jenny had no chance to show how they would have behaved if it had come to the crisis. They didn't know for certain and in the nature of things couldn't know when they looked back. Nor did those closest to them. In secret Alison Symington, loving her husband, believed he would have taken the line which, so she had to infer, David March had taken. He would have found it a moral strain, and he wouldn't have pretended it wasn't, but in the end he would have accepted it. He lived in this mundane world and there were limits to responsibility. Alison also thought that one day, perhaps only once, he would break through those limits. But it wouldn't have been this time. She was relieved that he hadn't been tested.

On the other hand, Lorimer, who had a simple faith in Jenny, didn't doubt what she would have done. She had her courage, she had her honour, and she would have lived up to them. Jenny herself wasn't by any means so certain. Splitting irrevocably with Swaffield—that meant security thrown away, and yet, after all, she was too practical not to count the credits. Any settlement, even with all the money she would have to repay Swaffield, would bring her quite a lot of cash down. And also (and here perhaps she underrated herself, and Lorimer was nearer the truth) she liked being honest and behaving according to her code. Perhaps she would have done so. Only God, in whom she didn't believe, could know. If she had, she would have enjoyed a rip-roaring row with Swaffield, as much as he would the one of which he had been deprived.

❧ 26 ❧

Liz did not realise how often she repeated herself. She was obsessive, of course, in her love: but it came out too on habits on which she didn't spare a thought. So, when once more anxious and adrift after Julian's coup at the lawyers' conference, she was once more engrossed about her father's money: and once more she telephoned James Ryle.

It was the call he had awaited so long, telling himself it wouldn't happen, it oughtn't to happen. When he received it, he was happy. How foolish could a sensible man be, he thought. He could console himself, though it wasn't much of a support, that at least he had behaved like a sensible man. He had taken no initiative, and wouldn't have done. Yet, talking on the telephone, he was happy. Eagerly, more eagerly than he approved of, he invited her to dinner. The Connaught? it was a decent place for dinner, or used to be. Yes, she wanted to talk. Yes, he understood.

Talk she did. She preceded him through the main dining room while he noticed her quick poised walk, something like an actress's strut, only possible if you had good muscles. He had secured a table in the corner, and almost as soon as they sat down she was describing the scene in chambers.

Ryle had begun with small, or even miniature, talk, saying that he used to dine here often in the war, when the American Ambassador had a table by the door. Liz had scarcely pretended to listen. Her manners, which had once been brisk but engaging, had that night completely dropped away. She had once been conscious that men found her attractive, and responded to them. Now she didn't even recognise that Ryle had feeling for her. The only important thing, the only thing that existed, was how, and why, Julian had "turned everything upside down."

Ryle was reminded—with sarcasm, not pleasure—of an occasion three or four years before, when his wife was gravely ill and himself worn down and looking for solace. He had asked to dinner a widow who had been intimate with both of them. She didn't enquire about either, but immediately launched into a monologue, informing him enthusiastically how, by endowing small prizes in schools, she was preserving her husband's memory. Well, there were plenty of egotisms, all of them hard, but you had to go a long way to find any harder than the egotisms of love.

"Why has he done it? Tell me that?" Liz demanded.

"Of course, you have to remember that I scarcely know him," said Ryle, giving a credible impersonation of a judicious old codger.

She was thrashing over the possible motives, as she had done obsessively to herself. Some were the same as the two counsel had discussed in their club, with more amusement, with considerably less pride. Through it all, Ryle couldn't help detect that there was pride, admiration, subjugation, because Julian had prevailed over them all. But why? Money—did anyone care enough about money to insist on a risk like this? Just for the chance, not too good a chance, of getting twice as much.

"I shouldn't," said Ryle. "But then I'm not a gambler, I never have been."

"The point is, is he?"

"You should know, shouldn't you?"

"I don't. There are times when I don't know him at all. After all this while."

She broke out, telling Ryle that, since the conference, Julian had been "extraordinarily nice" to her. Nice, what a word, Ryle thought. Did she mean tender or ardent or what?

Then she produced the motive which Lander and March had also played with. Was Julian really trying to make amends to his mother.

"Not very likely, I should have thought," said Ryle. "What good would it do?"

It was clear that Liz was jealous of Mrs. Underwood, with jealousy of the same nature, maybe not so active, as that— which Liz had been culpably slow to recognise—Mrs. Underwood bored her.

"What's she like?" said Ryle.

For the first time that evening she smiled at him, reacting to sympathy.

"She's not really my favourite woman, as a matter of fact."

"I doubt if she'd be mine."

"She loves him more than anything in the world, though," said Liz. "That's something in her favour."

Liz had been drinking more than he did, Ryle observed. He had seen that before: but then women of her age drank more than those he had taken out as a young man. While, though the food was good, she was only pecking at it. Not a good sign, the young Ryle might have considered. There had been one or two women he had been fond of, who had no appetite, and they had been choosey or frenetic about sex. Even that night in the Connaught, opposite this intent handsome face, he recalled that in the old English marriage service the wife promised to be "bonair and buxom in bed and at board." Enraptured with this woman he might be, but that didn't prevent him wondering or doubting.

At last she produced a motive which wouldn't have occurred to March or Lander. Was it all to do with her? This was an old fear. Was Julian designing this manoeuvre in order to escape her? Lose everything, and then tell her that he couldn't possibly marry her or anyone else?

"I don't think I believe that," said Ryle.

"Why don't you?" She was looking straight at him. In the shielded restaurant light her eyes, pigmented green in daytime, were full black. Her gaze was fierce, insistent, and suddenly trusting, because this was what she needed to hear. But she didn't hear quite that.

"We all imagine, don't we, that when someone we are attached to does something strange, that we've come into the calculation. It's not what I've found, more often than not. People are driven by their own wild horses, not by anyone else's.

We're not as central to anyone else's doings as we'd like to flatter ourselves." (Was that entirely true? Someone else could be central in one's thoughts, perhaps in one's actions, in the first grip of addictive love. At the moment, Ryle was about as central to Liz's thoughts as the waiter who had just refilled her glass.)

Ryle went on, talking as temperately about personal relations as another sensible man, David March, and coming to a similar conclusion.

"As I've said, I don't know the man. I'm prepared to believe he's out of the ordinary, nothing makes sense otherwise, but I don't believe he's utterly different from the rest of human kind."

Liz gave what on another woman would have seemed a sheepish smile.

"So I'm willing to bet a modest sum that whatever's making him perform like this—which sounds pretty near the confines of lunacy, between ourselves—whatever's making him perform, is just himself. He may be wanting to cut a dash. After all, he hasn't done much to justify himself, if you don't mind me saying so. Or it may be the money. He may have been telling the truth. People do, sometimes, you know."

"I suppose that's intended to be a comfort," said Liz.

"It's intended to be what you ought to come to terms with."

"Right." She said, very sharply: "Now about my father."

"Yes?"

"How much can you tell me?"

"Very little."

"Have you been to see him?"

"No." After a pause, Ryle added: "I offered to. But he didn't wish it."

"You're one of his closest friends."

"So I thought." Ryle said it simply.

"How ill is he?"

"Very seriously, I'm afraid."

"Yes, I had heard that."

The extraordinary thing to Ryle was that she seemed to have heard no more.

"How seriously?" she asked.

"I've only had a second-hand report."

"What is it?"

"I don't want to alarm you—"

"Tell me straight."

"It sounds like cancer, but I don't know for certain."

She sat, brooding, looking as she would when she was much older.

"I must go and see him," she said.

"I think you should. He'll be bound to see you."

"I must see him."

She didn't say much else. She had a glass of brandy, and then another. Ryle felt the years. At his age, brandy was one drink he kept off. He didn't relish waking up at three in the morning, his heart thumping.

Liz had accomplished her business and was ready to go, but a relic of politeness kept her sitting beside him. Another relic of politeness made Ryle help her to depart. He saw her into a taxi in Carlos Place. She kissed his cheek, the kind of kiss which men and women in their world exchanged every day of the week, unlike the manners of his youth. It was the only contact he had with her.

Next day Liz discovered that her father was in hospital, having deep X-ray therapy. He was too tired to see anyone. Shortly he would be returning to her sister's. He would still be fatigued after treatment, but in a fortnight or so he should be able to receive a visit.

It was not till late March that Liz, waiting restlessly, heard that he was well enough. Taking a morning off, she drove out to Beryl Road. Ryle, who had thought it extraordinary that she knew so little about her father's illness, would have thought it even more so that she only once before had been inside her sister's house. But then, Ryle had no experience of living in a family of strangers. As a rule, amiable and cordial strangers. Her young sister greeted her with pleasure. There was a gap of a dozen years between them, very little life had been shared. But some things didn't need to be said.

He seemed better, said her sister, a little better.

"Are you sure?" said Liz.

"No one can be sure," said her sister, as firmly as she spoke herself. "There might be intermissions, they might go on for some time. No one has much idea."

In the small neat living room (a little Etty over the mantel-piece, which Liz remembered, it must have been extracted from the Suffolk home) Liz, talking of their father, was having another kind of suppressed, subliminal response. At a first sight of that Beryl Road house, Adam Sedgwick, used to middle-class space, had thought he couldn't live there. Not so Liz, who had once been used to more luxurious space. She had a feeling, almost inadmissible, that if she could take Julian there for good and all, this would be her refuge. The narrow room would make them safe.

She went upstairs with her sister, and then alone into the back bedroom. Her father was sitting in an arm chair near the window, reading. She entered and called out. He turned to-wards her quite quickly and said:

"My dear girl, how are you?"

"I'm not interrupting, am I?" She was nervous, more ner-vous because she had said something so awkward, so imbecile.

"You scarcely could, in the circumstances, could you? But I'm very glad to see you. I was told you were coming, as a matter of fact."

"How are you?"

"More or less defunct. Slightly less defunct than I was a month or so ago. But I need hardly say, that may be wishful thinking."

In fact, though she couldn't know it, he looked appreciably better than during Sedgwick's visit. His cheeks were no thin-ner, and the jaundiced tinting was visible only under the lower lids. His manner was different also. Whatever she had ex-pected, she hadn't expected to find so much of his old ur-banity.

"What's that you're reading?" She couldn't prevent another foolish question coming out.

"To tell you the truth, Paléologue's memoirs. He was the French Ambassador to old St. Petersburg just before the Revo-lution. It's a slight comfort, don't you know, to read about peo-ple who are shortly going to be as unfortunate as oneself."

He was smiling at her, ready to be detached, discursive. She hadn't come for this.

"They were also quite remarkably inept. I wonder, I do wonder, whether in the same position our own upper classes would have been quite so inept. I daresay we should. I can't believe we have been very clever about the miners." (This was a reference to the strike that spring, said with an elder statesman's satisfaction.) "But I like to think that a few of us if we'd been in Petersburg might have shown a grain of sense. By the by, the chap Paléologue wrote very elegant French. I'm reading him in French. I had a French governess, you know. Not that I was anything like really first-class at it. I did get sent up for good occasionally once upon a time. I suppose that at my very best I might have sounded something like a Flemish Belgian, required to speak the other language, more or less educated, but distinctly out of practice."

He appeared gratified by the comparison. He gazed at her in his familiar hooded manner and said:

"My dear girl, what's your French like?"

"Awful."

"I don't suppose we ever had you taught properly. That was very remiss. What a pity. What a pity."

"How are you? How are you, really?" she broke out.

"Well, mortality is certain for all of us, isn't it? It's slightly more certain for me than it is for some."

Her voice became even harder, more intense.

"How are you? I want to know."

"If you want to know how long I've got, I am afraid that I can't tell you. They don't tell me, and I suppose I might be regarded as having a certain interest in the subject. The charitable assumption is that they haven't much notion themselves."

Did he realise how his manner was transformed from that in which he had talked to Sedgwick? Of course, he was a good deal of an actor. It was natural for him to put on an act. He was happy doing so, he felt more like himself. Physically this was one of his better days. Perhaps he only spoke as he had to Sedgwick when the metabolic tide was running low.

He enquired, as though with academic interest:

"But, my dear girl, why should you specially want to know? I can't matter to you all that much, I should have thought. That is, once you've accepted the fact of my comparatively rapid disappearance—"

"That's not so easy."

Suddenly he smiled at her, with the kind of smile which used to tease her when she was a little girl.

"Oh, there is a point, isn't there? I ought to have remembered. I have to survive another six years or so before that little gift of mine comes to you in full. You're right to think of that, it would be stupid not to."

"Not only that." Her expression was dark, blaming someone, herself or him. "Not only that."

"Not only that? But a little of it, wouldn't you say? You're not going to pretend?" He was still teasing her, more affectionate than she was used to. He was looking at her, seeing his daughter's face afresh. It was a good classical face, not fluid, not easily mobile. Good ivory skin, blood suffusing it now. He would guess that she cried more with rage than with pleading. She wasn't far from crying at this moment. All his life with women, he had wanted to lighten the moment in which one stood.

"Well, you know, I don't think you ought to reckon on that money. Six years is a long time in the present situation. Mind you, I'd do it to oblige, but I can't make any promises. I'd do it for my own sake as well as yours."

"For God's sake," she burst out. "I've told you, that isn't all of it."

"Look here, my girl, we are neither of us particularly sanctimonious, when it comes to the bone, don't you agree? You're more like me than you'd prefer to think. I've talked a lot of sugar-coated nonsense in my time. I don't expect you have. But I suggest that we might as well dispense with it now."

She forced a smile. The tears had retracted, but while she had been pretending her concern before, she felt it now.

"Better," he said. "It's very curious, don't you know," he took on his air of pleasurable discursion, "how entirely minor pieces of legislation can produce some rather surprising results. In my time, it was quite common to visit elderly relatives and have a lively interest in when they proposed to quit this mortal scene. The sooner the better, since one stood to gain a certain amount of money when they were safely put away. I remember watching the declining years of a very nice uncle of mine. Of whom I was distinctly fond. And from whom I had considerable expectations, which I am glad to say in due course were realised. But even when his demise was as good as published in *The Times*, he lingered on for years. I thought that was inconsiderate of him. I don't want to overpraise myself, my dear girl, but I very much doubt whether I'm enormously more selfish than the majority of the human race. One speculates on how many persons have spent too long a time dying, for the peace of mind of their nearest and dearest."

That was a reflection which would have seemed congenial, though he couldn't know it, to his heir, Dr. Pemberton.

"But now," Hillmorton said, "we have cleverly introduced a new refinement. Owing to our seven year clause about gifts, which we both happen to be familiar with, don't we? Now, instead of sitting beside an elderly relative, as I did beside my uncle, with a certain mixture of emotions, including both affection and a desire, possibly reluctant, that he shall shortly depart—we now sit beside an elderly relative, with the same mixture of emotions, except for one trifling change. We now have to desire that he should somehow remain. At least for seven years, or whatever is the term required. Very interesting. Should you say that was an improvement in civility, my dear Elizabeth?"

He was proud after this piece of exposition, as proud as when he had sat down after a satisfactory speech: not that any speech of his, at any time, in any place, could have been as uncompromising as this. Liz, other feelings dissolved, felt proud too. In her childhood she had always enjoyed him most when he wasn't on his best behaviour, or when, as she then thought, he was pretending to be bad.

Tired, too tired to talk much more, he asked out of politeness how her affairs were going.

"You mean Julian?" she said.

He nodded.

"No change," she said.

"I was afraid of that."

"There can't be any. Yet," she said, as tartly as when she first confronted him. Then she told him that they were going ahead with the appeal. Through his tiredness he brightened.

"Is that wise?" he asked. "Is that really wise?"

"He thinks so."

"Ah yes."

Liz explained that they could have compounded for a tolerable settlement, but he wouldn't have it.

"Ah yes," said Hillmorton again, as indicating both negative surprise and his opinion of Julian. He asked when the appeal would be decided.

No one was certain, she said. Towards the end of the year, she expected.

"Oh, I should like to hear the result of that. I hope I manage to. I do hope so."

He said that with a curious simplicity, not at all sarcastic, not pathetic, just telling her his wish. She thought she had stayed too long and that it was time to say goodbye.

PART THREE

❧ *27* ❧

More than once that summer James Ryle recalled asking Hillmorton in Brooks's whether anything was wrong, and being told that it was only a slight malaise. Ryle recalled it, because that seemed some sort of description of his own state. Not physically: he felt as well as he had for years past. But he was disturbed, nerves too near the surface, in a way he had not learned to cope with, as though he were living his life backwards.

The charm, and it had been a charm, of feeling the spring of love again had now quite left him. It was humiliating. It was ludicrous, to be hankering after a woman who scarcely noticed him. She never would. He hadn't seen anyone more totally surrendered to immolating love. He was enough in control of himself to accept that.

The more he saw of her, the more unarguable it was. He saw a good deal of her, unable to put her off when she called for his company, that early summer. Once she had managed to quarrel with Julian, and left him for a couple of weeks. Several nights running, she sat with Ryle in the Lords' guest room and went out with him to dinner in the town. Ryle had moments of ridiculous pride, when he noticed eyes following her. Then she went back to Julian. The telephone didn't ring any more. Again she had to be put out of mind.

Submerge one worry and another flooded in. Censor thoughts of Liz, and others, just as sombre, took their place.

They might have seemed impersonal. Perhaps they were less humiliating than an old man's youthful reveries. In fact, Ryle took to worrying about the fate of the country, more than he had since the beginning of the war, and he was as morbid as when he thought of Liz.

There were plenty of objective reasons for worry, he told himself. How were they all going to come out of this mess? He was still, in his fashion, tough minded. He didn't anticipate anything dramatic. The nation-states wouldn't suddenly collapse. The capitalist world wouldn't collapse, certainly not in the United States; it had proved remarkably resilient, and would stay so for foreseeable time. So incidentally would the collectivist world.

Ryle didn't envisage any cataclysmic change in his sons' time. His own country? Was it going to become a poor relation on the western side? Quite likely. It might turn into a bigger, more ramshackle, more internally fissured Sweden, social democratic, trade union controlled, nothing like so efficient. That might be the best prospect. Others were darker.

Ryle was finding an excuse for his discontents. If he had been happy, he would have searched for a different future. It was anyone's guess, whether he would have found it.

London, the summer of 1972. It remained, Ryle admitted to himself, the most comfortable capital in the world to live in. Unexacting. Presumably, when the English were more strenuous, it hadn't been so unexacting. Ryle, whom foreigners sometimes considered very English, liked it as it was. Manners, in shops, in the streets, were less gentle than they used to be: among his own acquaintances, rather more so.

He went out to dinner, not so often in private houses these days, the food much better than in his youth, more wine drunk, far more spirits (and far more than in the 19th Century, his historian's mind observed). He still had occasional business in the morning: he sat on the board of a merchant bank, and on a couple of others. Those would go on until he was seventy. In the afternoons and evenings, the House of Lords. For some men, getting near retirement, it would have been a tolerable way to pass their time, as until recently it had for him.

Were any of the people he met as worried as he was? He

didn't mean about a woman, though some must have been. One or two, he knew, were in various kinds of sexual trouble. As for himself, he believed that he had kept an imperturbable front and that no one, except perhaps Hillmorton, now beyond interest, had seen his secret. But was anyone worried about the future, short term or long?

Again some must have been, Ryle couldn't doubt it. Yet, if they were, they concealed it irritatingly well. Even in the luncheon room at the bank, secluded, leisurely, well fed, the faces weren't strained, they might have been conducting financial affairs in the City of London in the reign of Edward VII. Money was frightened, of course; but money had been frightened before, and would be again. They discussed it with interest, as doctors might have discussed a tiresome endemic disease. As for what they were doing with their own money, that was not discussed. Nothing was more unmentionable. Ryle had attended many board meetings, but he had never heard a hint which would have earned him a legitimate penny, except what he could have interpreted himself through reading the papers.

Meinertzhagen, who had once paid that friendly visit to Swaffield, was one of his colleagues on the bank's board. Meinertzhagen exuded absolute faith in the Government, like a bishop who was a shade more catholic than the Pope.

"All they have to do is to stick on course," he assured the luncheon table, not that they appeared to need assurance. "They'll keep their nerve." Meinertzhagen also exuded confidence that before long they would have "the country" behind them.

It all reminded Ryle of similar people when he was a young man, both before and during the war. It didn't add to his own confidence, that before the war they had been dead wrong. Yet, during the war, exactly the same phlegm and lack of foresight had turned out useful. It was only intellectuals who had confessed to one that we were going to lose. Phlegm was valuable when there was no point in foreseeing. There were plenty of occasions when, with enough foresight, one wouldn't act at all.

Nevertheless, there were times when Ryle, in his present

mood, wondered how many men had ever been as complacent as these. He had lived among acquaintances like Hillmorton for a long time now. But he felt, as though reverting to his youth, that he didn't belong there. Hillmorton used to have his flashes of detachment. As for the rest of them? Had any governing class, or one time governing class, been as thoughtless as these? Was this how a governing class slid out? Thoughtless might not be fair—Ryle was trying to handle his own gloom. Maybe short-sighted was nearer: and, even with men as shrewd as Meinertzhagen, preposterously uninformed.

Ryle needed some intelligent conversation. He wanted to know what the Treasury boys were thinking. It was for that reason, and not because there was the chance of filial intimacy, that he telephoned his son Francis and asked him to drop in one evening after the office.

Actually, since Whitehall was so near James Ryle's apartment, Francis not infrequently 'dropped in.' Those two were on affable terms, but were getting no closer. As Francis appeared, according to this unnecessary invitation, not wearing the old official uniform, black coat, pin-striped trousers, but the modern equivalent, a neat dark suit, his father viewed him with his usual approach to irritation. Francis was smiling and polite, his hair was short. James Ryle had not become acclimatised to long hair, and his younger son would have had his down to his shoulders. Nevertheless, that young man would somehow have eased the frets. He wasn't as competent or successful as this one. He was a schoolmaster, returning to family origins, not over-capable at that. He was no more like his father than Francis was. He had a streak of deep, inborn, causeless depression, whereas James Ryle hadn't habitually been depressed, anyway not without cause. Yet that streak gave his second son the sympathy which depressives sometimes had. He was kind, and just now his father could do with a bit of kindness.

Why, Ryle was moved by an entirely unreasonable fit of exasperation, was that son, whom he loved, unhappy, and this older one looked as though he hadn't had a day's unhappiness in his life? That was a fatuous thought. Ryle would in his normal equilibrium have jeered at it. For a balanced man to be crying out because there wasn't justice on this earth—injustice was prescribed from the moment one was conceived, it lasted all of a lifetime. Into one's old age. Into the way one died. Here was he, getting towards seventy, still vigorous. Better men than he, such as Adam Sedgwick, had received injustice the other way round. So had Hillmorton, more savagely.

As for happiness, that was a grace. No justice there. It descended at random. Sometimes it skipped those who should have had it, such as his younger son. Sometimes it elected for the silly or the wicked. It wasn't a prize for good conduct. Ryle had had as much of it as most people, possibly more. Liz had so far had less.

Ryle asked his son Francis to help himself to any drink he cared for, and enquired with routine duty about wife and children. Then, as Francis was sitting down, chair drawn up close to the sofa, just as when Liz had once solicited advice in this room, James Ryle said, with the over-hearty brusqueness that infected him in his son's company:

"What are you chaps playing at?"

"Do you mean—?"

"I mean, what are you really doing about the economy? I suppose you must be doing something."

Francis said: "Oh, we're plugging away."

"I've heard that before. It always means that things are going to turn out even worse than one expects."

Francis remained relaxed. He said:

"Well, you've seen a fair amount in your time, haven't you?"

Once more his father had a surge of unreasonable exasperation.

"I might feel a bit more confident—if your department occasionally showed rudimentary signs of being shaken."

"Would that do any good?"

"I suppose some of you get a shade uneasy, now and then. At least I hope you do."

Francis gave a wide smile, indicating cat-humour.

"Some people do. There was a case a couple of days ago. Someone had made an appointment to see my chief. About a private matter. He was a fairly prominent member of your House, as a matter of fact. I was called in to take a few notes."

James Ryle was able to interpret this in terms of official protocol. Francis couldn't, and wouldn't, produce the name of the visitor or give away anything about the private business. That was correct. It was stuffy, but it had its value. Francis's chief was one of the permanent secretaries, and the man concerned was probably well-known. Well-known enough for someone as senior as Francis to be invoked as a silent listener to the interview. That was the polite and open Whitehall equivalent of bugging, and it too was correct.

"Well," said Francis, "the piece of business seemed to pass off all right. Then this man—it had nothing to do with what he had come for—happened to mention that he didn't like the look of things. In your sense, that is. He had wondered whether it wouldn't be sensible to go somewhere where the future was more promising. Such as Canada. But after all this was his country. So far as he could see, it was a sinking ship. Still, only rats left sinking ships."

Ryle was thinking, who could this man be, he probably knew him. He seemed to have a sharp taste in rhetoric. Ryle asked:

"What did your chief say to that?"

Francis's smile appeared immoveable.

"Just—Well, you can't expect me to agree with that, can you? Referring to the first part of the statement."

Francis, even when amused, didn't lose his precision. Then he did say, reporting his chief again:

"But I do know what you mean."

Ryle, feeling for an instant warmer to his son, said:

"Spoken like a good civil servant." He added: "What do you really think? Yourself?"

Francis replied: "Officials have to be moderately optimistic, you know. Otherwise we couldn't do the job."

"I've seen more mistakes caused by over-optimism than by any other single cause."

Francis persisted, without expression: "If we hadn't a touch of optimism, we shouldn't do anything at all."

For a short time he did some technical analysis. His father thought it was competent and conventional. Expansion was theoretically right. The Treasury wouldn't have done it so fast.

This was a gamble. If it failed there would be a considerable shambles. Of course, there had been some contingency planning already. Francis was too discreet to say so, but officials like himself had some practice in making contingency plans, unknown to incumbent governments, methodically filed away.

In precisely the same equable tone, Francis said:

"As a matter of fact, I was just going to write you a letter."

It was so unemphatic, temperate, business like, that Ryle was totally deceived.

"Were you, by God? Anyway, you've said it now, I suppose."

"No, I haven't, you know."

Francis gave a smile, but it was neither amused nor polite.

"I wasn't going to write to you about the state of the nation."

"What was it, then?"

"Someone's got to tell you. I thought it had better be me."

"I don't understand."

"You're making a fool of yourself about that girl of yours. You ought to take hold of yourself." His voice was still unexcited and disciplined: yet lurking underneath was a vestige of the brusqueness with which his father often spoke to him. "People are beginning to talk."

Ryle had listened with astonishment and chagrin mixed. Suddenly he had an excuse for anger.

"What the hell do I care about that?"

"Why should you?" Francis was embarrassed: that had been a tactical mistake. "That isn't what we're concerned about—"

"Who is 'we'? Who are these people you are talking about?"

"You do have a family, you know. As for the people who've noticed something, you're not entirely insignificant. You've been seen about with her."

Ryle had, not for the first time, been falling into a trap, specially designed for acute and inquisitive men. They couldn't avoid the delusion that they were able to go about observing without being observed themselves, as though by a curious kind of uncertainty principle. At that moment, in his own sitting room, he was thinking, wildly, of modern surveillance. Would this son of his have access to intelligence departments?

He was blustering it out.

"Of course I've been out with her. If I had had the chance I should have been out with her a great deal more."

"She's no good to you," said Francis. "We don't want to see you waste your time."

"I take it you are speaking for my devoted family," said Ryle.

"That's fair enough."

"I'm very touched by this overwhelming interest. You might care to hear that if this woman would have me I should marry her tomorrow. She wouldn't have me. That's the only thing I think twice about. I take it that my devoted family wouldn't be over-pleased if I got married again. You wouldn't come into the money you're expecting."

It was Francis's turn to look at the other with astonishment. He had not once in his life heard his father speak like this. Few people had. Most would have said that this lurch of vulgar sarcasm wasn't in Ryle's character. Yet it had grimaced its way out.

Francis had reverted to his mechanical Japanese smile, but his colour had yellowed. He was one of those who blanch with anger. It was some moments before he controlled himself.

"That's quite unfair. I regard it as inadmissible."

He spoke, quietly, formally, as he might have done across the table in committee.

Ryle, equally angry, was also controlling himself. He had to call, not on affection, but on his pride. He had always prided himself on his balance and his sense of fact—and those indicators said that he had been wrong.

"I accept that. It was unfair. I'm sorry. I withdraw."

It was said harshly, not with any grace: but it was said.

"Look here," said Francis, "there's nothing we should all like better than to see you married again. I'd approve of it myself, more than anything that could happen to you. That's not to be doubted. You have to believe it."

There was a pause.

"Yes, I believe it."

Again, that was said without grace, but it was said.

"We should be glad to throw some nice unattached women in your way, if that's any use."

"It might be a good idea," said Ryle, tone still uninflected.

"There's no reason on earth why you shouldn't find a wife and enjoy yourself. We'd all like to see it." Francis was breaking into a real smile that wasn't in itself expressive but was actually lubricious. "I expect you can still make it all right."

If that remark had been produced by one of his friends, Ryle wouldn't have been displeased. He had the least complicated of recent proofs that it was true. He had attempted some of the recipes for escaping from a hopeless passion. They didn't work, as anyone who had lived his life ought to have known, but nevertheless, since a good many emotions were neither dignified nor grand, he had found himself walking away from a woman friend's house, breathing the night air, confronting faces in the street as boldly, as impudently set up, as he had after not dissimilar occasions as a young man.

Yet, hearing that remark from his son, the son whom he regarded as tight laced and priggish, he was outraged. Whatever those two said to each other that evening, as on other evenings, was wrong. Both were even-tempered men: and still they couldn't help stirring each other's temper below the surface. Ryle had long ago decided not to make sexual references, certainly not confidences, to his sons. Only the innocent did that, those who thought that life was hygienic and who knew nothing about fathers and sons. Now to hear one in reverse. It was meant kindly, maybe, but that made it crasser.

Whatever they said to each other was wrong. Possibly Francis, less wily than his father, was—when out of the duty mode, as his colleagues were coming to call it, having picked up a soldier's term—ready to be more open. It was too late. Like other fathers, Ryle had been surreptitiously gratified to guess, infer, and finally confirm, that his sons had had their first women, were virile and content. That had been a father's gratification in much stiffer times than these. Ryle had read what some Victorian fathers said to their intimates: they might have had orthodox beliefs, but they had felt as he did. But it was a different thing to have this son curious about, and ready to approve of, his own virility.

The only answer was not to answer. Ryle, easy with so many men and women, so often a social lubricant, fell into oxlike silence. Francis looked at him, first with a quizzical stare, then with something like disappointment, or even hurt. With an effort Ryle emerged from his thoughts and in an impersonal monotone asked another question about the economic situation.

❧ 28 ❧

If he had been invited to Swaffield's June party, Ryle would
have had another occasion to wonder whether people were
thoughtless, or just dancing as the English officers did the nights
before Waterloo, because there was nothing else to do. However, James Ryle wasn't invited: and, to come down to more
crude facts, there was no dancing. Swaffield had planned that
party with devoted care, and there was another entertainment,
which, when his guests received their invitations, aroused in
some expectation and, in a good many more, surprise. Certain
sceptical spirits enquired: "What's all this in aid of?"

Swaffield wouldn't have minded that question. The party
was in aid of Swaffield, or more exactly in aid of Swaffield the
peace maker. When the settlement had been quashed by Julian's master play, Swaffield was left in a position both ridiculous and irksome, having performed his Quixotic act, incurred
all the penalties, and then been cut off from any conceivable
satisfaction. That would have infuriated more harmonious men
than Swaffield, in the event, so unlikely as to be impossible, of
more harmonious men performing the Quixotic act.

Yet, Swaffield, despite that fit of pride or other eruptions
known only to himself, was capable of being as humble as a
young man on the make. He diminished pride as though it
wasn't relevant, and set to work to rescue what he could. If it
meant another hundred thousand to Meinertzhagen's party
funds, that was easy. If it meant being apologetic or sycophan-

tic to dear friends like Meinertzhagen, that was not so easy but could be done. Expressions of sincere friendship, sincere regrets for past mistakes and deviations, all the apparatus of a party member—when did dazzling insincerity stop and belief take over?—had been part of his progress up the ladder, and he could manage them again. He was too wilful a character to be supremely good at them, the people who were supremely good at them were those who did them by nature, not by trying. Still, he had energy and resource to draw on.

Of course Meinertzhagen and the party bosses knew what he was doing. They would have been fools not to have known, and they weren't fools. They were used to displays of penitence, and to aspiring persons wanting to make their credit good. That did no harm to others' morale, no harm at all. As for what was in store for Swaffield, that was their secret.

One odd thing was that, just as Swaffield underestimated them, so they did him. He thought that they were third rate caucus hacks, with the imagination of turtles in an aquarium. In fact they had senses which he hadn't. While they thought that he was a coarse-minded crook who had somehow made his pile, without much ability except a nose for money: whereas he was much cleverer, as Sedgwick might have said approvingly, than any of them.

So Swaffield, as one of his signs of redemption, organised his July party. Here his enemies and detractors had a point. Like other rich men, he seemed to believe with extreme naivety in entertaining as a source of good will. No one was less naive (as the Symingtons and Jenny could have told those detractors), but he acted as though giving a Cabinet Minister a good dinner was likely to make him a friend for life. Would it have been better, sceptics could have pondered, to avoid the ghost of Trimalchio and give that Cabinet Minister a cheese sandwich at the local pub?

There were, though, considerable departures from Trimalchio about the July party. It had to be stately, Swaffield decided before he got down to planning: and when Swaffield intended to be stately, he wasn't going to do it by halves. Thus the first decision, that this wasn't to be a dinner.

It also had to be an irenicon, or at the least a symbol of all

246

that Swaffield wished to do, though he had been thwarted, to meet his friend Meinertzhagen's request at that little friendly meeting once before. It was the other side—this information had been judiciously conveyed—who had prevented any kind of private agreement. While, as for Swaffield, all he wished in the world was to see them all happy together, mute down any noise which might reach the masses outside, and satisfy other men of good will.

Hence the selection of his guests. He decided to invite the principals and participants on both sides—Mrs. Underwood, Julian with Liz attached, their solicitors and counsel, and with symmetrical impartiality Jenny Rastall with Lorimer attached, and her solicitors and counsel. Nothing could be more placatory than that. It would demonstrate to Meinertzhagen, Haydon-Smith, other ministers and the central office dignitaries, all duly invited, the earnestness of Swaffield's intention. There were others whom he considered as suitable background or dilution, such as the Schiffs and half a dozen lesser magnates. Swaffield wrote down the name of Lord Clare, crossed it out, and then after thought reinserted it. Swaffield didn't forget old suspicions and accounts to settle, but he had trained himself to leave them in suspense.

All these people received their invitations, and as soon as they read them a number found reason for grumbling. The card was chaste. Mr. Reginald Swaffield invited the Lord and Lady Schiff to a *soirée* (no one's heard of a *soirée* for twenty years, said someone. That fellow over-doing it as usual) on Thursday July 20th 1972, at 9:30 p.m. at 27, Hill Street, W. 1. In the bottom left-hand corner, music by —— and ——. The initiated saw the names of an illustrious string quartet and two similarly illustrious performers on harpsichord and piano (why the hell is he going in for music, said someone else. What a waste of an evening). There was also the neat instruction— Evening Dress ("Good God, white tie," said Lord Clare. "No one puts on a white tie in a private house nowadays.")

Grumbles properly discharged, almost everyone accepted. The curious thing was almost everyone usually did accept, not only Swaffield's invitations but any others. Why did they, Hillmorton in his former lofty detachment might have enquired. Parties weren't so rare, few admitted to enjoying them. But they went.

The only notable persons who didn't go to Swaffield's that Thursday were those two odd men out, the leading counsel. Even they might have gone, but it happened to be a night, changed from their habitual Friday, for their dinner at the club. March preferred that to any music on earth: Lander, who would have enjoyed the music, didn't feel like disappointing him. They weren't aware that their clients and connections were all gathering in Swaffield's house.

Thursday July 20th took on an aura, or something like a hush, for anyone in the neighbourhood of Swaffield. Even passersby in Hill Street or Chesterfield Hill had intimations that unusual events were being prepared for. A very large lorry drew up in front of Swaffield's house. From it a ramp descended. Down the ramp came a sizeable conifer in a sizeable tub. After it, another. The series continued. Men in aprons took the conifers inside, Swaffield in shirt sleeves assisting, giving orders, working harder than his mates.

People watching counted thirty of the trees, there might be more to come. They were mystified. Actually, there was method behind this feat of tree conveyance. The party, Swaffield had decided, was to be held on the patio, leading out of the grandiose drawingroom. The patio was open to the sky, spacious enough to hold tables for the guests but distinctly bare. Apart from roses round the wall, it bore a disconcerting resemblance to the setting for a firing squad. Swaffield was altering that by the installation of his trees: perhaps too many trees, he had a flicker of doubt, but then he liked the look of them.

He had one graver doubt. The musicians would be protected enough inside the drawingroom, but all the guests were to sit in the open air. Swaffield, who had made dispositions for unlikely contingencies, had been showing uncritical faith in London's summer nights. Now he was cursing himself. He couldn't get the whole party into the drawingroom. Angry with himself and even more with everyone round him, all he could do was watch the weather. The morning was cold, cloudy but dry. A modest improvement on past days. He watched it with suspicion. No, that wasn't all he could do. He ordered half-hourly forecasts from the Meteorological Office and sat in his study with the sombre concentration of the combined chiefs of staff on D-day minus one.

Swaffield often imagined his enemies sneering at him, and he did so now. "Showers, probably heavy, between three and four p.m."—Swaffield could see them grinning at an absurd Little Man deflated. But Swaffield could behave with absurdity, and not be deflated. Later forecast: "Dry spell arriving from north east in early evening, becoming cooler." Inflation succeeded to deflation. Cooler—action had to be taken. Swaffield had a robust disregard for others' discomfort, and his own, if it interfered with beautifully planned festivities. Still, they mustn't get too cold. That would distract influential minds from the object of the exercise. Action at once. Swaffield gave orders for a supply of rugs, suitable for the promenade deck of an ocean liner. Electric heaters to be scattered round among the trees. Hot drinks in reserve.

The weather forecast proved correct. The enemies weren't to have their satisfaction. No raining off. After all his triumphs, Swaffield felt this was another one, felt simple and joyous because he had prevailed again. At nine twenty he was standing in his drawingroom, accoutred in his tails, the last of the sunlight streaming in. He wasn't looking particularly stately. That dress wasn't designed for short powerful legs. But his greetings were stately beyond compare. Jenny, who arrived early, had never heard him in form like this.

"Good evening, my dear Jenny, how good of you to come." Not a jibe, not a dig, not a hug.

"Good evening, Lord Lorimer. How kind of you to come. How nice to see you."

As Swaffield's own butler, assisted by auxiliary butlers recruited for the evening, took his guests out to their tables on the patio, there was one slight, almost imperceptible, departure from stateliness. When Meinertzhagen, who was one of the late comers, had been duly greeted, Swaffield held him back.

"There's something I want to show you," Swaffield said. They walked to the end of the drawingroom, and looked out on the serried tables, lights, not fairy lights, shining, not obtrusively, from each alternate tree, the limpid not-yet-night sky above.

Swaffield pointed to one group.

"Do you know who they are?"

Meinertzhagen considered.

"I don't think I do."

"That's Lord Hillmorton's daughter. He's supposed to be her fiancé. With his mother. They are the people who lost over that Massie will."

"Really."

"Now do you see those two in the corner?"

Meinertzhagen, with sapience, said that he recognised Lord Lorimer.

"The woman with him is the one who won."

"Really."

"I've managed to get them all together in one house."

Swaffield said this with the modest satisfaction of a junior diplomat who, no credit to himself, had been able to persuade Arab and Jewish delegates to sit at a conference table. Meinertzhagen made a cordial noise. He couldn't profess astonishment, since Swaffield had informed him in advance that this was one of the purposes of the evening.

"Now the whole business is still going on. It's a dreadful pity," said Swaffield. "Everyone wishes they would settle it without any more commotion. We've done our best. But it wasn't good enough."

Meinertzhagen nodded gratefully. One man of good will to another. He didn't think any worse of Swaffield for this revisionist version of history. He was used to politicians who behaved as if they had no memory. Life would be more difficult if all the facts were engraved on stone.

Soon the quartet was getting to work. Music of Vivaldi came to the ears of those outside. To a spectator out of earshot it would have seemed a placid, mildly pleasurable, London party. To some present, the musical, the elect (Schiff, Julian Underwood, both Symingtons, Meinertzhagen, Jenny, perhaps half the guests), it became more than that. To others, the goats as opposed to the sheep (Liz, Rosalind Schiff, the Clares, the other half), singularly less. The sheep enjoyed. The goats endured. With an uncomfortable feeling, as the noise tinkled away, that they had to go on enduring for some considerable time to come. As a rough, though not infallible, discriminant, the music lovers were happy with champagne. The others were supporting themselves on spirits. Before the music started, Liz had had the forethought to provide herself with a third gin waiting reassuringly on their table.

All things came to an end, including Vivaldi. Great applause, not only claps but shouts. The quartet emerged from the edge of the drawingroom and benevolently bowed. More cheers.

"They really have played marvellously," said Julian with genuine childlike glee.

"Have they?" said Liz.

Interval. People were stirring, some feet were cold. As one struck by a revelation, Julian said, again with childlike glee, not quite so ingenuous:

"Now's the time to pay a call on Mrs. Rastall."

"Oh no," said Liz.

"Oh yes," said Julian. "Can't miss the chance."

It was the kind of devilry Liz hadn't found a means to stop. Nor perhaps, ashamed of her submissiveness, did she want to.

Julian led her over to the opposite corner, from which Jenny and Lorimer hadn't moved. Jenny, who didn't appear to feel the chill, sat there with bare arms. Lorimer was draped in a rug, looking something like a British officer detached for duty with Bedouin guerilla forces.

"May we introduce ourselves?" said Julian, with a shining candid smile. He gave their names, easy and polite. He added, still smiling candidly; "I think we have something in common, you know."

Jenny met his innocent open eyes with her acute ones. Like others, she couldn't find a reply to his mischief—for which later on she and Lorimer were finding rougher words.

"How are you?" said Liz to Jenny.

"How are you?" said Jenny.

Liz might be trying to make some fugitive apology. Jenny was not prepared to entertain the excuse. She thought that Liz was a hard and brassy woman, looking older than her age. Liz thought that Jenny looked sharp and shrewish, condescending to allow her fine eyes. This was the only time they had caught sight of each other, outside the courts. There was a flash of, not liking, not understanding, not sympathy, but some inexplicable desire to come close, such as sometimes sparks between enemies.

"All this is rather fun." Julian spoke as though presiding over a celebration. "I wish we could have that last piece over again."

"It was good," said Jenny stiffly.

"Did you enjoy it, Lord Lorimer?" Julian's spontaneity wasn't damped.

"I'm not much good at classical music," said Lorimer.

"What a splendid night!" said Julian, patronising the sky. In fact, it was a serene July evening, except that the temperature wasn't more than forty-five degrees Fahrenheit. However, it had not become colder, the wind had dropped. Stars were coming out over the luminescent London haze.

Lorimer spoke to Jenny: "I think we ought to go and look for another drink."

Jenny responded: "I think we ought."

"Well," said Julian. "It has been very nice to meet you, I'm sure we shall hear something of each other in the nearish future, shan't we?"

Liz and Jenny nodded their goodbyes. When the others had departed, Lorimer and Jenny didn't go in search of drinks, but Lorimer muttered that that man was too smooth by half, he didn't like him.

"Do you imagine I do?" said Jenny rattily.

Interval over, the harpsichordist began to play Purcell. Once more, the invisible divide, arcadian pleasure and the rest. To Liz, it seemed an interminable spell before the next interval. To Swaffield, all was going according to plan. It would be wrong to intrude himself any further in high quarters. Thus, leaving well alone, when the interval arrived he allowed himself the luxury of seeking lesser prey.

At that moment, Azik Schiff, who was observant and had noticed the previous assault on Jenny, decided that she ought to be protected. He and his wife moved along to her table.

Julian's hoot could be heard not far away, and his mother had been left temporarily alone. It was she upon whom Swaffield had his eye.

"I hope you are enjoying yourself," he said, as he stood beside her.

"Enormously, oh, enormously, Mr. Swaffield."

"We have met before."

"Of course we must have, of course we have."

Swaffield had remembered all this time, and was remembering now, that she had once snubbed him at a party—though that might be one of the thin-skinned inventions which he cherished and hugged to himself. Whatever was the truth, and that was undiscoverable, Mrs. Underwood had long forgotten meeting Swaffield in his more primitive days. She wasn't an over-complicated being, she was prepared to be deferential to a rich man, a man of power, associate of Cabinet Ministers. When she expressed her enthusiasm for the party, that, though she was one of the non-musical, wasn't entirely a gushing lie. To her mind, this was a grand assembly, grander than she had been invited to for years past, and she was basking in it.

Swaffield sat down beside her.

"How's your son getting on?"

"Very well, thank you, Mr. Swaffield."

"When's he going to marry that girl?"

Like other women when Swaffield put out his full projective force, Mrs. Underwood didn't resist.

"Quite soon, that is we all hope quite soon. Of course, there are a few difficulties, they're not children, you know—"

"What difficulties?"

"Well, there's always money, isn't there? And—"

"And what—"

"Sometimes I think, perhaps they're not certain that they are right for each other."

"Do you think they are?"

"I hope so, I do hope so."

"Do you think it's a good idea?"

"All I can say is, I hope so. He ought to get settled down, naturally. Of course she's a strong minded person."

When he wasn't on one of his rampages, Swaffield had more

insight than most men. He had learned in a few minutes what Liz only hesitantly suspected, that Mrs. Underwood loathed her. There would have been a tincture of that in Mrs. Underwood for anyone who took her son away, even though, simultaneously, in principle and in conscience, she was pressing the marriage on. That was commonplace enough. In addition, Mrs. Underwood loathed Liz for herself. Probably, thought Swaffield, she didn't realise how much, or even more admit it.

Swaffield felt tempted to meddle. These people had stood in his own way, they had done harm to Jenny, of whom he was fond. What was more tempting, Swaffield liked meddling for its own delicious sake. As a rule he did so to increase, in his own view, the amount of enjoyment, in particular the amount of sexual enjoyment, in the world. He wasn't above doing the reverse. It would be easy to disturb this particular triangle. He hadn't the free energy for such diversions, but it was agreeable to secrete the thought away.

"He may be getting interested in someone else," said Swaffield.

"I suppose it could happen—"

"*How do you know he isn't?*" said Swaffield, getting up to go, leaving her with that obscure warning and encouragement.

This interval was a long one, somewhat protracted because several performers were walking in the patio. While they were doing so, two highly placed persons, much loftier than Meinertzhagen, were walking together beside the trees. They were discussing the pianist who was to be the next and final performer, one of the most famous then alive. But they were discussing, not his art, but his pay. Or more precisely what it had cost Swaffield to transport him from New York, entertain him and provide his fee. They made estimates, which, though high, were actually slightly lower than the truth.

"I must say," said one, "the man Swaffield does us pretty proud."

"If you ask me," said the other, "it's very civil of him."

If Jenny had heard that, she would have regarded it as a classical English remark and been filled with irreverent pleasure. However, she was soon listening to more music, and filled with a different kind of pleasure. No, it was more than pleasure. Other music moved her in the flesh and the dear mortal world where she was at home. The Bach did that, and transcended it. This was pure joy. She wasn't trying to define it. She wasn't thinking that this was how she might have felt once or twice in her life time, if she had been religious. She wasn't noticing the crystalline night—or nearer to earth the faces round her—or the wrapped up figure at her side, whom she had been teasing. She was separate from all of them, part of it all.

Nevertheless, looking back on those moments—they didn't last long—with happiness, she recollected them wrong. She believed that the resolve which had been forming within her for some while past, and which had strengthened itself at that party, became settled and clear while she was overtaken by that joy. This wasn't true. She liked to think so, and she blessed the party for it. Soon after the music had finished, she had returned cheerfully to her resolve again. Just for those moments, though, and it was rare for anyone, not only for children of this world like herself, she had been living where choice and decision didn't enter, that is outside the domain of the will. Though she would have thought it fanciful, and conceivably have been right, some would have said that she had been lifted out of time.

❦ 29 ❦

Through the late summer Dr. Pemberton was receiving regular reports about Hillmorton. They came from his contact at the hospital where Hillmorton had been first examined, for, contrary to his prediction to Sedgwick and his own wishes, that was where he had been moved. He hadn't been able to argue much, he was only fitfully coherent or capable of a continued effort of will.

The disease, after the lull in the spring, had gone faster than Pemberton had expected. As he listened to the reports, he thought that it was unlikely to take long now. He followed the progress exactly as he had followed the progress of others in this condition. He had seen it all before. There were one or two curiosities. The brain tumour had grown with untypical speed. Pemberton's nearest approach to feeling was the reflection that for himself, he would prefer another way of dying.

The mind, still lucid in March, had all of a sudden deteriorated. That would be hard to take if there was a threshold when the patient realised what was happening. No one likes the prospect of being gaga, Pemberton thought to himself. Paralysis had spread. There wasn't much the patient could do for himself. He wouldn't be able to handle his own bedpan. There were many days when the bladder was obstructed. Pain, catheters, the routine performance, the routine nursing. More severe pain in the back and pelvis.

Whether pain in this kind of terminal illness was actually more extreme than pain such as toothache, Pemberton hadn't found any scientific method of deciding: but fear made the pain seem more agonising, there was no doubt of that. Pemberton had heard men as controlled as Hillmorton scream, and go on screaming, in precisely this same condition. Analgesics every four hours. Analgesics didn't give him much help, his nervous system appeared to have unusual resistance. Finally they used one which softened the pain but made him slobbery, merry and giggling like a fatuous cheery drunk.

Presumably Hillmorton had once had some sort of dignity. This way of dying didn't leave one any dignity. Fancy giggling on the last stretch. Pemberton couldn't tolerate his own humiliations, but, if he had been in charge, he would have given the same treatment himself.

Three or four months now, was his estimate. There was some practical office work for him to do. He didn't propose to waste time about taking the succession, for whatever it was worth. There shouldn't be any delay. His father had had an amateur passion for genealogy, such as gratified some with— real or imagined—lofty antecedents and no other claim to fame. He had drawn family trees like someone hoping to be admitted to a Hapsburg court. Or alternatively proving that he descended from a woman who had been picked up by the Duke of Wellington.

These charts Pemberton had had checked by the Debrett staff. There was no doubt anywhere. No senior line had survived. Hillmorton might have hated the thought of such an heir, but he had no doubt that this actually was his heir. In his entry in *Who's Who* there was the bare line: Heir. Kinsman Dr. Thomas Pemberton, M.R.C.P., F.R.C.S.

Nevertheless the formalities would have to be performed. Several nights in August and September, after listening clinically to the hospital report, which normally came through once a week, Pemberton went into his surgery and did more office work. He wasn't given to wasting money, and so the surgery did double duty as his study and he himself did double duty as his own secretary. He wasn't given to literary exercises, but he was neat and methodical, a hulking figure bent over the desk, writing in a tidy, minuscule italic hand. From those holograph charts he typed, boxer's hands precise upon the keys.

Genealogies were collected and placed in dossiers. Entries in Debretts and Burkes were copied out, and cross references supplied. So were photostats of family correspondence and of the birth certificates of his grandfather, his father and himself.

In September all was complete, and one night—he had heard earlier in the week that there was no change in Hillmorton's state—he first wrote a letter, and then typed it out. It was addressed to the Lord Chancellor at the Crown Office. It read: Dear Lord Chancellor, I am enclosing documents in proof of my succession to the earldom of Hillmorton etc. as vacated by the late holder whose death has been announced. The documents are self explanatory and confirm (a) that I am a legitimate male line descendant of the first holder of the Hillmorton titles, (b) that all senior male lines springing from that first holder are extinct. I shall be obliged if you will ratify these proofs at your earliest convenience, so that you will feel able to issue to me a Writ of Summons. Yours faithfully, ...

Pemberton read the letter with the satisfaction of an author receiving his first set of proofs. Procedure suitably business like. He prided himself on being capable of discovering sources of advice for any human situation. He hesitated about the signature. He came into the title the instant the other man died. Should he sign himself Hillmorton, or keep to Thomas Pemberton? Just for once he vacillated. He would have despised anyone else for it, but he had a slight superstitious twinge. With great firmness, at the bottom of the letter he inscribed the name he was used to.

The one thing he couldn't inscribe on that letter was the date. That would have to wait. Delicately, with careful fingers, he put the letter, documents, and large envelope into a folder. The folder went into a special receptacle at the back of his files. He slid that layer of his filing cabinet shut, and with an air of accomplishment, of obscure triumph, turned the small key in the lock.

Within three weeks of that piece of administrative efficiency, his medical acquaintance was saying over the telephone:

"It must be getting near the finish now."

"With this kind of cancer one can't tell for sure," said Pemberton.

"One can near enough, this time, I think."

"Any change that signifies?"

"There can't be now, can there?"

"He might have gone off earlier. He must have pretty fair vitality."

The other doctor said: "People often hang on. Longer than you'd think possible. Not the most likely people, sometimes."

"He's hung on, it hasn't done him any good."

"Of course, he's not feeling anything now. That last drug really does work, you know."

Pemberton did know. The doctors had done what they could, within the orthodox limits. They had helped, so far as the patient could be helped. The giggling way to death. Finally the vegetable way to death. It wasn't grand. Perhaps it was human. Pemberton had faith in what his mind told him, and his mind told him that that final way was right.

❧ 30 ❧

That same September Jenny was feeling restive and happy, the moods combined and co-existing because she was coming near a point of action. On an afternoon in the week Pemberton heard that last bulletin about Hillmorton, she walked, steps springy as a girl's (in the midst of death we are in life, some supernatural Dr. Pemberton, omniscient about all mondial conjunctions, might have commented) up Philbeach Gardens on one of her visits. Nowadays she paid these after lunch, after getting through her work in Swaffield's office in the mornings. This was a visit to a favourite old lady, whom she always called deferentially Miss Smith.

Miss Smith rose to greet her in a bed sitting room about the size of Jenny's own, but crammed with bric-a-brac, postcards on the mantelpiece, photographs on the walls, on a what-not small replicas of St. Mark's, St. Peter's, the Taj Mahal, and Cologne Cathedral. Miss Smith, well into her eighties, was straight backed, bright eyed. She had been a school mistress, which accounted for most of the photographs and all the postcards. Her tone was high and clear, cultivated (educated rather than upper class, Jenny's ear told her), nice to listen to.

"How are you, my dear?"

"You're looking very well," said Jenny.

"And how is that trouble of yours?" Miss Smith never welcomed any sort of protective care, but dispensed it. Jenny, who didn't approve of self-pity, of which she saw plenty, approved of this—and hoped she would be as tough if she lived as long. By that trouble of Jenny's, Miss Smith was referring to the appeal. She had followed the whole process with critical vigilance from the beginning.

"Oh, it's down for hearing at last. This term," said Jenny.

"That means before Christmas, am I right?"

"Quite right."

"Oh, I *am* glad for you. It will be a relief to get it settled. It's bound to be."

"Of course it will," said Jenny. She had been told, only recently, that the appeal was coming on and that this particular waiting would soon be over. But it wasn't that which was making her happy and filling her with a sense of action.

Miss Smith, who let little slip, had also detected that Jenny had acquaintances in the House of Lords, and wished to talk of them. For two different reasons, Jenny wanted to steer the conversation away. One of these reasons was that Miss Smith had a taste for talking politics and, though Jenny herself was conservative enough, Miss Smith's politics were not entirely soothing.

She was living on a tiny private school pension (was she too proud to take her old age pension? Jenny had not dared to ask her). She would be content if some people stayed preposterously richer. That thought delighted her—so long as a large number stayed considerably poorer, if possible a good deal poorer than they had ever been. These desires Miss Smith managed to involve with extreme moral righteousness, and her good nature got lost. All this made Jenny uncomfortable. Those desires were rather too close to her own instincts. She had been forced to listen to other views these last two years. She had heard Symington say that Lord Clare was somewhere to the right of Nicholas the First. She couldn't help accepting that Miss Smith was somewhere to the right of Lord Clare. She and Lorimer couldn't change much and didn't want to: but somehow they oughtn't to be fellow-travellers with Lord Clare.

It was pleasant to get Miss Smith gossiping about former pupils, safely away from embarrassing topics. On former pupils Miss Smith was the reverse of embarrassing. She was a sharp observer, she was interested in their marriages, children, divorces, love affairs. She was interested in a curiously antiseptic fashion, quite free from prying or any kind of vicarious heat. Rather like someone from another planet, Jenny thought, observing domestic happenings here with intelligence but without feeling or sharing in their kind of mess: rather like Jane Austen, who seemed to Jenny to have as shrewd an eye as anyone could have who didn't really know what sexual feeling was.

Jenny had decided that in her long life Miss Smith hadn't been troubled by really knowing what sexual feeling was. She certainly hadn't been even in the most sublimated terms a lesbian, as credulous persons might have thought. She hadn't loved a man. Somehow she had been above, or on the safe side of it all. It hadn't made her unhappy. Jenny would have judged that she had been happier than most people. Jenny wouldn't have been, in those conditions: but then she wasn't Miss Smith, and Miss Smith had told her that there were more ways than one of living a satisfactory life.

Had Miss Smith been blessed? Was it a great gift, to be born with a temperament like that? As Jenny left Philbeach Gardens, the odd autumn leaf spiralling down to the pavement, those questions, as they had before, flooded among her thoughts. But not for long. Jenny was filled with other thoughts, some agreeable, some uncertain, all pertaining to actions in the near future. Whatever the risks or disappointments might be, Jenny wouldn't have changed with Miss Smith or anyone else who hadn't entered the battle.

On the way home, Earls Court Road was scruffy. Again under foot there were a few autumn leaves, and far more scraps, bags, sheets of paper, the ubiquitous London paper. Yet to Jenny that month the sloppy streets—and perhaps through the smells of curry cooking, came a faint aboriginal smell from gardens nearby, the old wistful autumnal smell—had their own promise. No one could have called them glamorous streets, but it was enlivening to be walking there on a September afternoon.

Jenny was thinking of marriage. She liked to believe, both then and afterwards, that she had made up her mind that night on Swaffield's terrace, the sound of Bach filling her with joy. It was all of a sudden that night, she liked to believe, that she had known marriage was right for her and Lorimer.

Like all such resolves, of course, this one had been grounding itself—either known to her or unknown, or sometimes between the two—for long enough. But Jenny had the kind of sense or wisdom which didn't always have a slavish respect for historical fact. Deciding about marriage was important, and if it was improved by a little gilding, decoration or editing, well, her memory could adapt itself.

Just as she had the kind of sense or wisdom which knew what not to think about. She had become fond of Lorimer, that she could think about. (Did one become fond of anyone one saw a lot of, when one was lonely? That suspicion was dismissed.) He was absolutely honest, upright, someone to rely on. (She had found him dull, even forbidding when they first met. He didn't brighten the air, he didn't inspire her. The less she admitted that, the better. It was the cynical, not the realistic, who took a full look at the worst every instant of the day.)

It would be nice to have someone beside her at parties. It wasn't good for anyone's self-esteem, particularly if one had as little as she had, to go about alone. (He wouldn't shine, he would be obscure and mute among Swaffield's stars. That didn't matter, he had his own presence, she had seen people respecting him, she could hold on to that.) She would enjoy having a title, anyone like herself would be a hypocrite to pretend not to. (If the appeal went wrong they would be poor, very poor—joint income about up to that of a good secretary's, unless Swaffield helped them out. Still, she was used to being poor. As for being poor and going along to the peeresses' gallery and having notes addressed to The Lady Lorimer—that would be a distinct improvement, whatever anyone said.)

She must bring him up to scratch. Sitting in her tidy, dusted room, she used that phrase to herself. There was no time to lose. She must get it settled before the appeal: not that she was afraid of the results of losing, but of winning; she couldn't be certain, but there were recesses of diffidence, pride and even arrogance about Lorimer she understood less than she had thought to begin with. If she became a rich woman, her marriage would be news. He might be frightened off or given an excuse to regress back into solitude—or into himself.

She must bring him up to scratch. That didn't mean, as others might have guessed, making him propose. Which wouldn't have needed persuading, encouraging or evoking. He had been on the edge more times than once these last few months. Because of what?—indecision, even a kind of delicacy?—she had averted it, slipped out of it. Now the indecision was over, she wanted to marry him. But she wasn't going to marry him, unless she could get some fun in bed and give him some.

As before, Jenny had the instinct to know what not to think about. It would be wrong to imagine she thought continuously about the erotic chances, as Liz might have done. She just thought enough for practical purposes, and was capable of misty girlish reveries alongside. She wasn't ready to marry for company: or for someone to go about with: she wasn't far gone enough for that, she might have limited her expectations, but she hadn't lost them. She still had plenty of hope.

So she wasn't prepared to marry Lorimer until they had got used to each other in bed—and, as she imagined with unusual confidence, had enjoyed it. Here she, so diffident that it had been a lifetime handicap, was, perversely enough, more confident than a good many women would have been. To her, the sexual life wasn't as difficult as all that. Most men—however much they were what she would have called 'tied up'—were capable of enjoying themselves. And she had had, in what had been on the whole an unlucky existence, one piece of luck. She had a temperament which gained pleasure—active, sensual, final pleasure—from helping a man get pleasure. Perhaps it was a greater piece of luck than she recognised. Women whom the world thought beautiful often totally lacked it, and found themselves miserable beyond their comprehension. Anyway, Jenny knew it of herself. She couldn't help knowing it, and had caught herself giving an inward acceptant grin. After all, if she could work out any plan of action about Lorimer, this would be a help.

But plans of action didn't come easy. She didn't want him to propose, not yet. She didn't want explanations or arguments, that would only frighten him off. She wasn't good at seducing. She wasn't cool blooded enough. It took two to make a seduction, and he was a non-participant. She couldn't manage the preliminaries, and until they got through those she couldn't bring him on.

In the event, something like a misunderstanding (it wasn't really that) occurred between them and she took her chance. She had the advantage that she had been waiting for it.

It happened on an evening about a fortnight after she had paid that visit to Miss Smith. They were still in September. Following a bitter summer, the weather was benign. So much so, that, after Jenny had called at the Lupus Street flat and she had taken him out for a drink at the corner pub, they decided to walk round St. George's Square. There, in the little garden which overlooked the river, they sat, not far from the statue of Huskisson, dressed—rather puzzlingly, since he had been run over by a locomotive—as a Roman senator. The sun was setting, the air still, insects humming, including a mosquito, rare in London at any time. There was the river smell, bringing whiffs of decomposing matter and oil, and yet, to some nostrils, seminal too.

Jenny noticed that Lorimer was more than usually jerky: and when he was in that state his scraps of talk were all over the place. Suddenly he told her that the smell from the Thames used to be much worse than this. In the middle of the last century, they had to hang towels soaked in chlorine all over the windows of the Houses of Parliament; that didn't work, and they had to suspend the sittings altogether.

Jenny was feeling peaceful, enjoying the light which softened their faces, anticipating nothing. She wanted to smooth him down, so that for both of them the moment could take care of itself, as it did for her. She said, cheerfully:

"Never mind, Jarvey."

(The first born males in his family were given the name of Jervis, pronounced Jarvis, after the 18th Century admiral. Hearty acquaintances who called him by his first Christian name Peter might produce an air of cordiality, but got it wrong. Even Hillmorton, usually punctilious, used to make that mistake.)

"That won't happen again."

"I suppose it won't."

"And if it did, it'd mean you could skip a few more speeches, wouldn't it?"

He gave a jagged unwilling grin. In a moment, in the same jerky tone with which he had interjected information about the 19th Century river, he said:

"I've been thinking."

She was alert by now.

"I've been thinking. I was wondering whether you'd consider—joining forces."

She gazed at him, for an instant at a loss.

"If you could stand it, or consider it anyway. Joining forces."

Her fine eyes were dilated. Impatiently, not indulgently or even lucidly, she felt the prick of a tear and blinked it away. Of course this was how he would manage to propose. Later on she had twinges of guilt, because she was forced to misunderstand. In the existential present, though, it seemed utterly natural, not at all blameworthy, to think of what was needed for them both, or what she had to do. As soon as she heard the first yammering words, she had been engaged in not exactly fast thinking (that had taken place before), but fast feeling.

"It's a good idea," she said, sounding brisk and matter of fact. "It's a very good idea. It'd save us both quite a lot if I moved in with you. The sooner the better."

"I meant, would you consider joining forces—? You'll have to think—"

"I'm not going to think too much. Let's take it easy. Look here, my boy" (often she said that instead of an endearment, it soothed him more), "this is a time to take things easy. We needn't rush anything at all. Nothing at all. You're not going to be rushed, are you? Nor am I. I'll move in as soon as I can. Then we'll sit back and relax."

She was taking a risk, she knew—and knew better when it was over. He was an obstinate man. Despite his muteness, or

266

maybe because of it, he resisted being taken in charge. She couldn't be sure whether he had any real need of her. Nevertheless, somewhere she had found the tone which, at least for that evening and the next days, established a kind of peace and settled him. Domestic logistics formed a recipe against strain. He came to Barham Gardens, wrote down lists, talked domestically about her 'bits and pieces,' one or two of which, like some of his, were valuable, helped carry them to a car. She observed, and with approval, that he was surprisingly strong.

There was one thing which no one knew but herself. She was not an apprehensive woman. Quite unlike Julian and Liz, she didn't go in for tics or superstitious rituals. She hadn't once touched wood, in the literal sense, in her life. And yet on this occasion she did the equivalent. The upkeep of this old bedsitting room of hers wasn't much, but even that she couldn't afford. She didn't want to see the place again. Nevertheless—although this she concealed from everyone—she made no effort to sub-let it. There was the chance that she might have to come back again.

❧ 31 ❧

The Underwoods, mother and son, were in a taxi en route for Skelding's office—as they had been precisely two years before, to listen to the announcement of the will. The same week in October: the only difference was that it was now the morning, not the afternoon. This reflection of similarity appeared to give Julian esoteric pleasure.

"Two years!" he cried, as though the stately processes of the English law were something on which he ought to be personally congratulated.

"Could you believe it?" he went on.

Much as she loved him, Mrs. Underwood was sometimes fretted by his impenetrable spirits. Day by day, she watched him for signs of anxiety over the appeal, and had seen none at all. Over his health, or catching a train, he maddened her in the reverse direction. Now, when it mattered, anyone anxious as she was couldn't help resenting a person who didn't seem to know the meaning of the state, even if it was her son.

She was hoping for some news that morning, trivial news was better than nothing. While he had dismissed that possibility, and talked as if was expecting some new piece of luck, some fresh manifestation that all was more than right with the world.

"You never know," he had told her as they started off. "We may hear something to our advantage, that's what old man Skelding would call it, wouldn't he?"

He said it with blissful ingenuousness. Those who knew him better than his mother did, such as Liz, could have told her that—when it came to action—he was not distinguished by ingenuousness. Perhaps his mother half realised that, and simultaneously didn't realise it at all.

They had each received letters from Skelding, the one to Mrs. Underwood longer and more cordial, the other formal, asking if they could make it convenient to call on him. She had duly fixed the appointment, and now they were on their way. When they arrived, whatever information either was looking forward to, they didn't get it. As soon as they were shown into Skelding's office—the same room as they had sat in two years before, so much more stately than David March's in the Inn across the Strand, mouldings above the panelling recently preserved, window seats fresh painted—Mrs. Underwood couldn't resist asking, while they were still shaking hands:

"Well, have you any news? Is there any news?"

"News?" said Mr. Skelding, pressing her hand in his parsonical manner. "No, now you mention it, I don't think I have any for you. Not what you'd be interested in, I'm afraid."

He was confronting her with a smile, such as she had been used to at all their meetings, since the earliest time she had heard his advice—face and lips as rubicund, smile as professional, though it would have been difficult to decide whether the smile or the profession had come first. He was wearing, which wasn't his invariable custom nowadays, his black coat and striped trousers. The only oddity Mrs. Underwood noticed was that, as he invited them to set round his table, he also invited them to have a glass of madeira. She thought that habit had vanished long ago, and promptly accepted. Julian gave bland open-eyed thanks, and refused.

"Ah well," said Mr. Skelding, "it's very good of you to put yourself out." He was addressing Mrs. Underwood. "I do apologise for dragging you here."

"But you really haven't any news? About the appeal, of course?" She couldn't let it go.

He broke into a smile even wider, even more polite.

"Oh, I'm rather out of things. That's really what I wanted to

269

tell you about. So I can't say anything fresh about that matter of yours. It's expected to be heard before the end of term, I believe, but then you've been apprised of that already. Naturally, I wish you every good fortune."

"I don't understand," said Mrs. Underwood.

"I assure you, this is nothing to upset you. Or even to incommode you." He was speaking with a curious kindness—blended with orotundities Julian hadn't heard from him before, though they passed Mrs. Underwood by.

"Since I saw you last, though" (that meant the conference in March's chambers), "I have been giving a certain amount of thought to my own arrangements. I have decided that it is time I stepped down from the management of this firm. I had slightly hoped to continue in the saddle for another three or four years, but then, you know, there are always younger men knocking at the door. So one oughtn't to linger on the stage too long. On the other hand, there are a few clients whose business I've tried to handle for half a life time and I should find it a deprivation, if you'll let me speak personally, not to continue with them—for at least a little while yet. I need hardly say"—he gave Mrs. Underwood another meaningless smile—"that you are one of those I should most miss working for. My colleagues have very generously considered my feelings in this situation. So if the suggestion is agreeable to you, I am still able to conduct your personal business and there needn't be any change in our relations."

"That's exactly what I should want," said Mrs. Underwood, immediately, earnest, direct. Then, just as directly:

"That's all right, but what are we all talking about then?"

"Ah," said Mr. Skelding, "there has to be some slight alteration, you see." He turned his countenance to Julian, affable, an unmysterious moon: and yet, it was more difficult to read than more romantic faces, and it would have taken an expert in Skeldingesque expressions to detect that it had become a shade more set.

"I am sure you won't be surprised to hear that our last meeting had certain consequences of a professional nature. As well as the little personal matter of my retirement" (this to Mrs.

Underwood), "but that of course isn't material. What is material is that I felt under an obligation to report what transpired at that meeting to my partners. To cut a long story short, the general consensus of us all was that it would be a disadvantage to all parties if this firm withdrew from the case, at the present juncture. It might raise a minor question mark about the firm, but it could raise more serious doubts about you as litigants. Reputable firms don't throw up cases for nothing, I'm sure you've heard the old saying." (To Julian.) "If I was still acting as your adviser, or even your man of business I should certainly say that in your own best interests you ought to leave well alone."

"We never thought of anything else," said Mrs. Underwood.

"Loud applause," said Julian.

"I'm glad you agree."

Julian's remark had been cheerful and amiable enough, but the puce in Skelding's cheeks had deepened. Nevertheless his tone stayed even, his speech measured.

"In those circumstances, I am sure you'll also agree that I couldn't possibly continue to handle the case for this firm. I explained the position as carefully as I could to my partners, and I think I can say that they came round to the same point of view. It is neither here nor there, but this was of course a factor pointing towards my retirement. I am sure it is obvious to you that, though this firm will continue to act for you and do what can be done, I could not conceivably remain in charge myself."

"Oh, I don't see why not."

"With respect, but you should see why not. I didn't give you my advice lightly, as I hope you will appreciate. In my judgment, for what that may be worth, it was the best advice I could give you. You made it clear that you had no confidence in it. On my side, I had no confidence in the course you insisted on. The more I think about it, I have to tell you across this table, the less confidence I have. I have been associated with your family and in particular with your mother altogether too long to assist you towards a disaster. With great respect, you should be able to understand that I can have no part in it."

271

"Can't you think it over?" Mrs. Underwood sounded flat.

"I'm afraid that I've done that." He spoke to her with the earlier curious stilted kindness.

"Isn't there anything we can do?"

"I'm afraid I couldn't be any further use to you in this business unless you had confidence in my advice."

"Oh look," said Julian, "we needn't get weighed down over a thing like this, need we now?"

"I am afraid that there you must speak for yourself."

Julian opened his eyes wide, twitched his shoulders, for an instant stopped being casual. There was a silence. Then, old habit prevailing, Skelding mentioned, in an undertone, some minor piece of business of Mrs. Underwood's.

"You may have to draw in your horns," he said, liking to be minatory again.

Julian stirred himself.

"Well, we seem to have come to a dead end, don't we? Which isn't a surprise to anyone, I take it."

Mr. Skelding was expecting him to rise from his chair. As he did so, Mr. Skelding said:

"All that remains for me is to wish you success in the appeal." He shook Julian's hand. This had been done with dignity, the automatic reflex of years in that office. Dignity not so necessary, with no fuss at all, he smiled at Mrs. Underwood and said goodbye.

As they reached the court outside, drops of rain were steadily descending. Equally steadily, Mrs. Underwood was not beginning to hurry: but Julian looked at the sky, and not prepared to minimise any attack upon his health said:

"Come on, we must get out of this." He rushed her into a pub in Chancery Lane and there Mrs. Underwood, still disappointed at having received no news, was thinking about the past half-hour with Mr. Skelding.

"He's a pompous old boy, isn't he?" she said.

"Oh well, he's had a good deal to be pompous about," said Julian.

"Fancy bringing us down here for absolutely nothing."

"Nothing?"

"He didn't say anything we didn't know already."

Julian said, off hand: "He happens to be heart-broken, you see."

"Whatever do you mean?"

"He's packed up. He didn't want to pack up. I don't expect he has anything else to live for. He's the sort of man who doesn't live long after he's retired."

Mrs. Underwood gazed at her son. When, which wasn't often, he talked to her about other people, she was accustomed to believe what he said.

"Do you really think so?"

"That's what he was telling us. Or telling you, rather."

"I suppose he didn't like you not agreeing with him over the case."

Julian hooted. "That's putting it mildly."

Mrs. Underwood's firm nose and mouth took on the stern expression of someone wishing to perform a benevolent act.

"He's always done his best for me. I don't like the idea of the old thing being miserable. Can we do anything about it?"

"You can have him round to dinner now and then, he'd enjoy that. But the only thing that would really make a difference would be if I changed my mind."

"Will you?" She knew the answer. She would have argued if it had been anyone else, but not with Julian.

"Of course not."

Julian, who was lightly meditating, went on: "Poor old buffer, he's an awful bore, but he can't help that. I wonder if he knows how boring he is? But he's not a bad sort. It's a pity he's going to be put on the dust heap."

He opened his eyes to their widest, and said, with an expression of consternation, discovery, and supreme innocence:

"Do you know, Mummy, I've noticed before, that when anyone gets in my way they tend to come to a bad end?"

"Really," she gave a dutiful frown, "haven't you any feeling at all?"

"What do you think?"

But her protest, like her expression, was only in the line of duty. Loving him as she did, she believed that he had feeling for her: and if he was callous, callous as an infant, about everyone else, that didn't make her think that he was defective at the heart, but simply drew her closer, as though they were conspirators.

So that she immediately asked him another question.

"Have you been thinking about Liz?"

"I don't get much chance not to, you know."

"I mean, are you ever going to marry her?"

"If you were me—would you?"

He asked playfully but she took her chance. She said, sounding to herself fairminded and detached, believing that she was keeping an even balance.

"I wish I knew. To tell you the honest truth I can't make up my mind. She has fine qualities, we all know that. She'd be utterly loyal. At least I think she would. But of course, if you did happen to win this appeal, and I'm crossing my fingers every day about that, you'll have plenty of others who'll be wondering about you as a very good prospect. Younger girls than Liz. After all, there's no escaping it, she's not as young as she was. That might have made her specially anxious to grab at you. I don't know whether you've thought of that."

Mrs. Underwood spoke to her son as though she were instructing an inexperienced boy in the tactics of women. He sat by, face as simple as though he were that same innocent boy, listening to novel wisdom.

"I've sometimes worried a little," said Mrs. Underwood, "about what she would be like if you did marry her. Of course, she had that long affair with Talland, didn't she? Then she ditched him. She doesn't seem to have thought about the consequences for Talland's wife. Or poor Talland himself, in the end. Marriage might make a difference, I know. But if she's going to be loyal to you, I'd like to have seen her show she can manage it with someone else."

This was, in literal truth, an entirely distorted account, like history turned on its head or attempts to prove the sanctity of Richard III or the Marquis de Sade, of Liz's other major love, in which she had felt and behaved almost exactly—dismayingly so if one was predicting her future—as she had with Julian. Mrs. Underwood was a truthful person. She was reporting information which had been, unknown to Julian, gently put to her by a not specially reliable source, which was

274

Swaffield. Not for any special purpose. He had sunk his old vendetta. He had talked to her almost casually, it seemed, just to keep his hand in, dipping into a human relation. Sometimes his dips did good, he scarcely cared. The process was its own reward. He had come mildly to like Mrs. Underwood but scarcely cared about that either. Once he had made his guess, a good guess, about her feelings for Liz, there was a matrix he couldn't resist playing with. It took only a little time, it cost him very little energy, he didn't care much about the result.

"You really think if I married her that she'd be unfaithful, do you, Mummy?"

"I don't want to say that, but could you guarantee she wouldn't?"

Julian gave a shining smile.

"It would be rather interesting, I must say. I expect she'd come back, you know, and that would be rather interesting too."

His mother was lost. Whatever he was imagining, apparently with pleasure, she couldn't reach. She said:

"Do you think you will marry her?"

"You know what I'm like—"

"Have you made up your mind?" she asked, not aggressively, quite gently.

"I never have been able to do that, have I?"

She smiled, she couldn't help it.

"Sometimes," he said blank-faced, "I wonder if I've got a mind to make up, when it comes to the point."

"Do you think you will marry her?" She spoke gently again.

"That's a good question," said Julian, like a confident lecturer who has just received a more than usually absurd enquiry from the back of the hall. "That's a very good question. All I can say, Mummy, is that I've listened very carefully to everything you've said. I'm very grateful. You've been a model of fairness in all ways. You've been absolutely unprejudiced, haven't you? About me. About Liz. Especially about Liz. I shall bear it all in mind, I can promise you that. Thank you very much."

❧ 32 ❧

D r. Pemberton was the first person, apart from the hospital staff, who knew of Hillmorton's death. It occurred late in October, a couple of days after the opening of Parliament. Pemberton's doctor friend reported that he had not emerged anywhere near to consciousness for days past.

"Just as well," said Pemberton. He would have said that about anyone in Hillmorton's condition. If any fool, Pemberton had been known to remark, blathered about last words or goodbyes, he ought to be made to spend his time at death beds.

Well, that was one sort of end. There were now actions for Pemberton to perform. He dated his formal letter to the Lord Chancellor, October 27th, and posted it that same night.

Hillmorton had died on a Thursday afternoon. That was one sort of end. But his world didn't let their dead depart without the formalities being satisfactorily prolonged. On the Friday morning there appeared a three column obituary in *The Times*, an adequate length, judged the connoisseurs in those matters, of whom there were many. The same connoisseurs also judged that he had come out of it pretty well. The obituary said that he had once been spoken of as a future Conservative Prime Minister: perhaps he had never entirely fulfilled the hopes of his admirers, but with his famous detachment he had continued in a life of selfless public service. Ryle reflected that obituaries made everyone sound very much the same, embedded in a porridge of nobility. Perhaps it was as well.

In the same mood, Ryle listened to the valedictory speeches in the Chamber on the following Tuesday afternoon. These were delivered only if the member who had died had once been a Cabinet Minister. They began immediately after the end of question time, and the House was full, decorous, quiet, attentive, quickened by the interest, the suppressed sense of liberation, which sustained elderly men at the news of someone else's mortality. The leaders of the three parties started off, followed by others who felt impelled to pay tributes, relate their school stories and call him Hallio, or alternatively show their talent for character drawing. Sedgwick, who had forced himself to struggle to his place, didn't speak. Nor did Ryle, who felt both sombre and more than usually out of tune.

Someone said, with great confidence, that Hillmorton was a born democrat. In his secret heart, Ryle thought, he was about as much so as the Duc de Saint Simon. Several references to the famous detachment. They didn't know him, they didn't know when a veil seemed lifted only to reveal another veil, sceptical, amused, and left him in precisely the position where the dullest dimmest representative of his class, time and millions, would by instinct stand. How supremely unselfish he was. In fact, he was good natured and liked to see people happy, provided that didn't interfere with any concern of his own. Maybe that was as much as one could expect from a public man, or most private men either.

Ryle had been as fond of him as had anyone in those rows of faces. Even while he was dismissing what was said, it was a comfort that something should be said. The formalities had their use: they were formalities which all were practised at, they had the comfort of a ritual, they warmed up the nothingness.

It didn't matter what anyone said. Though there was just one thing which gave Ryle pleasure. It came from the Leader of the Opposition. He remarked smoothly, courteously, that "we on this side, of course, have had our quarrels with the noble lord, Lord Hillmorton, but that doesn't prevent us sharing equally, quite equally, in the common grief. Of course some of us suffered from his tongue when we, like him, sat in the other place (the House of Commons). But we always recognised his gifts and his virtues. Above all we always admired his style. As much as anyone in politics in our time, Henry Hillmorton had style. Sometimes I wish that some of us could recapture it."

Dead true, thought Ryle, and the wish also. Any society needed style. When it went, you never got it back.

Later that afternoon, Ryle saw Adam Sedgwick being helped along the corridor by a badge-attendant. As Ryle joined them, he heard a couple of hearty eupeptic voices behind him. One was saying that it might be time for a drink. The other was agreeing yes, old Hillmorton always went in for a drink at just about this time. With the sublime certainty which those left behind felt about the wishes of the deceased, they assured each other that he would have wanted them to do the same. As usual with those certainties, this didn't impose inconvenience upon them. Somehow the deceased couldn't possibly have wanted them to be teetotal for an evening.

In the Bishops' Bar, side by side with Ryle, Sedgwick managed to steer a glass two-handed to his mouth. He had been remembering Hillmorton.

"I shall miss him," he said. "I expect you will too."

"Yes. I shall miss him," said James Ryle.

That was all that Sedgwick felt inclined to say. The intellectual aristocracy, Ryle had sometimes thought, were no better at coping with emotion than the old landed one. Yet he knew beyond doubt that Sedgwick had had a passionately happy married life, adored by his children. Maybe in earlier days he would have been more candid about his feeling for his friend. That evening, he confessed to Ryle that his disease had produced a psychological effect. More and more he wanted to avoid people, like one with claustrophobia. He even had to force himself to go to his laboratory. The mind was pretty powerless against the body, he said: then broke out irritably, that was silly, they were one and the same thing.

"Still, it won't be long now. One way or the other," he said.

The little room was filling, there was rollicking laughter

from the corner, men milled round, clubbable in their health and the pride of life. To Ryle that evening, the murmur, the bursts of noise, became nagging. It made Sedgwick's last remark take on an ominous sound.

Not protectively, over-sharply, he asked Sedgwick what he meant. Sedgwick gave an accurate account, without self absorption but with an air of relief. As he had told Hillmorton on that visit to Beryl Road, he had been trying to finish a piece of work. He had taken it as far as he could: it wasn't specially important, but it was worth publishing. His kind of science wasn't an old man's game anyway, but he had gone on longer than most (for once he showed a flash of vanity, which Ryle hadn't seen in him before).

The young men would push the work further, here at any rate this country was brimming with talent. As for himself, he had finished.

So now he was going to have his operation. He didn't tell Ryle, what he had told Hillmorton in extremity, that he had been frightened of it—and that this devotion to his work was, at least partially, a cover or excuse.

Now he had made the choice, he was as business-like as though no one alive had ever had qualms about surgery. He had been in correspondence with the American surgeon who had invented the operation. One of the English pupils whom Cooper had trained was said to be as good as they came. He would perform. Sedgwick needed a few weeks' grace, just to prepare this last paper for publication (was that another excuse, a final bit of devotion, or delay?). Then he would enter Queen Square just before Christmas. One way or the other, it wouldn't take long.

Just before Christmas. Like Hillmorton last year. That was a sheer coincidence of date. But Ryle couldn't break free from the chill, or shake it off. He said anxiously, as though he were the patient, not Sedgwick:

"Well. What are the chances?"

Sedgwick was quite controlled now. More so than he had been when he had had to give a similar answer to Hillmorton. He spoke with clinical calmness. If it went wrong, it went very wrong indeed. Possibly death. Possibly total incapacity, which was less acceptable. At his age, the probability of those results, added together, was something like two per cent.

Hearing that, Ryle, surprised and for an instant pacified, broke out:

"That's good. That's better than I thought."

"Is it?" Sedgwick gave a tucked-in smile. "It's distinctly worse than the chances we take in most affairs of life, you know."

But it was Sedgwick who was cheering up James Ryle that evening, not the other way round. As a consequence Ryle was glad to help him downstairs, help him into a taxi, say good-night—and then return alone. Ryle couldn't make himself see reason. The likelihood was that nothing would happen to Sedgwick. Ryle couldn't believe it. The omens wouldn't let go of him. It was ridiculous, as though he had been seized by the Roman augurs or the astrological prophecies in that evening's papers.

Maybe he was vulnerable because recently nothing had gone right for himself or the people close to him. A piece of good public news would be a lift. He read the tape, and as throughout those months the public news was sour. It might have been back in the war, when like other men who wished to think themselves stoical, in secret he was saying to himself, as with an unbeliever's prayer, we need a victory. When one was reduced to that, however, one believed that all would get darker, and that night, even the corridors—as he walked through them in search of a companion—loomed ominous.

That same evening, Liz, to whom he had let himself write a note of commiseration (the first contact for weeks), was also beset by the future, though in a different fashion. The news of her father's death, which she didn't hear until she returned from spending the night with Julian, had made her inordinately unhappy. Curiously, she was filled with remorse. Not that she had any cause to feel remorseful about, except the little bites of guilt (enjoying herself in the treacherous flesh, while he was dying or dead: wishing him to live longer, not for his own sake, but because of the gift). In objective truth, she had been loving, like one who didn't get so much love back. There might have been remorse owing from him. For his misleading ease, the appearance of affection and intimacy, had promised much more than it performed, and this had made her distrustful of him and other men. But it was remorse she felt: and, as with other attacks of remorse, this was shot through with fear. She had done badly. In some way that she couldn't begin to define, she ought to have given her father more. Underneath all his façades—for those she saw as clearly as his friends did—he had died dissatisfied and disappointed. Somehow, if she had used her imagination and behaved better to him, she could have made a difference.

Those wamblings, which she would have despised in another woman, sounded outside Liz's character or range—so clear cut, so sharply figured, so concentrated on her own vein of sexual love. Yet the remorse possessed her. It made her afraid that she would pay for what she had or hadn't done. Somehow it became interlaced with her fears about Julian.

The appeal was now expected early in December. She had lost her judgment, she could not perceive what either result would bring to her, or which to long for. She was possessed by remorse about Julian, close to that which she was feeling for her father. If she had behaved differently, loved him more unselfishly, demanded less, then there would be nothing to be afraid of, and she would be innocent and be given happiness.

This was self-torment. Again in terms of objective truth, it was more absurd than her remorse about her father. She had loved Julian with total surrender, too much for her own need, though not for his. But this kind of remorse wasn't connected with the truth. Perhaps it contained a kind of vanity. Somewhere, in the scraps of pride she still preserved among her love, it was a sustenance to make-believe that she had done wrong, rather than that she had had it done to her.

Thinking of her father and Julian, the figures indistinguishable as in a dream, perhaps she made the future less pathetic if she took the blame.

That was not altogether so easy to do, since she had not lost her sense or her sharp wits, as particulars of her father's will began to filter through. It would take months or years to settle the death duties, the lawyers said, as though proud of the complications that a man as clever as Hillmorton could devise. However, as Liz told Ryle, to whom she turned once again, two things were clear enough. First, Hillmorton, that exponent of rationality, had in his will displayed a remarkable lack of it. Money, property, pictures, possessions, there was a great deal, no one could value it yet. In disposing of it Hillmorton had shown a preposterous faith in primogeniture. Even if he had had a son he couldn't have gone to more extremes (that was the way the English aristocracy had preserved their fortunes, Ryle had once said, but now he didn't consider that that sociological reflection would be particularly strengthening to Liz).

The Suffolk home, as had been known previously, had been made over to his eldest daughter, but it appeared only as part of a trust. All the rest had been transferred sometime before, to this same gigantic trust. From this, his wife and daughters were to be allowed to draw annual sums, quite small sums without even an adjustment for inflation. In the end, the entire resources of the trust were to pass to the first male grandchild—on the death of Hillmorton's wife, or when the grandson attained the age of twenty-five, whichever was the later.

"All tied up," said Liz, "so that it can't possibly do any good to anyone." She didn't mind him being callous, she said, she had always known he was capable of that. Ryle didn't comment. Of course she minded. "But this is just fantasy. It's the work of a fool. He wasn't a fool, was he?"

"Very far from it," said Ryle. He knew that, just then, she wanted to hear him praised.

The second thing was that he had duly made the gift she had wrung out of him. He had kept his promise. The surprise was that it was less than he suggested. It was actually £20,000. This wouldn't have been an inducement to Julian on the first night they spent together, certainly not now. She didn't mention Julian's name, though, talking to Ryle. She had become less self-absorbed, perhaps sharpened by her own stress and not so oblivious of his.

In any case, as Hillmorton hadn't survived the seven years, his gift would, when the duties were worked out, be worth next to nothing at all.

"That's how I come out of it," she said. "I'm left pretty stripped and stark, shouldn't you say?"

"You've not been lucky."

"I wonder, how many of us have?"

She might indulge in self-torment, but that she hadn't told him. She didn't indulge in self-excuse, that he could read for himself. She had the kind of spirit he would have loved if she had been his wife. They exchanged looks in which on his side there was sarcasm and regret, on hers pity. That touch of pity, soon over and not to return, was not the pity which leads to love; but she enjoyed feeling it and it gave her some confidence back.

❧ 33 ❧

When Jenny moved into Lorimer's flat she, for once unwilling to tempt fate, was still keeping on her own. She never returned there. That told as much of the story as she would have told, even to herself. In her kind of realism, she knew when not to put sex into words. She might have repeated the saying she had picked up earlier in her life—the worst doesn't always happen. That had been the advice given her by a derelict acquaintance when her own existence was in one of its bleakest phases. The saying sounded to her grim, realistic, nordic, and she liked it. In fact, of course, it would have appealed so much only to a nature as sanguine as her own.

The worst hadn't happened this time. They both of them looked happy. He felt proud that he had made the decision that night in the embankment garden. She was satisfied that she had judged it right. Perhaps something could be inferred from noticing that he was showing signs of cheerful, almost flippant happiness, which none of his acquaintances had seen in him before: whereas Jenny wasn't so elated, but content and secretly triumphant.

She hadn't expected wonders, and didn't get them. She was much too sensible to believe excited virgin tales about the inhibited: how they were marvellous, irrepressible, when once set free. That wasn't true of anyone she had met. It certainly wasn't true of Jarvey. But yes, and this she did believe, most people were capable of enjoying themselves, with a little coaxing: and that turned out, equally certainly, to be true of him. There the happy side of her nature was kind to them both. Because he enjoyed himself, so did she.

She discovered something about him which she didn't know, didn't know because there were things you could discover only in bed. It wasn't that he was suddenly transformed into a wit or a verbal charmer. Speech came a little easier perhaps, not much. But he had, and this was the discovery, a remarkable capacity for joy. Not passion, no: that was ordinary enough: but joy, yes. That this had come to him, that here he was with someone he trusted and who was fond of him, who made everything light-footed and took anxiety away, so that at last he knew what it was like to live as man and wife—could he get joy out of a bread-and-butter assurance such as that? She was certain that he did. Joy out of the simple prospect of the night together: joy as they lay afterwards in bed.

Jenny had long ago perceived that he had always felt cut off from other men. With a touch of mute arrogance, with much more shrinking and humility. Somehow it was wonderful for him to have found his way back into the mainstream. She could understand that, but she was amazed that it so continuously lit him up. Humble he might be, but sometimes he surveyed her as though he were a pasha, or modestly modelling himself a Julian Underwood.

A month after she had installed herself in Pimlico, it was he who insisted on marriage.

"That's what I really meant," he said. "You know, when I started things off that night. Down by the river."

"Did you?"

"But you didn't get it right. So I took advantage of you, didn't I?"

He spoke with the complacency of a seducer. Jenny obediently smiled. She had no guilt. No harm had been done to a living soul. He was better off, and so was she.

He insisted not only on marriage, but on making a fuss about it.

"I don't want us to look ashamed of it, do you? May as well come right out with it. Proper announcements. Take place shortly. We won't go to a register office. We'll have it in the Chapel. That's the way to do it, you know."

There she was surprised again, as well as pleased. Religious service? She was sure that he believed no more than she did. Was this something he wanted to do for her? No, it was a signal about himself. She was more grateful because of that.

The engagement was duly published in *The Times*, the week after Hillmorton's death. "The engagement is announced, and the marriage will shortly take place, between Lord Lorimer, M.C. of 127 Lupus Street, London, S.W. 1. and Mrs. Jennifer Rastall, of 42 Barham Gardens, S.W. 5." That was all right, thought Jenny, as she read the paper. But she hadn't been born in her class for nothing, and she reflected (just as she and Lorimer had felt obliged to remark, the first time they went out together), humorously, but not entirely so, that the addresses didn't look very grand.

Congratulations over the telephone, piled up in letters which she had to collect from the deserted flat. More than she had received ever before in her life. That was pleasant. It was pleasant to be invited with Lorimer to parties. At one of these, with her acute directional hearing, in which respect, if in no other, she resembled Swaffield, she picked up two youngish women discussing the engagement, and to her delight using the same egregious phrase in which Lorimer had originally proposed.

"Two elderly people joining forces, I should say, shouldn't you?"

"Right."

"Just for company, of course."

"Of course."

This time Jenny's reflections were entirely humorous. To the puzzlement of the man speaking to her, she broke into a wide, toothy, unprovoked grin.

At this stage, early November, there was a complication. Lorimer might have insisted on the marriage, but Swaffield insisted on taking charge of the wedding. Jenny had to do some domestic diplomacy. Lorimer hated Swaffield, said he despised him, was jealous of him. He was rancorous at the thought of a rich man amusing himself with their wedding. He told Jenny that he wouldn't stand it. On the other hand, Jenny wasn't going to stand the loss of Swaffield. She was more prudent than Lorimer, they might both need Swaffield for jobs. She counted pennies more than Lorimer and neither of them had any. Swaffield assumed that he would pay for all.

It was no use battering at Lorimer with practical arguments. So she told him (which was also in part true) that she felt obligations to Swaffield, that she couldn't snub him just when her luck had turned, that she had to show some sort of honour and pay off her debt. Even if no one noticed that they themselves happened to be the pair getting married. This was the tone Lorimer had no answer to. She had to use his decency against him, and, she was acceptant enough to think, this wouldn't be the last time.

Thus, on the first of December, at eleven in the morning, Swaffield, carnation in his buttonhole, monkey-like in morning suit, stood as her best man in the Crypt Chapel, and Swaffield was providing the reception afterwards.

The Chapel, embedded below the old Palace of Westminster, was small. It was also venerable. A good many people in the congregation were accustomed to think of their country as venerable and the places they saw round them. Much of that was an illusion. There was little standing in London which had been built before the eighteenth century. As it happened, much of that existed in their particular Westminster corner. The Abbey across the road, and St. Margaret's (relatively juvenile). But the Houses of Parliament themselves had been created after a 19th Century fire, as a great confident 19th Century gothic fantasy. Scarcely anything was left that, say, the younger Pitt might have cast a cold eye on—except the dark and freezing Westminster Hall, suitable for State trials, some cellars, and this little Chapel.

That morning candles were blazing toward the vaulted roof, something like a scene out of a film of Ivan the Terrible, gilt gleaming off the pillars, gleaming off the medallion of Judas in the East wall: the whole picture was Kremlin-like, said knowledgeable peers, much to the puzzlement of Russians.

The Chapel used to be arctic before the heating engineers got to work. That morning it was uncomfortably warm, the more so because it was uncomfortably packed. Jenny was incredulous and didn't accept the obvious explanation—for her diffidence still stayed with her, and she didn't imagine that she was popular. Many of her clients had turned up, old people making their way by underground. Even older people, such as her Miss Smith, had had to afford the taxi fare. That meant a week's pinching, but Miss Smith was glowing with approval, as though this was a proper and natural occasion for a protégée of hers. Nearly all the Swaffield entourage had come, and the staff at the charity office.

As for Lorimer, he was an obscure back bencher, but, just as you didn't let anyone's death pass without a modest demonstration, so you didn't let a marriage either. If you lived in an enclave, you made the most of it. Everyone felt warmer when you closed the ranks. Members of his own party attended, who knew him only walking through the lobbies. The Government Whips were there, bonhomous, well turned out, shining faced. They were exchanging cheerful words with peers from the other side. Several of those had come—out of good nature (one or two observant eyes had noticed for years a sad-looking man, silent, often alone in the bar), general social emollience or just a desire for a party and a drink.

Bishop Boltwood took the service. He was a high Anglican, but his church didn't mind overmuch that both parties had been married before, and divorced. If the church did, the Bishop didn't. He might have the exterior of a Lancashire comedian, but he was shrewd and had formed his opinion of these two. They had been ill-treated. He was in favour of marital happiness. If anything he could do would help them, he would do it. So, shortlegged, sturdy, authoritative, he rolled out in his firm, not specially stately, voice the old and specially stately English words.

Soon it was done. Muriel Calvert, who was sitting with her mother and step-father, might have been commenting at that point—the irrevocable happened altogether too early on. However, the Bishop was not done. More stately words of the ritual, and then he felt it desirable to add some of his own.

"Jennifer and Jervis," he said, "some of us in this place know you both, and we want you to believe, as we believe, that you have the best of your lives before you. You are going on an adventure. . . ." The Bishop, a warm-hearted man, was not notably economical in speech. He developed this figure. Sardonic and hard-baked persons, and there were a number of those present, went off to the reception remarking that he made it sound as though they were off on a stiff trip of Amazonian exploration.

Jenny, who thought of herself as hard-baked and to whom tears didn't come easy, found herself irritatingly near to them. For the only time since she had decided on marriage. She found herself irritatingly and absurdly thinking that she had never had much of a father and that this peculiar little Bishop, who was younger than she was, might have been better than most.

She soon recovered, and she had some need to. They arrived at a big room at ground level, tables set for the party, awnings stretched over the terrace, a door open on to the swirling mist outside. For December, the morning wasn't cold. The mist wasn't the old London fog, by this time obsolete. It was the thick, grey, anticyclonic mist, no harm to anyone except to transport, shutting them all in, making them feel safe and cherished, like children looking out of the windows of their house, not needing to go outside on a raw winter day.

The walls of the long room were polished, and now that there were a hundred people in it the sound reflected clashingly in all ears. The trays of champagne were going round. One or two of the guests, glasses in hand, were walking out on the terrace, with the air of those accustomed to compulsory expeditions from country houses.

From the moment they entered, Swaffield had monopolised Lorimer and Jenny.

"That went O.K." He said it as though he had done it all.

"Very nice," said Jenny.

"Don't worry about next week." This referred to the appeal, which was down for the following Thursday.

"We're not counting on anything," she said.

"You'd better not." (She thought that this was cool, with the memory of certain ferocious advice.) "You'll manage somehow."

Lorimer had drunk two glasses of champagne and was less affronted by Swaffield than he had been.

"I got her to marry me, didn't I?" He was becoming argumentative. "I shouldn't have done that if we couldn't manage, should I?"

"Shouldn't you?" Swaffield gazed at him without excessive interest.

Then he said: "You won't get much of a honeymoon."

He meant, they couldn't go away until after the appeal. He couldn't resist—not that he tried to—the familiar note, proprietorial, private detective-like, ineffably salacious.

"Plenty of time for that," said Jenny, who was now as imperturbable against this specific probe as either of the Symingtons.

Then Swaffield put his arm round her and took her away from her husband.

"This is all right, is it?" he asked.

"Of course it is."

"I'm glad you fixed it up, my girl. I'm glad something's gone better for you. You deserve it."

For the moment, his manner was kind. It was also—she might be imagining it—vaguely chagrined, or even wistful. He had what others envied, power and money and his eventful life, including his roster of sleeping partners. She had envied him herself. For the moment, though, in reverse he seemed to be envying an unspectacular marriage.

She returned to Lorimer and moved on his arm into the middle of the room. Men, engulfing canapés, merry with champagne, kept coming to them. In Jenny's visits to the guest room, the peers she had talked to were middle aged and staid. Some of these were quite young and not so staid. Congratulations. Praise.

"Lady Lorimer, you've made a difference to him, you really have."

"He looks pretty well on it, doesn't he, Lady Lorimer?"

They had a knack of talking about him as though he wasn't there. Lorimer towered above her, decorously shy, with a fixed smile at the same time shamefaced and gratified. One man, so bald that she couldn't guess his age, introduced himself and gave a name which to her meant nothing. Later she discovered that he was an eminent physician. He had small, bright, abnormally piercing eyes: "I want to tell you that I think this is a very good idea. I've been worried about your husband. Just on inspection. It's a risk for anyone to live so much alone."

She was taken aback at how forthcoming some men could be, yes, how inquisitive, how they inspected her or perhaps liked to bring her into the party.

She had to do her duty, going off alone to talk to her clients, most of them overawed by the noise, the assured conversation round them, the uninhibited parliamentary voices, the place itself. She was, as usual, at home with them, made them have another drink (one or two dignified old ladies were showing the effects of their first), told them that she had expected to be ejected from the place when she was first invited there, but had enjoyed it when she got back to her bed-sitter. So would they.

Even Miss Smith had to struggle to preserve her customary air of patronage. She took refuge in acquiring information. Could her dear Jenny, now her dear Lady Lorimer, tell her about the titles in the room? Jenny did her best, which, since Lorimer didn't have so many acquaintances, was not a good one. Where was Lord Clare, whom Miss Smith had heard her mention? No, he wasn't there. (Not smart enough for him, Swaffield had been thinking meaningfully, and stored another note in his elephantine memory. For reasons of his own Swaffield had hired the room and the reception, not through Clare, but through Azik Schiff.) Then by a piece of luck Jenny noticed someone she did know, one of the whips, good at parties anyway, heritage modestly historical, though not so much so as Clare's. She attracted his attention, he turned his on to Miss Smith, and she was happy.

It was only a little later that Jenny had a curious, perverse experience, which she couldn't deny but of which later she was ashamed. She was elated: the lights in the room seemed more brilliant, with the mist closing in: looking out of a window, she couldn't see across the river, no Lambeth, just the nacreous, comforting and guarding swirl. Suddenly she felt more anxious about the appeal than she had ever been before. It was as crude as though, now she had something, she wanted more, much more, she wanted the lot. Here she was, being fêted, safely married, approved of, content: and she found that, just as when one dread had been cleared away then another flooded in to fill the vacuum in the mind (as Ryle knew too well all through those months), so it was with what one desired. She wouldn't have said, judging herself, that she was grasping, certainly not mercenary: yet now she wanted all which that last will snatched away from her, she wanted the money, she wanted to be well off. If she won in the Appeal Court, she wouldn't be rich, like a number in this room. But she and Lorimer could live in modest style. She wanted that.

It struck her, how sharp the longing was. She felt she didn't know herself. She didn't like herself. She couldn't repress it. She was retracing snatches of Swaffield's conversation. He had told her not to worry about next week, but when she said that they weren't counting on success, he had replied that they had better not. He couldn't have any inside knowledge not given to her? No, that was impossible, worry running away with her. Was it a guess or a forecast? More likely, just a dig at random. Swaffield indulged himself as a kind of emotional thermostat. If one was up, as she was on her wedding day, one ought to be brought down. If she had been down, Swaffield would have aimed to haul her up. Well, that was all about her money. She tried to stiffen herself and get back to enjoying the morning. Her spirits were so high, she could throw off thoughts which kept nagging into her mind—but they didn't leave her quite at rest.

For a while, during the reception, they revived, but in a fashion which seemed natural. The same whip who had been giving pleasure to Miss Smith had walked through a knot of guests, looking the reverse of purposeful, but actually in search of Jenny. She was still standing beneath the window, and the whip noticed her, with one of the chandeliers reflected snugly against the murk outside.

He said to Jenny:

"I know it's not a very suitable time, Lady L. But I'd like to drop a word in your ear."

"Right." She had a soft spot for this smooth pink man, who might be as pink as he looked, but wasn't as smooth.

"It's this. We'd like to bring Jervis into things more now. But you'll have to prod him, you know."

The plan was amiable, as produced by an experienced school master to an inexperienced parent. Jervis wouldn't be likely to become very easy on his feet (i.e. as a speaker): but he ought somehow to make his maiden speech, it didn't matter whether he read every word, the House would take anything from a maiden speaker, particularly someone they cared for (gentle, avuncular, though this man could have been Jervis's own son). Then another speech or two, an occasional question. Once he had done the barest minimum in the Chamber, there were all kinds of jobs round the place where a man like Jervis would be useful. They could put him on committees. They were always looking for men who weren't politicians searching for office, but who could devote a certain amount of time.

Jenny suspected that this smooth pink man didn't deserve the highest marks for candour—but this plan was well-meant, there couldn't be anything but good will behind it. It would be fine for Jervis. But it pre-supposed that he didn't need to earn money. Any such work in the House was done for love: unlike the whip's own job, which was part of the Government and paid. The whip, who didn't often get things wrong, must imagine that she had means. Of course, if she won next week—then the reservoir of worry began filling again, drip by drip. But it didn't fret her. This man was exuding well-being just because there was a bit of personal management to do. No harm to anyone, conceivably a little good. Part of the unexacting stream.

If Ryle had been present, and had heard that conversation (he had refused an invitation, not for Clare-like motives, but because he had a board meeting that morning, incidentally being prevented again from meeting Jenny), he might have had more of his forebodings. People of ability, energy, spirit, were playing round in the unexacting stream. There was no drug like habit. Or continuity. Even this cheerful morning, marriage, party, all safe in the bright weather-bound room, made them content that all was as it had been and was going to be. Human beings didn't look forward very far.

Yet Ryle would have had to allow for his own pessimism. Possibly he was no more objective than these people living in the moment. Jenny had lived an unexciting life, by most standards. The whip was full of well-being, trying to do a good turn to an unavailing man. They were doing no harm, except, as inimical critics would have said, by the sheer fact of their existence, or that of their country and their enclave within it.

Ryle would have been one of the first to remark, not many people had ever been persuaded to abdicate by the sheer fact of their existence. Those two standing by the window, were too healthy and happy to do so. They dealt with what came close to hand, and they didn't feel guilty because they did no more.

❦ 34 ❦

On the Wednesday following Jenny's marriage, which was the day before the appeal, Dr. Pemberton (he intended to keep that name on his doctor's plate) was sitting on the Government back benches in the House of Lords. This was the second afternoon he had attended, and he was viewing proceedings with a not unfamiliar blend of grievance and inspissated scorn. Grievance because he had expected the previous day, when he took his seat, to be something of a show, with himself on stage. Not a bit of it. He had signed the book at the table, walked up to the Woolsack, presented the writ which, with office efficiency and without comment, had duly arrived, and shaken hands. No one had noticed. No one appeared to enquire who was the very large man, black haired, pale faced, who had gone to sit beside complete strangers while a peer proceeded to ask the first question of the afternoon.

This next day, he was giving the place another chance. The only record of his entry was inscribed on a leaf of green paper which he had picked up in the lobby. Minutes of the day before. Date in Latin. Die Martis 5ᵉ Decembris 1972. Mummery, thought Pemberton. Prayers read by the Bishop of Chichester. Next line—The Earl of Hillmorton Sat First in Parliament after the death of his kinsman.

That was all it said.

As it happened, there was something of a show this afternoon, which Pemberton, now Hillmorton, had to witness. A newly created life peer was being introduced. More mummery, thought Pemberton, with increasing scorn. This was one of the English ceremonies, and the English were still good at ceremonies. Pemberton did not approve of them. Garter King of Arms in heraldic dress leading a procession: three peers in baronial robes (hired for the occasion, Pemberton judged), the new one in the middle, walking solemnly down the aisle, up to the Lord Chancellor, presenting the writ of summons—which Pemberton had done the day before, without all this fuss, as he now thought. The monarch's statement of the new creation, oath of allegiance taken in the name of God. Further solemn walking, taking off and putting on of hats, stiff necked bows. Final walk to the Lord Chancellor, hand shaking, disappearance among loud hear-hears.

In Pemberton, thoughts about mummery continued to rankle. This didn't happen when one succeeded to a peerage which already existed. They needn't have let him just slink in. Still, ceremonies were fatuous, he had no use for them, nothing of the sort would have appeased him. Human beings had a passion for putting on fancy dress. It showed they had nothing better to do.

Most men, even against their will or convictions, were impressed by forms, style, collective mana. All Adam Sedgwick's forebears and friends had with lucid rationality dismissed the idea of the Upper House. When he arrived there, in rational possession of his faculties, he had felt rather like an unbeliever going into church, with the kind of shiver that an unbelieving serious Larkin man couldn't shrug off. Not so Dr. Pemberton. He thought it was singularly silly.

He surveyed the faces round him and the serried faces opposite. Middle-aged faces, elderly faces. A doctor was used to looking at faces. A few were bright, some—Pemberton was under no temptation to give the benefit of the doubt—not so bright. Ordinary faces. In a moderately prosperous practice you could have picked them up off the street. One was breathing heavily not far away. Pemberton would have taken precautions if that had been a patient. And with one or two others he could see. Too much weight around. Pemberton had once sat in the gallery of the Commons. Still more weight there, still more signs of strain. To Pemberton's eye, politicians often looked bad lives.

Pemberton thought even less of politicians than he did of most people. To him, they didn't appear suitable persons to run a country. He didn't consider it necessary to think of anything better. He wasn't a Ryle, historically minded, trying to imagine the future. He didn't care so much and had nothing like Ryle's foreboding. Pemberton was neither a far-sighted nor a pessimistic man. He didn't often indulge in what he would have written off as profitless speculation. True, he hadn't much use for his countrymen, any more than he had for the rest of humankind, perhaps less. They were an idle lot. The workers didn't work, and the managers didn't manage. Nevertheless he took it for granted that things would go on. He didn't believe there would be much change. If there were, whatever happened, he was safe: a decent doctor wouldn't starve.

The new peer had just entered, unrobed, one more ordinary looking man, thought Pemberton, and took a modest place on the cross benches. Questions, which to Pemberton sounded like parliamentary pingpong, and, if it had been possible to make his estimate of the place sink lower, would have done so. Half an hour of questions. Waste of time.

The Clerk of Parliament had pronounced "The Lord—" and the debate began. This was a Wednesday afternoon debate such as Ryle had been listening to almost exactly a year before, the afternoon when he had first questioned Hillmorton about his limp. The subject didn't sound entrancing: the world's energy supply. Quite soon Pemberton, not without let-down, found himself feeling less dismissive. Pemberton gained internal warmth from general superiority to all round him, as had reinforced him so far that day: but he was honest, it was no good pretending superiority when others were doing better than one could oneself.

This man knew his stuff. He was also a practised speaker. Pemberton hadn't made a debating speech in his life, nothing nearer than delivering papers in front of medical societies. This was different. It might be more difficult. Leather-red benches, shining gilt, mummery, old men clutching their hearing aids, mummery. No, Pemberton was forced to attend to the accurate professional voice. This man wasn't a nobody. Nor was the one who followed: not so professional, slightly more futurist. If one was going to make any impact in this place, one would have to learn their techniques. These men seemed able to think on their feet. All Pemberton knew was medicine. He might learn to make a speech on a medical topic. He became thoughtful.

He recovered his superiority when he left the chamber to master the building. A competent man, entering a new hospital, identified the lavatories and the place where one ate. Pemberton was a competent man. He didn't think much of the architecture of the Palace of Westminster. Grandiose decoration was not for him. Crimson carpets, too many shades of red, tapestries, pictures of long forgotten peers—nothing to distinguish one corridor from another, the building was a functional frustration. Pemberton didn't think much of the mixture of luxury and frustration. He would have liked to design the place himself.

He walked into the library, no medical books, not much use to him. Into the guest room and bars, not much use to him, being a non-drinker. Might help with visitors. Visitors might be impressed by the place. He was going to make it work for him, for what that was worth. Pemberton wasn't as assured as he would have liked to be, walking as a stranger in a domain where everyone seemed to know everyone else. One felt the opposite of snugness, when everyone around was snug. It impelled Pemberton to think of past injuries. Some he could begin to pay off. He would call in at the Appeal Court (he had kept informed about the date) some time next day. Hillmorton's daughter and the rest of that family might as well face his existence now.

The big man walked along the corridor. Walked soft footed, like an old games player, thinking again that he had better give the place a second chance. He had actually formed that phrase, and in his mental ear it didn't seem a singular one. If he had considered, he would have thought it well-chosen.

Not long afterwards, he admitted to himself that at least the place had its value as a source of news. He had already discovered the tea room, and made his way there. More pictures of Lord Chancellors—more, although Pemberton didn't know it, of the Prince Consort's taste in mural ornament. Good taste of its kind, as usual, but then Pemberton would not have been interested in the Prince Consort or competent to make a significant statement about him. Pemberton saw a long table in the inner room, where, as at the more convivial clubs, one seemed to sit down at the nearest vacant place, not choosing one's neighbour. There were a dozen men, a couple of women, comfortably engaged over their tea, possibly not the most enthusiastic of debate aficionados. Pemberton sat next to an elderly beaming man, bald head so polished that remarks appeared to rebound off his forehead. He had beaming friendly manners and wasn't inhibited about asking questions. Shortly, he was saying:

"Excuse me, but I don't think I've seen you here before."

"You couldn't have very well."

"You must have come here recently, then?"

"Yesterday," said Pemberton.

"Ah. Really."

Cogitations were going on.

"Would you mind telling me who you are?" Pemberton's interlocutor introduced himself, and Pemberton said, as to the officials the day before, that he was Hillmorton.

"Ah. Now I get it. Let me see. Hallio wasn't your father, was he, he didn't have a son. Anyway—your uncle. Of course, I knew him very well indeed. I was at school with him, I knew him all my life. Hallio. I don't need to tell you he was one of the kindest men who ever lived. He couldn't bear to see anyone in trouble. He would go to any lengths to do anything he could. Even when he was working himself to the bone in office."

For once, Pemberton had lost his assertion. He made a nondescript noise. He was not to know that his neighbour had made a study, almost a profession, of saying the best about everyone. There were bleak persons who commented that by now he had come to believe some of it.

"I like to think of him, Hallio that is, your uncle," said the happy looking man, "helping his friend Sedgwick with his cigarette. That's Sedgwick the scientist, you know. One of the most distinguished members of this house, of course. But he has this nervous trouble and Hallio used to go to infinite pains about him. I am sure if Hallio was still with us he'd be helping Sedgwick through his operation. Of course he'd do that for anyone, not only a special friend."

Pemberton had not been disposed to attend to this old dodderer or do-gooder or bald headed man of glee (Pemberton might have considered any of those descriptions appropriate) bumbling away about the supreme benevolence of his predecessor. But, at the mention of Sedgwick, he did attend. He knew about Sedgwick as a scientist. Despite his abnormal lack of capacity for respect, Pemberton respected eminent scientists. He became polite. He put on his own kind of charm. He wanted to find out what was happening medically to Sedgwick.

To Pemberton's surprise, the old dodderer, even if he were also a dispenser of Christian charity, which made him still less congenial to Pemberton, turned out to have a talent for precise information. Men were curious about each other's illnesses when they became old enough, Pemberton didn't need telling: but this one was good at it. He knew the diagnosis. He knew the name of the surgeon who was to operate on Sedgwick. He knew the hospital. All he was uncertain about was the date of the operation, but he believed that it would be right at the end of the year.

"Very interesting," said Pemberton. He explained that he was a doctor. "I'll see if I can be some use."

He said it with massive prepotence. He hadn't enjoyed feeling alien, or out-classed by those smooth operators talking in the Chamber as he couldn't talk. Now he was making his own terms. He stared with slightly mollified scorn at the faces round the table, though he was clinically impatient because they were eating too many cream cakes. Never mind what he thought about this place. He could, and would, take advantage of it to get in touch with Sedgwick. That, at any rate, would be rational, if nothing else was.

✤ 35 ✤

The Law Courts were not old, but they could strike so.
Jenny and Liz were not old, but up there, in the Appeal
Court number two, they were waiting to hear a decision about
themselves in a fashion which was about as old as law. For
both of them, it was the only decision, or piece of official
news, that might make a difference to them: and it was coming
as it would have done generations before, face to face with the
deciders, without any mechanical aids, by word of mouth.

On the dais sat three Lord Justices, Fowke, Shingler, and
Gimson, bewigged, Fowke presiding, looking somewhat like
an incisive long-headed Arab, interventions courteous but sub-
liminally irritable. Shingler was heavier, more considerate and
gentle. Gimson was a small plump man, who appeared to relax
into dormouse reverie. (Their title of Lord Justices might have
been invented to baffle foreigners: they weren't lords, though
the job carried a knighthood. They were less elevated than
Lords of Appeal in Ordinary, who sounded humbler but actually were made lords, and sat in a committee room in the
House.) The Appeal Court number two was broader than
long, rather like Sedgwick's college rooms magnified and
equipped with a gothic glass-windowed roof: panelled walls,
bookcases with sets of shining volumes, a candelabra dominating the centre of the court, six wall-lights behind the dais.
Unlike the lower court, in which Bosanquet had sat, this contained only three rows of benches for spectators: which didn't

matter, since (lawyers, Liz, Mrs. Underwood, Julian, Jenny and Lorimer aside) there were no spectators at all. Except for Ryle, who came in after half an hour on the Thursday morning, and sat behind Liz.

It wouldn't have occurred to her that this kind of personal decision was quite different from anything in his experience, or her father's. But it was curiously true. Of course they had waited for news, about careers, jobs. But that news had arrived impersonally, cables, telex, over the telephone wire: good news travelled fast, at the speed of electrical impulses. Liz's father had received telephone calls from Number Ten. That meant he was in. (Once in 1935, he had waited by the telephone expecting a call which didn't come: that meant he was out.) Ryle's prosperity had been announced in business calls from New York. As for Adam Sedgwick, the only chancy event in his smooth career had been a call from Stockholm, a Swedish journalist telling him he had just been awarded the Nobel. Very early in the morning, too early to go to the laboratory and have a celebration. It was the public men who lived at the modern speed.

Jenny and Liz, private women, had to bear with the old-fashioned. That wouldn't have been an interesting reflection as they sat in court, nerves stretched and jangling.

It was not only an old-fashioned process, it was to both of them, clever people, who had by this time learned something of the law, semi-incomprehensible. That is, neither could judge, during almost any of the dialogue, whether the point was going for her or against. Lander was arguing, with manifest pleasure and enthusiasm, about 'influence' as discussed in a High Court judgment thirty years before. March called on his computer memory for verbal passages in 1891, 1903 and 1920. To Jenny and Liz, it was remote from themselves, or anything which had happened to people of flesh and bone in old Massie's house, or Jenny's memories of her father.

The counsel, and the three judges, seemed to be stirring with intellectual interest. Volumes with slips of paper protruding were opened and read as though the reproduction of printed documents hadn't been invented. To an outsider it would have seemed peculiarly amateur. The judges were industriously writing away in long-hand. Harwood and Baker, Hargreaves and Gray, to Jenny meaningless names, significantly repeated. Readings by both counsel from old judgments. It had something of the air of a theological argument between people with faith in revealed truth, Calvinists trumping each other with a text, or a Marxist producing six lines from Lenin. There were interludes in which one of the judges and the counsel became engaged, like a session of modern philosophers, in semantic or even grammatical exchanges.

Later on, but not in the court, Jenny might recognise that the law got more abstract as you went higher up. Before magistrates, in obscure courts of first instance (which she hadn't seen), you met people and heard what were supposed to be facts. At the assizes, or in her case before Mr. Justice Bosanquet, people still entered and facts were talked about. But in Appeal Court number two people and facts had somehow been purified away.

Later on, Jenny might recognise that that was part of the process. Not now in court. She had to concentrate on the sentences they were speaking, and then let them drift away. She was at the same time apprehensive, painfully more so than she had been at the earlier trial, and seepingly bored: apprehensive and bored, which was a state with little to recommend it. Though she felt it unsuitable or almost improper, in the middle of suspense, she even welcomed the odd diversion. There weren't many, but late on the Thursday morning, not long before the lunch-time break, her eye was caught by the sight of a very large man padding in behind the Underwood party. She wondered who it could be. She couldn't hear the conversation which began as soon as the court rose, but it would have distracted her.

This was Dr. Pemberton. He had touched Liz on the shoulder and asked:

"Aren't you Elizabeth Fox-Milnes?" She looked round into the big dominating face.

"Yes, that's me."

"I'd better introduce myself. I'm Archibald Pemberton."

"Sorry," she said, uncomprehending, uninterested.

"I've just taken your father's seat."

"Really?" Now she did comprehend.

"So in that way I'm the head of the family. I thought I ought to make myself known."

"Really?" Liz went through the courtesies, and introduced him to Mrs. Underwood and Julian as Lord Hillmorton.

"How's this business going?" Pemberton was at his most assertive.

"Your guess is as good as mine."

"I keep telling her it's all right," said Julian, casually possessive.

Pemberton ignored him, and exerted his maximum weight on Liz.

"Is there anything I can do?"

"I shouldn't think so, should you?" Liz replied. "That is, unless you can corrupt their lordships up there."

"I can tell you how to reduce the stress."

"I think we're coping," said Liz. "We shall have to go to lunch, shan't we, Julian? Thank you so much for coming," she said to Pemberton. "I expect we'll meet again."

Pemberton, enraged, felt as violent as when young, and could have smashed her teeth in. He felt he was being snubbed, which was true, and snubbed on social grounds, which wasn't. Liz might be a drop out of an aristocrat, but she was enough of one not to cherish the dear old middle-class illusion that aristocrats were incapable of snobbery: she was still more than capable of it herself. Not, however, with her father's heir, however he had arrived there (about which she was vague) and whatever he was like.

Her motive for snubbing Pemberton was quite different, singular, and unexpected. She was repelled by his overwhelming masculinity. Oh yes, she liked men, but they had to be men of a special kind, subtly devious, weaving veils of sexuality, not just embodying the plain brute fact itself. Although she had not yet accepted it, her instinct for men had been, at least in the eyes of other people, remarkably defective. As her father had remarked one night, she was one of those women who couldn't avoid being a bad picker. If Pemberton had been the only man around, she would never have picked him.

Pemberton watched them depart. With a total lack of hypocrisy or delicate forgiveness, he was devoutly wishing that 'that gang' would lose their case.

Jenny did not have to remain in that special fog, bored and apprehensive, for long. At half past four on the Thursday afternoon Lord Justice Fowke announced, conversationally, rattily, that they had heard enough. Bland nods from Shingler on his right, expressionless nods from Gimson on his left. They would need, Fowke continued, a certain time to write their judgments and would deliver them at eleven thirty the following day.

The following day, when it at last arrived, was a sparkling December morning. In the court, the chandelier as usual presided over what would without it have been a tenebrous room. The same company as the day before, not a single spectator, not even Ryle: he thought he could guess the verdict, and preferred to read it in the law reports. Front row, lawyers, next row, the Underwood party, on the left, Jenny and Lorimer on the right. The two back rows, quite empty, as in a remarkably unsuccessful backroom theatre. All the visitors who had spent hours at Bosanquet's hearing had dropped away. Curiosity about other people's concerns didn't last so long. As for disinterested stamina, that didn't last at all.

At eleven thirty precisely, flanked by his colleagues, Lord Justice Fowke began to read. He read without drama, without much intonation, and in a tone dry and only just over the audible threshold. Parliamentarians might have quoted the old maxim, the worst spoken speech was better than the best read one, though it was a maxim they didn't obey. Lord Justice Fowke's first words were:

"Among the many wise remarks Mr. Justice Bosanquet delivered in his judgment in this case, I wish to select two."

For Lander and March, he needn't have said more. They knew what his decision was to be: none of the rest did.

The judgment went on:

"I wish to give my support to Mr. Justice Bosanquet on the desirability, to put it no higher, of settling such cases as this without having recourse to legal process. The parties concerned should have reached an amicable agreement as soon as the will was disclosed. That is what all lawyers advise, and will continue to advise." He then proceeded to agree with Bosanquet on the state of the law about 'undue influence.' Of all the cases that came before him, these were the most unsatisfactory.

"But I have to deal with the law as it exists. I have studied the precedents introduced by learned counsel, and I have come to the conclusion that there is only one tenable basis on which to form an opinion. That is, what I shall define as the degree of influenceability of the testator. I have no doubt that we make the area of dubiety, which is already too great to be tolerable, enormously greater if we pay excessive attention to the environment and the personalities around him. Some men could be in such a state of mind and body that they could be influenced by the merest acquaintance. Some men could be uninfluenceable by those nearest to them, however strong their personality, uninfluenceable, that is, in any sense that the law should recognise or define. It is here, with reluctance, that I depart from the position of Mr. Justice Bosanquet. In his judgment, there is comparatively little reference to the character and condition of Mr. Massie, though a great deal of interesting material about the environment of his last years. I have no doubt that we shall decide the question of influence upon Mr. Massie if we search the evidence for how influenceable he was."

As the words had muttered on, Jenny accepted (almost without emotion, as in shock) that this judgment was going against her. Would the three judges have conferred together? Did he know what the others were going to say? Was there still a hope?

The judgment proceeded to analyse the evidence about old Massie (there was almost nothing said about Mrs. Underwood: March afterwards remarked that Fowke was deep, sharp and narrow, liked something he could get his teeth into, and was the last man to have patience with Bosanquet's intuition). There was little sign at any stage that he was more influenceable than other men, and many signs that he was less so. He had allowed his household to be rearranged by a competent woman. That could be interpreted as the attitude of a normal man having regard to his comfort. It had not been suggested, much less proved, that there had been any loss of efficiency. A reasonable man, who had been demonstrated in evidence not to have strong family ties, however unusual that might be, could decide without influence to alter his disposition about a daughter whom he had not seen, nor as the evidence again demonstrated, wished to see, for many years. This was no reproach to Lady Lorimer, the previous Mrs. Rastall. She had behaved with complete propriety in what must have been for her painful circumstances. The attitude of Mr. Massie was however as clear as a quantity of evidence could make it. He was regarded on all sides as a man of strong convictions and strong character. There was no effective evidence that those convictions and that character were seriously impaired by age, certainly not to the extent of his not knowing what he wished to do or merely acting as a passive tool. The position of Mr. Massie came out clear. He was as difficult to influence as most men could be, and that was the only certain ground which we could isolate for the purpose of decision in law.

Lord Justice Fowke looked up over his spectacles, although the words were in his script, and said with no emphasis:

"On this ground I would allow the appeal."

Lord Justice Shingler read in a rich good-natured voice.

"I can be very brief in the expression of my assent that the appeal should be allowed."

It was over for Jenny. They must have conferred last night, she thought. She stared, still blank-faced, at Lorimer, who didn't whisper but went on patting her arm.

She was too bemused to realise that Shingler was paying her compliments, to the last trying to act as a dispenser of good will. ("She mustn't depart from this court thinking there is the slightest reflection on her integrity or good standing. Nothing is further from any of our minds.") If there had been, or ever were, a clash of wills, or even opinions, between himself and Fowke, he wouldn't stand a chance: but he wasn't to be stopped putting in a bit of conciliation—and, as it turned out, a bit of practical charity.

The third Lord Justice, Gimson, took off his spectacles, shelved his appearance of repose, and read:

"I have to dissent from the judgments which have been delivered." A cool onlooker, such as Muriel Calvert, would have complained about the stage management: if Gimson had spoken second she would have had a few minutes more of pleasurable suspense. However, Muriel Calvert wasn't present, having long forgotten the entire process: actually, she had become occupied, not for the first time, with a man younger than herself.

Gimson had little to say about influence or uninfluenceability. His point was simple, and given with sharp quite undormouse-like authority. It is not enough that any of us trying the case might have come to a different conclusion. There must be such a preponderance of evidence as to make it unreasonable that the judge should deliver the verdict which he did. I find no such preponderance of evidence. The evidence is complicated and could be interpreted in several different ways. The judge interpreted it in a way any one of us might have differed from, but his verdict is not unreasonable. I should disallow the appeal."

Two to one for the appeal, and so the end. No, not quite the end. Lord Justice Fowke said, in his unpropitiating mutter:

"There is the question of costs. In the normal course, the appellants would be granted costs. In the somewhat unusual and needlessly complex circumstances of this case, it is considered that a somewhat different distribution should be made. I do not wish to hear submissions from learned counsel. It is decided that half the costs shall be paid from the estate. The other half to be discharged by the unsuccessful party."

To Jenny, that was more background noise. She didn't recognise until some time afterwards that this must have been a compromise, or in Aesopian language even a gesture of sympathy: presumably forced, so the lawyers agreed among themselves, by Gimson, with Lord Justice Shingler trapped between two strong minds. She didn't take in any of that. She turned to her husband, and as the judges made their bows and were departing through the door backstage, whispered:

"We've had it." She said it bright-eyed, without feeling, which had still not returned to her. She rose, back straight, and tapped Symington, sitting in the row in front, on the shoulder.

"Leslie. I want to thank you for all you've done."

"I'm sorry," Symington said. "I am sorry, Jenny." He meant it. He had come to respect her, and be fond of her. He would deal with Swaffield. He would make arrangements to see her again. But Symington was a professional, and a professional couldn't carry too much weight of personal regret. Even then, he was thinking that the conduct of the case had been sensible, not perfect: his own judgment had been right throughout: the proper tactic had been, as he had pressed, to reach a settlement: the only margin of doubt was whether they should have accepted the one and only offer.

In the same sharp, firm manner Jenny spoke to Lander, who was talking confidentially to David March. When she thanked him, he found himself, since she was smiling, smiling back.

"It's a shame," he said. "It's an awful shame." Then he sobered down. "I must say, it was a very near thing."

"A miss is as good as a mile, isn't it?" said Jenny.

He was an affectionate man, and an unusually kind one, but his piece of tactless comfort—far more than his hyper-reactive smiles—made her sag, as she left the court on Lorimer's arm.

Alone, March's wig thrown on to the seat, the two counsel were continuing their talk.

"This is a turn-up for the book all right," said David March.

"You did pretty well," said his friend.

"No. No." It was pleasant to win, but March had become cagey about success. He had had plenty, he liked to be honest about it when it was deserved.

"This was a piece of cake for anyone. The old boy had made up his mind before we started," he said.

"That comes better from you than me," said Lander. "Far be it from me to disagree. Which leaves the interesting speculation: why do you get more than your share of pieces of cake, and I don't?"

That was said innocently, with a freedom from envy which no one but March would have believed. March did believe it, gave a slow grin, and said that, as this was their ritual night in the club, he would pay for dinner. On their way through the great hall of the Law Courts, they were wondering how long Fowke's doctrine of uninfluenceability would stand: it was explicit, it must have been thought out for the wrong reasons (said Lander, with his lively unsuppressible tongue), and yet it might make some sort of unsympathetic, intelligible sense.

"The only disadvantage," said March, "being that that's not the way that people operate in real life."

While those two were confiding, Jenny was sitting in a bus on the way back to Pimlico. She sat beside her husband, but didn't speak until they got home. Then, as they closed the sitting room door behind them, she burst out:

"God, I'm furious."

"Never mind."

"What's the good of saying that?" She began to cry. Lorimer had seen her cry before, but only at sentimental films on television, at which, to their mutual pleasure, he was prone to tears himself. Now she was crying in wretchedness—in disappointment, and also in something like impotence. Lorimer stroked her head as though she were a dog, and then went and poured her a drink.

"Making a fuss," she said, as she put down a stiff whisky.

"Never mind. Who wouldn't?" He added, jerky, shy:

"I was proud of you. In court. You took it on the chin."

"Bless you, Jarvey." She could do with being praised. He might be jerky and shy, but to her he was by no means always inept. Yet he wouldn't fake his praise, and she couldn't fake it.

"No, it was easy, you know. I hadn't got round to it then either. Do you know when I realised? Not till we were waiting for the bus." (In fact, it was a few moments earlier, but that she suppressed.)

"Never mind," said Lorimer.

"It's miserable. I can't do the things I wanted to do. For us. I never shall."

Her face began to smooth, as though she were going to cry again.

Lorimer said: "Perhaps we're better off without it."

This time he was inept.

She said: "Oh, save me from that. How the hell can we be?"

Then he muttered: "I didn't like that man Fowke. I don't know what he was up to."

Strangely, that helped. She didn't want to cry, her face

flushed and lined and became active. They became conspirators like innocents in trouble in a kind of fighting paranoia. Yes, Fowke had been working against her. There must be some personal reason (this was absolutely without foundation, but nothing could have persuaded them, and it was a support). Whom did he know? Lorimer went off to fetch an old copy of *Who's Who*. Who was behind all this? Where was the enemy?

About this time, about two in the afternoon, as Jenny was recovering her spirit, another lawyer was not comforting himself with the serenity of those in court. This was Skelding. He had retired more completely than he had intimated to the Underwoods, and nowadays went to his office only for a couple of days in midweek. That Friday, he was getting used to his new routine at his home in Wimbledon. Not so satisfying as giving wise old man's warnings to his favourite clients, preferably well-connected: but habit was something, habit was better than nothing.

He was a widower, and he had an old housekeeper who gave him pleasant English meals, not too large for an ageing man who took care of his health. Breakfast at nine, later than it used to be. The *Times* took up an hour or two. Then a little reading, though he had never had time to read and seemed to have lost the knack. This particular Friday he had the vicar of his parish church in for an early lunch. Skelding had become a churchwarden, and that took up a desirable amount of time. The vicar departed, Skelding was just retiring for an hour's sleep (that was another new habit) when the telephone rang. It was from the office, to tell him that Julian Underwood had won the appeal.

None of Skelding's clients, who had seen him in professional form, would have believed his state just then. He was angrier than Jenny, at least as desolated, and more betrayed. He had given advice, which he was certain was right in law and in common prudence. It had been sneered at, and they had gone on regardless. Now they had won.

Skelding was unlike Swaffield in more ways than one, including some which Skelding would have been too proper to mention. He was not given to haranguing empty rooms. But this once, just like Swaffield after he had been genteelly threatened, Skelding couldn't help talking aloud to his chintz and flowery drawingroom.

"There's no justice in this world," he said. He repeated: "There's no justice in this world."

A very old habit asserted itself, much older than the rituals he was soothing himself with now. He went to his study, and wrote a stately letter of congratulation to Mrs. Underwood, as he had always written to clients all through his practice. It was a very stately letter: the old formulae flowed off the pen, there was no need to alter them. He addressed and stamped the envelope. He would post the letter on his walk—another bit of the new ritual—after tea. A moment's hesitation? Should he write to Julian? Habit, discipline, etiquette weren't strong enough. Be damned if he would.

Mr. Skelding performed his duty, with that small exception. Simultaneously Jenny was performing hers, cooking Lorimer an omelette: they lived as simply as they had begun, and she remarked, with resilience flooding back, they might as well face it, they would go on living simply. She was putting on a show of cheerfulness, partly for his sake, partly, perhaps mainly, because it wasn't in her nature to relapse. After all, she hadn't been over-optimistic, any more than when she left her flat to live with Lorimer: as then, she had taken out a bit of insurance, like a small-scale model of the Treasury operations, and made what she could—nothing exalted—in the way of contingency plans. First thing next week, she would have to talk to Swaffield. He must have heard the verdict by now. He hadn't telephoned. Nor had anyone else. She was letting herself go with semi-cheerful semi-sarcastic gibes. The telephone didn't ring when you had been beaten. If they had won, they would have been answering it all afternoon. Although she didn't know it, she was echoing one of old Hillmorton's quips about politics: when you're out you're out, and no one is interested in you any more. Lorimer didn't utter, but gave her a grim gratified smile. One of the things he loved in her was that she understood failure, its climate and results: he had had enough of that for one life.

The following week, Jenny had to dip further into her resilience: she went to the office on Monday morning, tried to see Swaffield, was told that he was busy all day. Probably he would also be busy on Tuesday. Jenny told herself (and realistic people didn't find these truths any more endearing than the rest of us) that, when someone tried to do you a good turn, and it went wrong, he invariably felt you were to blame and couldn't bear the sight of you. However, when Swaffield did consent to make an appointment, though he was far from intimate, he was also business-like, as though he were interviewing a somewhat disappointing, but nevertheless deserving, member of his staff. He would give her a full-time job (that meant eliminating her visiting round, which she so much enjoyed). This would bring in an income, not a big one, about as much as an executive class civil servant—enough to live on. And Lorimer? That was part of the contingency plan, that was urgent. She was intent on getting him out of his pathetic teaching job. She had already tried to persuade Swaffield that Lorimer could be useful in another charity, looking after ex-officers. After all, he was one himself. He wasn't used to office work, but he would take infinite pains. (If she had received her father's money, her first priority was secretly to subsidise the charity, and even more secretly to instal him there.) She had even, when she was in favour with Swaffield, played on his feelings, saying that this would set up Lorimer's self-respect. That had been—she thought as she did it—a mistake. Swaffield didn't like Lorimer, since, with his active antennae, he knew that Lorimer didn't like him. Yet Swaffield still had a fondness, an irritable fondness, for Jenny. Yes, he would do what he could. Lorimer couldn't expect to earn much; it might contribute to the housekeeping.

Finally, Swaffield would help them to buy a house.

"You can't go on living in that slum, my girl." That was the first time, in the Wednesday interview, that he had reverted to the old bullying, proprietorial, lurkingly amorous tone. Swaffield had never been inside the Lupus Street flat, but it was like him to have investigated it. Perhaps through one of his spies: just possibly, by himself, on one of his night-time prowls. He would get them a mortgage.

"Nothing grand, the sort of place I used to live in. As much as you can manage." That was the total of Swaffield's proposal for the Lorimers.

It wasn't generous, but it was fair. It was a little better than Jenny expected, and considerably better than she had feared. She had forgotten that Swaffield, despite all his diablerie, when it came to action wasn't at the mercy of his impulses. She was a competent woman, and he was prepared to have her around. It wouldn't do his own plans any harm to have a humble, and passably loyal, peer and peeress in his entourage. Further, he had a curious reason for a little benevolence. If he had been compelled to pay the whole costs, he wouldn't have felt it. Still, like other rich men, he enjoyed saving money, and the Appeal Court order had saved him a good many thousand pounds. So, though he wasn't displaying it, he felt good-natured towards Jenny. And perhaps, whatever had happened, he had enough solidity, underneath the mercury of his character, not to let her sink.

That was settled on the Wednesday morning. The previous Friday, just after the appeal, while Jenny was wondering and planning how she was going to live, there was a celebration elsewhere. It was a singular celebration, since one of the three present was as distracted, just as unsure of how she was going to live, as Jenny herself. Mrs. Underwood hadn't tempted fate by ordering lunch in advance, and so it took time for the cook to produce a meal. But in Victoria Road, Mrs. Underwood lived in modest luxury, and there was pâté de foie gras and caviar, not often eaten, reserved for occasions such as this. Not that there had ever been an occasion such as this, she said happily, as they sat in the drawingroom, spreading pâté on hot toast, drinking champagne.

"I don't mind waiting for luncheon, do you?" she said, showing a good steady healthy elderly woman's appetite for food and drink. "We'll go in when they're ready, what does it matter now?"

Liz was drinking hard, eating less. Julian had condescended to take half a glass of champagne, breaking his abstinence: he refused the pâté de foie gras, which had ill effects on the liver. He said, not with triumph but with seraphic equanimity:

"I always knew it would be all right."

314

"How did you know?" Liz asked, voice edged and barely steady.

"Oh, clairvoyance. Plus a little common sense."

"You couldn't know. No one else did."

"I always told you, didn't I?" he said, sweet-tempered. He said: "I told you right from the beginning. I told those damned fool lawyers too. Just as well I did."

That was incontrovertible. His record of optimism was immaculate.

"I couldn't have done it," said his mother, with love, with something like reverence. "I do admire your nerve."

"I think I must get that from you." He was as flattering as when he first met one of his women: as, Liz thought, when he first met her.

He was lying on the sofa, as he now did, as one of his principles, in any unoccupied moment when in this house or his own apartment.

His expression clouded.

"Of course, I don't like that business of the costs. That was monstrous. If March had been any good at all, he would have made trouble. He ought to have done. He *ought* to have done."

"Oh," said his mother, "don't spoil it now."

She was brave enough to scold him. He broke into a cheeky, then penitential grin.

"All right. All right. I won't."

He said: "I always knew it would be all right. Darling, that's what."

The two women were watching each expression on his face. They had been doing so since they left the courts. They had been anticipating the same thing, or the same indication: one with fear, one with anxious hope. But now the fear was diminishing, so was the hope. They had expected some mention, playful, oblique, sultan-like, whatever he chose, Liz was ready for anything—of marriage. It hadn't happened, not by the shade of an intonation. He appeared deliberately to elect not to be alone with her. When for an instant his mother had gone into the diningroom to consult the housekeeper, he had even asked Liz—politely, casually—to go and help.

His mother was watching him with devotion, voracity, increasing triumph. The hostility was not far from the surface now. She was even confident enough to ask:

"What's the first thing you're going to do with the money?"

"Dear Mummy, I've told you."

"What did you tell me?"

"Long, long ago."

"Well, what are you going to do?"

"I'm going to buy a ham."

"What?" Liz cried out.

"A ham."

There was hate in the room. She had let herself admit Mrs. Underwood's long before this, and now it was triumphant she returned it. She gazed at the babyish happy face on the sofa, and felt all the yearning craving love—and another kind of hate. She had once heard James Ryle, in one of his moods, tell her that happiness didn't come from virtue, not from effort, certainly not from merit, but was a grace.

If that was so, she felt with bitter longing, that grace had been granted to Julian, and in the delicacy-laden room she looked at him with hating love.

❧ 36 ❧

While others whom Dr. Pemberton wished to dismiss from his mind were assimilating, or trying to adjust to, the result of the appeal, he had a different preoccupation. To his surprise, almost to his consternation, he couldn't make himself professionally objective about a piece of surgery. A proper doctor—it was a life time maxim of his—didn't worry about operations in advance. It did no good. One knew the chances. So did the surgeon. So did the patient. It was weak to worry. And yet he found himself doing so about Adam Sedgwick's operation.

Shortly after the conversation in the tearoom, on his second day in the Lords, Pemberton had written a letter. He took unusual pains about it, and for him it was an unusually polite letter, signed in his new style. He explained to Sedgwick that he was the former Hillmorton's heir and that he had just taken his seat. He was a working physician, he said, and gave his qualifications. He had a motive for this, and in a first draft stressed that he had passed his Membership at the earliest possible age. Then he had unfamiliar qualms, and re-wrote the letter. He had heard that Sedgwick wasn't well. Could he call on him, and (Pemberton bit down his pride) revive a family acquaintance?

From Sedgwick's Cambridge home, Pemberton was told that there was an operation arranged for Tuesday January 2nd. Sedgwick was going into the National Hospital for Nervous

Diseases in Queen Square the week before, and Pemberton was welcome to visit him there.

Thus, a couple of days after Christmas, Pemberton drove into the Square, which from other calls at that hospital he knew well enough, though he didn't notice the peeling plane trees, the Georgian façades, the gaunt but temperate London winter scene. Unlike James Ryle, Pemberton wasn't borne down by omens. Last Christmas, paper-hatted, he had heard the news of old Hillmorton, not that that had afflicted him. This Christmas, again paper-hatted, he had been anticipating his visit to Sedgwick. No connection, for a hard-baked, rational man. The only connection was one which aroused his habitual contempt for the working population. The laziest brutes on earth. The whole country had gone into a stupor for ten days just like the year before. Pemberton had been making enquiries. He had discovered the name of the surgeon and had (once again smothering pride in a practical cause) telephoned him. The operation should have been performed this week, but owing to the holiday season it had had to be postponed till next.

Brooding on slackness, Pemberton was taken upstairs in the old hospital to Sedgwick's room. Pemberton was immune to hospital smells, or the air of suppressed anxiety or calamity surrounding him. Only laymen felt that. He was as indifferent as a airline pilot walking through the aisle on a rough flight. A hospital was a hospital. Just as Sedgwick's private room was a hospital private room, no more, no less: chest of drawers, a couple of chairs, a table, vases of chrysanthemums, bowls of fruit.

Pemberton had seen many such, and was blind to it now. But he wasn't blind to Sedgwick, who was sitting in one of the chairs, wearing a new grey suit—incongruously new for a patient in hospital. Pemberton wasn't interested in male tailoring either. He was searching the face for clinical signs: in passing it was a fine and intelligent aquiline face, but the point was, typically Parkinson-imprinted. Standard form, pretty far gone. By this time, Sedgwick's intake of the drug had been reduced, so that the facial grimaces weren't so violent, but they still happened, giving the effect of an entirely unexpected hilarious smile, as it might be a Japanese giving one news of his

318

brother's death. He had his fingers locked in his lap, so there for the moment Pemberton could observe nothing.

Sedgwick didn't get up, but said:

"Lord Hillmorton?"

"Lord Sedgwick?"

In that exchange, neither of them felt like Stanley and Livingstone at Ujiji. Sedgwick had lived all his life in the English extremes of formality and informality, and Pemberton, though he might be a rough customer, was getting used to it.

"I knew your relation very well," said Sedgwick.

"I didn't. Scarcely at all."

Sedgwick was fine-nerved. He didn't pursue that particular line of talk. For an instant, though, he made Pemberton impatient with another one. Sedgwick began speculating as to whether anyone who had the money, such as himself, ought to be able to buy a private room in a hospital. He did so in a detached manner, seeming to imagine that the other man had orthodox left wing opinions, or asked the orthodox left wing questions of the day, as the Symingtons might have done.

"Nonsense," said Pemberton.

"What?"

"Sheer nonsense," said Pemberton. "A man like you needs all the comfort he can get. If anyone tries to stop you, they're the sort of people who'd reduce the whole show to indistinguishable lumps of porridge if they could."

"You're slightly out of touch with modern thought, wouldn't you say?"

"To hell with modern thought. Look, we haven't time for this now. How are you?"

This was coarse, and more brutish than Sedgwick was normally confronted with, distinctly unlike the manners of the former Hillmorton. Though Sedgwick couldn't know it, Pemberton had never possessed any medical manners, which had sometimes counted against him. However, Sedgwick was sick, he wanted to talk about his sickness, this man was a doctor, even a brutish doctor was someone to talk to, better than no one. Further, he was soon asking the right questions.

How much of the drug had they been giving him? Sedgwick gave the amount.

That was a lot. It would have improved his speech (from

the first words Pemberton had picked up the slurring, but in fact Sedgwick's speech was more distinct than it had been twelve months before) but had produced the twitches in his face. With his passion for instruction Pemberton explained that the doctors had to keep a balance between the two effects, one positive, one negative. Whatever the operation did, it couldn't improve his speech: they hadn't learned how to touch the speech centres.

"Yes. I've been picking up a certain amateur knowledge of the subject, you know."

Pemberton gave a rough chuckle. Between hectoring from him, sardonic flicks from the other, they seemed to have established a common language.

"Now what about the movements?" Pemberton asked. "Walking must be difficult."

It had been so for months? It must be marche à petit pas?

Yes, it had been petit pas. Sedgwick was grateful for the technical phrase, less humiliating than the thing itself. Surprisingly, Pemberton's words sounded more like French than his own. Which side had been affected? The right.

"Try and touch my right hand with yours."

Pemberton, totally outside the case, was taking a great deal on himself, but that came naturally. It didn't occur to Sedgwick that it was odd for a G.P. to be so well briefed about this disease. But Pemberton, who read nothing but medical literature, hadn't minded reading more.

Sedgwick's right arm moved up from his lap, hand shaking a few degrees in the first instants, then violently, not with slow weaving purposelessness like an amoeba's tentacles, or an infant's hand, but more as though it were gesturing in autonomous rage. It made darts at Pemberton's hand, missed, went sideways, missed again. In the effort, Sedgwick's fine serene forehead had become lined. There was sweat, maybe of embarrassment, at his temples.

"That's a pretty fair amount of tremor," said Pemberton as the arm dropped back. He hadn't, as a layman would have, found the sight grotesque.

"I've noticed that myself," said Sedgwick.

"You ought to have had the operation before."

"That seems to be the general view," said Sedgwick.

"Well," said Pemberton. "Now the left hand. Try to touch me."

Just then Sedgwick's poise was shaken.

"No, that one's all right."

"Never mind. I want to see."

Sedgwick had a strained bright look which the other was inured to in men shrinking from a clinical test. Reluctantly the arm came up. Compared with the other, it was steady. It met Pemberton's hand. Soon it touched finger tip to finger tip. There was perhaps as much shiver visible as in a moderately heavy drinker's after a thick night.

Pemberton felt the fingers, bent the arm at the wrist. After he released it, he sat quiet for a moment, big face expressionless. Then he said:

"Well. I'm not an expert, of course. But I'd guess that the operation on the right side ought to give you most of what you need. All being well, you'll be able to walk decently, and you'll have your working hand."

"That would be a distinct improvement," said Sedgwick, composed again.

"That's enough to be going on with. But I don't know what your man has told you, but I'd also guess you'll have to think of an operation on the other side in finite time."

It was clear that Sedgwick had heard that before: and that was what he hadn't wished to hear again. Pemberton administered his own kind of encouragement.

"Anyway, you can cross that bridge when you come to it."

"I'm rather inclined to think the same myself."

"You'll find out next week what the operation is like. It's nothing very formidable. But it's rather unusual. I suppose they've told you something about it."

Some would have been fretted, or made more nervous, by Pemberton's unembellished or unrelenting treatment. Sedgwick wasn't. Perhaps it removed a veil of personalities.

He replied: "I've been doing a little research on my own. I've been through Cooper's book." With his left hand, he indicated a volume on the chest of drawers. "Involuntary Movement Disorders. Extremely interesting. I might find it even

321

more interesting if I didn't happen to be somewhat concerned. In a passive sense."

"Do you know the man Cooper?"

"Yes. Very impressive. I've always thought, he ought to have been an Englishman." (That could have seemed a singular remark to Sedgwick's international colleagues, from that international unchauvinistic dignitary. It sounded like the English soldiers talking about Joan of Arc.)

"Why didn't you get him to do the operation?"

"Why?" Suddenly that innocent question touched a nerve, where clinical probing hadn't. "Isn't Tompkin good? Is there anything wrong with him?"

Still unemollient, Pemberton thought it was time to give some reassurance. The operation was standard since the American perfected it: it was being done all over the world: Tompkin was first class, he had learned the technique at source: he was as good as anyone this side of the Atlantic. Pemberton had himself talked to him—

"So have I, of course."

"What did you think?"

"He went through the correct procedure, I take it. He produced the necessary warnings. He didn't commit himself too much."

"Don't you understand," said Pemberton, in his most overpowering style, "that he's under great strain? Just as much as you are, perhaps more."

"Do you expect me to find that remarkably invigorating?"

"For two reasons," Pemberton went on undisturbed. "In this operation, you're having to be fully conscious all the time, I expect you know—"

"Of course I know."

"That's a strain on both of you. And he's a young man and you're a very distinguished old one. He'll have to ask you questions right through the performance. It's a hell of a responsibility for a man of thirty."

"No doubt," said Sedgwick, "I shall be able to take a technical interest in the process. After all, I've done some experiments in my time, myself."

Pemberton let out an uningratiating laugh.

"No one would like performing on someone like you. Because you're what you are. And that takes in the other reason why he's under strain. Imagine that something went badly wrong. Say the worst chance happened. If you were taken out of this place feet first, it wouldn't do him any good, would it? After all, finishing you off wouldn't pass completely unnoticed."

"I'm not sure that I find that remarkably invigorating either."

"That won't happen. The chances are a hundred to one against, you must have gone into the statistics."

Sedgwick had, which made the hectoring, sarcasm, antiphon get sharper. But Pemberton wore the other down.

"Then you know the chances of coming out more incapacitated than you came in—they are about fifty to one against. We take that sort of odds plenty of times in our lives. It's rather better than the chances against being seriously damaged if you drive a car for twenty years. That doesn't prevent me getting my car out in the Fulham Road."

"Statistics are rather more convincing when they apply to other people. You are too young to remember some old mathematician saying that in an air raid he took refuge under the arch of probability. He may have done, but I confess I never could."

"The operation will be all right. I'm not worrying about it for a minute—"

"Now that ought to be very invigorating." The sarcasm wasn't unfriendly.

Pemberton continued: "The operation will be all right." He wanted to call the older man Adam, but at the last instant his brashness unaccountably failed him. Also unaccountably, what he had said about not worrying was not true. Reason was letting him down, as well as brashness. Still, he could fall back on his doctor's drill.

"It will be all right, I tell you."

Drill was a help. He asked Sedgwick about his general health. Good for a man of his age. They've done all the routine tests, of course? Blood pressure? On the low side. Weight? A hundred and fifty pounds.

"You'll live more years than I shall." (Pemberton weighed nearly half as much again, though he carried no fat.) "Large men don't last. Statistically, that is."

He said: "You'll sail through that operation, I'm telling you. By the way, I'd better tell you also that I shall be there."

"Where do you mean, you'll be?"

"There. In the operating room. It's all in order. I have Tompkin's permission. I've never seen one of these operations. I should like to. I might be able to take some notes for him. Or be another pair of hands with the X-ray plates."

Sedgwick said: "This is rather unusual, isn't it?"

"Oh, it's often done." (Pemberton didn't reveal that he had insinuated himself by pulling rank, that is by using his title.)

"I said I had Tompkin's permission. But I haven't asked yours. I'd better do so now, hadn't I?"

Sedgwick looked unforthcoming, stern, but slowly his expression changed from the austere into a curiously urchin-like smile:

"I have an idea that you'd be there whatever I said, wouldn't you? And I shouldn't be in a very strong position to resist, I take it."

The conversation didn't end there. Pemberton had come with a dual purpose. One discharged, now he wanted something for himself. He wanted advice, he told Sedgwick. He had always hoped to do medical research, he said, not just ordinary practice. What were the prospects? He duly got advice: and, though it was polite, it was as acerb, as candid, as that which he had been bestowing himself. The prospects were negligible, said Sedgwick. No money? That wasn't the prime difficulty. The trouble was his age. How old was he? Forty-seven. Too old to do anything first rate, or even decent second rate. Possibly, if he had started at the right age, he might have done good work. Too late now. Perhaps he could manage some clinical observations. Nothing of first class interest would emerge, except by sheer blind luck. It might be better than nothing.

Pemberton knew when he was hearing the truth. With his obstinacy and persistence, he would try to hack out a way somehow, but he would need an adviser with lower standards than Sedgwick's. Before he left that room, Pemberton said that he would raise the topic, later the following week, as soon as Sedgwick was fit after the operation. That was another bit of his doctor's drill, implying that the future was safe. It was intended to pacify Sedgwick. It was also intended to pacify Pemberton himself.

To his own puzzlement, he was not objective about this piece of surgery. Not that he preserved any hope, or really had ever had any, that Sedgwick would help his old, slightly pathetic, scientific ambitions (it would have enraged Pemberton to know that, to the other, they had a touch of pathos). If that had been true, it would have been a good, sound, selfish, egotistic realistic reason for being concerned about Sedgwick's condition. Pemberton would have understood himself for that, and have approved. But he had no such reason, and was still concerned. He respected Sedgwick. Surely that wasn't enough? After all, he was an old man, all he had done in science was already done. His effective life was over. In the nature of things, his physical life couldn't last very long. Pemberton had no use for people who got maudlin about mortality. Pemberton didn't like symptoms of maudlin sentiment in himself. Yet he was still concerned.

Eight forty-five, a.m. on Tuesday, January 2nd, 1973. Sedgwick's head, shaved and polished, shone under the spotlights in the operating room. Miniature pointed clamps, also shining out under the lights, gleamed at the sides of the head, held it immobile, so that he looked only upwards, at the X-ray box in the ceiling. He was as helpless as a sentient being could be.

It was a fine head, if anyone in the room had been disengaged enough to study it. He had always worn his thick gray hair, with its casual quiff, as carelessly as an undergraduate of the twenties. That had concealed the vault, not specially large, smooth-curved, which now pointed behind him towards Tompkin. Tompkin had just taken up his place after another ritual washing of his hands and arms, between a nurse on his right, an assistant surgeon on his left.

On the table, Sedgwick was covered up to the neck by green blankets. The room was large, immaculately tiled underfoot, packed with apparatus. No one present needed instruction in what the apparatus was: Tompkin had learned the technical lessons from his master, this had become standard form. Gleaming console, dials set and clear against the unyielding white, controlling the flow of liquid nitrogen: X-ray beamers, one in the ceiling, the other in the walls aligned at right angles to the patient's head. It could have been a scientific laboratory, with one function all purposes or intakes analysed away, except the single one. It could also have been a torture chamber, to which the same definition would apply.

As usual with any functional process, technological, official, there were more people in the room than an outsider expected. That was true of legal conferences at David March's, or cabinet committees, or police investigations: there were always people, more or less anonymous, whom no one counted. It was true that morning. They were all dressed in long coats, caps, mouth-and-chin masks, slacks all in uniform green, the same colour as the blankets which covered the patient—rather like a football team parading in their track suits. There was the chief surgeon himself, his assistant, an X-ray technician, another technician in charge of the liquid nitrogen apparatus, an operating nurse, another nurse at general disposal, an anaesthetist (as an insurance, not for use). There was also Dr. Pemberton.

On one wall stood a bold notice: SILENCE PLEASE THE PATIENT IS AWAKE. In fact, no one but Tompkin and the patient had spoken for the last quarter of an hour. Underneath the caps and masks, the faces round the table were barely identifiable, but Pemberton's massive shape took more disguising.

Sedgwick had said: "So you have come, have you? Good morning."

Tompkin had heard that, knew that Sedgwick was trying to sound detached, and immediately tried to sound detached himself, explaining to Sedgwick another detail of the operation, as though the two of them were surveying an interesting piece of experimentation. Tompkin was an impressionable and sensitive man: at least he was certainly impressionable, and wished to be sensitive. He had learned more from his master than the surgical techniques, and would have liked to feel as deeply.

Of course he was tense before the operation. He had a touch of what cricketers called the needle. They said you couldn't be a first class performer without it. He could understand one of the Cooper lessons: after hundreds of these operations, one knew at last when the anxiety and responsibility would have evanesced and the profession taken over: and the answer was never.

That was certain, for a man like himself. But perhaps he was cooler than he thought. Certainly he tried to appear cool up to the limit, that was right, that was the professional imperative. But perhaps that came easier than he imagined, and some of the lessons not so easy. He had to remember that this man helpless, an object on the table, was knowing the meaning of loneliness: ultimate loneliness, not too far from the loneliness of dying. You could remember that only if you had a depth of feeling. He had to remember something not so desolating but much uglier, more a kind of moral impotence in all of us. Human sympathy cuts off sharp, he had been taught. Our instinct for superiority is so harsh that we don't admit it: but the living feel superior to the dead, the well feel superior to the ill. Just walk with your nerves alive through a hospital. If this had been a torture chamber instead of an operating room, the torturer would be feeling superior to his victim: morally superior, which helps men to commit horrors. The surgeon feels superior to the object on the table. That has to be transcended, Tompkin had been taught, if we are going to stay human at all.

It was a difficult, alien lesson for a young man like Tompkin. Humility didn't come naturally to him, though duty did. He had been making an attempt, punctilious or comic according to taste, to find a way to cope. For this operation in particular, he had for days past been thinking of the formalities. Sedgwick was an eminent man, and he himself wasn't: he must preserve the right deference when he talked to Sedgwick on the operating table. What was the best form? "Lord Sedgwick" would be unwieldy: "Sir" might do: no, he recalled that in his own undergraduate days at Cambridge, Sedgwick, at the height of his fame, just awarded the Nobel, had a Royal Society Professorship and, in the English fashion, was always called Professor. That would put them both at the right distance.

So at nine a.m. precisely by the operating room clock, Tompkin said, in a light-toned but clearly articulated voice:

"Professor, I am just going to begin."

Tompkin was concentrating on the operation, and on nothing else. Dr. Pemberton, standing on Sedgwick's left side, would have assumed, and approved of, that. To him, there were no moral concerns. There was a job to be done. A good deal less prepotent or assertive than usual, he was eager to see it through. He had one small regret that he hadn't found a piece of work to help with. It wouldn't have mattered how mechanical it was.

"Professor, I'm ready with the local anaesthetic. You'll feel a prick, not much more."

In a moment, Tompkin added:

"That's all you'll feel. The brain is insensitive to pain."

"I know that." Sedgwick's reply struck strong and terse.

Pemberton was engrossed in the mechanics of the operation, and wished to follow them, step by step, but from where he stood, the first he could not see. Tompkin was making an incision on the left side of the scalp. Pemberton watched the nurse, practised, on her cue, handing him a small and shiny object. Must be to keep the cut open. Now the surgeon—it was all concealed from Pemberton—was looking at the bone beneath the scalp.

"We're going to drill a hole," he said. "Very little. It'll only take a few seconds. It makes a bit of a noise."

Sedgwick had learned the procedure off by heart. His voice came up:

"I must say, this is getting rather near the bone."

Sedgwick, who had thought about gallows jokes after his visit to Hillmorton's bedside, was vain about that one. Had it been prepared? No one there knew, or attended, or perhaps even listened. The whirr of the drill took over. Silence.

"Good," said Tompkin.

Nine fourteen a.m. The hands of Tompkin and the nurse were moving steadily, and nothing else. No sound. Pemberton was recalling the anatomy of the outer brain. Hook in Tompkin's left hand; then a scalpel in his right. Nerveless movements of the hand. Must be through the cortex surface. Tweezers. More work with the scalpel.

"All right," said Tompkin. "How are you, Professor?"

"Still here."

Nine nineteen a.m. Pemberton understood the next stage. As a mechanically minded man, he got fascination from it. A rubber tube was being inserted through the puncture on the brain surface, fluid withdrawn, replaced by air. Air formed a shadow when they took X-rays, and that would give Tompkin his map inside the brain.

Meanwhile the other surgeon attached an instrument to the head of the table. To Pemberton this was a beautiful device, working in three dimensions, driving the probe to the target. The cannula probe, more shining metal, was already in place, aiming, waiting, its purpose being to kill the target cells by freezing. Now they were all waiting.

Tompkin said:

"This is where we have to stop for the X-rays. The remaining X-rays will be quick. This takes a few minutes."

Sedgwick's voice: "I find it slightly tedious."

Tompkin reminded himself, he was finding it more than that.

The second nurse had, minutes before, placed X-ray plates under and alongside Sedgwick's head. The entire operating party, during the minutes of waiting, had moved over to the end of the room, close to a viewing box, just like a group of crystallographers during a new experiment. Would it have been better to have someone to talk to Sedgwick? Some prefer to be alone. Anyway, too late to detail anyone now.

The surgeon was at work on the X-ray film. Pemberton assumed that he was marking the target: there wasn't much tolerance to play with, millimetres at most. Nothing had been said, it was still dead quiet, while Tompkin whispered a couple of measurements. He went back to adjust the probe.

Nine thirty-two a.m. "According to plan, Professor," he said. The others had reassembled in their places, and he asked Sedgwick to hold up his right hand. It was shaking like something with its own will, more than anyone there had seen it shake before.

"Is that enough for you?" said Sedgwick.

"Quite enough."

Tompkin's tone was cool. Just as coolly, he began pushing

the probe into the brain. Quite slowly. By calculation, by reason, it should have reached home now. Coolly again, he asked Sedgwick to say something. There was a hesitation: the surgeon had a spasm of anxiety: but it was the hesitation of someone in a radio studio being tested for sound level.

"William I, 1066–1087. William Rufus 1087–1100—" came Sedgwick's voice.

"Fine. Fine." Tompkin was for the first time over-hearty.

"I take it," Sedgwick was making another effort, "you don't want to destroy the speech centre."

"That's why I have to keep you awake. To hear you talk, sir."

"It would be inconvenient. Not being able to speak."

More X-rays, rapid this time. Tompkin nodded: calculation confirmed.

More lifting of Sedgwick's arm. Quivering more violent.

Nine forty-three a.m. Tompkin spoke to the technician. Liquid nitrogen was now running into the probe. Tompkin asked for the temperature. Minus ten. He asked Sedgwick to speak again.

"Henry I, 1100–1135. Stephen and Matilda, 1135–1154." Speech as clear as Sedgwick's had been the day before.

"Lift your arm again, Professor."

Shaking, quivering, unchanged.

"So that's it," Sedgwick muttered into the quiet room. Without change of tone, Tompkin called for minus forty. Then, for an instant, his decisiveness was shaken. He seemed to begin asking Sedgwick to lift his arm again, stopped, and instead left his stool and walked round to the righthand side of the operating table. There without speaking he took hold of Sedgwick's right hand and wrist. Minus fifty, he called. Pause. Nothing said. More finger work. Longer pause.

Nine fifty-three a.m. Minus eighty. Longer pause. Tompkin, after pressing, relaxing, pressing once more, the hand within his grasp, let it go. He exchanged an eye-flash with the other surgeon and the nurse. Eyes in masked faces carried no expression to onlookers like Pemberton.

Tompkin said, voice also expressionless:

"Professor, will you lift your arm again?"

The hand rose, like a tired man's, as though not wanting to. The fingers didn't quiver. The arm went higher. To those watching, there wasn't a tremor visible. Arm and hand stayed steady; those watching wanted to turn their eyes away before the sign broke down.

"Professor, please separate the first finger."

The finger moved apart.

"Now bring that finger round and touch your nose."

With a slow, and almost graceful, sweep, the hand came round, and the index finger without a falter did as it was told.

Pemberton, astonished at the sight, astonished at what he was feeling, felt a pleasant choking sensation.

"Good God." Sedgwick spoke loudly. "I couldn't have done that for years."

"I thought it was coming right," said Tompkin. It was the only personal remark he had made since entering the room. This was what the eye-flash had conveyed, minutes before, to those who knew him best. Underneath the mask, he had been smiling, and so had they. Now everyone was smiling, and though they didn't see much of anyone else's face they took for granted that it was as joyful as their own.

It was a moment of communion. You didn't need to take a lofty view of human beings, you could take one as contemptuous as Dr. Pemberton's, to recognise that it was a moment of selflessness. Their pleasure was unique and pure. Later on, maybe, Tompkin would be less pure, as he thought about his own credit: conversely, the other surgeon might reflect that he needed one of the star operations for himself. But not now. They were all united in a kind of species loyalty. Viscera, mind and spirit were at one. A sick man was better. Something had been done. Life was shining bright, and they were happy.

None of them had known of old Ryle, in depression, brooding that people needed a victory. Perhaps this was a victory. Only a small one, of course. An elderly man (never mind his being a clever one, men were equal anywhere near the extreme conditions) had been freed of an affliction. Conceivably, not for the rest of his life. The surgeon would have to remind him soon that there might be recurrences, or the need for another operation on the lefthand side.

Still, it was a victory. It might even give pessimistic people ground for a little hope. They might think, and they mightn't be wrong, that much evil, and certainly much suffering had been caused by false optimism about human beings. It was better to start with a bleaker view: then what you built might stand. But there was something, perhaps not much, on which to build. Human beings were skilful. The people in this room had seen, inside one hour, a prodigy of skill. They had been visited by a totally selfless joy. They knew the pleasure of species loyalty. Human beings were capable of that. Combined with skill, skill above all, intelligence if you wanted to give it a more grandiose name, that gave something irreducible on which to build. Veils stripped away, old Hillmorton before he died, Ryle, Sedgwick himself (who had lived better than the other two) had seen much go wrong, but would have agreed on this. It wasn't much, but it gave the lot of them a chance, and reason to preserve some hope.

❧ 37 ❧

At breakfast the morning after Sedgwick's operation, Pemberton received a letter from someone whom he knew by name. The name was Swaffield, and the letter was almost word by word identical with that to Jenny over two years before which had started the law suit and disturbed a number of lives. There was nothing particularly strange about Swaffield sending such letters. He was used to summoning people to see him. It was one of the perks of wealth.

It didn't seem strange to Pemberton either, as he read it. One didn't play the markets as he did without some idea of Swaffield's doings. Pemberton assumed that this invitation was connected with money. In fact his first thought was that the man wanted to sound him. He had always imagined that, once he came into his title, he might be offered seats on a few boards. He had been disappointed that so far no one appeared to have noticed the desirability of this step. Very likely this odd man out (Pemberton had read profiles of Swaffield before now) was ready to lead the way.

It would be interesting to meet someone who understood money. Perhaps a more delicately organized man, or a more aspiring one, would have felt some let-down or incongruity after the nature of the day before. Pemberton didn't. Healing the sick, admiration for someone, was one thing. Money was another. Pemberton didn't worry about, or even notice, having to switch from one to the other. In a street near his house was a doctor who stood in for him when he took—reluctantly—his annual fortnight's holiday. He arranged for this doctor to look after his surgery patients the following evening: and on that Thursday duly drove himself to Hill Street.

When he entered the big drawingroom, the butler calling out Lord Hillmorton, he observed much less than Jenny on her original visit: but even he couldn't avoid getting a sense of opulence pressing upon him. So even he, not given to gratifying remarks, couldn't avoid saying, as the short dominant figure advanced towards him:

"Fine place you have here."

Which gave Swaffield a chance to make his favourite reply:

"It's a nice home."

The two men shook hands, Pemberton looming a full head above the other. Professional habit made him give a passing attention to Swaffield's physique: thick chest, low slung, the sort of body you met in professional footballers, unusually tense and active for a man in his sixties.

"So you've come, have you?" said Swaffield, the question making up in force what it lacked in the necessity for an answer.

Pemberton was dislodged from detached attention.

"Have a glass of champagne," said Swaffield, and explained, as he had to Jenny, that he drank two before dinner each night, never less nor more.

Pemberton said, only a little for him. He might be called out later.

Swaffield didn't enquire the reason, his intelligence service kept him well informed. He merely said:

"It must be a dog's life."

Pemberton wasn't used to meeting men as assertive as himself. However, he had an instant's satisfaction. They were sitting on the sofa, glasses on the table in front of them. Swaffield turned his full-eyed gaze straight onto Pemberton, and said:

"I'm glad you came. I sent for you because I wanted a word about a financial matter."

Pemberton felt like congratulating himself. Just what he had expected. But the instant was not a long one. When Swaffield continued, it was not at all what Pemberton expected.

334

"I suppose you know all about the Massie will," said Swaffield.

"Why should I?"

"Oh come man, of course you must. Your niece, or whatever she is, old Hillmorton's daughter, she's all mixed up in it, you know that better than I do. She's running round with that bleeding gigolo Underwood, and he's run away with the cash. Well, you'll have to make her do the decent thing."

"I have nothing to do with her or any of that family."

"Tell that to your Aunt Jemima."

"I tell you, I have nothing to do with them."

It was possible that for once Swaffield hadn't been completely informed, or that no one had discovered the relation between Pemberton and his predecessor. Swaffield shoved aside any disclaimer, and said that the result of the case was an outrage and the other man knew it. Pemberton, angrily on the retreat, began to defend the legal verdict and, to his own surprise, the integrity of Liz and the Hillmorton family. Swaffield, experienced negotiator as the other wasn't, said that meant that he was admitting responsibility. Also like an experienced negotiator, he gave away a point that the other was anyway capable of knowing. He, Swaffield, would have liked to carry the appeal to the House of Lords (that is, the highest judicial court, nothing to do with the Lords as a senate) on behalf of his friend Jenny, Lady Lorimer—but that probably wouldn't be permitted. So he was demanding a gentleman's agreement. Julian and Liz had to be made to arrange a settlement for Jenny.

"I wouldn't do it if I could," said Pemberton.

"It's easier to get a gentleman's agreement," said Swaffield, with a frog-like grin, "when you are dealing with gentlemen."

"I've heard that you are an authority on that."

"Then perhaps you've heard other things about me. You might have heard that Reg Swaffield isn't a good man to tangle with. Even if it means a bit of trouble. I warn you, it might result in making some of you uncomfortable."

"You're bullying me, are you? I warn you as well, I don't like being bullied."

"That's your privilege."

They were still sitting on the sofa, a foot apart. Quite unlike dramatic convention, they didn't get up and quarrel with their backs to each other. Swaffield's eyes had taken on the unblinking, unfocussed look which Jenny would have recognised. Pemberton's acreage of face, which at no time had any colour, had none now.

They were each of them outsiders, and hugged the image to themselves when no one else did. They went about much of their time in a state of subdued but comforting rage. Neither of them had much regard for the world. Whatever opinion each had of himself, he had a distinctly lower one of the people around him: and the longer they lived, the more that opinion seemed to them just. One might have thought that they would have been natural allies. Those natural allies had now met for ten minutes, and a spark had flashed between them. It happened to be a spark of mutual fury. Whatever Swaffield had set himself to achieve, and he could usually control his internal smouldering, as he had done with Meinertzhagen and the others, all his energy had gone into reducing this big fellow, as though in an old French cartoon of deux enragés.

While Pemberton, who like other persons with unqualified faith in their first-hand experience also had an unreasonable faith in folk wisdom, felt the old adage that bullies were always cowards running through his mind. It didn't occur to him that others, reasonably, thought that he was a bully himself, and that it would have taken an effort of absurdity to think that he was a coward.

So he began to threaten in return. And, with an effort of absurdity all his own, mentioned the topic of the House of Lords. Did Swaffield realise that questions could be asked? On anything? On business deals? Questions which were privileged, no libel or slander, no holds barred? Pemberton spoke with marmoreal ominousness.

"Oh, sweet Jesus, is that all you have to offer? That mausoleum. We'll soon get rid of that lot of nonsense." Swaffield gave a savage jeer. He continued,

"In the name of reason, man. That is, if you are capable of reason. Why should you be sitting there when people who have done something are not?"

"You mean, you're not."

"Yes, I mean that."

Pemberton became committed to a defence of the institution, in particular of the hereditary peers, whom in the flesh he had not surveyed with superlative admiration. Swaffield, falling back on his old irregular radicalism, produced a good sound radical critique, such as Adam Sedgwick's father and his Cambridge apostolic friends would have taken for granted in Trinity before the first world war. Pemberton, contemptuous but not suspicious, did not detect that Swaffield had invested considerable personal resources, and sizeable sums of money, in getting appointed to the place himself, and still had hopes.

"Coming down to cases," said Swaffield, "if we have any kind of second chamber, what blasted right under Heaven has anyone like you to get in? When I haven't."

"Coming down to cases," said Pemberton, "what blasted right have you to be a very rich man? When I'm not."

He gazed, balefully expressionless into a face not so expressionless, though difficult to read.

He went on: "That is, I suppose it is true what they say, that isn't a front as well? I suppose I have to call you a millionaire?"

"You can call me a multi-millionaire."

"I'd sooner call you something else. What right do you think you have to make money like that."

"I could make money at the North Pole. It's just as well for this country that someone can."

"Nonsense. Anyone can make money if he thinks about nothing else."

"Do you think you could? I should want some evidence of that before I paid you in washers."

Curiously, that piece of off-hand abuse, which might have been routine in the workshops of Swaffield's youth, silenced Pemberton. Or else the quarrel had exhausted its own dynamic. Swaffield, acting as though he had prevailed, offered another glass of champagne. Without any effort at politeness, Pemberton said no. The best he could think of, as he departed, was to utter, standing up:

"If you'll take my advice, speaking as a medical man, you'll

337

ask your own doctor to have a look at you. I'm not sure I like that tremor in your hand. You are a shade too restless for your own good, considering your age."

Driving home to Fulham, Pemberton was not too proud of that final remark. There was no use pretending, he had been outfaced. It wasn't that he was worried by Swaffield's threat or warning. Ten to one the man was bluffing. If he wasn't, Pemberton didn't care, or rather he cared with approval, since any trouble to Liz or her family was a contribution, only a little one, but still a contribution, towards settling the elephantine account.

Yet Pemberton was miserable. It wasn't that he minded himself and Swaffield not giving a demonstration of human beings at their best. Some, perhaps some among those he had watched the day before, might have disliked that drawingroom spectacle: but Pemberton had a less lofty view of the possibilities of others' behaviour and his own. He still didn't feel any incongruity between the day before and now. He was the last man to be irked by the grit of this our mortal life.

Nevertheless he was miserable. He had gone to see that man with faint but lively hopes of a directorship. All he had received was a despising grin, not even commonplace respect. He had been outfaced. The old fear, the old dread, was seething inside him. He had not only been outfaced, but humiliated. Humiliation, any more than when young, he couldn't bear.

At that same time, Swaffield was sitting alone in the drawingroom. He didn't feel specially successful. He had discomfited too many people in his time, and was a little discomfited himself. He had, as Pemberton guessed, been bluffing. But that didn't stay in his mind. One cut one's losses. He had had plenty of practice at that too. He had nothing solid to attack the Underwoods with. This had been worth trying, but he hadn't counted on it (if he had, he would have been more careful with Pemberton). He had come to the end of that particular game. Let it go.

He was a little discomfited though. He felt both lonely and old. Pemberton would have been happier if he had been told he had made an impression on Swaffield, and even inspired a kind of envy. But it was true. Envy chiefly—this was also true—for sheer brute force and strength. Swaffield held out a hand at arm's length. Were his fingers shaking more than an elderly man's ought to? In his own estimation, he was never quite well, never quite ill. Maybe a long voyage would be good for his asthma.

He felt lonely. No one was visiting him that night. He went in for homely self-pity. Reg Swaffield rattling about like a pea in a pod. He would whistle up Jenny—she was a sensible woman, he hadn't regretted taking her up, that affair was done with now, but she wasn't. He had better ask that dumb husband of hers as well. They could come in and sit with him after dinner, and after a few drinks maybe he would be able to sleep.

❧ 38 ❧

Course of a Year
1973

Ryle took to spending more time in the House. He was still a sociable man, and was not often alone. Once or twice, though, he reflected that, three years before, he, Sedgwick, and Hillmorton used to sit together in the Bishops' Bar. It would have taken supernormal foresight to predict what was going to happen to them. Hillmorton had looked in vigorous health, and now was dead. Sedgwick, whose state had distressed them, was walking about like a fit man. While to Ryle himself, nothing had happened—except that three years had passed, and nothing was likely to happen now. Ryle was too stoical to protest, like old Skelding, about the justice of this world. Still no one would have foreseen these three personal stories.

There were some who did feel like protesting against the justice of this world, especially when they witnessed Julian flourishing in excelsis. Mrs. Underwood's triumph continued but often seemed to her precarious. Julian had become worried about how to safeguard his money. None of the western stock markets were any good, investments were no good: should one buy jewels, pictures, silver? This needed as much cautious thought as his health. He bought a small house in Campden Hill (that might be a safer investment than most), and there allowed Liz to live with him. They entertained very little, since he decided it was a waste of money. Ryle was invited there once, and then not again. He thought that Liz had become thinner, and much more silent. Others, more disinterested, said that at least she had got some of what she wanted.

To Liz, with irrefragable reasonableness, Julian pointed out that one argument for marriage no longer existed. The great financial inducement had been taken away, since Liz's youngest sister (the one who had looked after Hillmorton at the end) had recently produced a boy. So, if money continued to mean anything, which Julian took leave to doubt, this child would ultimately inherit the Hillmorton fortune. Even if he and Liz married and had a son, they had lost that chance. To his mother on the other hand he sometimes ruminated that it was time he settled down for good.

Jenny hadn't got all she wanted either, but she was enjoying what she had. Thanks to Swaffield (though Lorimer grimly suspected that some of the payments on the mortgage filtered back to him) they acquired a house off the end of the Fulham Road, by coincidence not far from Dr. Pemberton's. After her days in the office, Jenny had enough energy, gusto, and long frustrated homemaking skill to make her house elegant, and to all appearances—despite the gross difference in wealth—they lived more comfortably than Julian and Liz. They entertained much more, and Lorimer's acquaintances in the Lords, including new ones made for him by Jenny, enjoyed going there. There was some talk of sliding him in as a junior whip, but by the end of the year he still had not managed his maiden speech. Jenny's conspiracy with the smooth young whip was still continuing.

In May Swaffield received a letter from Downing Street saying that the Prime Minister 'had it in mind' to recommend Swaffield for a knighthood in the Birthday Honours, if this was acceptable. Swaffield, despite disappointment and fury, was capable both of calculation and taking advice. At his age, they wouldn't offer him anything more. Paying him off at the lowest possible rate. He did accept. On the day after the list appeared, there were envelopes coming through the letter box at Hill Street addressed to Sir Reginald Swaffield. Effusive congratulations from Meinertzhagen, Haydon-Smith, the rest.

In his study, Swaffield uttered a number of words to the empty room. However, he wrote seemly letters of thanks: hope never completely died. He allowed himself one luxury or self-indulgence. That same week, he sent a message for Lord Clare to come to his office, sat at his desk reading papers when Clare came in, and kept him standing up. Then:

"Edward, I'm taking you off the Board."

"May I be told why?"

"You're not doing anything useful. All right? Bless you."

Also in June, David March was appointed a judge of the High Court. This wasn't a surprise, but had come early enough to mean other steps in prospect. Lander was bouncing with delight, and stood the drinks all evening, which cost him something, the recipient being David March. Under monumental phlegm, March had the fighting satisfaction of an ambitious man: but in secret, there was a vestige of worry about his friend, Lander's tongue had recently been disrespectful, even by its own high standard. March was beginning to doubt whether he would ever have the chance to return the celebration.

In the Lords, Ryle was finding that his black thoughts of the year before were being shared by others. In private (not in debate or in print), some were saying them. Ryle found this a kind of left-handed consolation. One brightfaced handsome man passed him going out through the swing doors.

"Did you ever know a time when no one anywhere had the slightest constructive idea? Or a grain of hope?" Most of his friends were more sedate than that. But men older than himself, on both sides, were being sad. He heard more insights and self-recriminations than he had heard in that place before.

Azik Schiff, so long above the battle, disposed to think that politicians were unteachable, was as sad as any. The new Arab war made him shrink as with an illness or as very old men do. He had, years before, lost his only son. He had done his duty by his adopted country, but Israel was his only emotional commitment and all he had left. With an unfamiliar burst of candour, one night he told Ryle, whom he didn't know well, that after the Poland of his childhood he recognised anti-semitism when he smelt it, and he smelt anti-semitism stirring again all over the western world.

Those were impersonal anxieties or calamities. Most of these people were as contented as they had been before, a good many of them happy, like Jenny and Lorimer or above all (to some outsiders regrettably) Julian Underwood. Some were having what their world regarded as success, such as David March. Bishop Boltwood, one of the cleverest and toughest men among them, was being tipped as a possible odds-against bet for Canterbury. Still, in a number of people selected at random, the statisticians would have said that there was likely to be, whether there were impersonal calamities about or not, a personal one. That was the reverse of sheltering under the arch of probability. It had duly happened. To someone who those connected with the Massie case would have considered one of the more indestructible. That summer Symington, at the age of forty, was struck down by an arachnoid haemorrhage. He could easily have died, the doctors said, but his strong nature carried him through—and his wife's will for him to live was as strong as his. By the end of the year, it seemed that he might get back to work again. Hubris, he said without a blench. I thought I could do anything. It was unlikely that he would ever be able to work as he once did. He had been rapacious under the lustrous surface. He would have to renounce that now. He had aimed to be one of the first solicitors to sit on the same Bench as David March. If any solicitor did, it wouldn't be Symington: and he accepted it.

Towards the end of the year, Ryle was waiting for Sedgwick in the Bishops' Bar. He had appreciably less of Sedgwick's company than he used to: for, on a sitting day in the Lords, between tea time and a quarter to six, Sedgwick was constantly escorted by Dr. Pemberton. To Sedgwick's friends, this was difficult to understand. To think that Pemberton—who had become known there as Archie Hillmorton—was popular in the Lords would be a misjudgment. Lorimer, since he lived

343

near, had made an effort to talk to him, but said to Jenny that he was a bounder. Others were more tolerant, but the unspoken consensus was that he took some tolerating. It didn't help that he neither accepted drinks nor stood them. A few, on hearing his views of national politics, his countrymen, and his fellow men in general, found them satisfying: but for those he had even less respect than for other members. His capacity for respect seemed to diminish as he grew older. He also had no capacity for pretending any. He had no more use for the place than when he entered, and no more for the people in it. He had delivered a couple of speeches during the year. One, his maiden, on funds for the Medical Research Council, was greeted with the normal congratulations for any maiden speech. The second, on student grants (in his view, at least one-half the students in the country should have no grants at all), was not received with enthusiasm. He didn't like the place, and didn't disguise that he never would. He came in at tea time, and left in time for his surgery at six o'clock. Yet Sedgwick, the fastidious and cultivated, put up with him. Ryle, who thought himself more suitable for coping with roughnecks, once asked him why. Sedgwick replied, urchin-grin taking over from austerity, that as one grew older unqualified admiration was good for any man. He added that the man was a hopeless philistine, uneducated, coarse-fibred, but had what ought to have been a good mind. It was refreshing to meet a good mind which had never been domesticated or tamed at all.

That December night, waiting for Sedgwick in the bar, Ryle wasn't thinking of Pemberton, in whom his interest was not excessive. He had just heard that his son Francis was being seconded to the European Commission in Brussels. His interest in his son Francis was not excessive either, but he couldn't help reflecting on his grandchildren. What sort of life would they have? From professional England, from anywhere in the professional West? Those children had some of his genes. If they had a specific gift, they would be fortunate. If not, if they were anything like himself, reasonably competent, reasonably forceful, he couldn't see them having so free or interesting a

344

time. True, they had been born more privileged than he had. But the real privilege was to be born in the right country at the right period. That they hadn't been.

It occurred to him to wonder, how would a historian of the future, a historian of his own type, judge the society he had lived in and the people in it. It was possible, it was more than possible, that historians of the future wouldn't be much fascinated. It might seem a period of confusion between great epochs, and those didn't shine very bright in history. But if they did give us any attention, it was certain that they would analyse our discontents, anxieties, the forces moving us, even our attempts at foresight and our hopes, quite differently from the way we had tried ourselves. And they would be right, or more right than we had been. If there was a lesson a historian learned, that was it.

But there was another lesson a historian learned. They will also read our feelings and our experience quite differently from the way we lived them. The present couldn't imagine the ideas of the future, that is one of the certainties. It seemed equally certain, from what Ryle knew of history, that the future couldn't live again the existence of any present. For what it is worth, that is our own. We didn't know much, but that was something only we could know.

A consolation? No, it just put us into perspective in the whole chain of lives, and that was humbling. Not that anyone should require humbling, Ryle thought, if he had lived in our time.